The MUSEUM
DETECTIVE

Greater Karachi City

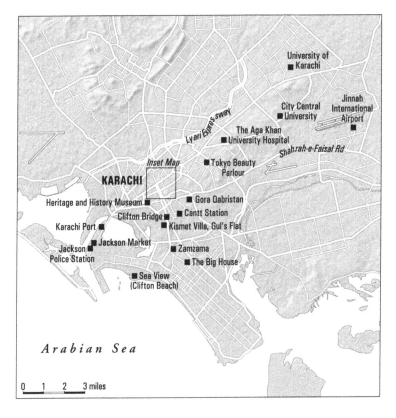

University of Karachi

City Central University

Jinnah International Airport

Lyari Expressway

The Aga Khan University Hospital

Shahrah-e-Faisal Rd

Inset Map

Tokyo Beauty Parlour

KARACHI

Heritage and History Museum

Gora Qabristan

Clifton Bridge

Cantt Station

Karachi Port

Kismet Villa, Gul's Flat

Jackson Market

Jackson Police Station

Zamzama

The Big House

Sea View (Clifton Beach)

Arabian Sea

0   1   2   3 miles

For Damien Phillips
& for Tia Noon and Fahad Khan

Published by Soho Press, Inc.
227 W 17th Street
New York, NY 10011
www.sohopress.com

Library of Congress Cataloging-in-Publication Data

Names: Phillips, Maha Khan, author.
Title: The museum detective / Maha Khan Phillips.
Description: New York, NY : Soho Crime, 2025.
Identifiers: LCCN 2024042004

ISBN 978-1-64129-656-4
eISBN 978-1-64129-657-1

Subjects: LCGFT: Detective and mystery fiction. | Novels.
Classification: LCC PR9540.9.P45 M87 2025 | DDC 823'.6—dc23/
eng/20241031
LC record available at https://lccn.loc.gov/2024042004

Map illustration © Philip Schwartzberg

Interior design by Janine Agro, Soho Press, Inc.

10 9 8 7 6 5 4 3 2 1

EU Responsible Person (for authorities only)
eucomply OÜ
Pärnu mnt 139b-14
11317 Tallinn, Estonia
hello@eucompliancepartner.com
www.eucompliancepartner.com

The MUSEUM DETECTIVE

MAHA KHAN PHILLIPS

Karachi Center

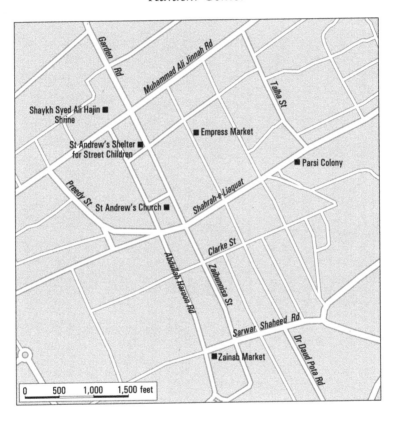

The MUSEUM
DETECTIVE

CHAPTER 1

GUL WAS DREAMING OF Mahnaz when her phone rang.

Her eyes snapped open and she reached for it, her fingers fumbling around the bedside table. "Mahnaz?"

"Is this Gulfsa Delani?" It was a man, his voice cutting in and out, sounding lost on the wind.

"Yes. Who is this?" Gul squinted at her clock. 3:06 A.M.

"My name is Deputy Superintendent Farhan Akthar, from the Jackson Police Station in Keamari. I'm sorry to be calling so late, Madam."

So this was it, then. Her knuckles were white against the phone. "You've found her?"

"Yes. We weren't sure whom she belonged to. How long has she been missing?"

"Three . . . it's been three years since we've had any word. Is she alive?"

There was a pause. "I cannot imagine why you would ask such a question, Madam."

Despite the shock of the call, Gul was not entirely awake yet. She sat up and tried to focus. "Surely it is the only question that matters right now, Deputy Superintendent. You said you found my niece?"

The man coughed. "My apologies, Madam. I don't know anything about your niece. That's not why I'm calling."

"No?" She swallowed down the tightness in her throat. What the hell was going on?

"We made a discovery earlier tonight, during a narcotics

investigation. We are in need of your expertise. Can you meet me?"

Gul swung her legs onto the floor and switched on the bedside lamp. "Deputy Superintendent . . ."

"Akthar, Madam. DSP Akthar."

"DSP Akthar. I think you have made a mistake. I'm not a narcotics expert."

"I know that, Madam."

"I am a museum curator. I work at the Heritage and History Museum."

"Yes."

Gul shook her head. Why on earth was this cop calling her? "For the last month I've been excavating a Sassanian fort in the Indus Delta, so unless your narcotics are deep in the mangrove swamps, I don't know how much help I can be."

"I am aware of your work."

"Then I really don't understand." Now that the adrenaline had passed, disappointment took over, leaving Gul feeling raw. The call was not about Mahnaz. Better to receive no news than bad news, but still.

"It's a little difficult to explain on the phone," DSP Akthar said. She could hear him barking orders at someone in the background. "If you could confirm your address, one of my men will escort you here. It's a long drive out of the city, so please bring everything you might need."

Gul pressed her fingers to the bridge of her nose. Her head was beginning to throb. This whole situation was bizarre. "You said you were posted in Keamari? I live in Bath Island. It's twenty, twenty-five minutes. Faster if we take the bypass."

"I'm not calling from Keamari, Madam. Please bring your things and expect to be here some time. I think you will find it worth the effort. This discovery . . . I believe it is unique."

Gul tried to interject, but the policewallah didn't seem inclined to provide any further details. Bloody man. What were the "things" she was meant to take with her, when she didn't even know why he was calling? She forced all thoughts of Mahnaz away and tried to focus.

As she got out of bed, Gul wondered whether she should wake Rahim Raja, director of the museum. She decided against it. If he knew about this—whatever *this* was—he had chosen to make it her problem. And if he didn't, he'd find out by morning, and she wouldn't get barked at for disturbing him without providing any useful information. She closed her eyes for a moment. There was always a logical explanation to everything. This was what Gul Delani believed.

The police weren't going to ask for her help without good reason. What had they uncovered? Some stolen artefacts, perhaps? Or maybe they'd stumbled into an ancient site. Though why that would require her presence in the middle of the night, she couldn't even begin to imagine. But now she was professionally curious, as much as anything else. She gave DSP Akthar her address and hung up.

Gul jumped into the shower and emerged a few minutes later, blinking shampoo out of her eyes and twisting her curly, rebellious hair into a messy bun. She paused when she got to her cupboard. Her normal excavation attire consisted of a pair of comfortable cotton trousers, a loose-fitting long-sleeved shirt and a distinctly unfashionable vivid orange tie-dyed bandanna she had picked up in Kathmandu sometime in the early 2000s. But today she had no idea where she was going, or who she would be meeting. You never knew with the policewallahs. There could be all types of official-doms hanging about, just making a nuisance of themselves. She opted for the safest option, an olive shalwar kameez made of khadi and an embroidered white dupatta. Simple enough to work in, yet versatile enough for any occasion, and sufficiently flag matching and patriotic for any government cronies.

She made herself a cup of tea and located the pair of thick-rimmed plastic glasses she used when doing close-up work at any dig, wondering whether she was meant to pack her excavation tools or not. She decided to pack everything—her picks and trowels, some ropes and markers, her laptop—everything that wasn't still in her office, left there from the weekend before, along with her well-worn camping gear, which lived there permanently.

It didn't take more than a few minutes to get ready. Once awake, Gul was brisk and efficient, so when a jeep with flashing lights pulled into the driveway, she was already downstairs waiting to meet it, wincing slightly at the thought of her neighbours. There were three flats in her building, and the cantankerous Mr. Dada, who had been ensconced in his for over fifty years, hated any kind of disruption. The man was the epitome of a curtain twitcher—though this being Karachi, he had to do it through metal grills rather than lace. Mr. Dada, long widowed and disappointed with all his children, was already up in arms about Gul's comings and goings "at all hours." He often tut-tutted about her "excavations"—he said that word with distaste, as though it were akin to prostitution, a trade Mr. Dada made clear he detested.

It was bad enough suffering fools, Gul thought, but suffering the self-righteous ones really got her goat. Once, when he had railed about rumours of an illicit brothel opening in the neighbourhood, Gul shot him a sweet smile. "Well, it is the oldest profession, you know, so there is plenty for historians and archaeologists to learn. Do you have an address? Perhaps we should go and record their stories."

If Mr. Dada had ever worn pearls, he would have clutched them in horror. He had to settle for gripping his taveez instead, shooting her a dirty look and muttering under his breath. Just thinking about the incident made Gul smile.

The cop opened the jeep door for her, and Gul nodded her thanks. Once inside, Gul texted Mrs. Fernandes to let her know what was going on. She didn't know how long this would all take, but she had several budget meetings in the morning, plus the museum tour for the orphanage kids and the National Archives people coming in the afternoon. Mrs. Fernandes would make sure that nothing fell through the cracks in Gul's absence.

The roads were clear at this time of morning, no need for the cop to turn on his sirens, but he did so anyway. They raced through the city, the streets of Karachi glinting in the semi-darkness. She used the time to push all thoughts of Mahnaz away, but only after offering a brief prayer to the Gods—every single one of them. Amun-Ra. Vishnu. Zeus. Tlaloc. Izanami. Pele. Whatever their culture or creed, she invoked them all. *Not Mahnaz. May it never be Mahnaz, not if it was bad news.* For a moment there Gul had felt hope, but she was used to swallowing down her disappointment as every lead, every potential "sighting" turned to dust. And now here she was, in a police 4x4, driving into the unknown. What a start to the day. Whatever this artefact was, it better be worth it.

DSP Akthar was right—the drive was long, far longer than Gul had expected despite the warning. They turned onto the Hub Chowki Road, connected to the Northern Bypass, and she was amazed when, just as the sun inched its way up the horizon, they pulled up at a military checkpoint between the provinces of Sindh and Balochistan. The cop, whom she now knew to be PC Shah, glanced at her from the rearview, and mistook her amazement for something else. "Don't worry, Madam, I am armed, and a second escort car will join us after the checkpoint. You will be perfectly safe."

Gul gave him a half smile, and then turned to look out the window. Balochistan. The supposed badlands. People weren't inclined to drive out here, not unless they had good reason. She felt the first stirrings of excitement. She had never been allowed to officially excavate in Balochistan, the police and security bureaucracy being too onerous, the kidnappings and conflicts too frequent. And now she had a chance to sit back and marvel as the landscape changed. The sun was rising, hues of orange and lilac were spreading over the vast horizon. Within minutes, the road was engulfed by tall sand plains on either side, etched from prehistoric times, looking like castles with crenulations, or dinosaurs with teeth, so jagged and razor-sharp in their appearance. The landscape was otherworldly, almost Martian.

After driving for another two and a half hours, PC Shah turned off the N-10 and into the vast openness of the desert—a land that time, and years of conflict, had left forgotten. They passed a trio of small mud volcanoes and Gul longed to get out and linger. But the moment was fleeting, the hard sand giving way to something more porous, to shifting dunes, acacia bushes and then, just over the horizon, the glinting Arabian Sea. She sat up. Unlike the beaches of Karachi, the one they were now driving alongside was pristine. It had no hawkers, no piles of rubbish, no plastic bags floating along the breeze. Up ahead, she could see the landscape changing again. Above the beach were cliffs and rock formations.

Gul knew they had reached their destination when she saw several police vans and an ambulance ahead, destroying the peace of this otherwise perfect ecosystem. They pulled up behind the vehicles, and she jumped out of the jeep, watching a group of hermit crabs scuttle out of her way. They were still only a few hours' drive from one of the biggest cities in the world, and yet, this place was as remote as they came.

PC Shah slammed his own door shut and motioned for Gul to follow him. When she did, hot air hit her like a furnace. It was the thick of summer, but even so, the heat was exceptional, and she was already sticky with sweat despite the sea breeze. They walked towards the other cars. She stopped when she saw two gurneys—their occupants covered with white sheets—being pushed up the beach.

Gul wiped the trickle of sweat that was already cascading down her cheek. People had died here today. What the hell had happened? Up ahead, she could see that the rock formations were actually narrow caves. And coming out of one of those caves was a paramedic pushing a third gurney, this time with a cop in uniform lying on it. He had vast amounts of blood congealed around his torso, and it was dripping down one arm onto the smooth, terra-cotta sand. She couldn't tell whether he was alive or dead. Her left foot hit a stone and she stumbled.

Another policeman came out to greet her, looking harried. "Mrs. Delani?"

She was used to people making assumptions about her marital status. "It's Dr. Delani, actually."

He nodded. "I am DSP Akthar. Thank you for coming."

"What the hell is going on here, Deputy Superintendent?" The policewallah was of average build and would have been impossible to pick out of a line of other men his age and weight, other than the curious birthmark on his forehead. It was almost question-mark shaped, as though the man had been branded as permanently quizzical. Well, he was in the right job for it, she thought. Gul motioned to the caves. "It seems to me like you've had quite the night. What is this?"

"It was a coordinated drug bust between Sindh and Baloch police forces. The Jackson Police Station received a tip-off that heroin was being smuggled out of these caves. There was a gun battle. The perpetrators were all killed, and several of my men are badly injured. We have recovered approximately two hundred and fifty kilos of heroin."

"Bloody hell."

The man had dark circles under his eyes. He looked exhausted. "Yes. Quite a haul. We found something else as well, and this is why I need your help. We have to move quickly. The tide will come in soon, and the entrance to the cave will become inaccessible until this evening."

Gul followed him, trying to take it all in, the policemen swarming around, the bodies, the blood spatter she now saw against the rock wall, the narrow entryway itself, which required her to turn sideways at times, before opening into a vast cavern, full of glinting stalactites. She took a deep breath. "Once again, I feel the need to reiterate, Deputy Superintendent, that I am not a narcotics expert. This is not my world."

He nodded. "Yes, but you are an Egyptologist, correct? At least, that's what I understood from your bio on the museum's website."

"Yes. Yes I am." What the hell could he possibly want with an Egyptologist?

"You spent several years in Cairo?"

"Yes, I completed my doctorate there, and did some years of fieldwork before returning to Karachi. Though, as I'm sure you can appreciate, there's not much call for Egyptology in Pakistan."

He looked grim. "I think perhaps there may be now." He pointed to a ridge at the very darkest corner of the cavern, raising his torch towards it.

Her eyes followed the beam of the torchlight. And what she saw took her breath away.

CHAPTER 2

GUL WALKED TO THE ridge. Lined up against her short frame, it was chest high. She used her arms to push herself up, brushed sand off her knees and accepted the flashlight from DSP Akthar. Then she put on her glasses and peered more closely.

Had she really seen what she thought she had seen?

Yes, yes she had. She was staring at an ornately carved wooden sarcophagus. She blinked and then tried to take in everything at once. It was . . . it was a lot to process. The casket was full of inscriptions—the writing was a variation of the cuneiform script—though she was far from being an expert on cuneiform, and it was difficult to make everything out in the half-light. If it was, in fact, cuneiform, it would make the sarcophagus at least 1,600 years old and likely much, much older. The box also contained carvings of trees and floral patterns that she could swear she recognised. Her heart started to pound. This was exciting. This was really, really exciting.

She peered closer and her gaze moved to what was inside the casket. A stone covering, probably alabaster, which was also inscribed in cuneiform. The stone was broken in three pieces. She would have liked to have a moment to savour the writings, even if she couldn't decipher them, but there was no time, no time at all, because DSP Akthar was now beside her, lifting the stone pieces out of the box so that she could see what was inside.

Now her head really started to buzz. It was a mummy. An honest to Gods, heart-stopping, breathtaking, bone-chilling mummy, just lying there in the cavern. The mummy was beautiful, in the perverse way that mummies could be beautiful and terrible at the same time. It was covered in some sort of resin-impregnated cloth that had formed a hard shell of amber but looked like it was draped around her—for this was definitely a woman, she realised—like a shroud. A beaten gold chest plate lay on top of the mummy's crossed arms. On her face, a gold mask, melted across her features, defining every contour, every nuance of her expression. And to top it all off . . . a gold crown carved with . . . seven . . . yes, she had counted correctly . . . *seven* cypress trees. This was insane. This was brilliant! Was this *real*?

"Is it authentic?" asked DSP Akthar, mirroring her thoughts.

"I can't say, not yet." Gul's mind raced, but she forced herself to pay attention. She inhaled deeply. Musty, yes. A little sickly, perhaps, but there was no smell of decay. This mummy's organs had most likely been removed, then. And she was not new—at least, not preserved in the last year. But how was that possible? Only the Egyptians removed the organs of their dead like this, and this was clearly not an Egyptian body. And what the hell was a mummy doing in a smuggler's hideaway?

"Is she from Pakistan?"

"No," Gul replied. "At least, she could have been buried here, without being from here." She bent over and examined the chest plate, already reaching into her satchel for her gloves and her tools so she could dust it down. "The religious heritage wouldn't support it. Islam, Hinduism, Zoroastrianism . . . none of these religions believed in mummification. Besides, the writing is cuneiform."

"Cuneiform?"

"It's a logo-syllabic script, used in many ancient civilisations, in Sumer, Mesopotamia, even in Old Persia."

"So definitely not Pakistan."

"Unlikely, but I couldn't rule it out, not yet. It could be that she is even older than our religions. Zoroastrianism is believed to have emerged from the common Indo-Iranian religion system dating back to the early second millennium BCE, but I suppose it's feasible, in the smallest way, that there were other, unknown influences. It would be hard to swallow, though. If I could have a few minutes to examine her?"

DSP Akthar nodded and stepped away. "Of course. Please."

Gul crouched against the sarcophagus and used the flashlight to take in as much as she could. Some of the carvings were deeply damaged, while others were entirely preserved. The alabaster stone pieces were covered in dirt and difficult to read, as was the mummy's chest plate, but a deep clean would help with that.

Sometime later she straightened and pulled off her gloves. "This body appears to be Achaemenid. The Achaemenid Empire is not my area of expertise, I'm afraid, but I can tell you a few things. The cypress trees and the rosettes are all emblematic of the city of Persepolis. See that large rosette carving there? Next to it is the emblem of the god Ahura Mazda. You've got a Persian mummy on your hands, Deputy Superintendent, not an Egyptian one. What's more, she could come from the royal family—at least, if the crown she's wearing is anything to go by."

"Persian?"

"Yes."

"Did the ancient Persians have mummies?"

She handed back the flashlight. "The idea that the Persians adopted some of the belief systems of the ancient Egyptians has been posited before. Nothing tangible has ever emerged, however. This is the first Persian mummy I have ever seen."

In the shadows of the cavern, DSP Akthar stared at her, unblinking. "So she's valuable."

"If she's real, then yes, certainly. If the ancient Persians mummified their dead and none of us ever knew about it, then this mummy would be something very special indeed."

"Careful there," said DSP Akthar. He pointed the flashlight to a pool of blood near where she was standing. She saw then that there was blood splatter on the casket itself, and quickly stepped back. For a moment, she had forgotten that this was a crime scene.

"One of the smugglers was shot here. He fought like a demon to keep us from reaching the mummy. He was more focused on protecting her than protecting the heroin. Any idea why?"

"I'm afraid not."

"How much is she worth?"

Gul cleared her throat. "Impossible to say. Millions. Again, if she's authentic, that is. But as I said, until now there's been no actual evidence to support the notion of the Achaemenids mummifying their dead. So, she's a conundrum."

DSP Akthar crossed his arms. "And what is she doing here?"

She shook her head. "Deputy Superintendent, I have no idea where *here* even is. You said this was a narcotics bust, but I can't help you without some context."

He paused and looked at her. Light dipped in and out of the cavern, as below them, other policemen used their torches to look around. Eventually, DSP Akthar spoke. "We have been chasing a Baloch drug baron, one who keeps slipping through our fingers. We only know him as Saayaa."

"Saayaa? As in *shadow*?"

"Yes. We have never been able to ascertain his true identity."

"Well, you know one thing, he's not very original."

"Sorry?"

"Shadow. It's not a particularly inspired moniker, now is it? Not even particularly scary."

"In my experience, criminals are not always the most imaginative people."

"Really?" She arched a brow. "I would have thought it would be part of the job description. So, this Saayaa, does he dabble in antiquities?"

"Up until now, not that we were aware of. There has been some sex trafficking, but really, drugs are his business." DSP Akthar rubbed at his stubble. "We thought we had him tonight, but he managed to evade us again. He wasn't here, just some of his men. Unfortunately none of them lived long enough for us to interrogate them. Why would he have this creature here? The casket, the pieces of stone, the body—it all weighs a great deal, and moving it around would be of great inconvenience to him." He combed a hand through his hair. "The heroin could have fetched him thirty-five million dollars on the international market. Why bother with a body?"

"I couldn't tell you, but I can only imagine that he was smuggling her out to sell on the black market as well, also for a great deal of money. Antiquities smuggling is rife, though I must say, I have never come across anything like this before."

"You understand why we thought she might have been stolen from the museum."

"Yes, I can see why, but she isn't ours. So what happens now?"

"Now?"

"What do you intend to do with her?"

He shrugged. "She's evidence in a narcotics case. We will examine her and then keep her in storage."

Gul squared her shoulders. "You can't do that."

"What do you mean?"

"Whoever she is, ancient or not, there's a body in there and she's fragile, even more so in this heatwave. Despite the various preservation methods used, mummies are delicate. Once they are unburied and exposed to the elements, it doesn't take much to cause a chemical reaction and start the degradation process. You may be left with a pile of goo on your hands, Deputy Superintendent."

It struck her then that the drug dealer could have had the same thought. "Perhaps this Saayaa character left her in this cavern because he knew it would help to preserve her body for longer, because it's cool and dark. It's what the Victorians did during their Egyptomania phase. They brought their looted mummies to England and buried them back in the earth until they were ready to reveal them, often at social events, where the mummies would be unwrapped in all their grisly splendour while people watched on with a drink or canapé in their hands."

He snorted. "I doubt that is what Saayaa intends for her."

"Me too. But he might have thought he was keeping her safe by bringing her here."

"She is valuable to them. Maybe more valuable than the heroin. I need to know why. Why was she worth the risk? Is she worth more than thirty-five million dollars?"

"Let me take her, and I might be able to tell you," Gul pressed. "There are no oxygen-free museum cases in

Pakistan—that's what she needs to stay intact. My team can fashion up some sort of hermetically sealed, inert gas–filled chamber to prevent further chemical and biological degradation."

"Impossible, Madam. This is a police case."

"And if she turns out to be authentic, then under the antiquities law, she will belong to the government, am I correct?" Gul was nothing if not dogged, and the chance to work on a Persian mummy was a once-in-a-lifetime opportunity, something too precious to leave in the hands of a bunch of inept cops. They would have no respect for her, no intellectual curiosity and no ability to keep her safe. They didn't understand that her very existence changed the past entirely, how could they? No, she was not letting this mummy go for anything. "I've worked with mummies for a large part of my career. I'm the best chance you've got at keeping her whole. I'm also the best chance you have of finding out what's going on. You want to know why a notorious drug dealer decided to veer into ancient mummy smuggling, given all the inconvenience? Well, I want to know whether everything we knew about history has just changed. If I have the time to examine her properly, I may be able to answer both our questions."

DSP Akthar stared at her again, clenched his jaw, and then nodded. "Today she will be transported to the Jackson Police Station and dusted for prints."

"But . . ."

He raised a hand. "Tomorrow, if my superiors give permission, you can transfer her to your museum."

Gul tilted her head in acknowledgement. "Fair enough."

"You'll take a police escort with you. She will be guarded at all times."

The last thing Gul needed was a bunch of ignorant

policemen underfoot, ruining her examinations. "You don't have to worry, Deputy Superintendent. We take our work seriously. We will not damage her in any way."

"I don't think you understand, Madam. The police escort isn't for her protection."

"No?"

"If she's as valuable as you say, then Saayaa will want her back. The police escort will be for your sake, not hers."

CHAPTER 3

IT WAS DUSK BY the time Gul got home. She was exhausted, hot and hungry. Other than her brief time with the mummy, she'd spent most of her day in the car.

She thanked PC Shah, who drove her home, waved at Mr. Dada who was scowling from his window, walked to a side door leading to the stairs of the apartment complex and took them two at a time until she reached the third-floor entry. Gul's building in Bath Island was falling apart, but in the most beautiful of ways, with an ivy of weeds growing through many of its cracks and crevices, and overgrown bougainvillea hanging from the roof like a waterfall of pink. Granted, the other plants were mostly dead in this heatwave—there was no way to justify spending money on illegal tankers of water just for gardening. But still, the whole thing was wonderfully atmospheric, from the two ancient banyan trees in the garden, to the old *Kismet Villa* sign on the side of the front door that kept falling lopsided, no matter how often she had it fixed. Gul had never really understood modernity, and these flats were as close as it got to old buildings in Karachi. She loved this place, despite the fact that the pipes got clogged on an almost weekly basis, and Shakir the plumber had to be kept on retainer.

Flat 3 of Kismet Villa had originally belonged to Gul's maternal grandparents. They had made their way to Karachi from Jamnagar during Partition, carrying untold stories and experiences that, though left unspoken, haunted them nonetheless. Back then Bath Island was still truly an island. It had been favoured by the British, who erected beautiful and expansive homes in an otherwise undisturbed locale, a place teeming with flamingos and kingfishers and very few humans. Land-reclamation projects began in the 1950s, and Bath Island, once accessible only by boat, became a peninsula, connected to the mainland on one side. Still Gul's grandmother told her many stories of being isolated from the rest of the city and even from the wider Clifton area, as the bridge was often submerged in times of high tide. Her grandparents would walk along the shore, collecting mother-of-pearl and other shells that Gul still kept in a jar in her bathroom.

Now, of course, Bath Island had become entirely unrecognisable. It was as much a concrete jungle as the rest of the city, the old houses torn down and replaced with nondescript high-rises, the streets congested with traffic, so much so that the thelawallahs stopped bringing their carts around in the mornings, shouting about their fresh fruit or cleaning supplies or anything else they wanted to hawk. The trees that had once stood sentinel along its broad avenues were gone, and the seagulls no longer swooped down to take a pakora from your hands. The sense of being separated from the world was lost.

Still, Gul had always loved the place. As a child, in the school holidays, her family had spent many languid days here. Every afternoon she would clamber up the banyan trees with some of the other neighbourhood children. She was always the fastest to make it to the top, and the last to come down. She loved the density of the leaves, and the banyan's thick, elongated vines, which looked like they belonged in a fairy tale. She'd always be told off about the climbing, of course, which was grossly unfair, because her brother, Bilal, climbed the banyans all the time. And even though he was six years older, Gul was always faster.

Bilal. She felt the old bitterness rise and she swallowed it back down again. She had made her peace with Bilal a year after Mahnaz vanished when she was just fifteen, but their relationship had never recovered. She shut her eyes. There was no point in dwelling on Bilal now, any more than there was thinking about Mahnaz.

Inside the flat, the air was cool, the old, tiled floors and ceiling fans doing an excellent job of keeping the heat at bay. She hung her keys off a tooth on the mounted crocodile skull near her door and tossed her bag on the side of the corridor, where it lay next to her partial whalebone, used as an occasional doorstopper, alongside dozens of dusty old books she had been gifted by an elderly gentleman from Parsi Colony, a historian named Mr. Davar. As ever, she looked at the books with a pang of guilt. She had been meaning to go through them for at least six months now, to dust them off, archive them and donate them to various schools and universities, as she had promised him she would.

But there was always so much to do. Between her regular work at the museum, the Young Archaeologists Club she ran once a week, the Braille exhibition she was organising, her work at the shelter, and the night classes she was teaching at Karachi University, her foot was almost always pressed firmly down on the accelerator.

Not that she would have it any other way. Being active kept her sane. It kept her from thinking about Mahnaz.

She shrugged off the metal taste in her mouth that lingered at the thought of Mahnaz's disappearance and decided to focus on the task at hand. There was a lot she would need to research, and she would need to do it quickly if she was going to give DSP Akthar the answers he was looking for. Why would a drug lord turn to the world of mummies? It wouldn't be exactly easy to sell a body like this on the black market, not unless you had a well-established network of smuggling contacts in the antiquities world. She would need to reach out to some slightly dubious contacts of her own, to see if they knew anything about this Saayaa character. She would also need to read up on the Achaemenid dynasty and establish the authenticity of the body. Was she right in her assumption that her organs had been removed, Egyptian-style? Or perhaps she was more like the mummies of Papua New Guinea, where dead bodies were placed in a hut and smoked until the organs desiccated naturally?

Gul's instinct, and her very brief examination of the body, made her feel that the death rituals used were more Egyptian in nature, but she was a long way from being sure. What would they find, exactly? It would be impossible to really tell until the body was forensically examined. The police had not given her much time with it, but hopefully in the morning, once his superiors had signed off, DSP Akthar would let her transport the body to the museum. She'd need to arrange an ambulance for that.

She paused, trying to think. She had told DSP Akthar she would keep the mummy safe in order to prevent further chemical and biological degradation. Fashioning an oxygen-free chamber big enough for the mummy would take some thought. The poor body must be disintegrating by the minute at the police station, and the long drive there wouldn't have helped. She would need to call Hamza immediately. He was the tech wiz on her team. They'd need to get started straight away.

Gul headed to the kitchen, then jumped when she saw the shadow. She exhaled, clutching her heart. "Mrs. Fernandes, you scared me."

Mrs. Fernandes was standing over the stove, her hair in its usual sixties bouffant, a style that looked more like Darth Vader's helmet with an up-flick than a legitimate hairdo. Many years ago, long before they met, Mrs. Fernandes had worked at Tokyo Beauty Parlour as a bookkeeper. The salon's signature style had not changed in over sixty years, and neither had Mrs. Fernandes. Today she was wearing a beige summer dress, cinched at the waist, which somehow managed to accentuate her stockiness. She wore her usual serviceable brown shoes, her only adornment being the cross around her neck, which she refused to put away, even when there was religious tension in the country. As usual, she was looking severe. But she had a Goan prawn curry bubbling on the stove, and she was putting on some rice.

May the Gods bless Manora Fernandes, Gul thought. The woman was a marvel, always looking out for her. She arrived wherever she went like a ball of furious, efficient energy, often a pen behind one ear, usually with a well-worn Filofax in hand. Mrs. Fernandes believed in evolution, but she didn't believe in change.

"Oh, brilliant. I'm famished," Gul said, reaching for a spoon to dip into the curry.

Mrs. Fernandes used a wooden spatula to smack her hand away. "Wait till it's finished. You're always so impatient."

Gul leaned against the kitchen wall. "It's been a long day, Mrs. F."

Manora Fernandes turned to look at her, spatula still in hand. Her jaw tightened. "And whose fault is that? Who told you to go trekking to Balochistan all of a sudden? Only last week the Taliban blew up that police van near Quetta."

"I wasn't anywhere near Quetta, Mrs. F. I was in the middle of nowhere."

"Even worse. If there had been some sort of attack, who would have helped you?"

Years ago, when they first met, Gul had wondered if Manora Fernandes had a screw loose, the way she harangued people. Now she accepted her harassment as a sign of her love. "It was fine, Mrs. F. And really worth it, for what we discovered. Now at least let me eat before you lecture me," Gul said. She opened the fridge door and grabbed a can of Coke.

"You consume too much sugar, and you never drink enough water," the woman grumbled, watching Gul with narrowed eyes.

Gul ignored her. "I'm going to wash up, and then we can chat."

To her credit, Mrs. F kept her opinions to herself until they sat down at the table. Then, as soon as Gul had eaten, she started again. "Idiot policewallah, calling you in the middle of the night and scaring you like that. And you haven't even told me what you found."

"It was a body."

"A body?"

"A mummy."

Mrs. Fernandes pursed her lips. "What do you mean, Charlie?"

She called everyone Charlie. That was another thing Gul learnt the day they met.

"A mummy, like an ancient, artificially preserved mummy. They were chasing down a drug dealer, and they found a mummy instead." She filled Mrs. F in on everything she had seen that day.

Mrs. Fernandes shook her head. "This sounds like trouble. You should let someone else handle this."

"Don't be ridiculous."

"I mean it, Gul. There are times when you get too emotionally invested. You have to be careful to avoid disappointment. You know what can happen to you."

It had been a long journey back. They had hit rush hour, and Gul felt exhausted by the heat and the fumes and the excitement of the day. She felt the sweat ooze down the back of her neck and she flushed. Really, sometimes Mrs. F pushed too far. Yes, she knew what could—what *had* happened in the past. "It was an acute stress disorder, Mrs. Fernandes, nothing more."

"A nervous breakdown is a nervous breakdown, no matter what polite term they use."

"It was three years ago. *Because of Mahnaz.* And I'm fine now."

"You've only just weaned yourself off the medication."

"It's been months now, and I haven't needed the pills."

"Gul, I am your friend. It is my job to be concerned about you."

"Yes. But you are not my mother."

Manora Fernandes bit her lip, and Gul winced. She'd been too harsh. They both knew what Mrs. F had been to her, all these years.

"If this mummy turns out to be real, and worth a fortune, then by tomorrow the whole of Karachi will know about it," Mrs. F said. "The government will get involved. You'll get pushed aside."

"They can't push me aside. There's no one else with any kind of actual mummification experience. Has Director Raja actually sat in a room and used the old methods to dry out a corpse? He knows nothing about how to use natron, or bitumen, or how to remove internal organs, or how to preserve the brain of a dead body. It's a complicated process, having your vital organs excised. And that's even before we get to the enemas that were used to dissolve guts and faeces in animals. Can you imagine a world where Director Raja, or any of the government experts, would ever get their hands that dirty?"

Mrs. Fernandes looked pained now. "That drug dealer may come after you. The police said the same thing."

"Not after me. Maybe after the mummy, which is why it's so important to find out more about her. Maybe we'll expose a black-market ring. Can you imagine? Besides, she'll be under police protection."

"Still . . ."

"This could be the biggest thing that ever happens in my career, Mrs. F. A Persian woman who was somehow mummified? The possibility that the rulers of Persepolis appropriated Egyptian customs like mummification, and we have *proof*? There will never be a more exciting discovery."

Mrs. F scowled again, and rose from the table, lifting plates as she did.

"I'll get those," said Gul, getting up as well. She was still feeling guilty over the mother comment.

"No, I'll do it," said Mrs. Fernandes. She headed to the kitchen.

Gul sat back down. Mrs. F was worried about her, that was all. Gul didn't know how she had managed before Manora Fernandes entered her life. Thirteen years ago, Gul had been working at the Department of Archaeology, on the government's payroll. She'd been there over a year—to the shock of many of the old-timers. Before she started, it had been the department's firm rule that women were not allowed to take on any nonclerical roles.

That rule had served the men in the department well for over fifty years. It was the reason—well, one of them—that Gul had gone to Cambridge and then on to Cairo and studied

Egyptology in the first place, rather than start her fieldwork in her native country as an archaeologist. But then, around the time her father died, new legislation was introduced to support women in the workplace, to ensure they weren't being harassed, but also to discourage discriminatory hiring practices. It meant the department had to consider her as a candidate for an assistant director job or justify their decision not to. For Gul, it was a sign. She wanted to move back to Pakistan. She wanted to spend more time with Mahnaz—despite Bilal's wishes—and she wanted to work on the ruins of the Indus Delta, not just on Egypt.

Gul read and wrote in four ancient languages. She had varied field expertise. She had completed her PhD from the American University in Cairo, on top of the degrees she already had from Cambridge. Just twenty-eight when she joined the department, Gul had more experience than most of the men in the office, even if most of that experience was Egypt focused. The department ran out of excuses to employ less-qualified male candidates, and so Gul returned to the country, and her new role.

But that didn't stop her new colleagues from doing whatever they could to "encourage" her to leave. She was not allowed to do any fieldwork. Instead, she was set up in a back storeroom. It was supposedly the exploration and excavation branch, but was really just a dark, dank space stacked with skeletons and forgotten antiquities. They thought she would give up and leave archaeology, because nobody wanted to spend their days cataloguing bone parts with no chance of promotion. But they had underestimated her determination.

Her first step had been to hand out flyers at Karachi University, where she was lecturing on ancient civilisations. The university did not have a dedicated archaeology programme, but, she thought, surely some of the students would be keen to learn? There was nothing in the department's rules that prohibited her from recruiting unpaid interns.

It had been one of the best decisions she ever made. Seven people showed up in response to her flyer. Five ran for the hills when they realised how mind-numbing the work would be, but two remained, curious. There was something about Hamza and Rana, even back then. They were misfits in their own ways—brilliant, out-of-the-box thinkers who were struggling with what their futures might look like. They were history students, kids with imagination who had wanted to study archaeology, but couldn't find a programme to teach them. Neither of them came from wealthy families, and ordinarily they would have joined the sea of aspiring accountants and lawyers and wannabe bank managers at their university—or worse, in Rana's case, the "only here till we get married" types. But they yearned for more. It was a feeling Gul recognised all too well, and together, they got to work. Rana and Hamza were whip-smart, but they were green. When they joined her as interns, she dedicated time just to teaching them the academic discipline required in categorisation and analysis. Most of their days were spent cleaning the artefacts for her to sort through.

Gul tried her best to make the work fascinating, and because her young team was keen to do real archaeology, she took them out to the field as much as she could. She put together module work they could do on the side, she taught them herself, and arranged online university access via her friends at universities overseas, so that they could do additional qualifications in tandem to what they were doing in Karachi.

All this from the dusty basement. Together, they taught themselves all there was to know about bones, from type to structure to function, from human to most of the less obscure animals. She dusted and cleaned alongside them and catalogued everything.

When the days were done and Gul emerged, blinking, from her dark rooms, she would wander around the building, reading the archives, looking at some of the exhibits that were in transit or being worked on, spending time with the many forgotten books. Then she would go home, get a few hours' sleep and begin it all again at 5 A.M. She knew her male colleagues thought cataloguing the bones would keep her busy for years, but she was determined to get them finished. In fact, she was nearly there, what with all the weekends she'd put in, and with the help of her interns. They'd simply have to give her more-challenging work after that.

After eight months of exhausting work with the bones, Gul decided that her interns needed a break and put in a request to take them on a trip to Rani Kot Fort. She'd thought it would be good for all of them to see the sunlight and experience a rare marvel. Rani Kot was the largest fort in the world, stretching over sixteen miles, its massive ramparts standing thirty feet high. In her biased opinion, its walls could rival China's own showing. Even more excitingly, the fort's origins remained a mystery, which made it all the more fun to explore.

She'd filled out the forms that all her male colleagues used for fieldwork, requesting a day away, the use of the museum's van and the money for petrol. She waited a week, but Director Hamid Kayani never replied. And so she filled out the forms again. This time, she went up to his office herself, to personally hand them over, striding across the hallway and up the stairs, determined not to leave until she got what she wanted.

And then . . . she faltered. A dragon with a bouffant sat sentry outside the director's office, her fingers clacking on an old Apple Mac. She barely looked up. "What do you need, Charlie?"

Gul cleared her throat. "I need Sir to approve this day away. Please." The woman was sitting in front of a battered fan, but even still, her hair wasn't moving. It was extraordinary.

Mrs. Fernandes looked up and said nothing for several moments. Then, she gestured to her in tray. "You can leave them there." She carried on with her typing.

"I've tried leaving them before. I won't do it again. Is he free? I'm going in."

Mrs. Fernandes's death stare was enough to stop Gul in her tracks. The clacking of the keyboard stopped. Manora Fernandes spoke very slowly, looking at her without blinking. "I said you can leave them in there. I'll make sure that he signs them."

Gul was outraged. "I'm not going to just—"

"You'll leave them if you know what's good for you, Charlie. I told you; I'll get them signed."

And for some inexplicable reason, Gul—who had once been confronted by an angry cobra in a newly explored tomb in the Valley of the Kings and had very casually knocked it on the head with her walking stick before carrying on with her work—backed down.

The very next day, Gul received the necessary permissions. She promptly phoned Mrs. Fernandes.

"I'd just like to say thank you."

"For what?"

"For your help with my forms."

"I don't know what you are talking about, Charlie," she said. "But I have work to do." And with that, she hung up.

Gul did not see or hear from Mrs. F again, until many months later. She'd come in one morning and found the exploration room ransacked. There were bones flung onto the floor in their hundreds, a tibia here, a parietal piece there, making it impossible to walk without crunching, all their tags removed, the shelves upended.

Bastards. Absolute utter madarchods. Somehow, as the anger built, she thought about the many times her mother had quietly congratulated Gul on her perfect marks, but then told her not to make a fuss, so that Bilal wouldn't develop a complex when he came home with his own mediocre reports. Why was it that men so often felt threatened by women who used their brains?

She almost gave up that morning. There was nearly a year's worth of work here, upended. There would be no investigations, she knew. Nobody would be blamed or implicated in the vicious destruction of museum property and invaluable artefacts. What was the point of continuing? There was no place for a woman here.

When they arrived, her team were devastated by the sabotage, though they tried not to show it. They stayed well into the evening, sorting what they could. Later, when she'd accepted she would be there until morning, she heard the door to the exploration room swing open.

Manora Fernandes stood in the shadows. "Well, hurry up, Charlie," she said. "We'll never finish if you work at that pace."

Behind her were some of the women in the secretarial pool.

It took months to properly sort out the mess, but from that day, Mrs. Fernandes was a permanent fixture and source of support. When Gul attended her interns' university graduations, bursting with pride alongside their families, it was Mrs. Fernandes who sat with her.

And when she moved to this new job at the Heritage

and History Museum, working under the slightly more amenable Director Rahim Raja, she insisted that her interns be allowed to come with her as full-time staff members. She was thrilled when Rana and Hamza agreed to join her, despite the long hours and pitiful pay. When they came, they were accompanied by Manora Fernandes.

Gul had learnt a lot about the woman in those initial years, about her quirks and idiosyncrasies. Mrs. F liked formalities. She wasn't happy unless she was making an itemised list about something or the other. She hated any kind of fuss or excess but had a secret passion for badam nankhatais and always had a tin of them in her car that she could nibble on while she was on the go. She was kind, but she was prickly, and was not one to share her emotions. She had a strong sense of justice, though. She had come to help Gul—who at that point was a total stranger—because she was outraged at the notion of a group of men trying to bully a woman.

Though she never showed it, Mrs. F was also permanently exhausted. She was raising her small grandson, Francis, because his parents had died in a car crash. And in her free time, she was devoted to a street kids shelter, one which had originally been set up by Mr. Fernandes, who had been a deacon at St. Andrew's Church. Mrs. F could be found there after work on most days with Francis in tow, cooking, cleaning, feeding.

As their relationship developed, Gul began to join her there. Francis was an adorable child who was obsessed with outer space. Spending time with him, helping him with his homework and science projects, and sneaking him chocolates when his grandmother wasn't looking brought her peace. Being at the shelter supporting Karachi's most disenfranchised and lost street children was just the balm Gul needed, given her own messed-up family life. Her parents were now dead, and she was not close with her brother, Bilal or his wife, Sania, who'd both discouraged Mahnaz from spending too much time with Gul. She only saw them at the odd family gatherings that Gul felt it necessary to attend, at the weddings, birthdays and Eid luncheons. It took several years for them to come around, and for her to establish a relationship with her niece.

But when Mahnaz vanished—only a short time after Bilal and Sania had finally relented and let Gul back in their lives—it had been too much to bear. The only thing Mahnaz left behind was her schoolbag, found near the gates of her convent school, her phone still zipped in the front pocket. It was Mrs. F and Francis who had come and spent that first anguished night with Gul. And when hours turned to days, and days to weeks and weeks to months, and Gul's body and mind had both shut themselves off and embraced depression, it was Mrs. F who looked after her, prickly and sour as usual, but always there for her, with cups of tea, removing old unwanted trays of food and replacing them with fresh unwanted trays of food, never pushing, never demanding. Never leaving.

It had taken many months for Gul to emerge from the fog, and more for her to make her peace with Bilal and Sania over what had happened. And Mahnaz . . . well, wherever she was, Gul could only pray that the Gods would protect her.

Gul listened to Mrs. F clattering about in the kitchen, putting on the kettle, washing dishes. She followed her there and pulled out two cups, ready to make the jasmine tea.

Mrs. Fernandes looked up. "What time are you picking up the body tomorrow?"

"As early as possible. I haven't had any confirmation from DSP Akthar yet, but I'm not going to leave the station without her, not without a fight."

"I'll drive you."

"There's really no reason, Mrs. F. You have enough on your plate."

"I said I'll take you there, Charlie."

"All right." And then, after a pause: "Thank you."

Mrs. Fernandes gave her a slight nod. "You are such an obstinate girl."

"I love you, too, Mrs. F."

CHAPTER 4

GUL BARELY SLEPT. SHE was too wired. She stayed up most of the night, trying to learn more about the mummy and hoping beyond measure that DSP Akthar would pull through for her the next day. Just who was this mysterious woman, so beautifully encased in gold, now lying in the dusty confines of the Jackson Police Station? Her wooden casket was covered in the emblems and motifs of the city of Persepolis. That linked her to the Achaemenid Empire because the city thrived during the Achaemenid dynasty.

Gul already knew some amount of information on the Achaemenids from her studies. They had created one of the most powerful civilisations of all time. Their territory stretched from Persepolis to Susa, to Ecbatana via Pasargadae, and to the east, all the way to modern-day Punjab. The great kings and pharaohs of Egypt, Assyria and Babylon all bowed their heads to their Persian conquerors.

The rest, she'd have to cull from her own limited library of history books and other resources—online articles, academic papers, the like. Unfortunately, many of the accounts of the period came from the Greek historians Ctesias and Herodotus. They wrote about the great kings of the time, of the epic battles and the shattering betrayals. Those accounts had to be taken with a pinch of salt, however. Their reflections were deeply biased, given the long-standing conflict between Greece and Persia. To the Greeks, the Persians were barbarians, torturers, and louts, whereas Gul knew that they were also great statesmen, engineers, nation builders, and explorers and—unlike many of the Greeks—they were tolerant of the religious and cultural practices of the people and land that they took over. Studying history was always like this, Gul had learnt: you had to piece together narratives that were conflicting, biased and human if you were going to create a logical arc. It would never be a whole picture, of course. But understanding history required understanding the stories that people told themselves, the ones that were inevitably flawed.

It was Cyrus the Great, the founder of the Achaemenid Empire, who conquered the city of Babylon and freed its slaves, giving people the right to choose their own religion. It was Darius I who went on to build an administrative system that organised the empire into satrapies, created a tax regime and fostered some of the most innovative architecture of the time. And it was Xerxes who welcomed women warriors into his armies, promoting some of the best strategists to the rank of general. Telling the truth was revered in Achaemenid societies, and lying was a cardinal sin, so much so that to be caught often meant a torturous death. A culture of banquets and feasts became the norm, in part because of the notion that those who drank wine together would speak the truth to one another.

Cyrus the Great might have founded the Achaemenid Empire, but it was Darius I who built Persepolis, which meant that if the mummy *was* from Persepolis, it was likely that she would have come from his time, around 522 BC, or the time of his son, King Xerxes.

Gul traced her fingers along a map she found in one of the books lying by the front door that had belonged to Mr. Davar, the old Parsi gentleman. *A History of Persia's Greatest Kings*. With delight, she saw that it had been written by Mr.

Davar himself. The ancient Persians were enlightened in many ways, one of which was the way they treated women, Mr. Davar had written. Women held positions of influence at court, owned businesses, and were in some cases able to join the military and civil service. But nowhere did the book mention anything about the practice of mummification.

At some point, Gul had started pacing up and down her bedroom, all thoughts of even attempting sleep forgotten. Was the body even real? Would the government take it away from her before she got the chance to find out? Eventually, she lay on her bed and shut her eyes. There was too much to speculate about, and too few answers.

She must have nodded off because she dreamt of Mahnaz again. It was the same recurring dream she'd had for many years—discordant, jarring—a memory, actually, of a day when the child was six years old, and Gul had been on summer break in Karachi.

It was the day that changed everything, the day that Bilal and Sania had inexplicably banished Gul from their lives. It had been a perfect day, not too hot, with a gentle breeze. Gul had taken Mahnaz swimming, blissfully unaware of what was to come. They'd had a wonderful time splashing in the pool, Gul throwing Mahnaz in the air and then letting her fall into the water and splutter her way back up, listening to her giggle afterward. Mahnaz would wrap her arms around Gul's neck, begging for her to do it again and again, her breath heavy and hot and smelling of chlorine. Then they indulged themselves at the nearby bookshop, both of them buying more than they should, even Mahnaz, who was reading at a nine-year-old level already. After that, they had bought some ice cream, and Mahnaz had dribbled strawberry all down her chin, which she had allowed Gul to wipe away only if she didn't have to put down the cone while she was doing it.

But later, on the way home, at the crossroads turning into Phase 5, another car broke the traffic light and ploughed into them.

It had not been Gul's fault. Of course it had not been her fault. She'd known that even then, in the aftermath, in the smoky silence that followed the screech of twisted metal, after she'd checked on Mahnaz, pulled pieces of glass out of her hair, and removed her from her car seat, fuelled by shock and adrenaline. The gathering crowd agreed that the man in the other car had been reckless. Seeing an injured woman with a weeping child only heightened their anger towards him. One of them cuffed him across the head, while the others decided to physically drag him to a nearby police station.

Gul had broken her collarbone and suffered a concussion. As for Mahnaz, the pinky on her left hand had shattered into so many small pieces, the doctors could never put it back together again properly—it remained stiff and immovable forevermore.

It could have been a lot worse. But Bilal and Sania were full of rage, and that rage had been directed at Gul. Why had Gul not left the pool earlier, when there was less traffic? Why had she been driving herself, and not hired a driver like Bilal had suggested she do? Why hadn't she noticed the other driver coming at her, and moved her car out of the way? The accusations kept on coming. How could she have let this happen; how could she have done this to their beloved child? And eventually Bilal announced, in his cold way, that it was better if Gul stayed away from their daughter.

Gul woke up with her hair plastered to her face, her stomach churning. She blinked a few times and saw pale light inching its way through the bottom of her blinds. She gave up on the idea of sleep. She did not want to think about

Mahnaz, not today. She would think about the mummy instead.

The woman in the sarcophagus—whoever she was—deserved to have her story told. And to give her that, Gul would have to unlock her mystery.

She got up, showered and got dressed. And then she waited for Mrs. Fernandes to come and pick her up.

CHAPTER 5

DESPITE THE HEAT, GUL'S teeth started chattering en route to the Jackson Police Station. Perhaps it was the excitement of seeing the mummy again, or perhaps it was because Mrs. Fernandes was driving them across town in her thirty-year-old, mustard-brown Toyota. Ordinarily, Gul would have insisted on driving herself, or calling a Careem taxi, because there was nothing worse than careening across the city with Manora Fernandes behind the wheel. The woman was a speed demon. She literally had no fear. And she never, ever stopped long enough at the red lights.

Today, however, Gul simply lacked the energy to argue. In fact, for the first time, she did not ask Mrs. F to slow down. She needed to get her hands on the body as quickly as possible. She thought about how Director Raja was going to react when he found out she was bringing a mummy to the museum, assuming the cops would release it. He wouldn't be thrilled at the police investigation, she imagined, but he would at least acknowledge her resourcefulness in preserving the body. Still, she wasn't his favourite person at the moment.

Gul had got in trouble only a few days earlier, when, at the weekly Young Archaeologists Club meeting she had set up at the museum, she taught her students how to mummify a basket of oranges. She told the children to close their eyes and imagine they were removing human guts, and they had been enthralled. Then they'd filled the insides of their oranges with cinnamon and cloves and bicarbonate of soda and salt, wrapped them up in bandages, and left them in the sun to dry out and shrivel. Some parents had complained, however. Apparently, mummification was un-Islamic, and, therefore, not something their children should be involved with. Even a simple orange was offensive. Gul's response had been to offer the kids a chance to watch her mummify a dead goat.

Gul sat quietly as the car lurched from one side of the street to the other. She watched Mrs. Fernandes hunched over her steering wheel, her eyes never leaving the road. You didn't talk to Mrs. Fernandes when she drove. Not if you wanted to live, or at least survive with your limbs intact. Not as she weaved her way through cars and rickshaws and lights, and dodged fruitwallahs and stray dogs at breakneck speed. It was such a strange thing, because ordinarily Mrs. Fernandes loved rules, and loved enforcing them even more. Perhaps this was the only way for her to let her frustrations out.

Mrs. F had lost almost every member of her family, and if that wasn't enough, because of her work at the St. Andrew's Shelter for Street Children, she spent most of her evenings and weekends dealing with other people's pain and suffering. It was a lot to carry, even on her broad shoulders.

She could often be spotted in her car, collecting her various kids. Those who did not want to leave the streets could still be cajoled to come to the shelter for meals. Others needed ferrying to a health clinic or needed a place to dry out. And even those kids, who were at their wits' end, who had suffered the combined indignities of poverty and assault, balked at getting into Mrs. Fernandes's rust bucket of a car.

Luckily, the Toyota wasn't really up to her driving ambitions. The air conditioning had never worked, and the windows' antiquated handles were all stuck or so difficult to maneuver that passengers pretty much gave up, and so the windows remained at four different levels of open. Instead, anyone in the car held their noses and tried furiously not to breathe in the dust balls of the city while the Toyota groaned and moaned under Mrs. Fernandes's expectations.

Today, they had raced through traffic all the way from Bath Island to the docks, passing the ships anchored at the harbour, swollen with freight, almost running over a man carrying a bundle of books on his back as he entered Jackson Market.

Jackson Market—one of Mrs. Fernandes's favourite haunts when she was trying to save a buck, Gul knew. It was said that anything and everything could be found at Jackson Market, the old bazaar where smugglers had been trading in goods pilfered off ships for over a century. The entrepreneurs, the chancers, those who knew how to have a good time—they all made their way to Jackson Market at some point or another. Need a specialty, one-off item? It might take a while, but one of the merchants would get it for you, no matter what it was, no questions asked. Whole lives had been built, and destroyed, by what Jackson Market had to offer.

These days the place had gone upmarket and lost some of its lustre, with many of its shops now housed inside proper concrete buildings, rather than in the fresh air. Many of the merchants refused to even bargain anymore. It was still a good place to go for second-hand bicycles and electronics, and "duty-evaded" items of all kinds, but there was a new-found snobbery to the place, as though it had aspirations of grandeur. As they drove by, Gul saw a shopfront that looked like a layer cake of oddly sized air conditioners—they were round, and smaller than anything she had seen before, presumably because they were repurposed from some ship. She then remembered that she needed a new fridge; the last one was on its way out. Every time the electricity went off and then came back on a few hours later—a daily occurrence these days—the fridge would shudder its way back to life with less and less enthusiasm. It wouldn't survive more than a few more weeks of Karachi's summer load shedding.

At that, Gul grew concerned. What was happening to the mummy's body in this heat? "You can go faster, if you want," she said mildly to Mrs. Fernandes. "I don't mind."

The engine roared in response. The car flew in the air for a moment as they raced over a speed bump, and then slowed a few minutes later after a dramatic right turn and a lurch to the left, as they reached their destination.

She was never happier to step out of a vehicle.

From the outside, the Jackson Police Station was a reminder of the city's colonial past. It was a simple building made elegant because of its tall archways and windows. It was constructed from yellow limestone and speckled with white paint that had clearly been left to peel off some years ago. *Police Station, 1924*, read the fading sign above the entrance, partially concealed under a mass of criss-crossing wires that formed a concentrated tangle and then spread in every direction, like a spider's web, until they reached the electricity poles.

A cop escorted them up some old wooden floors, made grey with dust and dirt and paan spit, and through a maze of interconnecting hallways, until they arrived at a door. They were ushered inside, into what could have been any corporate office building in the city—there was a glass desk with a PC on top, a ceiling fan and a filing cabinet. Only the certificate for bravery on the wall reminded her that this was a police department.

DSP Akthar was sitting behind the desk. "As salam alaikum."

"Wa alaikum salam."

Gul made brief introductions, then DSP Akthar rose from his seat. "I have good news for you."

"You're going to let me take her?"

He seemed amused by her eagerness. "Yes. I have spoken to my superiors and they are worried that if the body is not preserved, we will lose face in the international community. Those UNESCO types might create a stink, and the government doesn't need any more problems. Lucky for you."

"Lucky indeed." Gul smiled.

"Please, follow me." He led them out of his office and through another warren of hallways, into a dark room. His hands went to a light switch, and for a moment, there was an unsteady hum, and an even more unsteady flickering of fluorescent, until the lights clicked into place.

There she was, the mummy, looking even more splendid than she had in the cavern where she was found, her gold chest plate catching the light. Gul heard Mrs. Fernandes inhale sharply.

They got to work. With the help of a couple of cops, Gul carefully lifted the mummy out of its wooden coffin, using three bands of cloth passed underneath it to maintain its structural integrity. It was strapped into place into the ambulance she had arranged, while its sarcophagus was lifted into a police van and tied down with protective sheets and bungee cord. DSP Akthar had not been exaggerating about a police escort—there were three outriders waiting to escort the convoy, and a van with two armed cops behind. Bloody hell.

He motioned to a couple of the policemen, both of whom gave Gul a quick salute. "One of them will remain inside with the body at all times. The other will monitor the museum from the outside."

Gul arched her eyebrows. "You do know the museum has its own security guards? A mummy isn't exactly something someone could hide under their shirt and run away with."

"Nevertheless. I want you to keep me informed as soon as you have translated all the writing on the box."

"Of course."

"And there can be no forensic examination, no opening her up, not without police permission."

"I wouldn't dream of it, DSP Sahib," she replied slowly, climbing into the ambulance. Ever since Mahnaz's disappearance, there had been no love lost between Gul and the Karachi police force. However, as much as his officiousness was grating on her, DSP Akthar seemed committed to his job. Maybe, just maybe, there were some good ones out there after all. For now, she would reserve judgment. "I'll keep you posted."

The ambulance zoomed through the city. The driver did not bother to put on its sirens, because the police outriders on their bikes were moving traffic for them. They raced up Napier Mole Road, skirted the edges of Chinna Creek, and passed through the chaos and bustle of I. I. Chundrigar, navigating a mosaic of offices, banks, trade centres and burger joints. The usual congestion seemed to dissolve when they hit the Arts Council off Strachan Road. A quick turn at the FBR building and they were there—the twenty-minute drive to the Heritage and History Museum in Saddar was done in seven. It was amazing what a police escort could do. This was the beating hub of the city, where there was money to be made and deals to be done. Sometimes, during the commuter rush, the traffic could be gridlock for over an hour. But not today.

Gul texted Director Raja. Now that she had custody of the body, it would be all that much harder for him to refuse to allow her to investigate.

When they got there Hamza and Rana were at the gates, bright-eyed and excited. Together, they wheeled the mummy into an empty room on the ground floor. It then took five of them to bring in the wooden box and the three pieces of stone that had covered it, which they lifted on to one of the museum's unused wooden displays.

Gul stood over the mummy as they lifted her from the gurney and onto the table she had prepared, anxious that she not be damaged in any way. If they had been in Egypt, this would have been a far better thought-out procedure. At the caves, nobody would have touched the body without an expert there to ensure its stability, or without gloves. But this wasn't Egypt, and this was an unprecedented moment. They had to make do with what they had, and what had been done up until this point. From now on, though, she was in charge—unless the police changed their minds.

Gul shivered. She'd chosen this room because it was air conditioned, and Hamza had cranked it on high before their arrival. He had also somehow found a dehumidifier. The kid was enterprising, though the dehumidifier wasn't strong enough to really make a difference, not in a room this size.

Hamza pushed his glasses onto his forehead and rubbed his tired eyes. Gul wondered if he'd also been up all night. Sometimes, when he couldn't pull himself away from a game—at the moment his obsession was *League of Legends*—he did that. Hamza was a tech guru. He had shown her how to use photogrammetry to build 3D models of photographs for deeper analysis. He had endless patience, undeterred by her own technophobia and basic inability to use a computer without pounding on the keys in aggravation. He was scrawny and pale, someone who hated sports and only spent time in the sun when he was on a dig.

Gul looked at him now as he carefully laid out one of the

pieces of stone and marvelled at just how far he had come in the last few years. Hamza's father had died suddenly, leaving him to support his younger sister and mother. It was a heavy burden, though amazingly enough, his mother had pushed him to do what he loved, rather than to sell his soul to the world of accountancy or IT for their sakes. Of course, the rest of his family was far from pleased. His father's brothers phoned him up often to remind him that he was too soft. He was the man of the house now—he had to make something of himself because his mother and sister would be his burden for the rest of his life. And Hamza, who hated conflict and was a classic people pleaser, had been overcome with guilt on many occasions, and even tried to quit archaeology entirely. Luckily, his mother had intervened, and he had stayed the course.

It was also lucky that Hamza loved computers. When he wasn't obsessing about the eating habits of the ancient people of Mehrgarh, he did some programming on the side, and used the money to put his sister through university. Still, money was tight, his uncles were overbearing and it was costing him a lot to do what he loved.

Today, it turned out, his lack of sleep was her fault. "I saw your email about building a chamber for the mummy, to remove all the humidity from the air. I've already been working up some of your ideas. I think I can make it work, but I'll need at least until tomorrow, Apa," he said.

Gul put her hand on his shoulder. "Thank you. I'm very grateful."

Both Hamza and Rana looked stunned, their eyes barely leaving the mummy. Gul could hardly blame them. This was the most exciting thing that would probably ever happen in any of their careers. This was *it*, the moment every archaeologist would die to have. To be the first, to discover something new, to change the way history was viewed. Hamza and Rana had already done more in their field than she could have ever hoped for, producing stunning research and presenting their work internationally. They were building a name for themselves, and yet, nothing could have prepared them for this.

It was difficult even for Gul to pull her eyes away from the body. It was the mummy's face that struck her so deeply, the serenity of her visage, captured in a shroud of gold leaf.

Gul cleared her throat. "Right. When working with a mummy, it's important to document everything. And I mean *everything*, both visually and textually. We need videos, we need photographs, we need verbal and written descriptions of everything we observe. It's even more vital in this case, because none of us have knowledge of this particular type of cuneiform writing to translate what's been written, so we'll need to send visuals to experts further afield. By the way, there will be plenty of our colleagues who will come in here to gawk, and there won't be much we can do about it. Just remember that anyone who comes even close to the mummy should use gloves and masks to avoid contamination and protect the body as much as possible. Hamza, you continue to work on preservation. Let's find a way to keep her safe from the elements."

"Yes, Apa," he said.

Gul gazed at Rana next. Tall and slender, with blue-tipped hair, the girl looked far too hip to be an archaeologist, with her long, ethnic earrings, silver bangles, flared jeans and bright purple khussas. Rana was as different to Hamza as it was possible to be. She spent her days with a set of noise-cancelling headphones wrapped around her neck or on her ears, listening to dance music and tapping her fingers on any surface she could find. It should have been annoying, but really, it was endearing. Rana was a DJ; she often played at underground raves or house parties on the weekends, and had built a cult following.

Like Hamza, Rana was an outlier. She drove a second-hand motorcycle, swearing at the men who swerved into her because they were either outraged to see a woman driving a bike, or amused by it. Several times, Rana had been knocked off, but she always got back on with a curse on her lips. Now she was an expert, veering in and out of the traffic like she owned the place. If a man tried to play chicken on the road, he soon found himself flat on his back, choking on her dust.

Unlike Hamza's mother, who recognised his needs as an individual, Rana's parents were keen that she "find some-one" and settle down. They were the classic *log kya kahenge* types, but Rana simply rolled her eyes and got on with it. She attended protests, was a regular at the Aurat Marches, taught other women how to ride motorcycles and smoked like a chimney.

Rana was also a skilled linguist who had become obsessed with deciphering the Indus Valley script. Working with Gul was her chance to do some real archaeology, she had told Gul once. It was also her chance to have a female mentor, and "rage against the patriarchy." Gul had had to smile at that.

"Rana, start visual analysis," Gul said. "Record everything that you see, take as many pictures as possible, but without using any flash, please. Start with the sarcophagus, then make your way to the body. When you get to the body, both the recto and the verso need to be examined and photo-graphed. I can help with that."

Gul pointed at the coffin. "See that large rosette carving there? It's emblematic of the motifs of Persepolis. Next to it is the emblem of the god Ahura Mazda, also carved every-where at Persepolis, particularly on the doorway of the main

Council Hall. That's an encouraging sign. And the cypress trees? I learnt last night that seven cypress trees was the royal emblem of the ancient city of Hamadan, which lay next to Persepolis. You can see the motif on her crown, and on the side of the sarcophagus. As I told the police, this body, if it's real, could be of royal blood." The very thought of it made Gul's pulse quicken.

She pointed to the mummy's mask. "We need to find out if the Persians ever used masks like these, in any time period," she said. "Hamza, when you're done with your schematics, can you have a quick look to see if there are any other examples of gold-leaf work like this in Achaemenid Persia? And after that, see if you can find us some forensic help. We'll need a medical professional who can provide X-rays and CT scans, even an MRI if the director and police-wallahs allow. Someone who can tell us what has happened to the body internally."

Hamza nodded. "No problem Apa."

"I'll work on dusting down the writings on her chest plate and wooden box, and on the stone covering her, so that we can start having the writings translated. Then, we'll start working on the body itself. Let's put together all our findings later today, and then I'll send them to Harry at the British Museum. I'm sure he'll be able to provide some valuable insight."

At the mention of Harry, Hamza's face lit up.

Harry—really Dr. Harry Gilbert—was an old colleague from Gul's Cambridge days. He was an eminent forensic historian and a professor at University College London. In the last few years, he'd taken on a part-time role as South Asian curator at the British Museum, which meant that the two had reconnected. Harry had started coming through Pakistan a fair amount, always chasing after some artefact or the other, trying to get it to be put on loan for a museum exhibition. There was nobody whose expertise Gul had more respect for.

Harry had helped her team get their archaeology degrees through various remote-learning programmes, and so they knew him well. He was always fun to be with, always up for an adventure, and far cleverer than he let on.

If anyone could tell her what kind of mummy she was looking at, it would be Harry Gilbert. She would record her findings, and get them to him today, Gul decided. At least that way, even if the body was taken away from her, she could continue some kind of independent investigation. As her team scattered, she became absorbed in her work, dusting the sarcophagus, lingering over the crown of cypress trees, trying to loosen as much dirt as possible.

Eventually, she paused, making space for Rana to take her photographs. She stood back, examining the body now. The study of mummies was a multidisciplinary endeavour. It required an understanding of medicine, of chemistry, of textiles and anatomy, even of agriculture. There were certain visual and physical examinations that the team would need to make once Rana had finished taking her photographs. They would need to measure the entire body and its dimensions, as much as they could with the shroud of resin over it.

If the body's wrappings were more accessible, she would have been able to use the cloth—poring over its quality and thread count, its colour and patterns—to draw conclusions about who the mummy was and when she had lived. But for now, if the police allowed, samples of the resin would need to be removed and examined in the right conditions to tell her anything about the wrapping itself. Would the wrappings bear inscriptions, as some mummies had? Were there tampons of linen in the body's nose and ears, as some Egyptian mummies were preserved with? She could see that there were stains on a straw mat that lay inside the sarcophagus, indicating the presence of oils, resins or body fluids. So far, there was nothing to suggest that this body had not been mummified many thousands of years ago. If this was a hoax, then it was a remarkably sophisticated one.

Gul was so focused on the mummy that she did not notice Ali Mahmood, the museum's Mughal archivist, come through the door, red-faced and huffing, until he cleared his throat. His eyes took in the mummy, and then turned to her. "So it's true," he said. "Why were we not informed?"

Gul ignored him. Ali Mahmood was an odious man. He was Director Raja's de facto second-in-command, but that was only because he was the nephew of the Minister of Antiquities. And he never let anyone forget it. Ali liked to throw his weight around, bullying those who worked for him. Rumours had been swirling around the department—a secretary disappearing, paid to leave and keep her mouth shut after Ali tried his luck with her. Then the only female intern working under him abruptly handing in her notice and nobody, besides Gul, asking any questions . . . The man made her skin crawl.

Ali was stocky and solid, and oily in every sense of the word, from his slicked-back hair to his Dolce & Gabbana shoes. Despite their mediocre pay, he only ever wore branded clothing. It sometimes amazed Gul that he would still be working at a place like this, given the scope of his ambitions. But here he was, and she was stuck with him and his glinting gold Rolex, which had to be a fake, unless he'd won the lottery and she hadn't known about it.

She carried on with the work. "I informed Director Raja this morning, as it happens. But this is not a Mughal body, Mahmood Sahib. I wouldn't think it would be of interest to you." Her brush wasn't making much impact on the harder pieces of dirt. She'd need to use something stiffer.

"Wouldn't think it of interest . . . My dear Madam, this is very wrong." Ali cut across her and Rana, trying to examine the body and sarcophagus for himself. They carried on regardless, forcing him to move every few minutes.

"The Egyptians must have taught the Persians," he said at last. "Proof that mummies exist outside of Egypt! Who would have thought!"

Gul couldn't resist. The man was insufferable. She stopped dusting and smiled sweetly at him. "What a sense of humour you have, Mahmood Sahib. Of course, we both know that mummies exist on every continent of the world. Why, just think of the Chinchorro mummies of South America. They are fascinating examples of artificially mummified human remains, and quite something to look at. I have some photos of them hanging in my dining room, if you'd like me to bring them into the office for you to see?"

"You keep photos of their dead bodies? In the room where you eat?"

"Only the interesting ones," Gul countered. "The older ones are quite marvellous, really. Quite ingenious, the way they have been preserved. They used to peel the skin away from the bodies of the dead, a bit like a sock. Then, when they had undertaken their preservation work, they pulled the skin back on. Every time I see their images, I feel like I learn something new."

He was turning a peculiar shade of plum, and Gul was satisfied.

"Yes, well. That may be the case. But they are not as important as the Egyptian mummies. Those are the oldest and most important mummies in history."

"I believe you'll find the Chinchorro mummies to be at

least two thousand years older," Gul replied, putting down her brush. "Then there are the mummies of the Scyths in the Pazyryk culture of Siberia, of course, and the mummies of the Han dynasty . . . Why, even the Canary Islands had its Guanche mummies. In fact, the Indian subcontinent is one of the rare regions where human remains have never been artificially preserved in that way, as far as we know." She smiled blandly at him, enjoying his pained look.

"Yes. Well, obviously, I am not an expert."

"No," she shot back. "You are not."

At that, his face darkened. "Director Raja will be here soon."

"Good," she replied shortly. "Now if you'd be so kind as to give me some space?" Bloody man.

Ali Mahmood's indignation lingered long after he'd left the room, and Gul asked Rana and Hamza to work as fast as they could. She had no doubt that even at that moment, he would be on the phone to his uncle, the useless Minister. Director Raja was a diligent but weak man. If the Minister demanded that he let Ali take over the police investigation, he'd cave, even though they both knew what a disaster that would be.

When Director Raja arrived, he reaffirmed her fears. "Work fast," he said, surveying the body. "Minister Mahmood has already been on the phone, but I've emphasised that this is an independent matter between you and the police, who chose you because of your expertise. I'm sure the Minister is calling the head of the Sindh police even as we speak. I bought you some time, but I'm not sure how much."

And so Gul worked quickly, dusting, recording, cataloguing, ignoring the ache in her back. There was a significant section of the chest plate that was so dirty she couldn't reveal the cuneiform on it, and she spent a long time cleaning it, determined not to make the slightest injury to the metal. Eventually, some of the letters began to form, and she felt the thrill, once again, of being the one to uncover something new.

By midafternoon, they had made decent progress. Hamza had found records of similar gold-foil funerary masks in Persia, and he'd been on the phone with a doctor at the Aga Khan University Hospital, who was willing to help with a CT scan and MRI, if the police would let them go that far.

"But he's not a forensic expert, Apa. He can just run the tests."

Hamza was right. They would need someone with an understanding of the forensics of mummies. Gul paused long enough to have a cup of tea. There were so many things to think about. She needed to make sure that she wasn't missing anything.

She collected everything they had and compiled it into one digital file, and then emailed it to Harry. She followed it up with a phone call.

"Gul," Harry said. "What's up?"

"I've sent you something." She couldn't wait for his reaction. Would he think this was all crazy?

"Don't tell me it's that deadly new book on Pharaoh Akhenaten and his mystery illness by Professor Hotchkiss. I know you idolise the man, Gul, but a lot has changed since Cambridge."

"Not that kind of something. I've sent you a file. Can you have a look?"

"Now?"

"Yes, please."

"I'm about to go into a seminar . . ."

"Check your email and call me. Please, it's important."

Harry rang back in three minutes. "It's a fake. It has to be." Still, she could hear the excitement in his voice. He wanted it to be real, just as much as she did.

"What if it's not?"

"Well then, history has become a hell of a lot more interesting, hasn't it?"

Gul had been unaware that she was holding her breath until she exhaled, deeply. She knew it. There was something here. If not, Harry would have told her straight out not to waste her time. But he was intrigued too. "Can you have the cuneiform translated for us? I would find someone here, but it will take longer, and whoever I find might try and take over the case for themselves."

Harry laughed. "And here I was, thinking that the back-stabbing old goats in London had no competition."

"Seriously, Harry, I need this done quickly. It would be a big favour, and I'd appreciate it."

After a pause, Harry said, "I'll get one of the Persian scholars to give this their immediate attention. I should have something for you in a few hours."

"Thank you."

"Is this all of it?"

"No. In some places on the casket the dirt is too stiff to remove. Some of the writings will take time to clean up, but at least her gold chest plate is readable now. I focused on that first."

"Fascinating. There are, of course, records of multiple funerary gold-gilded plates in various parts of the world, but Iran is not one of them."

Gul hesitated. "Harry, can you come?"

"Where? To Karachi?"

"Yes, obviously to Karachi. I don't have the forensics background you do. If I manage to get an eminent British forensics expert on the case, I might buy myself a bit more time with her."

He sounded amused. "The things we do to keep the backstabbers away. I've got to be in Tehran in a few days, as a matter of fact. There's an artefact I'm trying to purchase for the museum. Wait till you see it."

"Even better. You can combine the two trips. Come on, Harry. You know you'll be able to provide some valuable insights, and this is too exciting to be missed."

"You really think this is real?"

"I . . ." Gul said, then paused. She was a scientist, after all. "We don't have all the facts yet."

"But what's your gut telling you?"

"Yes," Gul blurted. "Yes, I think she could be real."

Harry said nothing for a moment, but he didn't have to. She could hear, just from his rapid breathing, that he was in. "I'll have to move my schedule around."

"But you'll come?"

"Try and stop me."

CHAPTER 6

IN THE EVENING, GUL headed to Mrs. Fernandes's shelter.

It was a wrench to pull herself away from the body, but on Tuesday evenings she taught English and mathematics to whichever kids were around and interested. Teaching at the shelter was something she was committed to, and wouldn't forgo. So she locked the door of the room where the mummy was stored and left the police escort standing outside in the corridor. She'd only be away for an hour, after which she planned to pull an all-nighter with the body. There was no way Ali Mahmood would be given permission to move the mummy until morning, assuming he was able to get his grubby little paws on her.

The shelter was actually a former residence, now a dilapidated heritage house like many of those peppering the old colonial enclave of Saddar, tucked on a street behind St. Andrew's Church and not far from Empress Market. As usual, the place was engulfed by a sea of traffic and pedestrians, a cacophony of tooting horns and cart vendors hawking their wares. In the heat, everything baked, and Gul could smell the tarmac melting off the road, wafting alongside the body odour of the collective mass of people on the pavement. Gul parked up the road next to the lines of motorcycles three or four deep that took up a large part of the street.

Inside the shelter, an army of volunteers, mainly from the church, but also from the Tokyo Beauty Parlour, was corralling children to the kitchen. It was dinner time.

The shelter both inspired and depressed Gul. Kids came in, hollowed out by the streets. Some were zombies, exhausted by life. Others were quick on their feet and would grab what they could and then disappear with a cheeky wink. Some of them spent their days in the disused fish section of Empress Market, now a bed of heroin addicts, returning only to sleep and dry out. Others never left, incapable of leaving, and others still were indefatigable, always cracking jokes, delighted with their buttered rotis and meagre portions of sabzi. Many were teenage prostitutes, massage boys who plied their trade on the streets, with their little bottles of oil showing the world who they were, while others spent their time walking around Sabzi Mandi or Lea Market or hanging out at some of the cold drink spots around the city where they would be picked up by men. Many didn't have families, and almost all had been abused or let down in one way or another.

Gul spent her time with the kids that had somehow retained that most elusive thing of all: hope. They were mostly younger, some were regulars, others were just passing through or had been dropped off by parents too poor to feed them. The shelter used a network of charities to move the little ones to orphanages or schools wherever possible, but there were so many of them, and very few places. The older ones were offered the odd apprenticeship when it came up, though even those were few and far between.

Gul set up in the front room, which served as a makeshift school, populated by a chalkboard, a bookshelf of workbooks and some old desks and chairs. An over-sized Christ was being crucified in painful glory on the wall behind her, dominating everything. The kids would start trickling in soon, so she had a few minutes.

Ejaz stuck his head around the door and grinned. "Salam, Apa."

Gul smiled. "Ejaz. Where have you been hiding?"

Ejaz entered, scratching at some stubble. "I've been busy. I haven't had time to visit."

Watching him, Gul felt the familiar pang. When they'd first met, Ejaz had been just seven, scrawny and watchful. Now he was seventeen, tall and filled out, fine boned and handsome, with thick, shoulder-length hair. Whenever she saw him, she couldn't help but think of Mahnaz. In the months before her disappearance, she'd volunteered here and taken Ejaz under her wing, acting as older sister and co-conspirator in turn. Ejaz and Mahnaz, firecrackers both. He had been devastated when she vanished.

Gul looked at Ejaz, who was beaming at her. She had thought for a while that he might stay off the streets, but Ejaz was a chancer, a wheeler-dealer, an occasional massage boy and a sometimes runner for the local gangs, selling hash at the nearby colleges and around Zainab Market. He was smart and resourceful, and above all, he valued his independence. Maybe if Mahnaz had still been around, she would have convinced him to find another way, despite all the obstacles and challenges.

"I hear you found a body. One that could make you rich."

Gul looked at him sharply. "Who told you that?"

Ejaz shrugged.

Well, that didn't take long. Mrs. F had been right. In this city, nothing was ever a secret. "Yes, as it happens, we did find a body, but it's a police matter."

"Can I see it?"

"Why?"

"Why not?"

"As I said, it's a police case, Ejaz. Off-limits."

"They say the body is the property of Saayaa. Is this true?"

"How did you . . ." It was a redundant question. Of course he knew. Nobody had a better network than Ejaz.

Ejaz shrugged again.

"What do you know about him—Saayaa?"

He picked up a piece of chalk from the blackboard and began to move it around his fingers. "If you're asking, it means the rumours are correct."

Gul hesitated. At this point, it seemed, Ejaz had more information than she did. "It's true. This man, Saayaa, with the silly nickname, had possession of the mummy when they found it. At least, his men did."

Ejaz's expression was troubled. "Be careful, Apa. Saayaa is not a joke."

"He sounds like a villain from a fairy tale."

Ejaz shook his head. "He's a bad man."

"So I'm told. But he's a drug runner. I want to know what he was doing with a mummy. Tell me about him."

He dropped the chalk and looked at her, slyly. "I will be happy to answer all your questions . . . on the drive to the museum."

She couldn't help but smile. "Curses, you're like a bloody bloodhound. All right, if you're that curious, I will take you. But you need to respect that this is a police case. No touching anything. Deal?"

"Bilkul, Apa," he replied, putting his hand over his heart.

"We can go tonight, after the class if you want. I don't know when the police might take her away, so this may be your only chance."

Ejaz grinned and then picked up the chalk once more. "Do you want me to teach the mathematics? We both know I am better at it than you are."

"That's because you had a good teacher. Come on, then. Stand up here with me and show me how smart you are."

After the class, Gul went to the kitchen to say goodbye to Mrs. Fernandes. In the corridor, she ran headlong into someone, and moved back to apologise. It was Sania, Gul's sister-in-law. Bloody hell.

Sania stood near the kitchen doorway, her face impassive. She was perfectly manicured and curated, as usual. How did the woman never, ever have a single hair out of place?

When Sania and Bilal had first got engaged, Gul had been optimistic. She liked Sania. Gul thought Sania could be a bridge between her and her brother. Sania was bright and engaging. In some ways, despite their arranged marriage, she was the perfect match for Bilal. She made no bones about never wanting to have a career, about wanting to raise her family, and she was grateful for the opportunity to marry up—her own family's wealth was relatively new, and they had no real political connections, unlike the Delanis. Bilal's star was on the rise at work, and Sania was determined to support his career. She was vivacious, interested in world events and international politics, in Sufism and experimental film too. She would keep Bilal on his toes.

In the early years, Gul thought they had really hit it off, two women with "big personalities," as her mother often said. But it didn't take long for Sania to start to freeze Gul out. For reasons she never fully understood, their relationship had soured.

Whatever happened, something shifted. Sania stopped talking to Gul about secret cinema, or the state of the world, or her love of Latin American literature . . . and more or less stopped talking to her about anything at all. Sania, who once used to scoff at these things, seemed to become a pillar of the Memon community overnight, celebrated amongst the largely merchant, entrepreneurial class of Gujrati speakers. She embraced her role as a member of one of the leading banking families in the country, a woman whose husband regularly went to Friday prayers and didn't drink but still enjoyed a good party or two, demonstrating just the right amount of piousness.

Sania began hosting community networking events and stood by Bilal's side when he launched a scholarship fund for Memon kids to get to university. She was seen by others as an icon, and seemed content with being perfectly poised and opinionless. A puppet princess amongst her people. There were family luncheons and society functions and the Club and charity events, fashion and Hermès bags, blow-dries and foreign holidays, and her daughter. This was Sania's universe, and where she seemed happy to be. And there was no room for Gul in that universe, no quarter given, especially after Mahnaz was born.

Gul nodded. "Hello."

If Sania was fazed by seeing her, she didn't let it show. They made it a point these days to politely ignore each other. Sania knew Gul would be at the shelter on Tuesdays, and she was never there at the same time, not usually.

It still amazed Gul that she was there at all. Getting her hands dirty wasn't really Sania's speed. But Mahnaz had loved her time volunteering here, and for that reason, both Bilal and Sania had developed an interest in the place even before her disappearance. Sania popped by every so often to check in on things, to help with logistics and the admin. Sometimes, she took some of the older kids home and offered them part-time work to ease their financial plight. Bilal threw money at the place via the Delani Foundation, which was his way of addressing any problem he came up against. His desperately needed funds kept the lights on, so Gul tolerated the situation. Still, they usually ensured their paths didn't cross.

"Gul," said Sania. "It's nice to see you."

It was something she always said. Both of them knew she didn't mean it.

"Hi, Sania. How is everyone? How are you both?"

"Bilal and I are both doing well, by the grace of God."

Everything was by the grace of God with her brother and Sania, Gul thought. "Good, that's good."

"Are you heading out?"

Gul cleared her throat. "Yes, yes. I'm going back to the museum with Ejaz."

"At this time of night?"

"He's keen to see something I'm working on."

"The mummy?"

"How did you kn—"

"They're all talking about it in the kitchens."

Of course they were. "It's a police matter. I'm just helping out."

"I see."

"Well, it was nice to bump into you."

Sania nodded, in an almost regal way. "Take care, Gul."

Gul let Mrs. Fernandes know she was leaving, then she took Ejaz to the car. Her stomach was churning after her encounter with Sania. Why did they always go through the charade of pretending they were okay with each other?

On the drive to the museum, she distracted herself by peppering Ejaz with questions about Saayaa in an effort to understand any tenuous link to the mummy, but the character Ejaz described was more myth than man. Saayaa was a gangster who had his fingers in many pies, it seemed. Drug running, money laundering, human trafficking and more. Any time a body was found within a few miles of Saddar, beaten and bloated, drowned or electrocuted, it was Saayaa's handiwork, according to Ejaz. And yet, nobody knew what Saayaa looked like. The street kids all claimed to have seen him, claimed he had bright red blazing eyes and was in league with evil spirits who helped him stay one step ahead of the police.

"He's a monster, Apa. That's why you have to be careful."

"I will be, I promise."

Ejaz gazed out the window. When he turned to look at her, his eyes were shiny. She glanced at him briefly before turning back to the road.

"Ejaz . . ."

"Yes?"

"You know you can tell me anything, right?"

"Yes, Apa."

"Good. You seem a little upset this evening. Is something wrong?"

"Nothing, I'm just tired."

Gul tried again. "You've never been remotely interested in my work. What is it about this mummy that interests you?"

Ejaz looked down and straightened the edge of his kameez.

"Ejaz, you know I'm not someone who interferes. But if you're in some sort of trouble, I need to know."

"It's nothing," Ejaz said at last. "Nothing for you to worry about."

Gul left it there. Whatever the kid was upset about, it would come out eventually; it always did.

They reached the museum and she waved at the night guard and parked in the semi-darkness. Idly, she wondered where DSP Akthar's extra cop had positioned himself—she couldn't see him at all. She took Ejaz first to her office, where she'd left the keys for the room downstairs. Her office was, as usual, a wreck of a place, files and books piled up high, pieces of relics and antiquities that needed analysis, student reports to grade from her evening lectures at the university, thank-you cards from the swathes of school children that came on tours, her excavation and camping gear flung into a corner. Organised chaos, she liked to think of it as, conceding that it may be more chaos than organisation.

Gul grabbed the keys. "Come on, let's go."

The hallway outside was encased in half-light, prompting her to look at her watch. It was nearly 10:30 P.M. The cleaners would have come and gone.

As they walked down the hall, their footsteps echoed on the polished marble. They moved through the Humans in History Gallery, passing the odd display of mannequins—the ones that always left her feeling mildly disconcerted. Here was the Life in Mohenjodaro exhibition, the mannequins dressed in brightly coloured ajraks, posed in a domestic scene outside a mud hut. The male was lighting a fire, and the female was weaving on a loom, which seemed arduous, given that she was also wearing a headdress full of beads and stones. A child was playing with a bull-cart toy. They were meant to look serene, but Gul had always found their expressionless waxwork faces a little creepy, especially now, with most of the lights switched off. It was almost as though they were on the verge of melting in the summer's heat, like they were watching her go by.

Gul picked up her pace, Ejaz following, and they walked briskly past all the dummies until they reached the turn for the entrance to the Rare Manuscripts Gallery. There, they took a left and walked down the stairs. After that they made their way down to the side room, where the body of the mummy was being kept. She opened the door and stopped. She could make out shadows, moving in and out of her vision. Heavy breathing, the scuttling of feet, and the stench of sweat. There were people in here.

Gul's fingers found the light switch on the left, and she pressed, hard.

The room became encased in fluorescence. And there, in the middle of it, was the police escort himself, his hands lifting one end of the body out of its chamber. On the other side, the cop who was meant to be on guard outside held the mummy's head, the body suspended between them about a foot above the sarcophagus. The duo looked as shocked to see Gul as she did to see them. For a moment they were all like cartoon characters, jaws on the floor, in suspended animation.

Gul pushed Ejaz out the door. "Run," she said. "Get help."

He didn't need to be told twice.

It took a moment for the men to react, and another moment for them to drop the body and come for her.

"Stop the boy!" one cop said to the other.

The second one tried to push past her, but she stood her ground.

"Haraamzaadi. Get out of the way or I'll snap your neck," he said. He came at her then, so quickly that she barely saw him move. They wrestled at the door, Gul thinking only of protecting Ejaz now. She kicked him between the legs as hard as she could, and for a moment, he stopped and grunted, and she turned to reach for the door handle. Then he lunged again, going for her throat this time, his forearm snaking across her neck. She clawed at his arm, desperately trying to pull him off her, even as he dragged her backwards. She dug her fingernails deep into his arm and for a moment, he let her go. She twisted around, trying to anticipate his next move, but it came too quickly. With a violent shove, he pushed her into the wall. Her head snapped back against the corner of a display case and her knees buckled. And then there was darkness.

CHAPTER 7

THERE WERE VOICES. IN the distance, someone was shouting. And then lights, bright, flashing lights, a jerk, a sense of movement, the voices fading in and out. Then both the lights and voices disappeared, only to be replaced by an incessant bleeping, the slow steady ticking of a pulse monitor.

Gul opened her eyes, blinking against the fluorescent light. She lifted her hands to her face, staring at the pulse monitor on her finger. She tried to sit up and moaned. The world was moving too fast for her to keep up, and everything tilted in and out of focus. Gentle hands guided her back onto her pillow.

"Rest now."

Was that Mrs. Fernandes? Gul tried to open her eyes again to see what was going on, but they were too heavy. Within moments, she entered oblivion once more.

WHEN SHE OPENED her eyes again, she was staring at the stars.

Gul blinked and tried to focus. No, not just stars, but a pattern of stars. Sticky glow-in-the-dark stars on a ceiling. Cassiopeia, the constellation, named after the queen of Aethiopia in Greek mythology. In her pride, Cassiopeia had boasted that her daughter, Andromeda, was more beautiful than the daughters of the sea god Nereus. And Poseidon, full of anger at her vanity, ordered the sea monster Cetus to plague the coastline and wreak havoc on its people. In the end, Cassiopeia had to sacrifice her daughter in order to appease him, to watch as her precious child was chained to a rock next to the sea, waiting for the monster to claim her as his victim. Only the heroics of Perseus saved her.

Gul blinked again. She was in Mahnaz's bedroom. She had helped her put that constellation on the ceiling, had watched as Mahnaz mapped out the space between each sticker so it could be as accurate a representation as possible. What the hell? How on earth had she got here? She sat up. Someone had stolen the mummy, and she'd hit her head. She had vague recollections of the hospital, of the bright lights and beeping machines. And now, somehow, she was across town in upscale Defence Phase 5, just past Zamzama and all the bougie restaurants and designer clothing stores, in the last place she ever wanted to be.

There was a glass of water on the bedside table, and she drank it with shaking hands. Gul looked down. She was wearing pyjamas. She sniffed her hair. Lavender. She'd been here long enough to have a shower, then. But why couldn't she remember? She looked around, hoping for a clue. Even when Mahnaz was alive, even when they were back in each other's lives, Gul was rarely encouraged to be in this room. Why would she be here now? Bilal and Sania must have brought her here, but why?

The room hadn't changed one bit. They'd left it exactly as it had been. There were the posters of the bands and musicians Mahnaz loved plastered on the walls—Muse, Abida Parveen, Ali Sethi, Nirvana, Junoon, and Queen—Freddie Mercury's raised arm curling slightly at the edge. He was next to a pithy poster with an image of Schrödinger's cat in the Wild West, which said WANTED: DEAD AND ALIVE, a poster that most of Mahnaz's friends had never understood. On the other wall, a framed quote from Maya Angelou:

There is no greater agony than bearing an untold story inside you.

She'd asked Mahnaz about it once. "Do you have untold stories bursting out of you?"

Mahnaz had laughed. "Doesn't everyone?"

Gul's eyes swept the room, her heart aching. Here, on top of the corner bookshelf was Blinky the sheepdog, the large plushie Mahnaz had slept with ever since she was a baby. Her tangle of silver bracelets and necklaces hung over her bedpost. And books, so many books. Books everywhere. Science books. Music books. History books. Books about politics and feminism. And on her bedside table, a fossil. *The* fossil.

Gul picked it up and cupped it in the palm of her hand. She squeezed her eyes shut. Mahnaz had been thirteen when she turned up at the museum, wearing a Queen T-shirt, holding this same fossil in her hand. She'd gone to the reception desk and demanded to see her aunt. The staff had called Gul, who was so shell-shocked, she hadn't known what to do. But she'd gone down to the lobby.

"I found this, in the back garden," Mahnaz had announced, her arm thrust forward, when she saw her aunt. "I've been digging for fossils, and I found this. I thought you could tell me what it was."

She held out the stone, which Gul took carefully from her hands, not trusting herself to speak.

"It's an ammonoid," Gul said at last. "It's a marine mollusc. It's extinct now, but this is a very well-preserved example." She handed it back.

Mahnaz nodded. "I thought it must be. I looked it up. I wanted it authenticated, but Baba said there was nobody who could do that for me. Then I thought about you. It's been nearly a year, Gul Phupi, since you came to the house for that big family Eid lunch."

"Gul. It's just Gul. Please." She'd never wanted to be called Phupi, which meant father's sister. It didn't sit well, and they'd all agreed she would be plain Gul to her niece. But now their relationship had become so distant that Mahnaz had chosen to formalise it, she thought with a pang. "And look how much you've grown since then."

Mahnaz had taken her hand. "I miss you, Gul."

Gul had stared at her hand, cupped so naturally, effortlessly against the other. "I miss you too, darling."

And that meeting changed everything once again. Gul had swallowed her pride and called Sania, and appealed to her. "I don't need to see her all the time. But you can't cut her out of my life entirely. It won't work, not if she's come looking for me herself. And I don't deserve it, Sania, you know I don't."

Amazingly enough, Sania had relented. Perhaps it was because she was feeling guilty about everything that had happened. Or perhaps she recognised that Mahnaz was an unstoppable force once she put her mind to something. For whatever reason, Sania had talked Bilal around, and Mahnaz once again became part of Gul's life.

The next few years had been the happiest of Gul's life. Mahnaz often dropped by after school and did her schoolwork at the museum before going home in the evenings. For two precious hours, a few days a week, she belonged to Gul.

Mahnaz had a keen scientific mind. She had explored the length and breadth of the museum within days, including all the dimly lit storerooms. She had a lively intellect, and she was curious by nature. Like Gul, she read voraciously. She loved detective stories and whodunnits, always pleased when she was proved right at the end of the book. She carried a journal with her at all times and recorded everything in it. Her day-to-day life, her explorations and discoveries, and her ideas. She was always full of ideas. Ideas for experiments. Ideas for ways to improve the shelter. Ideas for new and increasingly complex ciphers in multiple languages, overlaid on top of one another. Mahnaz was obsessed with secret codes and puzzles.

After a while, Gul affectionately nicknamed her niece "Jane"—a nod to Agatha Christie's famous sleuth, Miss Jane Marple. Mahnaz was thrilled with the moniker. At home, her parents still called her princess, which she hated, and which Gul agreed, one afternoon when they were sorting a box of ancient coins, demonstrated an appalling lack of originality, and a suffocating smugness.

Later, when Mahnaz had read every Miss Marple story there was to read, and when she learnt about Christie's own life in the Middle East, and the author's pursuit of archaeology, she began to call Gul "Agatha." And so they were bound by a mutual love of mysteries and archaeology, and became Agatha Christie and Miss Jane Marple, and wrote silly emails to each other, signed off as Jane and Agatha.

Oh Jane, won't you come over and partake in some tea with me?

Oh Agatha, I can't today, because Miss Ibrahim is making me write an essay about why it is bad manners to talk back to a teacher, even when the teacher gets things wrong.

Dear Jane, she sounds like a beastly woman. Love, Agatha.

Dear Agatha, if there is a Murder on the School Express, nobody should blame me.

As she grew older, Mahnaz discovered feminism. She read Wollstonecraft, Chughtai, Wadud, Friedan, Jahangir, and Steinem. She joined the Women's Action Forum and went on the Aurat March, despite her parents' beleaguered attempts to keep her at home, and despite the backlash and threats of violence marchers received. Mahnaz proudly carried one of the signs that said *Mera Jism Meri Marzi*, even though she knew, from previous years, how much controversy it could bring. Sure enough, a blurry image of her holding the sign appeared on social media, where she was called an obscene woman, a *randi*, a bitch. The next year, she carried another popular slogan—*Main Awara Main Bad-chalan*. Several attempts were made to identify her, and then Mahnaz helpfully posted a picture of herself on social media, and the vitriol dutifully followed.

Bilal and Sania were terrified, but Mahnaz could not be contained. She was formidable, and so intensely focused for one so young, so full of zeal and gumption, despite her dour, unimaginative parents. Gul felt blessed to be able to join her in her journey. She walked alongside her in the march. She drove her to her meetings and engaged with her politics. She spent long hours at the shelter with her. It was extraordinary that a child could be so committed to changing the world. Mahnaz wasn't like her contemporaries, who talked idealistically about what they would do when they were older, even as they were flicking through their social media. She moved at super speed, determined to make a difference.

Until her disappearance.

Gul put the fossil down and stood, ignoring the slight dizziness that came with the movement. She had to get out of this place. She looked around. Where the hell were her clothes? She checked the cupboard, the adjoining bathroom, the chair in front of the desk, but nothing.

The desk . . . on Mahnaz's desk was her stash of diaries, left there, as though she were still writing in them, or just about to walk through the door. Mahnaz's diaries—how had she forgotten about them? Gul trailed her fingers along the covers. She hadn't seen the diaries in years. She loved that Mahnaz had never been precious about them. She scribbled in old school notebooks, in fancy leather-bound volumes, in actual girlie diaries with locks and keys. Over the years she had scrawled her thoughts and her ideas and her sketches on every medium possible and kept them all. There was no chronology to them, exactly. She wrote when she pleased, some of the notebooks were half empty, some were totally full, and written on in the margins. Others were just scraps of paper, stuck together. It was a beautiful, chaotic, inspirational, wonderful creation. Just like Mahnaz.

Why had they never done anything with these? Gul picked one up carefully. Why had they never stopped to celebrate the marvel that Mahnaz was, instead of just waiting for her to come home?

Today I sprained my ankle, because stupid Aisha Chaudhry tripped in front of me in gym and fell down. And instead of apologising when I ran into her, she acted like it was my fault. I tried to explain basic physics to her, but she just flicked her hair and huffed. Aisha Chaudhry has the brain capacity of an amoeba.

And underneath, a sketch of a cartoon amoeba, labelled "Aisha."

The door creaked, and she looked up. Sania stared at her, her expression unreadable, as always. She stood in the doorway carrying a tray with a bowl of soup and some toast.

"Feeling better?"

Gul felt guilty, and then annoyed. Why should she be

ashamed of reading Mahnaz's diary? She put it down, none-theless. "How did I get here?"

Sania walked into the room and placed the tray carefully on the desk. "The police called us. You have a concussion. Bilal brought you here to keep you safe. The mummy is all over the news."

Gul sat on the edge of the bed. "It was a couple of the cops. They were trying to steal her."

Sania nodded. "And they succeeded, unfortunately. By the time the authorities got there, they were long gone. Turns out they were corrupt—someone paid them a lot of money for her. It's like everything else in this country. Men with money get what they want, and everyone's on the take. Especially the police. But one policewallah seems to be honest, at least. A man named DSP Akthar. He's the one who called us."

"What about Ejaz?"

"He's fine. Luckily, he moves like the wind. He sounded the alarm. Then he went back to the streets. God knows what he's up to now."

"And the mummy?"

"They haven't been able to catch the buggers yet. But your policewallah seems rather dogged. I'm sure he'll get her back."

Gul pressed a hand against her temple. Her head was pounding.

"Lie down," Sania insisted.

"No. I need to go. The mummy . . ."

"It can wait. There's nothing you can physically do about it now."

Gul shook her head. "My notes, they're all we have left now . . ."

Sania pulled Mahnaz's desk chair up. Two delicate, per-fectly painted hands came to hold her own. "Gul, you have a concussion, and some bruising around your neck. It could have been so much worse. Those guys were brutes; you're lucky you are okay. You need more time to recover."

"How long have I been here?"

Sania hesitated. "Two days."

"Two *days*?"

"You were in the hospital for the first night. You don't remember?"

"I don't really remember anything." She felt her anxiety rising. "Where's Mrs. Fernandes?"

Sania scowled. "You mean the army sergeant? She's probably standing outside our front gate again. She doesn't seem to understand that you need your rest. I thought she had enough on her plate, what with the kids and all."

"Sania, give me back my clothes, please." And where the hell was her phone? She looked around. She was going to have to call Mrs. Fernandes and get her to pick her up.

"At least wait until Bilal is home from work. You two should talk."

"Sania . . ."

"All right, but have a bit of soup first, please. You need your strength."

"I don't want it, but thanks."

"You can get as fucked off at me as you like, but you still have to eat."

For a moment, the comment reminded Gul of the Sania of old, and she grudgingly took the bowl. "All right, fine." She had a few spoonfuls before putting the bowl down again. "Thanks."

"You're welcome."

"Clothes?"

"Gul, Dr. Pirzada has been in to see you. He said that with this type of brain inflammation, it's important to stay in bed. If I let you go, you would never do that. You can go home in the morning."

"Sania, you're really starting to piss me off."

"You're tired. Why don't you rest a while? I'll wake you up later."

Sania's voice was fading. With effort, Gul forced her eyes to open. Her sister-in-law was watching her. Waiting. She should have guessed. "You put something in my soup?"

"It's for your own good, Gul," said Sania. "Dr. Pirzada says you need rest. He gave us something that will help you sleep. Things will be better in the morning."

All that nonsense about wanting to help. "Underneath all that lacquer and makeup, you're the biggest amoeba of them all, do you know that?" Gul said. With that, she closed her eyes.

CHAPTER 8

WHEN SHE NEXT WOKE up, Gul was fuming. Just who the hell did her sister-in-law think she was?

She got out of bed and saw that her clothes had been washed and ironed and were on the bureau, next to her keys and her mobile phone, which was charged to 100 percent. There were a few small brown spots on the shoulder and back of her beige kameez, and it took her a moment to realise that they were blood stains that stubbornly persisted. Gingerly she touched the back of her head. She felt no pain anymore, so that was something. She fanned out her hair, which always looked better unbrushed, even when there wasn't an injury to avoid hurting. Gul didn't have the time or patience for the hair creams and sprays that might otherwise discipline her voluminous and often frizzy curls.

She put on her jeans and chappals and went hunting for her watch and silver jewellery, which she spotted on the bedside table. She lifted up the Ayatul Kursi necklace her grandmother had given her when she turned eighteen. Nani had been so sure it would protect her against all evil, so much so that Gul continued to wear it in her honour. What would her Nani say now?

Once she had gathered all her things, she texted Mrs. Fernandes and headed to the door. Then she hesitated. Mahnaz's diaries. Bilal and Sania did not deserve them. She pulled the pillowcase off one of the pillows on the bed and stuffed them inside. Then she headed downstairs.

Near the bottom of the stairs, she inhaled. The Big House, as the family called it, still smelt the same, a combination of tobacco and fragrant jasmine. Her hand rubbed against the familiar rosewood banister, touching every old groove and nick. She had grown up here.

"Gul?"

Gul squeezed her eyes shut. Bilal.

She carefully left the overstuffed pillowcase behind the staircase where it was out of view and then made her way to the study, which was on the right of the front door as you came in. Gul had always thought it would take an apocalypse to get her back here. To be alone with her sanctimonious brother was not something she could really bear anymore. The guy had practically had to kidnap her to bring her here. But he'd heard her coming down the stairs, and there was nothing for it.

"Bilal," Gul said, nodding as she entered the room. For a moment, she felt a familiar pang. The study had been her father's once. It still embodied every aspect of male entitlement, from its tufted tawny leather sofas to the intricately carved brass Victorian inkwell that had been gifted to Gul's grandfather by Lord Mountbatten himself. And here was the mahogany desk with its curved recess where Gul had spent many childhood evenings curled up with a book, and, on the table behind the desk, the large bronze sculpture of a panther that looked like it was about to leap into the air, its teeth bared into a snarl. Gul had loved the panther when she was a girl. She'd broken one of its teeth, because she played with it so often, and one side of its body was smoother and shinier than the other from the number of times she'd rubbed the thing. She hadn't seen it in years.

In front of the panther, in a large frame, was an image of her brother himself, on the cover of some glossy finance magazine. Bilal at the Delani Investments office, looking managerial with his arms crossed, wearing a perfectly tailored navy-blue double-breasted suit with a pale-pink silk tie and matching pocket square. *King Delani's Midas Touch* ran the coverline.

Gul grimaced. She remembered when that article came out, Bilal bristling with pride when the media adopted the moniker King Delani. Whatever financial bets King Delani made, investors were sure to follow. Typical. Bilal never read books. He didn't understand critical thinking and wasn't remotely interested in philosophy. He was mediocre in every way. Except in this. When it came to investing, Bilal had some serious skill, and people thought he was a bloody genius. Unsurprisingly, he agreed with them.

It pained her, because she felt the family business could be put to far better use than the continuous pursuit of personal profit. Still, she had to hand it to Bilal. Whatever her issues with him, Bilal had proven himself to be a shrewd financier, and more than doubled the revenues at Delani Investments since her father's death. Gul was never offered the opportunity to run the company, but it was just as well. She had absolutely no interest in making more money than she really needed. She would have handed over all the profits to the Dawood Foundation, if it had been left in her hands.

Bilal was sitting on an armchair in front of the desk, a lit cigar in hand. He'd been waiting for her.

Gul clenched her jaw. "This is totally unacceptable, Bilal. You had no business bringing me here without checking with me first."

Bilal raised his eyebrows. "When exactly was I meant to do that? When you were bleeding from the back of your head? Dr. Pirzada said it wasn't safe to leave you alone."

"I was in the hospital."

"And when they released you, they said that we needed to keep a constant eye out. Who would have done that if not for us?"

"I wouldn't have been alone," Gul muttered.

Bilal had changed a great deal these last few years. The stockiness of his youth had given way to fat; the paunch on his tummy had become more beer belly than stomach. Unfortunately, the Delanis were not blessed with height, which only served to accentuate things. He still had a thick, full head of hair, though. But it was greying at the edges. In his expensive suit and silk tie, he looked every bit the CEO, the president of the Rotary Club, and the philanthropist around town. Bilal had been born into stodgy respectability, and, unlike Gul, he'd stayed that way. Gul noticed the tight expression on his face.

Bilal stood. "Typical. Even when I try to look out for you, I get abuse for it."

"What am I doing here, Bilal?"

"Do you have any idea what a furore this mummy of yours has caused? It's all over the news. The Iranians are claiming this mummy belongs to them and they are demanding the police get her back. The religious right are saying her very existence is un-Islamic."

"So?"

"So we already have enough on our plates, Gul."

"This has nothing to do with you."

"Doesn't it? I'm your older brother, and the elder in the family, and you are putting yourself at risk."

"I didn't ask . . ."

"Some drug dealer nearly killed you. I've had the whole story from Bob. You can't put yourself in danger again."

It was amazing how Bilal always managed to sound so pompous these days. It was hard to imagine that they had once been close, or at least, nowhere near as estranged as they were now. What had happened to her brother's wicked sense of humour, or his ability to laugh at himself? And then there was Bob . . . Bob was Ibrahim Bhatti, head of the Sindh police force. Bilal played poker with Bob and his other cronies from their school days once a week. It was such a cliché, it made her want to roll her eyes. Bob was always hanging around. Ever since they were children, Bilal had worshipped him. If Bob was in Bilal's ear about Gul dropping the case, then Bilal would listen.

"Well, you can tell Bob that the drug dealer never laid a hand on me. It was his own cops who did that."

"Gul, you know that Bob is working hard to rid the police force of corruption . . ."

"Is this the same Bob who stopped the investigation into Mahnaz's disappearance just because you told him to?"

Bilal flushed and stubbed out his cigar. "After four *months*. Because we weren't getting anywhere, and you were going crazy and upsetting the whole community."

Gul watched the remaining cigar smoke waft up to the ceiling. "I was trying to find her. I'm not sure what the hell you were doing. Four months is nothing, Bilal, we both know that."

Bilal shook his head. "I'm not interested in having this conversation with you again."

"Well, I'm not interested in having any conversation with *you*, but I wasn't given a choice, was I?"

"I knew it. I told Sania that if we brought you here it would be a thankless task. This is what I get for trying to protect you."

"Oh, please. Don't do me any favours."

"Stay away from this whole mummy debacle, Gul. Surely you can understand what a sensitive time this is. For many

people, a mummy is sacrilegious to begin with. A creature
that should not exist. If they find it again, walk away. You'll
be in trouble if you don't. Let someone else handle it."

"Oh, for God's sake," Gul exploded. "Not you too. I'm a
scientist. Do you understand what that means? I don't have
time for other people's religious convictions."

"I'm only trying to help. These types of situations can get
ugly very quickly."

"There is no 'situation.' There's no bloody mummy anymore either."

Bilal huffed. "It's so typical of you to react this way. You
are so easily outraged, when all I'm trying to do is protect
you, and to protect our family name."

"Well, now we have it."

"What?"

"The truth. You're worried that the family will look bad.
Well, don't worry about that. I haven't been a part of the
family for years. Everyone knows that."

"That's not what I—why do you have to make everything
so bloody hard?"

"I guess I'm just one of those difficult women, Bilal.
Thank you for the warning. I'll be careful not to upset anyone while doing my job."

Gul's phone pinged, and she looked down. Mrs. Fernandes was parked outside. "I've got to go. I'll see myself
out."

Gul left Bilal there, glaring at her, and went to the front
door, grabbing the pillowcase en route. There was no way
she was leaving Mahnaz's diaries with her brother.

CHAPTER 9

MRS. FERNANDES WAS STANDING outside, leaning against the door of her mustard-brown Toyota. She wasn't alone.

Gul's eyes lit when she caught a glance of the man standing beside her. "Harry!"

Harry grinned. "Surprised?" He gave her a brief hug, and she stood back to gaze at him. His hair was its usual tousled brown mess, and he looked smart in a pair of expensive jeans and a blue linen blazer. A weathered leather satchel slung across his chest completed the image, painting him as the epitome of a London professor in his mid-thirties. "You made it."

"I've been here for a day actually, but apparently your nefarious brother decided you needed your beauty sleep. Mrs. Fernandes was about to storm the castle."

For a moment, Gul smiled. Then she bit her lip. "The body is gone, Harry. I'm afraid it was a wasted trip."

"It's never a wasted trip to be in Pakistan. Besides, there's plenty of research material for us to work with."

"It's not the same."

"I beg to differ." He opened the passenger door of the Toyota, leaned in, and pulled out a manila envelope. "I have the translation you requested. It's a real corker, Gul. If this mummy is real, we're all going to have our socks blown off, and you'll have my undying gratitude for bringing me onto the case."

Gul took the envelope from him, but Mrs. Fernandes promptly snatched it out of her hands. "There'll be no more talk of that. Come on, let's get you home. You and Mr. Harry can bore yourselves to death with translations once I can take a proper look at you."

"They drugged me, Mrs. F. They're lunatics."

"Yes, well, it did get you to rest, didn't it?"

GUL SPENT THE day with Harry, sitting on her balcony, looking out past the banyan trees and on to the dust bowl of Karachi, poring over the translations, drinking nimbu pani and occasionally topping herself up with painkillers. The narrow road in front of them was a hive of activity—at one point, a rickshaw nearly swerved into a van, both drivers making obscene gestures to one another, the rickshaw driver leaning out so far that he almost toppled over. A group of children walked home from school, the boys sweaty in blue shorts and white T-shirts, the girls the other way around, blue kameezes with white shalwars and dupattas, everyone jostling each other good-naturedly as they shared little packets of saunf supari. By the time of the Azaan for Maghrib prayers, a group of crows were lazily making circles in the sky, occasionally swooping down when they spotted something of interest.

Against the tapestry of neighbourhood life beyond the balcony—the laughter, the tooting horns, caws of the crows and the rumble of the buses—Gul sat down to focus on the work. Harry's translations took her breath away. On the gold chest plate, the marking had been clear enough for the full writings to be revealed.

Adama Ducta Sayarasa . . . I am the daughter of the Great King Xerxes

She looked up, paper in hand. "Jesus."

Harry was reclined on a chair at the other side of Gul's cane coffee table, arms crossed, one leg resting on the rail of the balcony. He grinned. "I told you it was good."

"King Xerxes? Really?"

"Keep reading."

I am the daughter of the Great King Xerxes. Ahura Mazda, protect me. I am Artunis, the Lost Princess . . . I am.

"I've never heard of any Princess Artunis, let alone a Lost Princess. Have you?" A crow came and perched beside her and she flicked her hand to shoo it away.

Harry dropped his leg and turned towards her. "I hadn't . . . and then I did some digging. I don't suppose you've crossed paths with Priya Baxter? She's one of UCL's top Achaemenid experts."

"No."

"Next time you're in London, I'll introduce you. She's great, climbs mountains in her spare time and all that stuff. In any case, she translated this for me, and then referred me to the work of Hecataeus. Do you know of him?"

Gul shook her head, always disappointed when she felt there were gaps in her knowledge. "Should I?"

"Not really. He was an obscure historian who wrote a treatise nearly a century after Ctesias wrote *Persika*, his twenty-three-book history of Persia and Assyria."

"So?"

"Well, as you know, not many of Ctesias's twenty-three books have survived the ravages of time. In some cases, we have only fragments. But a hundred years after his death, Hecataeus quoted Ctesias's work in his own writings. Apparently, in the original books, Ctesias talked about a Lost Princess, a daughter of King Xerxes who vanished. That's all it was, I'm afraid, a passing reference by Hecataeus, about something Ctesias had written a hundred years before."

Gul rubbed her neck absentmindedly. "So it's rumour-mongering from over a millennium ago? One guy writes about a Lost Princess, and a century later another guy cites his work briefly, but because the original manuscript doesn't survive the test of time, we don't know what was actually said?"

"Exactly. However, we *do* know that someone was talking about her, at least."

Gul read the translation again. "Tenuous, at best. Was Priya Baxter able to make out the rest?"

"Turn the page and be prepared to be stunned."

She did exactly that, then swallowed. "Is this real?"

He beamed. "Well, I suppose we'll find out."

I am the seed of Eternity, the page read. *All evil which was upon me has been removed. The Wardens of the Sky await my soul but let them hear my vow. My soul cannot rest without vengeance. Oh Faithful Ones, the riches of a city are buried within me. Ahura Mazda, grant my treasures only to the true believers, so they may work their hands for the glory of Persepolis and bring peace upon my soul.*

Gul sat up. "You're right, I'm stunned."

Harry lifted his glass in a mock salute. "Well, who wouldn't be? If she's authentic, you have a real find on your hands, Gul."

"What does this mean, 'the riches of a city'?"

"Who knows."

"And how could they be buried within her?"

"Well, if this is Egyptian burial rites we're looking at, then perhaps if we find the mummy again, there will be some inscriptions on the wrappings that will shed some more light. Or maybe she was buried in a tomb somewhere surrounded by all her earthly possessions or something."

Gul's mind was buzzing, already thinking about next

steps. "We have to find her, Harry. We need a detailed forensic examination. CT scans, X-rays, autopsies and the lot. She's such a marvel, and such a mystery."

"Do you think your law enforcement friends will be able to locate her?"

Gul shook her head. "Who knows. My past experience of the police has left me a bit jaded. Of course, there's always good apples and bad."

Harry stood and cracked his back. "We still have the wooden casket. Once you're finished dusting it, we can send those images to Priya—perhaps they will give us some more information."

"We should go and do that now," Gul said, standing as well. Her vision became blurry, and she sat down again.

"Gul," Harry said, crouching beside her. "You're in no condition to do anything right now. Plus, from what I've been told, your team has been hard at work cleaning the casket. Once we have images, Priya says she'll be happy to translate them immediately. You can take the evening off."

"There's too much to do."

"I'm afraid that Mrs. Fernandes will skewer me alive if I let you leave. So, for my sake, let's pick this up in the morning? She's quite a dragon, your Mrs. F."

"But . . ."

"It's going to be dark soon, anyway. Besides, I've got my own tale to share."

Reluctantly, Gul nodded. Her head was beginning to hurt again.

"Good girl. Now, sit back. Drink your nimboo pani. Let me tell you about the Early Dynastic Period exhibition the museum is putting together. There's a green-glazed faience amulet being sold by an Iranian man who found it in his recently deceased mother's bathroom when he was clearing out her things. Can you imagine, something so priceless being left in a loo? It was under the sink, wrapped up in a plastic bag, apparently. She'd been using it to ward off evil."

Harry pulled out his phone. "You have to see the pictures, Gul. It's the form of the head of the Egyptian dwarf god Bes, wearing a feather crown. There's a circular lateral perforation through the crown itself, and it's stunning. Ordinarily, the goal would be to have the thing on loan, of course, but the man is eager to sell it apparently. I'll need to fly to Tehran and meet with the seller tomorrow evening to make sure that the piece is real, and then charm him into giving it to us—the Smithsonian is after it too."

Despite her headache, Gul had to smile at Harry's enthusiasm. "Will there be a bidding war?"

Harry rolled his eyes. "Oh, please. The Smithsonian's sending John Devereaux. The man couldn't find his way out of a paper bag. Besides, I've got a plan."

"A plan?"

He smirked. "I'm going to let it slip that Devereaux callously threw his own mother into a cheap nursing home where she died, abused and neglected. I can't imagine a grieving son—especially one from Tehran—wanting to do business with someone who would let their mother suffer, could you? Neglecting mothers is very taboo in this neck of the woods."

"And did he?"

"Did he what?"

"Throw his mother in a nursing home and let her die of neglect?"

"How the hell would I know? But come now, Gul, it's the dwarf god Bes, depicted in a way we haven't seen before. All is fair in love and the pursuit of history."

Gul said nothing then, neither condoning nor condemning, and they sat in companionable silence for a while. Then she looked at him. "It is conceivable, isn't it?"

"What?"

"That the Achaemenids would have appropriated mummification? I mean, Darius had a reputation for religious tolerance, unlike his predecessor Cambyses II. It could have started with him, couldn't it have?"

Harry nodded slowly. "It is conceivable."

"I didn't have a chance to transcribe everything on her body. There were still pieces we were dusting off. I missed my chance."

"You did everything you could, Gul. It's not your fault that you weren't able to start the physical examinations."

"I guess not."

"Of course not," Harry insisted gently. "You're an excellent practitioner. We both know that. It was never a sure thing, you being allowed to keep the body anyway. Your notes will give us plenty of information to get on with." Harry cleared his throat. "Not to be indelicate, but I felt I ought to tell you. When you were in the kitchen, I checked my email. There's one from your brother."

"Bilal? I didn't realise you were still in touch." During her university years, Harry and Bilal had met and got on. When Harry started passing through town on a regular basis, he and Bilal got in the habit of meeting for lunch, not frequently but a couple of times a year at least. It wasn't something that either hid from her, nor was it something that they particularly advertised.

For Gul, it irked. Perhaps it was childish, but Bilal had his own friends, his own occupation, and his own life. Yet, somehow, he was always enmeshed in hers, by building a friendship with Harry, by using the Delani Foundation to donate to the shelter, and even—for some inexplicable reason—by becoming a patron of the Heritage and History Museum. It was almost as though he didn't want anything to be just *hers*.

"Well, not that often, not anymore," Harry said. He didn't have to explain. *Not since Mahnaz disappeared.*

Harry looked down. For a moment, they sat in awkward silence.

As far as Gul knew, most of her international colleagues were unaware that she had a niece who had gone missing. They knew she'd taken time off work for personal reasons, but once she'd returned, she'd been as professional and efficient as always. Harry, in contrast, had a relationship with Bilal and knew the rest of her family. Plus, he had been coming and going often enough for the last few years that it was impossible to hide the whole saga from him. Until now, they had never spoken of it.

Harry was now looking at her with pity. "There's been no further news since the police closed the case?"

"How could there be? They closed it after a few months."

"Am I right in thinking it's been three years?"

"So what? Does that mean I should give up?"

Harry cleared his throat. "No, no, of course not."

"What did Bilal want?"

"To know what you were going to do about this mummy business. He said he didn't want you to single-handedly 'turn the city upside down' looking for the body, that it was dangerous. Given what happened to you, I'm sure he just wants to look out for your welfare."

Gul felt the burn of anger on her cheeks. "He's worried that any negative publicity around the mummy and me will reflect badly on him. I'm sorry he dragged you into it."

"Not at all. I told him that, as your colleague, I support

you entirely, though between us, I do think he may have a point about your safety."

Gul glanced at him sharply. "When did we start worrying about safety in our pursuit of history?"

"You're right, of course. In any case, I doubt he'll be reaching out on this topic again, or indeed on anything else."

"Thank you." The whole conversation was making Gul feel uncomfortable. "I would appreciate your discretion on this. Our family . . . situation . . . isn't exactly something I want to advertise professionally."

"And of course, you will have it." Harry cleared his throat again. "Gul, why don't you come and stay with me in Somerset after this? A change of scenery might do you good."

"Somerset? The place your aunt left you?" Harry's favourite aunt had passed away a few years earlier, but not before incurring the wrath of the rest of her family by gifting him a large house in the country and enough money for him to upgrade his central London flat to a two bedroom.

"Yes, and it's in shambles. You can help me renovate."

"Perhaps one day."

Harry inclined his head, with a look that suggested he knew that day would never come. "Right. Well. On that note, I suppose I should go back to the hotel. It's been a long day, and you need your rest. What's the plan for tomorrow?"

"I have a contact in the antiquities-smuggling world."

"Of course you do."

"I need to meet with him, to find out if anyone's trying to sell the body."

"Can I help?"

Gul shook her head. "I'll reach out. But he's not always available. I'll let you know if I get anywhere."

But as she was seeing Harry out, she had another thought. There may not be much online about a missing

Achaemenid princess, but there were other, more legitimate sources of support they could tap. "Perhaps you and I can visit Mr. Davar tomorrow."

"Mr. Davar?"

"He's a Parsi gentleman, a local historian. He might have heard rumblings of a Lost Princess."

"Sounds good. Should I pick you up in the morning?"

Gul shook her head. "I'll pick you up. There's something I have to do first."

CHAPTER 10

THE NEXT MORNING THE shelter was quiet. A handful of the younger kids were still asleep, but many of the older ones had left for the day in search of odd jobs or entertainment. There was always churn amongst the children; it was difficult to keep track of who was coming in or out. Unless you were Mrs. Fernandes, of course.

Somehow, Mrs. F knew all the kids and their issues, even better than the full-time administrator who kept all the records did. The only other person who came close to keeping track was Farzana, the cook and housekeeper, who could be found most mornings in the kitchen. Gul made her way there now.

The kitchen was simple and unadorned in every way. There had been no money for more than a second-hand stove, some hand-me-down orange Formica countertops from a well-meaning benefactor and a basic sink station. It was an odd assortment of styles from different decades, which somehow, together, gave the place a great deal of character. There was even a microwave, which Farzana refused to touch, because she said it was a dangerous thing full of radio waves that would give her cancer. Farzana had heard that said on TV once, and now it was deeply ingrained in her psyche.

Farzana was there, sweating in the heat, separating out little balls of atta, ready to be turned into chapatis for lunch. She moved the dough through thick seasoned fingers, stopping only occasionally to dab her face with her dupatta.

Gul cleared her throat from the doorway, and Farzana looked up and smiled. "You're here early. How is your head?"

"Fine, thanks," replied Gul. "I don't see Ejaz anywhere. Is he around?"

Farzana shook her head. "I haven't seen him since the other night when those police goondas attacked you. I'm glad to see they didn't break that thick skull of yours."

"Me too, believe me. He didn't come back?"

"He came, but only for a few minutes. He picked up some of his things and disappeared. You know how that boy is."

"I need to speak to him."

The other woman shrugged. "You could try the shrine."

"The shrine?"

"Where Shaykh Syed Ali Hajin is buried. It's not too far away. I go there once a week to be blessed. I have done so ever since I was a child. Why do you think I've never been ill a day in my life? Even when I had that toothache, I prayed to the Shaykh, and he made my tooth fall out and took the pain away."

"I see." She had no idea Farzana believed in mystics and superstitions. "But why would Ejaz be at the shrine?"

"I hear he's running errands for the beggar gang these days. That's where they operate from."

Gul frowned. The mafia who ran the local begging ring was no joke. The group often kidnapped children, forcing them to work the streets, or selling them into slavery. "He knows better than that."

Farzana stopped long enough to dust flour off her hands, and then looked up. "It's a tough world."

Gul nodded. "Will you let me know if he turns up?"

"Of course."

She left Farzana to her work and went to ask around and see if one of the other kids might know where Ejaz was. She made her way upstairs to the boys' dormitory but stopped when she saw Bilal and Sania coming out the door of the administrator's office. Sania again, *and* Bilal? The universe really was conspiring against her.

When he spotted her, Bilal straightened. "Gul."

"What are you doing here, Bilal?"

"I have as much of a right to be here as you do."

"I didn't say that you didn't."

"Who do you think pays the bills around here?"

"It's just that I don't see you here very often. Not really your kind of thing, is it?"

Sania smiled tightly. "We've cared about these kids ever since you first brought Mahnaz here all those years ago. You know that."

Bilal snorted and crossed his arms. "Typical. She introduced our young, impressionable child to this world without even bothering to inform us, and yet here she is, making judgments."

He pointed an irate finger at his sister. "Even though we supported Mahnaz's decision to volunteer here, and even after we devoted our own time and resources to this place, you still act like you're morally superior. Why? So you can continue with this mythology that I'm the bad brother and you're the good sister?"

Sania put a hand on her husband's arm. "Gul, since you're interested, we're here because the Delani Foundation is hosting its annual charity ball. We thought this year we might showcase how the funding we are providing to the shelter is making an impact. It's all about raising money for these kids, right?"

Gul waved in irritation at the fly that had landed on her cheek. She'd been an active member of the Delani Foundation's board—even attending meetings virtually when she was at university—until her car accident with Mahnaz, when Bilal had used his clout to boot her out. All these years later, it still stung. Still, Mahnaz had always been so proud of her parents for supporting her decision to volunteer here. As far as Gul was concerned, their spearheading of the Foundation was more about retaining their place in society than anything else, because it was out of character for them to think about anyone but themselves. Even still . . . "Mahnaz will be happy that you are continuing to support these kids," Gul said, as neutrally as she could.

"Mahnaz won't be happy, because Mahnaz is gone, Gul," snapped Bilal. "You're the only one not willing to accept it."

Sania pulled her husband away. "Come. The driver is waiting for us outside. Lovely to see you as always, Gul."

Gul watched them go with a knot in her throat. *Mahnaz needs us to find her*, she wanted to scream. But nothing came out.

Instead, she made her way to the dormitories. None of the boys had heard from Ejaz, which was worrying. The kid was a free agent, but he usually checked in with one of the regulars at some point.

She was nearly at her car when Rana called. "We've dusted everything we can off the casket. There's still parts we can't get to, particularly in the corners and crevices of the carvings. But we have enough to send most of the writing for translation."

"Well done," said Gul. "Can you take some photos and email them to Harry, and copy me in, too?"

"Of course."

"Harry will forward them to his contact at UCL. Hopefully, she'll be able to turn them around very quickly."

"Theek hai. Is he with you now?"

"No, but I'll see him later. There's still stuff I have to do. But we'll both be by in the afternoon."

"See you then, Apa."

Gul got into the car, her mind on Ejaz now. Something wasn't right. She could feel it.

CHAPTER 11

LIKE SEVERAL OF THE mausoleums that pocketed the city, the Shaykh Syed Ali Hajin shrine was devoted to a mystic whom many considered to have been a saint. Long embraced by death, he cured the incurable of illness, brought luck and prosperity to those who needed it most, and performed all manner of miracles. Gul had no patience for religion, but she had a grudging respect for the power of faith.

She pulled up at the shrine, noticing that it was smaller than those of some of the more high-profile saints of the city. She squeezed her car next to a silver Pajero jeep, which was boxed in by several motorcycles, and had a long scratch gashed across its bonnet. She felt sorry for its owner. This close to the centre of town there weren't many parking spaces, and the notion of a designated "space" was fairly fluid in any case. Cars had to squeeze into nooks and crannies and were often the worse off for it.

The shrine was a lively place, full of pilgrims providing enough foot traffic to appease even the most egotistical of martyrs. The building itself was painted green and covered with colourful bunting and flags. The air was smoky—devotees were burning some sort of incense, something sharp and tangy that assaulted the senses. Outside, food vendors offered up their wares on wooden carts, and shopkeepers sold garlands of flowers and head coverings. A pilgrim was paying homage to the saint by feeding the poor. Cauldrons of rice were cooking nearby;

a line of people had gathered, waiting their turn to have their plastic bags filled.

Gul stood for a while and surveyed the scene. There were plenty of beggars in the crowd trying their luck. Some were very young children, as little as three or four. A few were missing limbs, others an eye or ear. Gul knew many of them would have been deliberately maimed by the mafia in order to ensure they could garner plenty of sympathy from those who came to worship. A blind child made more money than one with his sight. It had been the same old story in Karachi since the time of the British Raj. She swallowed, wanting to bundle all the kids into her car and take them to the shelter. The beggar gangs were bastards, merciless and cruel.

She walked towards the shrine now, moving past throngs of people, looking for Ejaz. He was nowhere, not amongst the beggars, not amongst the pilgrims milling around outside. She covered her head with a grey dupatta that matched her kameez and made her way up the steep steps into the shrine itself. A man in a bright-orange turban smoking a hookah asked her for some money, which she handed him, and she was motioned inside.

Through the wooden doors, a haze of smoke made everything seem almost otherworldly. Unlike some of the other shrines she had visited, this particular saint was not alone, she noted with interest. There appeared to be eight relatives around him, each set up in magnificent splendour, resting in deep, latticed bed frames, beautifully and intricately carved, their coffins covered in cloth and then, on top of that, fresh rose petals. The saint himself had pride of place in the centre, his bed frame had four pillars, a mattress of red velvet, and a little terraced roof, under which his sarcophagus lay. His resting place looked like a scene from

Arabian Nights, a place where Scheherazade should have been spinning her tales.

Gul squinted through the smoke but couldn't spot Ejaz amongst the devotees, so she left. Neither was he with the food vendors or shopkeepers outside. After a hot and frustrating forty minutes, Gul pushed sweaty tendrils of hair off her face and decided to check out the streets around the shrine. There were some narrow alleys crisscrossing into a nearby bazaar, half under the shadows of electrical cables and clotheslines. Maybe he was there, or at the bazaar itself.

In the first alley there was only a stray dog and a large pool of urine. The second was littered with used needles, and there were several men sitting on a bunch of burlap sacks injecting themselves with heroin. They watched her go by, their faces gaunt, their eyes hungry, a momentary distraction from the task at hand. Gul felt her stomach churn. They were so young. It wasn't the heroin that would kill them first, she knew. It would be the hepatitis and other diseases they picked up from sharing needles.

The third alley was the narrowest, and it was difficult to see down it because residents had hung up lines of their washing. She stepped forward carefully, ducking beneath some sheets. It was quieter here, the noise of the shrine receding with every step she took. The alley was long, and she walked for several minutes without coming across anyone.

Then she saw a silhouette behind a drying chador and she recoiled. The chador was pulled back by a bearded man wearing a stained shalwar kameez. Had he been waiting for her? "You lost, Begum?"

Gul stopped. "No."

"What are you doing here?"

"Minding my own business, just like you should be doing."

"This place is off-limits. Go home to your rich husband, before you get yourself into trouble."

"Why does everyone assume I have a rich husband?" She tried to sidestep, but he held out his arm. It was only then that she saw the knuckleduster in his hand.

"Are you here looking for a husband, Begum? I can help you."

She heard someone chortle behind her and swung around. She hadn't even heard the other man sneaking up on her. She moved to the side, her back against the wall. "If you could kindly get out of my way, I'll go."

The first man shook his head and winked at the second. "Not without a kiss, Begum Sahiba." The other laughed, amused.

She had already pulled her homemade concoction of pepper spray out of her satchel when he came towards her. She sprayed it as liberally as she could, satisfied when he wailed and fell to the ground, eyes covered, even more satisfied when he began to curse.

The other man stopped, unsure of himself. Gul waited, her body tense. If she ran, he would run after her. If she stood her ground, he may give it up.

In the end, neither of them did anything, because Ejaz emerged from the shadows and stepped in front of her.

"Why are you bothering my mother?" Ejaz asked.

The first man got up, his eyes red. "This whore is your mother? What's she doing here?"

"Don't call her that."

"She's too rich to be your mother. Look at her. She's one of those Defence or Clifton Begums. You think I'm stupid?"

"You're meant to be watching for Saayaa, not harassing

women on the streets," hissed Ejaz. "Do you want me to report you to Big Galloo?"

The man looked sullen. "I can barely see. My eyes burn. Your mother burnt me. It is I who should report you."

Ejaz shook his head. "Go wash your eyes. You'll be fine in a few minutes."

The man spat on the ground. "You're nothing but a boy whore yourself, why should I listen to you?"

Ejaz went up to him then and said something that Gul couldn't hear.

The man stared at him for a moment, and then nodded, sullenly. "You watch your back," he said. They disappeared down the alley.

Gul exhaled. "Dammit, Ejaz."

He turned to her. "Are you hurt, Apa?"

"I'm fine."

"What are you doing here?"

"Looking for you, of course. What the hell is going on? Why are you here with these people? Who is Big Galloo? And what did you say to that man?"

When Ejaz had satisfied himself that Gul was unharmed, his face lost some of its tension. "I told him I knew all about the boy who he's been using to satisfy his urges. Big Galloo doesn't allow the men to stick their pricks into his boys, not without payment."

"Big Galloo? Does he run the beggar gang?"

He grabbed her arm. "Not here."

"Ejaz . . ."

He shook his head. "Please, Apa. It's not safe. They're watching. Already there will be questions about who you are and how I know you."

"Ejaz, why did you want to see the mummy? What's going on? If you're in some kind of danger . . ."

"I'll come to you when I can," he whispered. "Please. Please go now, for both our sakes."

He grabbed her arm and pulled her out of the alley, and then disappeared into the crowd.

A few minutes later she was back in her car, hands shaking. She'd been right, then. Ejaz was in trouble. And somehow, it had something to do with the mummy. She thought about calling DSP Akthar but decided against it. The beggar gangs had the police in their pocket, and she hadn't made up her mind about him yet. Ejaz could get into even more trouble.

There was only one person who could tell her anything useful. She got back in the car, pulling out of the shrine and heading down the twisty streets until she came to the main thoroughfare, oblivious to the silver Pajero behind her.

FARZANA WAS STILL in the kitchen, now chopping vegetables.

"Can you take a break?" Gul asked.

The other woman looked up. "Give me a moment. Let me get my cigarettes."

They stood outside, Farzana lighting up a Capstan Pall Mall Original. "What's going on?"

Gul watched the smoke waft off into the street. "Do you know someone called Big Galloo?"

Farzana pulled tobacco off her lips. "The gangster?"

"Must be." Gul filled Farzana in on what had happened.

"That boy better know what he's doing," Farzana said, shaking her head. "Big Galloo runs all the beggars around here. He can have people picked up and disappeared anytime he wants. They say he has half the big politicians in his pocket. He knows people who are rich and connected. They owe him favours."

"Do all the criminals have ridiculous names?" Gul asked.

"What?"

"Never mind."

Farzana was stubbing her cigarette out with her toe now. "He sells children, you know. To the traffickers. All the prostitutes work for him. That's what they say, anyway."

"He sounds a lot like this drug dealer I heard about. Could be they're working together."

"Could be," said Farzana.

"What should I do?"

Farzana placed a hand on her arm. "Nothing. You have to trust Ejaz to look after himself."

"I don't even know what the hell he's up to."

The other woman grinned, quick and toothless. "That boy, he's a survivor. When he's ready, he'll find you."

CHAPTER 12

PARSI COLONY WAS LARGE and rambling, full of majestic mansions with sprawling gardens, and picturesque bungalows with latticed verandas. But many of those structures were dilapidated, in desperate need of repair. The place was eerily quiet, only two pedestrians on the street. If this had been a Western movie, a large ball of tumbleweed would have rolled through.

"Where are we?" asked Harry, getting out of the car. "I thought I knew most of the city after all these visits." He put on a pair of sunglasses.

Gul locked the car and pocketed her keys. "This is Parsi Colony, or what's left of it. A lot of the Zoroastrian community has left."

"Left, why?"

"Karachi used to be a cosmopolitan place, a safe haven for minorities and those fleeing persecution." She stepped onto a narrow strip of pavement. "But many minorities feel that has changed."

"Extremism?"

"Among other things." Gul led Harry to the centre of the colony, where a beautiful, gated park was padlocked shut. "The community doesn't marry outside its faith, so its numbers are dwindling. The younger ones don't want to live here anymore. They get hassled for practicing their religion. They feel there is more freedom and career advancement to be had by moving abroad. Only the old guard remain. Sad, really.

Their ancestors came here from ancient Persia because they were being persecuted, and now their descendants feel they have no choice but to leave once again. This city owes so much to its Parsi community, but memories are short."

Despite the air of neglect, the place still had its charms. They made their way past an elegant fountain, to a cheerful white-and-yellow-painted bungalow. "Local library," said Gul. "Mr. Davar is going to meet us here."

In fact, he was already there, standing on the veranda, beaming. Mr. Davar was a small, elderly man with a cane, wearing a beige safari suit that had clearly seen better days. "Gul," he said, holding out a shaky hand. "It's been a long time."

Gul took his hand, and then introduced him to Harry. Mr. Davar's eyes grew bright. "It's been years since a respected academic such as yourself visited our part of the world, Sir. What brings you here?"

"We wanted to talk to you about the Lost Princess," said Harry.

"The Lost Princess?"

Gul reached into her bag, rummaging to find her phone to show the historian some photos. "An apparent daughter of King Xerxes, who no one seems to have heard of. I thought if anyone knew who she was, it would be you, Davar Sahib."

His eyes widened, and he looked at both of them. "Who no one credible has heard of, you mean. I'm surprised, Gul, that this has brought you all the way here."

Gul glanced at Harry, and then turned back to the old man. "You know something of her?"

Mr. Davar nodded. "Of course. But she's a folk story, a legend, nothing more. Who's been filling your head with such nonsense?"

They sat on the veranda as Gul told him about the

discovery of the mummy, the subsequent theft of the body and what they had uncovered so far. After seeing some of the photos, Mr. Davar grew pale. "Can it be true, then? All this time, have the stories been real?"

Gul noticed a slight tremble in his hand when he handed back her phone. "Mr. Davar, let's get you a cup of tea, and maybe you can fill us in on what you know?"

"Yes, good idea, Gul. It's remarkable, all this."

Mr. Davar led them to a back room in the library, which was piled high with books, loose-leaf records and papers bound with string—a chaotic and dusty treasure trove. He sighed. "Please, ignore the mess. Not very academically rigorous, is it? It's only been me, all these years. I haven't had much time to catalogue it."

"You have no one working with you?"

He shook his head. "Very few people come here. Except thieves, that is. A few years ago we had a big robbery and they turned the place upside down. Can you believe, I'm still trying to reorder it? I suppose they think we keep things of value back here, and they are correct. Of course, they can't see the treasure in ancient records, the way you and I can. They trashed the place, but they left everything behind." He swept an arm across the room.

Gul looked around. The place was so disorganised, she couldn't imagine anyone stealing anything with any degree of efficiency. "Do you know who broke in, or what they might have been looking for?"

Mr. Davar pointed to one of the bookshelves. "Some of the books and chronicles we have are very old, passed down from one family member to the next. Some are mundane. Title deeds and family trees. Others are records of the stories that have historically been told in the oral tradition of our people. You won't find these on Google."

"No?"

"Most of these books have been out of print for over fifty years." Mr. Davar pulled out some dusty tomes, showed them to her, dusted them off and put them back again. "Nobody has ever been interested enough to digitise our archives, and only the local academics come here. It's a shame, really. When I'm gone, who will look after all this?"

He put some tea bags into a pot, the pot chipped and placed precariously on top of a pile of books on a table at the end of the room. There was a little sink and a kettle too, and Gul washed out three mugs and handed them to him. Once the tea was ready, they sat on a small round table in the corner, amidst all Mr. Davar's dusty treasures.

The old man began to speak. "You'll forgive my surprise. The thing is, none of us ever took the story of the Lost Princess seriously. Even now, I would have told you both that you were out of your minds, except the body you found was a mummy."

Gul's heart quickened. "You *knew* she was mummified?"

Mr. Davar nodded. "The Lost Princess. I still can't get my head around it. We thought it was a fairy tale, you see, one of those myths that gets passed down from generation to generation. Nobody really believes that Theseus killed the Minotaur, do they? It's a tale about honour and bravery. I always thought, the whole community thought—those of us who are old enough to remember the story, that is—that the tale of the Lost Princess was the same. There aren't even any records of Princess Artunis being alive, there's no scientific or academic basis for any of this, you see."

Harry leaned forward eagerly. "But there's a story."

"Oh yes, there is a story. And there's always the odd conspiracy theorist or fortune hunter who believes it, though I haven't had one come through here, not for a very long time."

Gul looked at Harry. His eyes were gleaming. "Fortune hunter?"

Mr. Davar used his finger to wipe away a dot of tea that he had spilled on the table. "According to the legend, Artunis grew up in Persepolis under the reign of her father, King Xerxes, and became a celebrated military strategist. She disappeared the night her father and brothers were murdered. Some of the tales say she was involved in their murder, that she killed them and robbed the Treasury of its gold and disappeared with all the King's riches, enough to raise an army against the city of Persepolis. Others believe she vanished in order to take revenge on the real killers, to use the gold to remove them from power. Until now, conventional historians—those who have even come across the obscure tale—have considered the whole matter to be hokum."

Once again, Gul and Harry looked at each other. "There's a reference to the wealth of the city on her gold chest plate," said Gul.

Mr. Davar raised his eyebrows. "It was said that she left with three caravans full of gold, silver and precious stones."

Harry whistled and leaned back in his chair. "That would be worth a hell of a lot in today's market."

"Oh yes, hundreds of millions of dollars I would think, at the very least," agreed the older man. "Still, I can't quite believe it would be true, can you?"

It was getting hot in the room. With Mr. Davar's blessing, Gul got up and opened a small window by one of the many dusty bookshelves. She looked at all the piles of books and papers and couldn't help but think about how much Mahnaz would have loved this place. How much knowledge was lying here, how much history that no one was aware of. Were the answers they were looking for somewhere in these books?

She came to sit down again. Could Princess Artunis have
been the holder of a secret treasure? Is that why a drug dealer
like Saayaa became interested in her? "Mr. Davar, according
to the legends, how is it that Princess Artunis came to be
mummified?"

"Ah, now that's an interesting tale." Mr. Davar shuffled
to one of the stacks. He spent some time searching and then
pulled out a tattered file full of loose pages. "Yes, this is it.
I'm not sure why I kept it, probably because it was entertaining, but I'm glad I did." He put the pages on the table
between them, spreading them out in a fan.

Gul lifted a page. The writing was in a typed Arabic
script. The paper itself was a faded curling printout with
holes running the length of both sides. These had likely
been printed decades ago, then.

Mr. Davar cleared his throat. "I was given this, many years
ago, by a conspiracy theorist who claimed to have come
across some of the writings of an Egyptian high priest of
Ptah, who lived in Egypt during the Achaemenid conquest.
Have you heard of a high priest named Isu?"

"Hard to say. There were so many priests in ancient Egypt,
at different levels of seniority," muttered Gul. "Including in
Memphis, where there was a temple dedicated to Ptah."

"Well, one of the reasons that the conspiracy theorist
I met believed the story of the missing gold is because of
this priest, Isu's, supposed account of the life of Princess
Artunis."

"May I see those?"

Mr. Davar pushed the rest of the papers towards her side
of the table. "Be my guest. I'm afraid they will be of no use to
you. They are in Farsi. The man I met said he copied down
the account, translated from a text in Old Persian that he
had seen. He wanted me to help him find the missing gold.

I told him it was all rubbish, but he left these with me, in case I came across something that would help him."

"So it's rumours and folklore again. Nothing tangible," said Gul, shaking her head.

"You see why we don't take these things seriously?"

"Would you be able to tell us what these say?" asked Harry.

Mr. Davar cleared his throat. "Yes, of course. My Farsi is not that good anymore, so you'll have to bear with me." Mr. Davar put on a pair of horn-rimmed glasses and began to read aloud: "'I am Isu, son of Anhurmose, hem-netjer-tepi, the first servant of God, royal seal bearer and sem of the temple of Ptah in Memphis.'" He looked up. "As I understand it, the sem priests were embalmers, correct?"

Gul nodded. "Yes, in a sense. Some of them were very senior, and they oversaw the mummification of the corpses of the dead and recited the incantations that were needed to help them on their journey. They possessed the knowledge of which exact spells, said in what exact ways, would grant eternal life to the dead. It was a very specific skill set."

Harry took a sip of his tea. "At the temple of Ptah, the high priests often served as the sem priest as well, performing the opening-of-the-mouth ritual so the dead could speak and drink in the afterlife. Memphis was an extremely important place, and the temple of Ptah a key political posting. It sounds as if your priest was a highly placed man, Mr. Davar." Harry grinned.

"He seemed to be an ideological man as well," said Mr. Davar. "This is what he writes: 'This is an account of how I came to be in the service of the Princess Artunis, daughter of the Persian King Xerxes. Those who cast doubt on her should know that none was ever truer to her cause and to her peoples than the Princess Artunis, beloved by Horus, true of voice and blameless.

"'I met Princess Artunis in the third month of the growing season, on the sixteenth day, when she and her followers appeared in Memphis. Her suffering had been long and heavy. Artunis had traversed the lands for some years, and her Gods had cursed her and left her spirit broken. As we grew in friendship, she told me about what had come to pass, and now I have asked my servant, the good priest Nakht, to take up the scribal palette and papyrus scroll and commit to writing these words and delivering them to Persepolis when I am gone from this place, so that her own peoples might heed them.

"'Princess Artunis was raised in the palace of Persepolis, honourable and possessed of great intellect. She was skilled in hunting and a gifted horsewoman. Her sister, Princess Amytis, was married to General Megabyzus, satrap of Syria, but another path was chosen for Artunis. She was sent to the army, to train as a soldier. Artunis left the court when she was eight years old and did not return for ten growing seasons.

"'Artunis grew to become a renowned warrior commanding armies of men, fighting alongside her brother, the good and most revered Prince Darius. All of Persia celebrated her strength and courage then. All of you Persians who damn her now, how quickly you have forgotten what she achieved in your honour.

"'After quelling an uprising in Babylon, Artunis returned to Persepolis with three caravans of gold and jewels relinquished by those she had conquered. She also brought incense, lapis lazuli, ebony, elephant tusks, cattle, and goats. On the streets, her people cheered as she entered the city. But when Artunis returned to court, she discovered that her sister, the beautiful but . . .'" Mr. Davar paused. "'Licentious'—yes, I think that's the word." He continued:

"'Licentious woman Amytis, had returned to court from Syria with her husband, Megabyzus, having grown power hungry and jealous of Artunis's fame.

"'The great King Xerxes was growing old at this time and weary of mind and body. One night, after a banquet, someone stabbed him and left him to die inside a chamber in the harem. Later that night, the most revered Princes Darius and Hystaspes were also found murdered in their quarters.

"'On hearing the news, Amytis, the evil woman, let out a cry and claimed she had seen her own sister enter the harem with a dagger, aided by the eunuchs. Artunis was arrested, and three hundred eunuchs of the harem were sentenced to death by scaphism.'"

Mr. Davar stopped there and took off his glasses. "Tell me, are either of you familiar with the practice of scaphism? The very idea of it makes me shudder."

Gul shook her head.

"It was brutality at its finest, I'm afraid. The condemned suffered a slow and agonising death. They were secured between two boat-shaped pieces of wood almost like an open-sided coffin, with only their arms, feet and head sticking out. They were forced to eat and drink, and their faces were covered in honey in order to attract a multitude of flies. Confined between the planks, they lay in their own excrement, until they were eventually eaten alive by insects over several weeks. They would have begged and screamed for mercy, but there was none to be found. If they resisted, if they tried to starve themselves or die of thirst, their eyes would be plucked out."

"Jesus," muttered Gul.

Mr. Davar put his glasses back on and continued reading. "'Artunis was devastated. Her beloved family lay slain and she had been accused of their heinous murders by her very own sister. For some days she was stunned into quietness, as she contemplated the depth of her sister's betrayal.

"'Luckily there were still many who were loyal to her, and eventually Artunis escaped from the prison. She took her men and the three caravans of gold and jewels she had brought to Persepolis and fled in the night. She swore to raise an army against Amytis and Megabyzus and take back Persepolis, but it was not in her power. Long was the course that Amytis and Megabyzus pursued against her. Riders were sent to all four corners of the Empire to instruct the peoples that Artunis had slain her family. For many harvests, Artunis and her men hid from the Persians and tried to raise rebellion, but time after time they failed. After several seasons they grew weary. They hid the gold in some remote caves in a land to the south and the west of Bactria, in order to travel faster. Amytis's poison had worked quickly and effectively, for few believed Artunis's claims.

"'After some years, Artunis came to Memphis, having heard about the rebellion launched by Prince Inaros against Persia. Inaros, son of Psamtik, hailed from Tjehenu, and allied himself to Athens when King Xerxes was murdered, determined to overthrow our conquerors once and for all. He needed more men to command, and he coveted Artunis's gold.

"'For two planting seasons, Artunis spent time with Inaros in Memphis, but she was undecided about whether to give him her gold. Inaros, she felt, was an arrogant zealot impressed by his own intellect. She was worried his campaign would fail, even with her riches. But she was growing tired of retreat and longed for revenge. In her indecision, she refused to give Inaros what he wanted and begged him for his indulgence, using one excuse and then another, until he grew angry.

"'It was during this time that Artunis came to the Temple. She was magnificent, tall and lithe and well muscled. She was eager to learn our customs and our ways, and she was cast down by the poverty she had seen on the streets, poverty inflicted upon the people by the heavy taxes imposed by the usurpers in Persepolis. She vowed that she would end this on her triumphant return.

"'For two harvests I taught her about our ways and our Gods, and she delighted in them. She was not superior or arrogant, she was eager to understand, to pay respect to our way of life. She felt the injustice of our plight, and the suffering of the peoples.

"'Often she thought about bringing her caravans of gold to Memphis, to help ease the plight of the poor, but then she reminded herself of the promise she had made to free Persepolis of her sister's rule. Many a time, Inaros demanded her gold, and many a time she chided him to be patient. Eventually Inaros grew tired of her games. He removed his protection from Artunis and sued for peace with Persia.

"'And so Megabyzus and his army came to the gates of Memphis, demanding that Artunis be returned to them.'"

By now, both Gul and Harry were leaning forward, utterly absorbed by the story. Mr. Davar stopped and cleared his throat and took a sip of tea before continuing.

"'Most of Artunis's followers were killed in the bloody battle that followed. She herself took an arrow in the shoulder, and hid bleeding in the Temple for three nights. The Creator-God Ptah came to me in a vision, and told me that I must protect Artunis, even at the cost of my own life. And so my scribe Nakht and I took her and fled the city.

"'Artunis was strong. She removed the arrow in her shoulder herself, and we began the journey to the land southwest of Bactria, to a place called Mak, to retrieve the gold. But over the weeks, her wound began to fester, and she weakened. When we reached the caves and her treasure, she collapsed. In her dying moments, she begged me to keep her treasure safe and make certain that the gold was used to remove Amytis and Megabyzus from the throne. She wanted me to ensure that her only brother still alive—the young Prince Artaxerxes—knew the truth. She wished to restore her honour, to bring glory to Persepolis and peace to the entire Empire.

"'You who vilify her, know that she dedicated her life to you, and to honour, courage and glory. She died with the name Persepolis on her lips.

"'I lay with her body in the caves of Mak, and I most sorely grieved. I who know naught of your customs and knowing well how much she had come to love and respect our own Gods, have sent Artunis on her journey, guiding her to Osiris so that she may be reborn. I have recited many spells and transformation magics.

"'I have given Artunis all that she deserved, as much as was in my power in this place, with the help of the kind man Nakht. Even as her earthly life has ended, her eternal one has begun.

"'And now I will make my way home. I wish to be in the Temple one more time before I myself meet Osiris. What my fate will be when I return, I do not know.

"'But as my part in this tale draws to a close, I bid you, you who were so quick to judge Artunis, heed my words. Rise up. Rise up against Megabyzus and against Amytis. Come to Mak, and lay alms at Princess Artunis's place of rest and beg her forgiveness, even as she is reborn continually. And then, perhaps, if you are worthy, and with Nakht's help, she will guide you to her wealth, which you may use to further her cause and her name. May Persepolis be bathed in glory, as she had hoped.'"

When Mr. Davar put down the pages, nobody spoke for a moment. Then Gul got up and started to pace. "So, let me make sure I'm understanding. King Xerxes had a daughter named Artunis, who fled Persepolis after being accused of Xerxes's murder, apparently with three caravans of gold. And it was Artunis's own sister, Amytis, who was behind the assassinations. But after failing to raise an army against her sister and brother-in-law, Artunis was wounded in a battle and succumbed to her injuries near the very spot where she concealed the gold. Then she was mummified by an Egyptian priest named Isu whom she'd somehow managed to win over to her cause? It's all ludicrous, surely. The tale would have been thoroughly investigated, I'm certain."

Mr. Davar nodded. "Yes. That's what I thought, until now."

Harry blinked in quick succession. "I think it's marvellous."

Gul turned. "You do?"

"You had the mummy in your hands, Gul. She was flesh and blood, and this tale proves it."

Gul shook her head. Sometimes Harry's enthusiasm took him too far. "I'm an Egyptologist, Harry. If there had been a tale of a revolutionary priest who fled the city with an Achaemenid princess, I would have heard about it."

Harry leaned back and cupped his arms behind his head. "Not necessarily. You know the ancient Egyptians were good at erasing history, and if this priest went back to Memphis, Inaros may have had him killed, or removed him from any prominent position. Or Isu may have died on the return journey, who knows?"

Mr. Davar stood as well and went back to his stack of

books. "It's rare to hear the tale of the Lost Princess these days. I don't think anyone has mentioned her to me for at least three or four years, and before that, I hadn't heard anything for decades. It's only us oldies who remember the story now. What an amazing discovery this is."

Gul stopped pacing. "Three or four years? Who did you talk to about her? Perhaps they can help us gather more information?"

Mr. Davar shook his head. "I'm afraid I can't remember the woman's name, but she belonged to one of those history clubs or societies. City Central University was putting together an event, I recall. It was a silly thing, a way to lift the spirits during the exam period, she told me. They decided to debate some of the more far-fetched tales from local history that have excited treasure seekers over the years, tales that couldn't be proved or disproved. You'd be surprised how many of those we have in Pakistan."

"You wouldn't have any contact details for the woman you spoke to, would you?"

"I'm afraid not. All I remember was that she seemed like a lovely girl and was very polite. I don't know how she had come across the story in the first place, but she asked me if I could tell her a bit about Artunis, so we chatted on the phone. She told me she was going to share the tale at her event, that people would enjoy it, but that's the last I heard about it."

"I see," Gul said. "Well, I have a contact at City Central University, so I'll try to follow up and see who runs their history club or society."

"You'll let me know if you find something?"

"Of course, Davar Sahib."

Mr. Davar straightened and beamed. "A treasure hunt. Whether she's real or not, I think you'll have quite the story to tell by the end of this, Gul."

GUL AND HARRY left Mr. Davar amongst his books and papers, and headed back to the museum, both quiet for a time in the car. Then Harry spoke. "The text referred to a place called Mak, beyond Bactria."

Gul knew what he was thinking. Bactria was an ancient name for the land that was now central Asia and Afghanistan. To the southwest lay modern-day Balochistan, which several ancient civilisations had called Maka. Maka had been a satrapy of the Achaemenid Empire, in fact.

"You think it's Maka?"

"I think perhaps it's a derivative used in local dialects to describe the region, yes. I think her burial chamber could be in Balochistan, maybe even near the cavern where her body was found."

A rickshaw cut across them, and Gul braked sharply. You had to have your wits about you, driving in Karachi. "There is a whole network of caves around there. But let's say that, hypothetically, you're right. Whoever found her body would have also found her treasure by now, don't you think?"

"If they had, then they wouldn't have wanted her back so badly. Gul, the inscriptions say the riches of the city are buried *within* her. What if the secret lies inside her, on her bandages? A location, perhaps?"

"You're thinking like the Egyptians?"

"Why not? She was mummified by an Egyptian priest. Perhaps he thought this servant of his, Nakht, would ensure that the right people found her body?"

They had both seen Egyptian mummies with linen bandages inscribed with spells from the *Book of the Dead* and other prayers, even ones inscribed with locations.

"What if Isu placed the exact location of the gold, rather than prayers, on her wrappings? She could be an elaborate treasure map, Gul. Just think, it could have been a way to ensure that her secrets remained with only those most devoted to her cause."

"Well, we don't have the body anymore, so that's that."

"But we have the rest of the sarcophagus. Maybe there are other clues."

Gul smiled. For all his technical expertise and training, Dr. Harry Gilbert was getting carried away. She forced herself not to do the same. They had to focus on the facts, and the facts were that they still didn't know what they were dealing with.

When they got back to the museum, Rana and Hamza were busy with measurements, tracings and analysis. They'd dusted down everything they could, though there was still embedded dirt in a small section. It would have been easier if Ali Mahmood hadn't continuously interrupted, they told her. The man kept coming in, trying to take over. Gul put a stop to that immediately, letting him huff and bluster about his uncle, the Minister of Antiquities, but refusing to let him take the casket away. She may not have Princess Artunis's body anymore, but there was no way she was letting go of the sarcophagus, not to a man like Ali Mahmood, not unless Director Raja forced her to.

Sadly, Harry had to leave them to catch a flight to Tehran in order to bid on his coveted amulet. He promised to be back in two days. "And if you find out anything at all, no matter how small, you better bloody call me," was his parting shot.

In the evening, Gul dismissed the team and continued the work herself. They were pretty much done with cleaning the sarcophagus. The cuneiform phrasing was all about prayers for Artunis in the afterlife, and curses on her enemies. Nothing to indicate where she died or was buried, or where her missing gold might have gone to.

Gul sighed. Her head was throbbing. It was time to call it a day.

It was dark by the time she left the museum. She made her way to the back gate where her car was parked, carefully avoiding the broken step, and a patch of paan spittle that was shaped, oddly, like Italy's boot. The lights were off and the place was still, though beyond the gates, she could hear the lively sounds of the city at night. Cars and rickshaws honked, and motorcyclists with noisy engines were weaving in and out between them. A group of men squabbled good-naturedly with each other as they walked by, though about what, she couldn't tell.

Once in the car, she hunted around for her glasses—Gul was always misplacing the bloody things. She found them under her seat, where they must have fallen when she was getting out of the car. After that, she tried to call Ejaz again, but there was no response. She tapped her fingers against the steering wheel. The kid was in serious trouble; she knew it. She would go to the shrine again tomorrow. There was nothing else for it.

She felt too wired to go home. Instead, she called Mrs. Fernandes. "Is Francis there? I tried him earlier and he's not picking up his phone."

Mrs. Fernandes harrumphed. "He's here. Well, nearby. At the usual place. This better not be about you trying to pay for that new Wi-Fi service he's been eating my head off about."

"I need his help with a contact at City Central University, that's all."

"Shall I get him to ring you when he's back?"

"It's all right. I'm in the car anyway, I'll just pop over and have a quick word on my way home."

"Don't you dare give him any money. He has to learn to live on what he can earn."

"I wouldn't dream of it, Mrs. F."

CHAPTER 13

DESPITE BEING NESTLED IN the bustling heart of the city, Cantt Station still managed to evoke a sense of the past, a sense of time standing still. Its imposing yellow-and-red brickwork, elegant archways and geometric mouldings were all majestic in their faded grandeur. Victorian lamps—now electrified—lit the steps into the station, and a line of crows gazed dispassionately down at passengers from the ledge above.

Inside, the place still maintained much of its colonial heritage, from its original clock tower to its large canopies with curved metal trusses. The dial face of its massive, scarlet weighing scale still read W&T AVERY BIRMINGHAM AND CALCUTTA.

But modernity also jostled for position. The station bustled with people, with chaiwallahs carrying their trays, faded leaflets never taken down, piles of rubbish, used ticket stubs and mounds of cigarette butts. Porters in their red-and-orange turbans and shirts, identified only by the large black numbers printed on their backs, raced up and down the stairs to different platforms, some balancing suitcases on their heads. Others looked like escaped convicts in their uniforms, completing jobs as fast as they could in order to move to the next and to build on their day's meagre earnings. The air was thick and filled with the smell of bhuttas from the street vendor standing at the corner.

Gul walked past the rows of improvised tuck shops that

were walled with crates of Coca-Cola, 7UP, and Aqua-
fina, and which sold everything from razor blades to bags
of chips—the chips hung in garlands on top of makeshift
counters. She shook her head at the hawker trying to sell
her candy floss, and pushed her way through a large, disorganised family who had stopped suddenly for some reason,
taking up almost the entire width of the platform with their
bundles and bags and their prams and their children. The
Karakoram Express to Lahore would be here soon; perhaps
the family was collecting itself before the inevitable push
onto the train.

For a moment she closed her eyes, remembering her family's own train journeys from this very station. When she
was a child, her parents would often book a four berther
on the Khyber Mail to Rohri to visit their extended family.
It was one of the happiest memories Gul had of them all
together, of the growing excitement as they packed mountains of food ahead of time, parathas and shami kebabs,
but somehow, still, always having room in their stomachs
to stick their arms out at every station along the way to buy
something, sometimes hot boiled eggs, or chole or pakoras,
or sometimes, if she was lucky, her favourite, twisty jalebis
soaked in sugary syrup that always made her stomach content but her mouth feel dry afterwards.

On those trips her parents were always in genial, indul-
gent moods, their evening picnics followed by a card game,
the cards perched precariously on the small table between the
berths, someone's hand reaching out to keep them safe every
time the train jerked and jolted. Back then the train itself
was another relic of a time gone by, the racing green car-
riages seemingly untouched for a century, with their reading
lights with short metal chains you had to pull to turn on,
and their silver-plated ashtrays.

Gul could still hear her mother's laughter and smell her father's pipe smoke. It permeated the berther and all their lungs because Baba refused to wait until they had reached a station to set his tobacco ablaze, engulfing the small cabin in a delicious aroma of woodland and cherry, and second-hand cancer risk, no doubt. And then, before bed, Gul and Bilal would share their comic books—it was the only time that Gul ever read them—and swap their different chewing-gum flavours before crawling into the top bunks and letting the sway of the train and the clacking of the tracks lull them to sleep. In the early morning, the train attendant would knock on the door and wake them up with hot milky tea and warn them that Rohri was approaching, that they would have to be quick getting off the train, because it wouldn't wait for more than a minute at the station, no matter what. And Bilal would turn and smile at her and wink, ready for the next stage of their adventure, so much lighter in those days, so much less domineering.

Gul opened her eyes and swallowed. There was no point dwelling on all this now. The past was the past, and she had spent far too much time thinking about it recently. She pushed determinedly through the family with all their accoutrements and carried on down the platform. She stopped when she came to the small eatery optimistically named Food Court, which served a variety of inexpensive meals from all around the globe from a single grill and kitchen. She spotted Francis sitting under the eatery's green tarpaulin, on a bright blue plastic chair, munching on a burger while scrolling through his phone. The kid came here a lot because the food was cheap, and because the flat he shared with his grandmother nearby was small. Being here gave him some space away from his Dadi, whom he loved, Gul knew, but who sometimes loved him a little too fiercely in return.

She watched him now, thinking fondly of the boy he once was, with his obsession for outer space and rocket ships and nebulas and weird equations she never could get her head around. Not much had changed in that regard, though now he was a young man with thick black hair sporting a pencil-thin moustache that should have made him look foolish but in reality made him look like a 1940s aviator or movie star. Rockets were still his passion: Francis was studying engineering and had hopes of getting a scholarship to go to America one day, to get his doctorate degree in astrophysics.

He looked up just before she could reach him. His eyes widened and he stood hastily. "Apa, how are you?"

"You didn't pick up when I called, you wretch."

He flushed. "Sorry, Apa, I was going to call you back when I got home, I swear. It's just that I was talking to my girlfriend."

"Your girlfriend?"

"Don't mention it, please. I'm not ready to tell Dadi about her. Not yet, anyway."

"Your secret is safe with me." Gul knew from experience that the burgers here could unsettle even her hardy stomach, and so she ordered a Coke and sat across from him. "I need your help."

"My help?"

Gul pushed his burger towards him. "Eat. It's going to get cold. There was an event at your university about three or four years ago, a history club event."

"Do you mean the Historical Society? They call themselves the PastMasters, you know." Francis made a show of rolling his eyes.

"It's likely to be them, yes. I have to track down the people involved back then. I thought perhaps, since you're there every day, you could ask around and try and get some details for me. What do you think?"

His phone was back in his hand. "Do you know what the event was called?"

"No."

"The exact year it took place?"

"No. All I can tell you is that it was an event likely hosted by the Historical Society or PastMasters or whatever they call themselves, and that it was meant to be fun, something about treasure seeking or myths. I need to find the woman who organised it and ask her where she heard about a particular treasure that she highlighted in her presentation. It could be that she knows something I don't."

"Is this about the mummy?"

"Yes."

Francis grinned. "That's great."

"Just ask around, okay? Get some information for me, but don't go anywhere with anyone."

"You can't possibly think that anyone who calls themselves the PastMasters are dangerous, Apa? They're a bunch of stoners and pseudo-intellectual nerdy types, mostly."

"I don't know what I think anymore, Francis. But I'd rather not take any chances."

He nodded. "I'll ask around tomorrow, and call you when I hear anything, okay?"

"That would be great." Gul took a sip of her Coke. "Now, while I'm here, why don't you tell me about this girlfriend of yours? Is she the reason you need better Wi-Fi?"

CHAPTER 14

CITY CENTRAL UNIVERSITY WAS located close to the airport, just off Rashid Minhas Road. A relatively young institution, it had been set up five years earlier by some of Karachi's biggest industrialists in a bid to keep talent in the city.

And why ever would they want to leave? thought Gul, as she now walked around the American-style campus in amazement. Everything was sparkling new, from the state-of-the-art science labs to the spacious auditorium, sports complex, gym, and wellness centre.

Gul was used to the shabbier feel of the campus at Karachi University, which hosted over forty thousand students and charged far, far lower fees. As a result, it struggled to maintain its vast facilities. Karachi University was like a city in itself, a complex, highly politicised ecosystem spread across more than twelve hundred acres, with a diverse student body and an even broader academic curriculum. City Central, in contrast, had the air of a small village, easy to wander around and admire, even easier to navigate. It had plenty of coffee shops and a restaurant called Good Vibes, and knew how to keep its three thousand students happy, Gul thought, wincing slightly at the thought of the astronomical tuition fees that Francis was paying.

But ever since a suicide bomber had killed three Chinese academics and their Pakistani driver near Karachi University's Confucius Institute, Mrs. Fernandes had refused to allow Francis to attend. "What good is a dead grandson?" she'd said to Gul. The Balochistan Liberation Army had claimed responsibility, saying the perpetrator was the organisation's first female martyr, and to Mrs. F, this was proof that anything could happen at any time to Francis there. If it wasn't the BLA, it would be the Taliban, or the government cracking down on student activists. But nobody cared about a small liberal arts college full of upper-middle-class children. It barely made a blip on the radar.

Luckily, most of Francis's tuition was covered by his scholarship, but the kid had been enterprising in paying the rest. Mrs. F thought that Francis worked after school at Dolmen Mall, but really, Gul knew he was making money by frequenting the few legal liquor shops still left in the city, purchasing his quota of beer and wine each month, and selling them to other students at five times the price, which was still lower than what the bootleggers would have charged them. He'd even got some of his friends from church involved in his scheme, and collectively they shared the spoils. Being a Christian in Pakistan had little to recommend it, Gul thought. If Francis had figured out a way to leverage his religious status to make a rupee or two, who was she to argue?

Francis pointed ahead. "See that building? It's the faculty of social sciences. Yasmine is going to meet us in the lobby."

They passed a group of girls and Francis winked at one wearing a hijab. Then he grinned at Gul. "It's okay, Apa. That's my girlfriend, Dania."

"*That's* your girlfriend? Your grandmother is going to kill you, you know." She didn't have to say more. What would Dania's family have to say about her dating a Christian boy? Serious trouble had occurred over much less.

"Well, there's no point telling her, then, is there?" He

opened the door to the social sciences building, and Gul followed him inside.

Yasmine Premjee was tall and lean, with long, straight hair and a parade of studs in both ears. She was wearing a sleeveless burgundy kurti on top of jeans, and had several tattoos on her forearm. One simply said "NO" and another, Gul was pleased to see, was an image of the statue of the Dancing Girl of Mohenjodaro.

Yasmine followed her gaze and rubbed her tattoo. "I've always loved her. The original female icon. It was hard to find a tattoo artist who could draw her, though, so in the end I sketched this myself and had them ink it."

"You're an artist?"

Yasmine shrugged. "It's not really what I'm passionate about, but I can draw. Sorry about asking you to meet me here, but my friend is bringing her car around. I've got to put these leaflets in her diggi."

Gul noticed the cardboard boxes behind her. "Leaflets?"

"We're protesting next week. You should join us."

"May I?" Yasmine nodded as Gul reached into one of the boxes. *Stop the Harassment, Stop the Discrimination. Dress Codes Don't Equal Respect. Patriarchy ki Vaccine Kab Aye Gi?*

Gul smiled. "You think we need to vaccinate people against the patriarchy?"

The look Yasmine gave her made Gul feel like an out of touch boomer. "Over forty sexual harassment and assault cases have been lodged by women at City Central, some of them against teachers here. They have all been ignored by the administration. Instead, they've turned around and introduced a new conservative dress code. No jeans, makeup, or jewellery allowed. Clothing has to be modest and cover up to the ankles and wrists."

Yasmine opened another box. "This is meant to be a

liberal university, and we're in Karachi, not Peshawar, where all the universities are caving into this bullshit. Whether or not a woman wants to dress conservatively should be up to her, not them." She picked up another leaflet and showed it to Gul.

Dress by Choice, Not by Code.

"They think we're inviting the sexual harassment on to ourselves because we have the audacity to dress as we want. It's clever. They can blame us, instead of blaming their own faculty and administration. It's essential that women come together to fight this and make our voices heard."

Gul felt the familiar queasy hollowness that came at the sudden thought of Mahnaz. "You sound like someone I know. I hope you get some traction."

Yasmine inclined her head. "Thanks."

Gul pocketed the leaflet. Perhaps she would attend the protest. Why not? Just because Mahnaz was no longer around to spur her on, didn't mean she should give up supporting the causes that Mahnaz—that they both—believed in. Maybe she could bring Rana, who would love the notion of people needing vaccination against the patriarchy and had attended plenty of Aurat Marches herself. For now, though, she had to focus on the task at hand. "You know why we're here?"

"Only what Francis told me on the phone, which was that you needed to speak to someone involved in the PastMasters a few years ago."

Francis cleared his throat. "Faraz told me that you used to be a history major and that you hosted an evening all about hidden treasures and myths back then."

She looked surprised. "That's what you have questions about? It wasn't even that well attended. I remember it because I did a lot of the organising, but I was just a first year."

"What time of year was it?"

"In December. Just after our first set of exams. So, three and a half years ago or so?"

"Do you recall the story of the Lost Princess?" asked Gul.

Yasmine nodded. "Hanh, it was a lot of fun."

"How did you come across it?"

The other woman looked thoughtful for a moment. "That was one of Mala's leads. Mala was too busy to follow it up because she was graduating that year. She's half Parsi, so I think she had heard the story in her community but didn't really know much about it. But she got the number of a local historian who I spoke to on the phone. He told me about the Lost Princess, otherwise I would never have even come across the tale. I can dig out his details for you if you want?"

Gul swallowed down her disappointment. Mr. Davar had already told them everything he knew. A dead end, then. "Are you still in touch with Mala?"

"No, but I heard from someone that she moved to Lahore. Some of the history alums must be in touch with her, or I think she and I are following each other on social media? I don't have anything to do with the PastMasters anymore. I switched to social justice."

"Social justice?"

Yasmine shrugged. "What good is a history degree when you want to effect change today?"

"I would respectfully suggest that the answer is that it's worth a great deal, but I understand your reasoning. Is there any more you could tell me about the treasure-seeking event?"

"I'm sorry, Dr. Delani, but this was all a while ago, and everyone except me has graduated. I'm only here because I switched degrees, so I have another year to go. I don't think Mala could tell you any more about the story though. Really, if it wasn't for my phone call with Mr. Davar, we wouldn't have included it at all."

"I understand. It was a chance, but I was hoping you might know more about the Lost Princess than I do. I've already spoken to Mr. Davar, in fact."

"It *was* a fun story, though. Mummies and caves full of treasure. Who wouldn't get excited by it?"

"Yes, really remarkable."

Yasmine looked at her for a moment. "Is this important?"

"It could be."

Yasmine's phone pinged and she glanced down and exhaled. "I'm so sorry, I have to dash. My friend is here with the car." She grabbed a cardboard box, and Francis went to help, picking up another.

"Thanks." Yasmine hesitated and turned. "Would it help to have a list of attendees who came to the event?"

Gul's eyes widened. "It certainly couldn't hurt. Do you have that?"

"Yes. We got all their email addresses because they had to register. We streamed it online and did it in person too. It will be on the PastMasters SharePoint, and I'm sure I can get one of them to email it over."

"Well, you never know who else might have accrued some knowledge on the story, so that would be really great, thank you."

Yasmine bit her lip and put her box down. "You know, now that I think about it, a strange thing happened afterwards. A few weeks later, a man showed up at one of our meetings. He asked us for more details about the Lost Princess. I don't remember seeing him at our original event, but he was really insistent. He was a real chutiya—excuse my language—but he put everyone off, acting like we should know more about her than we did. Mala told him that he should speak to Mr. Davar in Parsi Colony if he wanted to know more, but the man kept harassing us for information anyway."

Gul's heart beat a little faster. "A man? Do you have his name? What was he like?"

Yasmine shook her head. "I don't really remember. It was just that he made everyone uncomfortable, asking lots of questions and then getting annoyed when we told him we had no more details to share."

"Did he speak English or Urdu?"

Yasmine frowned. "It was so long ago, I couldn't be sure. I think he was middle-aged though, that I remember."

A honking sound from outside caused her to pick up the box again. "Sorry, I better dash, but I'll email you, okay?"

"Thank you, I appreciate it."

"See you at the protest?"

"I'll certainly try to be there," Gul said.

AS THEY WALKED back to the parking lot, Gul gathered her thoughts. They had no new information about the mummy, but it was interesting that someone else had been trying to find out about her four years ago. Could it have been Saayaa? What if he had come across the mummy somehow, and had wanted to work out who she was and what she was worth?

And then she had another, unnerving thought. She picked up her phone. "Davar Sahib? It's me, Gul."

"What can I do for you, Gul?"

She cleared her throat. "You said you had a break-in a few years ago?"

"Why, yes, yes I did. I still haven't been able to properly reorganise my things. The rascals upended all my work, you know. There were papers and folders everywhere, the whole floor was carpeted in my files."

"But nothing was taken?"

"No, not that I'm aware of. Then again, there is so much in the archives, it will always be difficult to be sure. Probably those dacoits were looking for some antiquities to palm off for fast money."

Francis was walking ahead of her, and now turned around to wait. She waved him on, picking up her pace. "Could it be that they weren't ordinary thieves, that they were after some specific information instead?"

"What could you possibly mean, Gul?"

"Mr. Davar, when was the robbery?"

"It was . . . well, it was four years ago now."

"Four years exactly?"

"Well no, not exactly. It was late December. I remember because it was the year of that awful weather. It was bad enough that all my files were destroyed, but then I had to spend New Year's Eve clearing through the chaos in the freezing damp. I remember that. So not quite four years ago."

They were at the parking lot now, and Gul tried to remember where she had left the car. "December was when the City Central history event took place. So the robbery happened not long after Yasmine from the university called you?"

"Oh, good, you found her. Yes, I believe that was her name! Will you please pass on my regards?" He paused. "I think, if I remember correctly, the robbery was a few weeks after that phone call. It must have been, because when we spoke I still had all my files in order."

"I see."

"Gul, you can't possibly think that someone broke in here to find out about the Lost Princess myth?"

"I'm not prepared to rule anything out, Davar Sahib."

"Well, they wouldn't have found it. The papers are all in

Farsi and they were in a folder within a folder, full of loose-leaf pages on all manner of things. I have a system, you see, but for anyone else it would be the proverbial haystack. Not very elegant, but there you go. This is why I need some help."

"And nobody else asked you about Artunis, apart from the girl from the university?"

"Not for years."

"There was no gentleman who approached you about it?"

"None whatsoever. I'm sure you're overthinking this, my dear."

Francis found the car before she did.

Gul fished her keys out of her bag, pressing the fob to unlock the doors. "I'm sure you're right. In the meantime, though, I'll ask around the university. Maybe someone would be interested in doing some archival work for a little extra credit."

"You're a godsend, Gul, thank you."

Gul hung up and her phone rang immediately, causing her to jump.

This time, it was DSP Akthar. "Madam, I need you to come to the port first thing in the morning."

"The port? Why?"

He sounded excited. "We've found her, Madam Gul. We've found the mummy."

CHAPTER 15

THERE WERE TIMES IN her life when Gul felt small. When she'd walked across the glaciers at the foothills of the Himalayas, or when she'd first stood outside the Temple of Edfu, staring at the towering figure of Horus etched into the stone above her, she had felt the weight of it, of her own insignificance in the world.

But Karachi Port always brought a true sense of disproportion. As one of the region's busiest seaports, the place was like a city in itself, a maze of gargantuan ships. From a distance, the freight liners' shipping containers were like stacks of matchstick boxes. But up close those ships were disorientating. The vessels docked here could carry 75,000 tons of dead weight each. Some of those containers were the size of small houses, and there were hundreds of them, in some cases even a thousand, on each ship.

DSP Akthar had a police escort waiting for Gul when she got there. What he hadn't told her was that she would be leaving the port itself. The body the police had found, that they thought was Princess Artunis, was on a ship a mile away from the wharf, she was told. For whatever reason, the freight liner had yet to dock. She was escorted down to the jetty, where she climbed aboard a small motorboat that was bouncing up and down in the salty, monsoon sea.

They left the jetty behind and passed the two main wharfs of the port, the ships growing smaller as they pulled away, but still large enough for her to read their names. Some had

Chinese lettering; one said it was from Singapore. Several were German companies she recognised, and she was fairly sure one was Canadian, because it had a maple leaf painted next to its name.

The ship they were approaching was black, its deck was nearly flat, and it was heaving with a variety of coloured containers. When they pulled up, Gul could see that something was amiss. Some of the containers seemed to be resting on their sides on top of others. They had tumbled over each other like children's blocks, no longer the rigidly neat stacks that they once were. She came aboard and stood on the deck; her head tilted up. DSP Akthar came to greet her, looking hot and harried, his question-mark birthmark looking redder than normal. "Thank you for coming, Madam Gulfsa."

"What has happened here?" Gul asked.

Sweat was trickling down DSP Akthar's forehead. "The twist lock on one container somehow came apart. That container crashed into the others, causing them to fall. The ship had only just pulled out of port when it happened. As a result, insurance adjusters have been examining the cargo."

"How unlucky," Gul murmured.

DSP Akthar smiled grimly. "Unlucky for them, but lucky for us. All of the containers have had to be reopened and re-examined for insurance purposes, even the ones that weren't directly affected. And when the insurers saw the contents of one of those, they called us. Come with me. You will see for yourself, Madam. It's her."

Gul found herself climbing several ladders to the very top level of the stack. She looked down. They must have been at least forty-five feet above the sea, if not more.

"Watch your step, Madam Gulfsa," said DSP Akthar, moving from one container down to the second, which had its door open. Surrounding this container were cops, crew-men, and army commandos, all watching as she made her way towards it. She jumped down, walked past them and peered inside. It was dark, but she could make out that there was a large green electrical generator, strapped in with some sort of bungee cord.

"I don't understand," Gul said.

"You have to come to the side," DSP Akthar replied, walk-ing into the container itself.

He turned on the torch on his phone. "Careful. It's slip-pery. This is an industrial diesel generator, Madam. But when you walk to the back of the container, you see that the front is a façade. At the back, many of its parts are missing. Instead—come this way, please—you'll see that here, there is a space for a body. Whoever did this managed to pass it through customs. Can you see?"

"Yes," Gul said, numbly. "I can see." There was the hard cover of resin, ever so slightly pushing out of the back of the generator. She stepped as close as she could without disturb-ing it. It was the body. She leaned forward. Was it still intact? It would be difficult to examine her properly until she was removed. But she could see that there were the motifs from Persepolis, the cuneiform writings. Her throat tightened. "It's her."

Someone else came inside to hover, a burly man in a cam-ouflage uniform, his expression inscrutable behind a pair of sunglasses, which he didn't take off, even in the dark. "Are you sure?" His voice was clipped with irritation, and she wondered why.

"This is Kareem Mustafa. He's with the Port Security Force," DSP Akthar said.

Gul nodded distractedly at the other man. "As much as I can be, in the dark. Unless there's another mummy running around the place. But this isn't exactly a great angle; she could get further damaged. Can you pull her out?"

Sunglasses shook his head. "Not yet."

"Whose container is this? Where was it heading?"

The man shook his head again. "That is confidential." With his shades, his crew cut, and his uniform, he looked like he belonged in a *Top Gun* movie.

Gul glanced at DSP Akthar, who seemed to be simultaneously hot and uncomfortable. This man, Kareem Mustafa, whoever he was, clearly had more authority here than DSP Akthar did.

"I will arrange for you to be escorted back, Madam Gulfsa," DSP Akthar said, quietly. "Thank you for your help."

He climbed down the ladders with her, and when they reached the deck, she turned and faced him. "Why is she here?"

"Sorry?"

"Why is she on this ship?"

"Saayaa must be panicking." DSP Akthar dusted down his trousers. "He is selling her. He must have a buyer lined up."

"I see. Deputy Superintendent, when you phoned, I had just come across some new information." She filled him in on the three caravans of gold and the Lost Princess.

His expression barely changed. "So she is no longer valuable for just her antiquity. She could be the key to something bigger."

"This is still all a great deal of supposition, Deputy Superintendent. And I have to ask, if your drug dealer thinks there is a missing treasure, why get rid of the body, why not find the treasure for himself?"

"This ship is bound for the Gulf. Do you know if there are treasure seekers there?"

Gul thought for a moment. "There are certainly buyers

with deep pockets, some willing to bend the rules to procure unique items, I imagine, regardless of whether there are treasures to be found or not. For those who have come across the tale of the Lost Princess and can afford it, I imagine she's a compelling acquisition. I have been trying to connect with a black market contact I have, but he sometimes takes a few days to get back to me. When I do, I'll let you know."

DSP Akthar squinted against the morning sun. "I would appreciate the name of your contact."

"I'm sure you would, but I'm afraid that's out of the question. The man has helped me save several artefacts from being smuggled out of the country, so I owe him. But I promise you, if there's any information to share, I'll let you know." She glanced at the group of men still circling the container. "How come customs didn't pick up the body the first time they checked? Doesn't each container get searched thoroughly?"

DSP Akthar frowned. "All the containers had been scanned, and they were all approved by customs. Perhaps the customs officers overlooked this generator, perhaps they were negligent. But more likely, someone accepted a bribe, in which case nothing we do will make a difference." He followed her gaze and turned his head towards the Security Force personnel and the cops and the crew, and, it seemed to her, Kareem Mustafa particularly, and cleared his throat.

"I believe I understand you," said Gul.

"Until we know who we can trust, Madam Gulfsa, it is better not to trust anybody."

"My dear DSP Akthar, you are beginning to sound more and more like me. Am I going to get her back?"

He nodded. "I think so. I will have to check with my superiors."

"I'll need to autopsy her. It's the only way to really know what's going on."

"I understand. I'll see what I can do. I'll be in touch. For now, please take care, Madam Gulfsa. Whatever is happening, Saayaa knows who you are."

"Will do, I promise."

Gul was walking back to her car when she spotted Ali Mahmood stride into the port entrance. She watched him make his way to the police escort who had taken her to the ship. She followed.

"What are you doing here?"

Ali Mahmood turned, startled. Then his eyes narrowed. "I could ask you the same thing."

"I was here to confirm that they found Princess Artunis."

He straightened his tie. "My uncle has asked me to do the same. It appears that cop of yours overstepped his bounds by inviting you here without informing the Ministry first. The government has taken control of this case. It's been mishandled from the beginning, frankly."

"And how will you authenticate her? Are you a specialist on ancient funerary rites?"

"I am as capable of reading and of independent study as you are, Gul," Ali Mahmood snapped. "It doesn't take a genius to know what we are working with."

Even here by the sea, where the wind was picking up the smell of dead fish and leaving it to linger on nostrils, Ali Mahmood's cologne assaulted the senses.

"So, what now? You're in charge, is that it?"

He flushed. "It's up to the government to decide who takes control. I am merely here representing my uncle."

Gul relaxed. If Ali Mahmood's uncle had given him any real authority, he would have kicked her out of the port by now. The man was just showboating, trying to stake a claim. "No one taking you seriously, Ali?"

"You're an infuriating woman."

"So I have been told. See you later." She smiled sweetly and left him there. She was going to have to rush to the museum and make her case with Director Raja before Ali Mahmood got his grubby paws on Princess Artunis and ruined everything.

She got into her car and drove towards Napier Mole Road. When she turned onto Native Jetty Bridge, she noticed a silver Pajero turning behind her. Odd, she thought. She could have sworn she had seen a similar jeep with a distinctive gash on its hood before. The Pajero was still behind her when she passed the Turkish ice cream place on the corner and crossed into M. A. Jinnah Road, and even when she turned onto I. I. Chundrigar. It stayed with her all the way to Strachan and pulled away just before the museum. Was she being paranoid, Gul wondered, or was the Pajero following her? Her heart skipped a beat as she drove up to the museum gates, but she told herself there was nothing she could do about it now. She had bigger fish to fry.

CHAPTER 16

THE NEXT MORNING BROUGHT both welcome and unwelcome news. Princess Artunis had been returned to the museum and forensic examinations were going to proceed. Ali Mahmood remained sidelined for now, largely because news of the attempted smuggling of the body had leaked, and media scrutiny had intensified. The Minister of Antiquities couldn't be seen to be indulging in nepotism, not now.

Unfortunately, news of the mummy's return had provoked differing reactions. This was a country that buried its dead before sunset on the day they died, where religion required people's remains to be treated with the utmost reverence. When Gul pulled up to the museum gates, she realised that this was also a country with limited imagination, and she cursed.

Protesters had gathered outside, protesters of all ages and creeds, by the looks of it. Some of them were supporters of Tehreek-e-Labbaik, the extremist party, judging from the signs they were carrying, and the sea of turbans, prayer caps and long beards Gul was driving past. Others were students, both women and men, from the nearby arts college probably, and from some of the other local universities and schools. It was a motley crew, people of different ages, and clearly differing ideologies, because some of the women were in jeans, and the Tehreek-e-Labbaik types would normally have been trying to ban *them*.

And yet here they were, shouting at her that holding on to

the mummy was un-Islamic, unethical, an abuse of human rights . . . (the students and the liberal types were shouting about human rights and ethics, the Tehreek-e-Labbaik crew were unsurprisingly calling her a kaffir).

Gul had little patience for the religiously motivated protesters. Princess Artunis had lived her life a thousand years before Islam emerged in the world, and so they had no right to impose their views. She had more empathy for the liberals. The mummy was, after all, a body—a once living, breathing woman, worthy of respect.

Either way, she was not in a position to argue her case now, amongst the shouts and placards of the protesters, whose collective point was that the mummy should be buried immediately. Who knew the liberals and the religious fundos could agree on anything?

Gul was grateful her window was raised when a piece of spittle thwacked, and then oozed down it. She turned to look. The thug who'd spat at her looked like a poster child for anger management classes, his face a mask of rage, his fists waving at her, his turban askew. She shot him a dirty look, and quietly invoked the wrath of the Arai, the ancient Greek spirits of curses, upon him. And then she waited for the gates to open.

The mob had everyone spooked, and Director Raja had decided to arrange a press conference to reassure everyone that Princess Artunis was in safe hands, and to launch a PR campaign to calm people down.

Director Raja looked more tense than Gul had ever seen him before, his usually artfully tousled hair and well-pressed suit more than a little ruffled as he wiped his glasses clean. "There's been a lot of pressure, as I'm sure you can imagine, but for the moment, the government recognises that it needs a certain expertise to push this forward. I've made it clear to them that the optics of Ali being in charge won't be great, not with his lack of credentials. You, however, will play well with the Western press. Oh ho, don't look at me like that, we both know it's true. You come across as very credible. Plus, well, there's the matter of the Delani Foundation's generous patronage of the museum. So, for now, she's in your hands."

Gul exhaled. "Thank you, Director Sahib." As much as she hated that Bilal had involved himself in her life by becoming a patron of the museum, she reluctantly acknowledged that his money was helping her make her case now. The Delani name, the Foundation and all its work, held a lot of sway in this city.

Director Raja put his glasses on and blinked. "Don't thank me, Gul. Just do well at the press conference. You know how fickle this government is. They can change their minds at any time."

And so the museum became a spiral of activity. Gul had gone to work and commandeered all her colleagues. The Anwar brothers, both accountants and amateur birdwatchers, and both annoyed at being pulled away from their spreadsheets, had been prised from their desks and cajoled into helping move chairs to the Ancient Weapons Gallery, where the conference would take place. Honestly, she had never met two odder characters. They reminded her of the bumbling detectives from the *Tintin* comics—Thomson and Thompson. Both in their fifties, neither was married, or had any significant partner that she knew of. They lived together, often dressed in the same cut of suit or same-coloured shalwar kameezes and seemed oblivious to the joys of the artefacts around them, focused only on the numbers and business side of the museum. And now they were grumbling about moving chairs, incredibly put out, even though everyone else was lending a hand. Even Ahmed Nawab, a short-sighted junior curator who spent most of his time on numismatics, was perched under a podium, trying to get the mic wired up. Everyone was making themselves useful with the exception of Ali Mahmood, who was walking around scowling. It was all fairly chaotic—nobody had seen the electrician or the museum's PR manager for hours, and the police were crawling all over the place, guarding the mummy and generally getting underfoot.

In the midst of the madness, Gul somehow snatched a moment for herself. She found herself alone with the mummy for the first time since Princess Artunis had been stolen. There she was in all her majesty, her gold visage serene, dignified, resting next to her carved wooden box. She lay in state in the half-light, immune to the frenzy she was causing just outside the room. Just what had really happened to Artunis? Did she really leave a treasure buried deep within the caverns of Balochistan? Had Saayaa found that treasure already, or were there more secrets to unravel? Thank the Gods the government had finally agreed to let her conduct some forensic examinations. Day after tomorrow, the body would be transferred to the AKU Hospital, and their examinations would begin. If Harry's flight arrived in time, he would hopefully be joining them there. Maybe, finally, there would be some answers.

Footsteps echoed, and Gul could hear a murmur of voices reverberating from the high-vaulted ceiling of the nearby gallery. She focused on the body. Hamza's make-shift display case was holding up well. It was equipped with a special ventilator of her own design, one that would gradually pump oxygen out. The body would have to remain in the case at all times, except when being examined forensically. It was hardly an elegant solution, but it would have to do until something more permanent could be arranged.

For now, however, Gul had access to the mummy, and she was grateful. She trailed her fingers a hair's breadth away from the wooden casket lying beside her, admiring the delicate carvings, some of which actually depicted scenes that mirrored those etched into stone at the Hall of a Hundred Columns in Persepolis, scenes that were richly portrayed and perfectly proportioned, images of the beneficent king granting his people an audience, of him with his soldiers, and of his many battles.

It made her wonder what life must have been like for the woman who had inhabited this sarcophagus for over two thousand years. Had Artunis known love? Had she ever thought beyond revenge, or was her whole adult life spent trying to reclaim her city?

Gul thought about the princess's murdered father and brothers. What was it like to live in a world where people would fight and claw and burn each other to the bitter end?

Stop it, said the scientist within her. *Stop fantasising. Focus on what you can prove.*

But that wasn't a lot. Now that she finally had permission to take things forward, she would need tissue samples for histological tests to tell her whether Artunis might have suffered from any diseases of her time, and whether it was really a septic arrow wound that caused her death, or something else. Malaria, tuberculosis, trichinosis, leishmaniasis, and many more ailments killed people in droves back then, though an arrow wound would have made for a better story amongst the treasure-seeking community, no doubt. Bone and teeth samples, put through isotope and strontium analysis, would give her information about Artunis's diet and her overall health, while gas chromatography and mass spectrometry could reveal what materials were used in preparing the mummy, and therefore, potentially, what region she was in when she died.

Those were the things she would be able to prove, over time. But still, her gaze lingered, at the cypress tree on the mummy's chest plate, at her crown of gold, and once again, she could not resist speculating. Princess Artunis carried the symbol of a whole city on her head. What a burden that must have been.

For a moment Gul closed her eyes. She did not believe in God, not in any singular, religious way. But she believed in all the Gods together, in the rituals of all faiths, in all the paths that humankind had taken, and were still taking, to comfort themselves and achieve a measure of spirituality and grace throughout the centuries. And so she sent her own wish to the Gods, to that energy now. *May this woman have peace. May telling her story to the world, may revealing her secrets help bring her peace.* The ancient Egyptians believed in an afterlife. By saying the name of the person who had died out loud, by invoking them, you could help them live on forever. And here was a body, preserved in the Egyptian way, presumably with Egyptian sensibilities. *Artunis. Artunis. Artunis.*

The door opened with a bang, and she jumped. But it was only Rana, come to tell her that the arrangements at the hospital had been confirmed. She thanked her, and together they headed to the press conference.

The room was packed full of eager journalists, police, and government officials, all of whom were puffing their chests in pride. The journalists wanted to know who stole the mummy and why, and whether it was true that a notorious drug dealer was involved. The government refused to comment on an ongoing police investigation, leading to

several mutters of complaint. Then journalists asked what
the Minister of Antiquities thought of Iran's request for the
mummy to be returned. Would Pakistan be willing to give
up its new treasure?

Absolutely not, replied the Minister. The mummy was
found on Pakistani soil. It belonged to Pakistan.

A lively debate followed. Was it sacrilegious not to rebury
the mummy? Against Islam? And who did she belong to?
The Baloch government were demanding the body back
because she was found on their land, and they wanted to
build a new site especially for her. Meanwhile, the Taliban
were insisting on having her, too, but only because she
would fetch a pretty price.

Then a question from a British journalist. Shouldn't
the mummy be taken somewhere where she could really
be taken care of and examined properly? Did the Pakistani
team really have the expertise and the technological ability
to ensure that she was safely looked after, especially consider-
ing that the body had not long ago been snatched by the very
police who were meant to be guarding her? Surely Princess
Artunis belonged to the world, and not to any one nation-
state? This was followed by an insinuation, from a Reuters
reporter, that all of Pakistan's treasures had been looted, and
Princess Artunis would be sold to the highest bidder, which
caused Director Raja to step up again and bristle.

By the end, Gul had developed a headache. Photographers
piled into the room with the body, and it was a difficult task
getting them to leave once they'd finished taking their photos, with one or the other coming back for more. Rana and
Hamza managed the process with as much efficiency as possible, so much so that even the Minister congratulated them
on their way out. After that, they moved the mummy into
its special chamber. Gul thought about all the questions that

had been posed at the press conference. For now, there were no real answers to give, but she would press on, determined to unlock the truth of Princess Artunis.

IT WAS HOURS later that Gul was finally alone with the body again, having sent her team home. With some trepidation she turned off the remaining lights, said goodbye to the line of cops patrolling outside the door, and headed back to her office to pick up her things. She knew the cops were all men that DSP Akthar trusted and that the world's eyes were on the museum. She just had to have faith that there would be no further attempts to steal the body.

Once at her office, she saw that Hamza had left some expense claims on her desk for her to sign for the mummy's chamber he'd built. She perched on the corner, sorting through the pile. A different form for every little nut and bolt. The bureaucracy of this place drove her mad. No wonder the Anwar brothers worked late every single night and came in early every single morning. Asif Anwar, particularly, lurked around waiting for her to finish her paperwork. What bean counters they were. Everything in triplicate. Everything signed by everybody. It was a management consultant's dream, one she would have happily ignored for the night, except that Hamza had spent his own money buying what they needed, which was something he could little afford. As it was, it would be weeks before the museum paid him back.

And then she found herself sucked back in to work, answering long-overdue emails, looking at budget requests, dealing with research proposals.

At least an hour had passed when Mrs. Fernandes phoned. "Have you seen the news? The story is everywhere already."

Gul sat back and closed her eyes. It wasn't surprising.

"It's big business, mummies. It captures the imagination. It always has."

"The Iranians are going crazy. They say we can't be trusted with her. The religious right is calling you an infidel and demanding we rebury her. And you've somehow managed to cause a furore among the political left as well. They say that displaying the body is immoral and disrespectful."

Gul couldn't help but laugh. "It's quite something that I've managed to piss them all off at the same time. But it's a complicated thing. The archaeological community is still arguing about whether it's okay to display mummies publicly. On the one hand, it's educational and provides rare research opportunities. On the other, nobody consented to have their bodies gawked at by strangers centuries after their deaths. That's what the students were protesting about, and they aren't entirely wrong."

"All I know is that there's one mad fellow on social media demanding that we hold a séance to send her spirit back to the afterlife."

Gul rubbed her tired eyes. "Mummies have always elicited strange responses, Mrs. F. In medieval times, grave robbers dedicated their whole lives to unearthing mummies and bringing them back to Europe. People would eat their flesh to help them with a variety of ailments from acne to liver disease. Sometimes they would boil them first, and turn them into soup. Ironic, really, that the Europeans abhorred cannibalism, when they embraced the practice themselves."

"That's disgusting, Charlie."

"Oh, that's not the half of it. The Pre-Raphaelites used the mummies for pigment. They'd crush them into powder and turn them into 'mummy brown' in their paintings. Guess how many years paint companies sold the colour until they ran out of body parts to make more?"

"I don't know."

"1964. It was 1964 before the last paint company informed the world they had run out of bodies, and just had the odd limb lying around."

"You really are ghoulish."

Gul smiled. "So is the rest of the world. Princess Artunis is going to be all over the news for a while, especially since she's already been stolen once. Such dramatic events cause people to sit up and pay attention. See you in the morning, Mrs. F."

"Don't work too hard, Charlie."

"I won't, I promise."

But later, just when she was about to turn off her computer and head out, she heard the familiar ping of her email box and couldn't help but take a look. There was a message from Yasmine Premjee at City Central University.

Hi Dr. Delani,

I hope all is well. Attached is the list of the attendees of the PastMasters event. I have email addresses if you want to follow up with any particular attendee, but given that I'm usually the one ranting about the lack of privacy laws in Pakistan, I thought I'd hold on to them unless they're needed. I've also attached the Power-Point presentation we did, so you can see what the conversation was all about. Let me know if you need anything else. Yasmine

Gul opened the attachment. *X Marks the Spot: Myths and Treasure Seeking in Pakistan* said the first page of the presentation. She scrolled through it and couldn't help but stop at the tale of Alexander the Great's Macedonian general,

Seleucus Nicator, who became a king in his own right after Alexander's death. Seleucus established the Seleucid Empire, which included territories in modern-day Pakistan. While many historians believed that Seleucus was buried in Pieria in Macedonia, local legend had it that he was laid to rest in Pakistan, in a tomb filled to the brim with gold and other treasures.

Gul smiled as she read the tale. If the Lost Princess could be found in Pakistan, who was to say that Seleucus might not be one day as well, with all his accrued wealth? What other treasures lay waiting deep under the earth of the country?

She scrolled past another story of a high-profile Hindu family that had buried their immense riches somewhere on their lands, lands that were confiscated when the family fled during Partition. Their wealth had mostly been converted into antique coins, worth several million dollars at least. And yet they had never been found.

Gul made her way through the stories and myths and on to the list of attendees. The event had been open to anyone, she saw. She might have attended herself had she known about it; it sounded like it would have been a laugh. But Yasmine was right, only a few dozen people registered for it. None of the names jumped out at her, until very suddenly, one did.

Mahnaz Delani.

It was a moment before she remembered to exhale. Mahnaz had attended an event at City Central only a few months before her disappearance? What was she doing there? Gul turned off her computer and reached for her phone.

"Yasmine?"

"Dr. Delani?"

"We need to talk. As soon as you can, please."

CHAPTER 17

AFTER ANOTHER NIGHT OF tossing and disorientation, Gul woke up feeling emotionally and physically depleted. She couldn't stop thinking about Mahnaz. Mahnaz had come across the story of the Lost Princess. The coincidence unnerved her. How had Mahnaz even heard about an obscure event at City Central University in the first place? She was only fifteen at the time. It wasn't like Francis was studying there then, and she wouldn't have had any friends who would have known about it.

That question was answered a few hours later at least, when Gul sat down with Yasmine for coffee at Good Vibes, after a couple of futile hours of wandering around the shrine in search of Ejaz. She'd shown the other woman a photo of Mahnaz—the last one she had ever taken of her, grinning over a cupcake she was eating, the cupcake purple with sprinkles, a single sprinkle plastered to the rim of Mahnaz's curled top lip.

Yasmine had shaken her head. "I can't say that I recognise her."

"Is there any way to tell if she came to the event or if she logged on remotely?"

"I don't think so." Yasmine was already pulling out her laptop from her backpack. "But I can try and find out. I can check her email address. Maybe there's still some data on the server. The IT baandas might know. Let me just look it up."

"I can tell you now. It's pickaletter@gmail.com."

"Pick a letter?"

"She thought it was funny when she was young. Then it just stuck." Gul smiled at the memory of Mahnaz sending her an email for the first time.

Yasmine twirled one of the studs in her left ear. "Dr. Delani . . ."

"Gul, please."

"Gul, I've been through the list myself. As you know, I took out all the email addresses to keep people's data private while still trying to support your research. And I want to be as supportive as possible now that you've told me about your niece."

"I appreciate that."

"What I'm saying is, I would have remembered that email address. It wasn't on our list."

"What do you mean?"

"Hold on, let me check." Gul waited as Yasmine connected her laptop to the café's Wi-Fi. "Mahnaz Delani . . . aik minute." She looked up, and then turned her laptop around so the screen was facing Gul. "That's not the email she registered with, see? It's something else entirely."

Gul squinted and looked at the screen.

Mahnaz Delani – PakistaniJane@gmail.com.

Gul blinked several times. Mahnaz had another Gmail account? "Are you sure it's hers?" The question had been automatic, but Gul already knew the answer. Who else but Mahnaz would call herself Pakistani Jane?

Yasmine tilted her head and looked back at the screen. "PakistaniJane. Yup, that's definitely her." Her expression changed. "Aree bhai, I've come across that name before, I think."

Gul's mind raced as she watched Yasmine typing on her laptop again. She thought she knew Mahnaz, knew practically everything there was to know about her. And yet here was a whole other Mahnaz, who, it seemed, was good at guarding her secrets.

"Yes!" shouted Yasmine in triumph, and then grinned sheepishly as patrons turned to look at her. "Sorry, but I'm just so impressed with my brain for remembering this." She swivelled her laptop around again.

"What am I looking at?"

"It's my Instagram."

"The Feminist Collective?"

"I'm a community organiser. PakistaniJane followed me for a couple of years, and after a while I followed her back because she made some interesting comments on my posts. She sent me DMs for ages, and then she just vanished. I never knew why." Her cheeks flushed and she went back to awkwardly twirling her stud. "I'm so sorry, Dr. Delani."

"Gul. It's Gul, please," she said listlessly.

"I'm sorry for what you and your family have been going through, Gul. But look at the date here. I posted about the PastMasters event a couple of weeks before it took place. That's how she must have heard about it, why she must have turned up. But maybe she just logged in, because she never came and introduced herself at the event itself."

"What did she message you about?"

"What?"

"You said you messaged back and forth?"

Yasmine pushed the laptop further towards Gul. "Please, please have a look for yourself. It's nothing important. She wanted to know about different modalities in feminism, and about intersectionality in particular. She also wanted to know about various initiatives and activism in Karachi. I mostly just sent her links. She was clearly really interested. It's just here, see? There, there's our correspondence. Why don't you have a look while I get us some more coffee?"

Gul pored over the messages, her heart breaking again and again every time she finished reading one. There was nothing here that would help her, and yet, there was Mahnaz, in some tangible, meaningful way. Here were her passions, here was her voice and her tone and texture and humour. She let her fingers trail against the screen. This was as close as she had got to Mahnaz in three years.

When Yasmine came back she handed her the laptop. "Thank you," Gul said quietly. "It means a lot to me that you shared this."

Yasmine put the laptop back in her bag. "She seemed like a really engaged and motivated person. I hope you find her."

"Well," said Gul eventually. "You've given me an unexpected lead. That's more than I had a few hours ago."

"I have?"

"Mahnaz had another Gmail account we knew nothing about. She had an Instagram account I didn't know about, either. The police scoured her computer, and so did her family. But we never came across this in her web history. There may be something here that can help us."

"Shukar. I'm happy I was helpful."

Gul took the other woman's hands. "Thank you," she said.

Yasmine cleared her throat. "You're welcome. If . . . when you find her, tell her mujhe call karna. I would love to have her in this fight with us."

"I will, I promise."

ONCE OUTSIDE, GUL phoned Hamza. "How easy is it to hack into a Gmail account?"

"Hello to you too, Apa."

"Hamza, this is serious."

"I think it's near impossible. Google has implemented multiple layers of security to protect users' accounts, like two-factor authentication and advanced protection programs. People's accounts usually only get hacked if they fall for a phishing attack or use really weak passwords. But you're not doing that, right, Apa? Not after we put all your passwords on that one encryption site and made it easier for you to remember them?"

"My passwords are still safe, don't worry. What about Instagram? How easy is it to hack into someone's Instagram account?"

"Not easy at all. I'm sorry I can't help, Apa." He paused. "Apa, is this about . . ."

"Don't worry about it. Thanks, anyway."

Gul made her way to the university car park and then picked up her phone again. This time, she rang DSP Akthar and told him what had happened.

She could hear the man's brain working overtime as she filled him in.

"This is the missing case that IG Bhatti Sahib closed three years ago?"

Gul's heart sank. Would DSP Akthar be willing to help given that it might cause ripples with his boss? "Yes. Closed prematurely. I know I am asking a personal favour here, but is there any way to access the account, or reopen the case on the basis of this discovery?"

"I have no authority to open a case that has been closed, Bibi. But I can do something else. We can go to the magistrate and issue a court order and ask Google and Instagram to hand over the passwords. It will take some time, however."

"I'm exceedingly grateful. How much time are we talking about?"

He hesitated. "A few months. Because of the bureaucracy and jurisdictional issues, these things work slowly. Even then, both companies have strict privacy policies. They may not give us access to the account, but grant limited access to anything that they deem pertinent to her disappearance or the time frame in the run-up to her disappearance."

"That's insane. How could they possibly know what's pertinent?"

"I think you have to accept that this process will take time, Madam."

"It's been three years already, DSP Sahib. There's no time left."

"Just so, Madam Gulfsa. But I'm afraid that's all that we can do. For the moment, anyway."

Gul balled her hand into a fist. "Thank you. If you can get the things going, I would appreciate it."

GUL'S MIND WAS still churning long after she returned to the museum that afternoon. Mahnaz knew about the Lost Princess. Mahnaz had a whole other email address and an Instagram feed. What else had the girl been up to?

Instead of joining the others, Gul went straight to her office and onto Instagram. PakistaniJane had posted nothing at all, and was only following a handful of feminist feeds and advocacy groups. Some of those groups were following her back, but there were no obvious red flags, not anything she could see without getting into Mahnaz's account, anyway. She moved on to Gmail. She tried the most obvious passwords first. "Blinky" for Mahnaz's plushie toy. "Gloria," the name of her long since deceased goldfish. She then tried the names of some of her idols: "mayaangelou," "malalayousafzai," "asmajahangir," "ladygaga." And then again, combined with the digits of Mahnaz's birthday, and then with just her birth year. She knew she was grasping at straws, knew it was desperation driving her, but she would have tried anything, she would have continued forever. Then, to her horror, she was booted out. Google was locking the account for five hours, the screen informed her.

"Shit," Gul muttered, slamming her laptop shut. What would happen if she tried again without a password? Would the account be locked for good? Would the same thing happen with the Instagram account? It would drive her crazy, but she knew she needed to wait. This was too important to fuck up.

Gul thought about going to the Big House and hunting around, seeing if she could find a password stuck on a Post-it or something. But Mahnaz was far too technically savvy to do the things that Gul herself did, despite her assurances to Hamza. She wouldn't just leave her password lying around, especially not for an account nobody else knew about, would she? Besides, Bilal had caused enough damage when he had the investigation into her disappearance shut down. Why give him an opportunity to set obstacles on the path to her discovery again?

Gul took a deep breath, exhaled, and then left her office. The team were downstairs, working on finalising the arrangements for transferring Princess Artunis to the AKU Hospital. She joined them there, and the rest of the day went by both achingly slow and in a whir. There was so much to do to organise the mummy's transfer—and for Gul, more than the others, it involved paperwork and bureaucracy, from the museum, from the government, and from the hospital itself. Drowning in paperwork was usually the last thing she wanted, but today it seemed like just what she needed.

The team finished their final external examinations and measurements, and Gul sent them home. It had been a long few days, and tomorrow was unlikely to bring any respite, what with the early start and the forensic investigations.

Gul returned upstairs to her office, unsure about whether she could face going home. She sent some emails, did some more research on Artunis, and wrote her next university lecture. Eventually she got up and collected her things. There was nothing to be gained from staying here. Besides, she was starving. She needed to eat, and she needed to put thoughts of Mahnaz away until she could do something about them. For now, all her thoughts had to stay focused on the Lost Princess.

As she grabbed her satchel, she inwardly cursed. She'd left her glasses in the room with Princess Artunis. She was going to have to retrace her steps.

Walking down the hall, Gul felt a chill. The last time she'd been here this late at night she'd been knocked unconscious by a couple of corrupt cops. At least this time the place was still well lit despite the hour—DSP Akthar had insisted on it. Plus, he'd lined up men on every floor so that when she got to the creepy mannequins there was a policewallah blocking her view, standing to attention. She nodded at him. DSP Akthar had told her he'd picked the men out himself. After their meeting at the port, and their conversation about corruption, she had come to trust DSP Akthar, Gul realised. The cop nodded back, and let her pass.

Downstairs, she greeted Princess Artunis once more, again struck by her majesty. If it hadn't been such a long couple of days, she would have stayed, feeling more connected to the body of this woman than with anything else in her life right now. Where had she left her glasses?

She eventually found them next to the sarcophagus but groaned when she reached for them and accidentally dropped them on the floor. She was all thumbs today.

As Gul straightened, she glanced at the sarcophagus and frowned. She thought they had removed all the dirt there was, but here, in the very bottom left corner, embedded in the large rosette, there was still a smudge. She considered leaving it for the morning, but it would bother her, she knew. It would only take a few minutes to clear, so she picked up her brush and dusted. It was a particularly tricky corner, and she swept back and forth methodically, occasionally blowing some loosened dust away before continuing. There. She had got it all. She put on her glasses to check, and then blinked. There was the faintest of lines coming off the rosette, about two centimetres to the right. She leaned forward and peered more closely. Then she stood back, shocked. It couldn't be.

She leaned forward again, this time using her phone for light, and then exhaled, deeply. It was.

She rang Director Raja.

"Gul, it's late. Is everything all right?"

"No. No, it isn't."

"What's going on?"

"I was inspecting the wooden casket. The rosette on the very bottom left corner. I saw a line coming out of it. I—I can't be sure, not entirely, but . . ."

"Yes?"

"It looks like a pencil mark to me."

"Could it be a piece of dirt, that you've mistaken somehow?"

For a moment, silence lingered between them. They both knew the significance of what Gul was saying. Lead pencils had only been invented two hundred years before, which meant that the body could not be from the Achaemenid period. Suddenly, something that Gul knew all along could be true was making itself known. Was Princess Artunis a fake? "I dusted very carefully. I don't think it can be dirt or sediment."

Director Raja said nothing for a moment. "Let's not jump to conclusions. It could be contaminated by someone who walked past it, perhaps literally with a pencil in their hands. The mummy has been exposed to materials in several locations. It's been transported; it's been sitting in a police facility. We don't even know how long she's been above ground. Anything could have done this."

Gul shook her head and swallowed down the searing disappointment that had rendered her breathless. This is why she hadn't wanted to get carried away like Harry, and yet, it was a bitter blow. "Or it's the residual left from a tracing mark. If someone wanted to forge that carving, they could have used a tracing."

"And why on earth would they do that?"

She looked at the sarcophagus. "For the money, I assume. What if Saayaa is not a smuggler of antiquities? What if he's the one making the antiquities?"

Gul heard a door slam outside. Footsteps echoed in the hall. The police must've been changing rotas.

Director Raja exhaled into the phone. "Even if you did see a pencil mark, and even if its provenance is questionable, that's not to say that the wooden box and the body itself don't come from two different time periods. It's happened before. We won't know anything until you've completed your autopsy and all the carbon dating comes back. Look, why don't you go home and get some sleep? Tomorrow you'll start the forensics and get some answers."

Gul peered at the rosette again. She was sure it was a pencil mark. But let Director Raja inspect the sarcophagus in the morning and judge for himself. "You're right," she said. "It's been a long day. We'll look at it with fresh eyes tomorrow."

With a heavy heart, Gul locked up and left the museum. The traffic was light this time of night, the streets quieter than usual. Thankfully it was a short drive home, just past the police checkpoint, down Abdullah Haroon Road, past Frere Hall and then over the Clifton Bridge.

She had made it as far as the bridge when a vehicle came careening up behind her. What the hell? What was this idiot thinking, coming in so close? Her heart started to pound when she checked her mirror and moved to the left to give the driver a wide berth and saw that the car was a silver Pajero, with a large gash on its bonnet. It sped up so they were driving side by side. Shit. Why hadn't she taken it more seriously when she'd spotted the car following her earlier?

In the darkness she couldn't make out the driver's features. She tried to make out the license plate instead, so that she could give it to DSP Akthar later. And then she had no time for thought, because the Pajero was ramming into her left, trying to push her into the heavy concrete side of the bridge. She felt the violent jolt, heard the shriek of metal on metal, saw sparks flying out of her window, even as all her focus remained on straightening the car, her muscles already protesting about the speed at which she was turning the steering wheel. Jesus Christ.

Gul pushed down on the accelerator, trying to extricate herself from the concrete, but it didn't work because the jeep was ramming into her again and again. She felt the shock of it travel up her arms and into her neck, her head jerking to the left. The Pajero had firmly embedded her against the side of the bridge. She could smell rubber burning, even as something crashed through her back passenger window. What the hell was happening? She couldn't turn around, but the smell of kerosene hit her nostrils.

They remained locked together for several seconds, her

car becoming increasingly compressed into the wall, her focus now entirely on trying to keep from being flattened into the side of the bridge until heavy honking forced her to look ahead. A truck was coming right at them, and the jeep was directly in its path. With a sudden lurch, the Pajero pulled away and U-turned into the other lane. For a brief second in the glow of the oncoming headlights, she saw the silhouette of a man before the car disappeared entirely.

The oncoming truck screeched to a halt just inches from where the Pajero had been, and she was able to stop her own car, stumbling out just as the burnt rubber and twisted metal caught fire. She was unsteady on her feet, but was aided by the trucker, who had jumped down from his cab, and was pulling her away faster than her legs would allow.

They watched as the fire spread. Within minutes, the car was an inferno, the trucker staring at both her and the vehicle in amazement. Soon after that, crowds of onlookers formed seemingly from nowhere, just as they had all those years ago when she had been in the crash with Mahnaz. The rest of the night went by in a blur. The police were called; DSP Akthar appeared amongst the sea of faces. Witness statements were taken, and Gul described what happened as best she could, trying to keep her voice from shaking. Then, after she categorically refused any medical assistance, DSP Akthar drove her home and escorted her into her apartment.

He stayed for a cup of tea. "This is serious, Madam Gulfsa. Very serious. Saayaa wants you dead."

She shook her head, already aware of her aching body, the bruises and her strained neck. Tomorrow was going to be a bugger. "Yes, but if Saayaa wants the body back, why try and mow me down now? What good could that do?" She told DSP Akthar about the pencil mark she had seen. "If the mummy is a hoax, forensics will soon reveal it, so why bother getting rid of me?"

DSP Akthar's expression was grim. "I'm posting a unit outside your house," he said as he got up to leave, raising a hand when she started to protest. "No. Don't argue with me, Madam Gulfsa."

"My neighbours won't like it. Mr. Dada already thinks I'm up to no good."

"Well, I'm afraid he's just going to have to deal with it, Bibi."

WHEN DSP AKTHAR left, Gul jumped into the shower, wiping off the sweat and grit and tension of the attack. She crawled into bed, but couldn't sleep. She stared at the ceiling where a fly buzzed around the fan. What if Saayaa was watching her even now?

She picked up her phone and dialled Ejaz. Despite all the craziness of the last day, he had never been far from her thoughts. But his phone was dead, no ringtone, no nothing, just a void. He'd asked her to wait, to trust him, but that was too much to ask for after tonight. It wasn't enough to try to do this on her own anymore. Tomorrow, she would talk to DSP Akthar about the shrine.

Two hours later, she gave up entirely on sleep. She got up, made herself another cup of tea and opened a drawer in her bureau, the one she'd stashed Mahnaz's diaries in.

She touched them all, all the notebooks, with all their scraps of paper sticking out of corners, in their various shapes. She closed her eyes and picked one out at random. It was pink, a *My Little Pony* book with a lock and key, obviously something that had been bought for Mahnaz, because she would never have chosen something pink for herself; she violently hated the colour. Just holding it for a moment was enough to calm Gul, and she cradled it in the palm of her hand. The Gods only knew how she missed Mahnaz. The girl was still alive. She had to be.

Gul opened the diary. The key was long gone, and the lock was broken, but the diary itself was a treasure trove, full of funny illustrations, pictures and little anecdotes. There were no dates in it, but the writing was childlike, and Gul guessed Mahnaz must have been seven or eight when she filled its pages. Old enough to hate pink, but young enough to still like the idea of a plastic diary with a lock and key. On one of the first pages, Mahnaz had written:

> *Today I went to the beech and went on a camel.*
> *It was hot. Amal is my best frend.*

A crayon drawing of Amal and Mahnaz, two stick people with bright red smiles and yellow eyes, holding hands in a garden. Behind them was something indistinguishable—a block of blue. After staring at it for a while, Gul realised it must be a swimming pool. She remembered one in the garden at Amal Hashwani's house; she'd gone there four months after Mahnaz's disappearance. She'd wanted to speak to Amal, to find out what she knew. Kids didn't just disappear, and Amal was a party girl. Maybe she'd got Mahnaz into something dodgy.

Tact had never been Gul's strong suit, and in those days, she was still too upset to be rational. But Amal's parents were real chutiyas. They would not let her see their daughter. They were all pursed lips and politeness, telling her Amal and Mahnaz had stopped being friends years ago, that "their interests diverged." The mother in particular was pouty and waif-like—she was an expensive-handbag type, like Sania. And Gul understood what she was saying. Amal was popular. Mahnaz was a nerd, someone their daughter no longer associated with.

Gul remembered then how angry it had made her, the marked insinuations that she was being too hysterical, the judgment about who Mahnaz was, and what value she held. She made a show to leave them, but then snuck around the back of their house. Amal was in a pink bikini, sunning herself by a swimming pool with two of her friends.

Gul didn't want to think about the rest. The furore, the shouting, the heads silently shaking while she grew angrier and angrier. Sania had come to collect her, and soon after, Bilal had used his clout to end the police investigation.

Gul lay on the bed and continued flipping through the pages of the diary. She'd been hoping to wash away the memory of tonight, but had been left with a sour one from the past instead. Luckily, there were plenty of other images to take its place—Mahnaz sitting on top of an elephant in Sri Lanka, her hair blowing behind her, her eyes glinting in the sun. And then, on the next page, a list of things she wanted for her birthday, the top of which was a microscope, under-lined several times. Gul flipped the page again—whatever Mahnaz had drawn or written on the next page had been vehemently crossed over in dark, swirly lines. The whole page looked like it was a mass of interlaying shadowy moving circles. Mahnaz had had a bad day. Whatever it was, she had chosen to—literally—blot it out. Gul traced the pencil lines for a moment with her own finger.

And then she closed her eyes. If Bilal and Sania had not kept her from Mahnaz back then, she might have known what was being crossed out, what had troubled or annoyed the girl that day. Instead, they'd lost so much time. Long before the world had snatched Mahnaz away from her, Bilal had tried to do it first.

Gul got up, wincing when her body protested. That Pajero had done a number on her. She placed the diary back in the drawer, and reached for another. This one was a black leather notebook engraved with Mahnaz's initials. Mahnaz Alina Delani. MAD. Mahnaz had always got a kick out of that.

Gul recognised this notebook. She had sent it to Mahnaz on her thirteenth birthday, just a short while before they'd reconnected, when the lost years finally ended. Who would have known that they would have such little time together before they were lost to each other once more?

She got back into bed and took the diary with her.

Property of Mahnaz Alina Delani
Unauthorised access will be subject to the most stringent prosecution

Gul thought of Mahnaz at thirteen. Physically, it was an awkward stage. The girl had opted for red metallic braces instead of traditional ones, and they took over her face. Already, the hormones were raging, her breasts were large on her small frame, and they caused her to hunch over in embarrassment, which, combined with the blue slouch beanie she insisted on wearing every day, made her look more Smurf than teen. At thirteen, Mahnaz was even more of a loner than before.

There have been 359 deaths by selfies in the world. 359. What is wrong with people?

Minar keeps copying my homework. Should I:
A) Tell her to go away
B) Let her because she's my only friend
C) Tell her to go away, and then let her because she's my only friend?

She'd circled C on that one, in bright red ink. Gul smiled as she traced her fingers along the circle. Her finger against Mahnaz's pen.

I went to see Gul at the museum today. She looked totally shook to see me. I dnk why she and Babaji don't like each other. But I can't stay in the house anymore. I hate them both so much. When I got home, Mama told me I could go to the museum after school and do my homework there if I wanted, so it all worked out.

It shocked Gul, seeing it written out there, in meticulous ink strokes. She shut the diary with a thud and put it down. Then, after a moment, she picked it up again.

Mama won't tell me what Gul did, but it must be bad—worse than the car accident—because Mama is fake-nice with everyone.

It was a moment, and then it was gone. There were pages now, pages about her English homework, which was to build a model of Shakespeare's Globe. It was a class competition to see who could do the best job. Mahnaz had used pieces of a broom as the thatch, and built a cardboard structure for the theatre itself, stuffing it with Lego figures acting out *Macbeth*. She'd even put bubble speech coming out of their mouths. She'd painted matchsticks black, glued them together, and used them to show the timbers on the outside of the structure. The windows opened, the roof could be pulled off to look inside, and she'd used pieces of actual plywood for her stage. Here, in her diary, was an illustration of everything she'd done, with pieces of matchstick and thatch stuck in for extra effect.

And the next entry was all about her disappointment. Despite all her efforts, she'd lost out to Danish Hamdani. Danish's parents had clearly helped him—his Globe was expertly carved from wood. It was so unfair, so unfair because she had done her project by herself.

The next entry was a couple of weeks later. A flyer for the World Wildlife Fund, asking for pledges, combined with a description of the snow leopard she was planning on sponsoring. Snowy the snow leopard, Mahnaz wishing they'd given him a more original name. And then, a couple of pages later, the disappointment. Bilal and Sania refused to allow her to spend her allowance on the WWF sponsorship, suggesting that she support one of their many human causes if she wanted to, but not seeing the point in wasting money on animals.

I wish Gul was here. She's the only one who would understand.

Gul's breath caught, and she choked back the tears. But they came, nonetheless. She held the diary in her arms and started to sob. She couldn't handle reading any more—not tonight.

CHAPTER 18

THE PENCIL MARK WAS gone.

Gul stared at the sarcophagus in utter disbelief. The rosette was dusted and clear, exactly as she had left it. But the pencil mark had vanished.

It was early, the museum still empty save for the police and a lone janitor who was polishing the hallway with something that smelt of apples. Unable to sleep, Gul had called a Careem taxi and been there since dawn, managing to avoid both the protesters and her colleagues. Now she pulled up a chair and sat by the body, deep in thought. The only person she had told about the pencil mark was Director Raja. Was he somehow involved in this? The thought made her heart sink. Director Raja was sometimes too fussy and bureaucratic, but she had always felt they were on the same side, trying, against all the odds, to preserve the country's heritage.

Or what if their phones were being tapped? It happened all the time in Karachi. Or even more likely, had someone been lurking around the museum watching her? She'd heard noises the night before—could someone other than the police have still been in the building? Or were there more corrupt cops on the loose?

Gul rubbed her neck, which was bruised and stiff from the attack the night before. What if she had imagined the pencil mark? She'd been tired, it had been a long day, she'd been upset about Mahnaz, and it had happened before.

When Mahnaz first vanished—before Gul started taking the meds—she'd seen the girl everywhere. At the supermarket, and at Cantt Station. Even at the khoka next to where she bought her naan. Gul had been convinced Mahnaz was there buying cigarettes one night and had chased her down the street, only to run into an empty lot, greeted by a stray dog and a pile of rubbish.

Gul accepted now that those sightings had been her imagination, fuelled by stress. So maybe she'd imagined the pencil mark too. Mrs. Fernandes had been trying to warn her about this when she cautioned her about overextending herself to the point of exhaustion.

But she hadn't imagined it. She knew she hadn't. And someone had tried to kill her last night. She hadn't imagined that either. She had the bruises to prove it.

She sat there until the doors opened. It was Rana, come to check up on things before the body was moved to the AKU Hospital for its autopsy. The girl looked bright and excited, wafting in cigarette smoke, her hair even more electric blue than normal. Today she was wearing black leggings and a grey kurti, accentuated by a large belt hanging loosely at the waist—the eighties had made a comeback in Karachi, Gul thought.

If Rana was wearing it, then so would others. Gul had gone to several of Rana's gigs over the years, and she was always so effortlessly stylish. Music was as much a passion for her as archaeology, she got lost in it, her turntable an extension of her body. Today, as usual, her noise-cancelling headphones were around her neck. Those things never seemed to come off—Rana was practically a cyborg. The headphones came in handy when her mother lectured her about her future, and marriage, she'd once told Gul.

Gul smiled wanly at the girl. For a moment, she relaxed.

There was no point worrying the others about the Pajero, not until she knew what was going on. She helped Rana with all the preparations, moving stiffly, hoping the girl wouldn't notice.

When the others arrived, the mummy was placed in an ambulance and transported to the hospital. The traffic was heavy, the usual cacophony of honking frustrations and rickshaws trying to punch above their weight. They drove through Shahrah-e-Liaquat, where a truck carrying bales of wheat had burst a tire. It took up at least half the road, precariously tilted but pretty with its intricate patterns, bright colours and flamboyant embellishments. Karachi's truck art had always fascinated Gul. It was a vibrant medium of expression and cultural preservation, and showcased the idiosyncrasies and humour of each particular driver. In this case, the trucker was a fan of Nusrat Fateh Ali Khan, the legendary Qawwali singer whose face was painted on the back. But he fancied himself a bit of a philosopher too, Gul decided, when she read the words painted over the side. *Zindagi ek safar hai, aur hum sab musafir hain.* Life is a journey, and we are all travellers.

When they passed him, Gul winced. Life wasn't a particularly safe journey for this driver-philosopher at the moment, because he was crouched on the ground near his tire, oblivious to the cars that were coming so close to him they were making his kameez blow in the wind. She glanced back, watching him become a smaller figure in the distance, and found herself hoping the rest of his journey would be less eventful.

On National Stadium Road they slowed down again, and Gul felt her mind churn once more. What did Saayaa want? If he wanted the mummy, why go after her?

It took them half an hour to reach the hospital. Gul

started to think about what Director Raja had said the night before. In their short time with the mummy, it had been transported back and forth from the hospital, it had been placed in and out of ambulances and specially designed chambers, it had been photographed by hundreds of journalists, all of whom jostled for position and rubbed against parts of it despite the requests to stay at a distance. That was only a few days of Princess Artunis's existence. In the last two hundred years, she could have been out in the world and exposed in lots of different ways.

Except the pencil mark was now gone.

She sent the team ahead and waited outside the hospital for Harry, who was on his way from the airport, having landed back from Tehran. He arrived ten minutes later, hot and sweaty, an overnight case in hand. "I got it," he said, beaming. "The amulet. There was a bidding war, but I played the dying-mother-in-a-nursing-home card and I got it. It's beautiful. They'll send it to London next week."

Gul forced herself to smile.

His eyes narrowed. "Is something wrong?"

She thought about what to say. Gul didn't want to cause any alarm, but she had to speak to someone, she decided. "There was an incident last night."

"An incident?"

She filled him in on the attempt to run her off the road the night before.

Harry paled. "Gul, this is insane. I think it's time to call this whole thing off. Let the government do what they want with the body. It's not worth taking on a drug lord, not if you've been targeted."

"You think we should just give up? Now, after all of this?"

"It's not worth your life, Gul," he said quietly. "Just think about it."

She could feel her jaw clenching tightly. "I have to know the truth."

"Gul . . ."

She shouldn't have told him, Gul realised now. Harry would always put a colleague's well-being ahead of the work. It was natural, but it was frustrating, and she wouldn't give up, not because of Harry or Saayaa or anyone else. "The team is setting things up. Let's go join them."

GUL LED HARRY through a maze of hallways and utilitarian stairs. They entered the belly of the building, passing pathology labs and operating theatres, waiting at some double doors until Rana let them in with a swipe card she had acquired from the hospital. The body was being prepped for its CT scan and X-ray.

Rana took them to an imaging room. Hamza was already there, crouched over the mummy. Princess Artunis lay on a tray outside the large CT donut, covered in a white sheet, just like any living, breathing human would have been.

Artunis reminded Gul of the images she'd once seen of the body of King Ramses II, travelling to France. Ramses, also known as Ramses the Great, was the third pharaoh of the nineteenth dynasty of Egypt. He had originally been buried in the Valley of the Kings, but was moved many times by the priests, who worried about looters. He spent as little as three days in some places, and the priests recorded their movements on the wrappings on his body. By the 1970s, he was in desperate need of preservation, and required an irradiated treatment to prevent a fungal growth. But even the corpse of a king had to follow the rules. Egypt required that anyone leaving the country, living or dead, have proper documentation. Ramses was therefore issued a passport, and his passport photo was that of his mummified face. His occupation was listed as "King (deceased)." It was a calculated move by the Egyptians. They were worried that once the mummy arrived in Paris, the French would refuse to return him as they had the many objects and antiquities they had plundered over the centuries. A passport, ironically, would afford Ramses legal protections under international law.

So there he was, a three-thousand-year-old corpse, his date of birth listed as 1303 BC, the only person ever grinning in a passport image. And here was Artunis, looking—almost—like any other patient going through a CAT scan.

Gul and Harry were introduced to their volunteer medical staff. Dr. Nadir Chinoy came up and smiled warmly, and Gul liked him immediately. He seemed to be in his fifties, and with his nearly all-white beard, ruddy complexion and rotund body, he looked a bit like Santa Claus in scrubs. Gul now learnt that he was a cardiac surgeon, not a pathologist. But there was nobody else available, and Dr. Chinoy had, from his earlier training, some forensic pathology experience. What's more, he was an amateur archaeology buff, and he was beyond excited to help with the examination.

Dr. Chinoy smelt of surgical soap and peppermints. But she smirked when she saw what was in the right-hand pocket of his white medical coat. He caught her glance and pulled out the Marlboro Lights. "You'd be surprised how many of us smoke," he said sheepishly. "And yes, it does make us hypocrites. But you know, stressful jobs and everything."

"Well, Doctor, you're only human."

"But listen," he said, putting the cigarettes back in his pocket, "we have to be quick about things. The hospital administrator has given us permission to be here, but he has not asked our board of trustees. Some of them . . . well, you know how it is. They are a pious bunch, and they may not like the idea of this, especially with all the media ruckus over the body." He shook his head. "What an opportunity this is. It could have been such a learning experience for some of our forensics students. But it is not to be. Just myself and Owais over there, that's all the hospital will allow." He nodded towards a technician who nodded back from behind a partitioned glass wall. "Owais will set up the images, and I'll tell you what I can. I don't know how much use I can really be, but I'll certainly try my best."

"We can't thank you enough," replied Gul. "I know what we are asking is extremely unorthodox."

"Yes, well." He cleared his throat. "Nothing in this country is ever orthodox, is it? Even its orthodoxy. Now, I'm afraid I'm going to have to ask you to step outside, to limit your exposure to radiation. If you wait in my consulting room upstairs, I can come and meet you there. We'll complete X-rays by then too, and we can have an informed discussion about it all. I can put all the images on a memory stick for you or email them wherever you'd like."

Gul thanked him again as she followed the others out of the room. She sent Rana and Hamza to the cafeteria. It was well past lunch, and they hadn't eaten all day. Harry accompanied her to Dr. Chinoy's office, which was really a consulting room with an examination table, two chairs, and a desk. Within minutes, Gul started to pace again, until Harry rolled his eyes. "Stop being so fidgety. It won't help it go any faster. Sit down, why don't you?"

Gul shot him a look but then sat, occasionally glancing at her watch.

Eventually the door opened, and Dr. Chinoy walked in. "All done. We got some beautiful images." He came to sit behind his desk and turned on his computer.

Gul messaged the others, letting them know the results were in.

"I'll start with the X-ray," Dr. Chinoy said, "as I think it's where I can be most useful. As you know, we X-rayed as much of the body as we could. I can tell you that she was unfortunately a small lady, only five-two."

Gul smiled. "Nothing wrong with us 'small ladies,' Dr. Chinoy."

He coloured. "No, no, of course not. Well, I say 'lady,' but I should say 'girl,' really," Dr. Chinoy continued. He turned his screen around, and enlarged an image, pointing with a pen. "Can you see the pelvic bone here? And this white sliver of material that is sitting here? This is the epiphysis of the bone, the growing end. You see, in humans, the first elements to fuse are the ischium and the pubis, which form the ischiopubic ramus between the age of four and eight. Next, the ilium fuses to the combined ischiopubic portion at the acetabulum between eleven and fifteen years."

"I'm afraid I don't follow," said Gul.

"Sorry," said Dr. Chinoy, shaking his head. "I'm so used to discussing things with my medical students. You see, these bones tell us a lot about what we are dealing with. For most people, by the age of twenty-one the epiphysis closes, and that hasn't happened to this body. But the ilium has fused. You must, of course, send these results to a specialist, because sex and genetic factors can have an impact on timelines. But if I had to guess, I would say that this is a girl who was somewhere between the age of fifteen to twenty when she died."

Gul looked at the X-ray. "It's amazing how much one image can reveal."

"Oh, that's not all," said Dr. Chinoy. "I've had a good look through the CT scans as well. Let me bring them up."

He tapped furiously on the mouse, then enlarged a photo on his screen. "There you go. The X-ray couldn't show us everything, not through the chest plate. But here we get a good look at the thorax. Do you see?"

"Yes," said Gul, leaning forward.

"Well, normally, we would see the lungs on both sides here. Instead, there is something else there, some sort of material."

Harry jiggled his leg. "Material left over from the mummification? I haven't seen that before."

"I should imagine so," replied Dr. Chinoy, clicking on images. "As we go through the abdominal cavity, you can see that all the organs have been removed."

"So this is definitely an Egyptian embalming process," said Harry, beaming.

But something didn't look quite right to Gul. "Could we stop here for a moment?" she asked. "Is that the incision there?"

Dr. Chinoy nodded. "Yes, where they went in to remove the organs."

Gul looked at Harry. "Egyptian embalmers never made incisions of this size. They were careful, meticulous. It would have been a three-inch cut at the most. This looks like eight or nine inches, at least. The Egyptians would never have been so brutal; they believed in precision."

"I think you're overthinking this, Gul," Harry replied. "She was not mummified in Egypt, but in some cave somewhere, with only two priests to attend her. I can't imagine what resources they had or didn't have at their disposal. Remember Pettigrew?"

"This is not that, Harry."

"What is Pettigrew?" asked Dr. Chinoy.

"Not a what, but a who. Pettigrew was an English surgeon and antiquarian in the 1800s. He became obsessed with unravelling mummies, so much so that he was sometimes referred to as Mummy Pettigrew. He became something of an expert on Egyptian embalming methods and was asked by the Duke of Hamilton to embalm him after his death. And he did exactly that."

"An English Duke was mummified?" Dr. Chinoy's jaw was practically on the floor. "English nobility? Truly?"

Gul nodded. "Yes. The duke managed to purchase a sarcophagus from the Ptolemaic period and left instructions to be mummified after his death, and placed inside. When he died, however, he was too tall for it, so Pettigrew had to be creative."

"Creative?"

"He either cut off his feet, or broke his legs, depending on which account you believe. The Duke of Hamilton had managed to procure a second sarcophagus for his wife, Susan Euphemia Beckford. But she was so horrified by what happened to him that she refused to be interred inside it when her own time came. There are a few stories like this that pop up over history. Emperor Nero had his wife Poppaea Sabina embalmed in the Egyptian way, and we think the same happened to Alexander the Great. He died in Babylon, but was buried, we think, in Alexandria, and his body was preserved. But they don't mean anything in this case."

"That's what I'm saying," interjected Harry. "This could be a similar story. Princess Artunis is an outlier, mummified the Egyptian way but not in Egypt. Everything would have been so much harder for the priests. They would have had to change parts of their own rituals to mummify her, because there were only two of them."

"Yes, but . . ." What Gul wanted to say was, *What about the pencil mark?* Then she had a thought. "May we see the nasal cavity, and the cranium?"

"Yes, of course," replied Dr. Chinoy. He printed out a series of images from both the CT scans and the X-rays, then placed one on the table in particular. It was an image of the mummy's face. "Here's the nasal cavity."

Gul looked carefully and exhaled. She turned to Harry. "Can you see it?"

At once, Harry's expression turned grim. "Yes."

Dr. Chinoy looked at them both quizzically. "I don't follow."

Gul borrowed his pen and pointed at the image. "Can you see the ethmoid bone here, Doctor?"

He nodded. "Of course."

"It shouldn't be there."

"Achaa?"

"The Egyptians were very ritualistic in their mummification practices. They would go through the nasal passage and through the ethmoid bone to get to the cranium, to preserve the body as much as possible. But here, the bone is intact."

"Is it really such a big deal?" Dr. Chinoy looked confused.

"I'm afraid it is," Gul said firmly. "They would never have countenanced this, even if they were hiding in a cave in Balochistan. Look at the palate below. It looks like the priests came under the chin and broke a few bones to get to the brain. To the Egyptians, this would have been sacrilegious."

For a moment, nobody said anything.

Dr. Chinoy stood. He walked over to his printer and handed over the rest of the papers to Gul, looking unhappy. "I imagine, then, that you are thinking this has the potential to be some sort of forgery?"

"Yes," said Gul, feeling the sharp sting of disappointment. On one level, she had known it. Ever since the pencil mark, she had known. And yet it was a bitter blow, and difficult to accept. Princess Artunis was a fake.

"No," said Harry at the same time. "We still need forensic evidence to back up any conclusion, either way. It seems to me that the priest who preserved this body intended to follow Egyptian customs but did not have the correct implements and tools."

Gul shifted in her seat. She had told Harry about the silver Pajero, but she hadn't told him about the pencil mark.

"There was one more thing that I had to show you," Dr. Chinoy said. "Can you see her vertebrae? There's a significant disruption and distortion here." He pointed at the lower spine. "It's clear, to me anyway, that the body received a violent blow. Her back was broken. Her organs probably ruptured on impact."

Gul's heart began to thud. "A fall, perhaps?"

Dr. Chinoy shook his head. "Extremely unlikely, looking at the dispersion. I'm not an expert, but I cannot see how this could have happened by any natural means."

"Just what are you saying, Doctor?"

"I'm saying that this occurred from blunt force, probably from the right-hand side, given the fragmentation of the vertebrae. I'm saying that this lady—that this girl . . . Well. You see, she was probably murdered."

"We need to get the results of the radiocarbon dating, as soon as possible," Gul said quietly. "We have to test the mat and the wood, but we need to open her up and get under the resin to the body itself. We need to know how old she is." She looked at Harry, but he seemed stunned. He was going through all the printouts of the images, saying nothing.

"Thank you, Dr. Chinoy," Gul said at last. "You've certainly given us a lot to think about. Could I ask that you

keep this information to yourself, for now? We'll have to wait
for the results before we do anything further."

"Zaroor, of course," he said, standing. "This is the most
curious case indeed. I'll email the images to you now."

"Thank you," she said again, standing as well. It was
heartbreaking to think of Princess Artunis as a forgery, and
even more haunting to think of her as a murder victim. Gul
decided not to speculate. There was no point jumping to
any conclusions, not until they had more evidence. "Doctor
Chinoy, may we take these printouts with us?"

"Bilkul, please," Dr. Chinoy replied.

"Perhaps you can email the images to me as well?"

"Consider it done."

"Thank you for being so generous with your time."
Gul gave Harry a nudge, and he stood reluctantly, looking
shocked and more than a little disappointed. She gathered
the papers, and was headed for the door, when she saw
something that struck her. "Dr. Chinoy, have you seen this?
The lines here? Why does it look like that?"

She was staring at an X-ray image, one that focused on the
mummy's right hand.

"Oh, yes," said Dr. Chinoy, walking towards her. "That's
simple enough. At some point, probably in her early childhood, this girl, whoever she was, broke her pinky. It's fused
together well, but you can still see where it broke, in several
places. Can you see?"

"Yes," Gul muttered. "Yes, I can see."

Dr. Chinoy patted his pocket. "I think, after all of this, I
deserve a cigarette break, don't you?"

They walked out with him and joined the others. Gul
arranged for the ambulance to come and collect Princess
Artunis and take her back to the museum, strapping her
into the gurney with the help of her team. Rana and Hamza

went back to the museum as well. There was still so much work to be done.

Neither Gul nor Harry spoke much for the rest of the day, both of them lost in thought. Gul kept coming back to the same place. The mummy was a hoax, she had to be. If she was a contemporary body, then in all likelihood, she was a modern murder victim. That thought was enough to keep her up that night when she curled into bed and willed herself to finally sleep.

Hours later, Gul's eyes snapped open in the darkness. Another thought came, unbidden. As a child, Mahnaz had broken her pinky in several places as well.

CHAPTER 19

THE AUTOPSY TOOK PLACE two days later under the cover of darkness, with the help of Dr. Chinoy and Harry. No one at the museum was informed other than Director Raja. Gul did not want the word to get out, not when the mobs were still gathering most days, and not when this could be a possible murder case. Not when she herself had a target on her back, when she was constantly looking over her own shoulder.

She had spent the day trying to shake off the disquiet that had somehow permeated her entire being, ever since she had accepted, with near total certainty, that Princess Artunis could be a hoax, a murder victim with a smashed-up pinky. It was ridiculous to think that there could be any link between her and Mahnaz, other than the fact that Mahnaz had heard about her myth. She knew it, she could rationalise it, even accept it. But somehow the thought of it lurked, impossible to shift entirely. Illogical, but there it was.

It was strange being at the museum in the middle of the night, conducting the autopsy here instead of at the hospital where it should have been done, but the hospital had refused to help any further after a group of protesters turned up at the gates, angered that the mummy was not being reburied, given Islamic last rites. Mindful of the corruption within his own department, DSP Akthar had agreed that the museum was the best place to conduct the work, but even then, in secret. They'd lowered the blinds and cleared out the building before they began. The room smelt of floor polish and sweat, all of them nervous about what they would uncover, and all of them working hard.

Cutting through the amber resin that coated the bandages covering the body proved to be no easy task. The resin—whatever it consisted of—was thick and hard and took hours to saw through, until it cracked open in an explosion of earthy dust.

After the dust settled, they could, for the first time, see the body of the woman who had been such a mystery. Inside the mummy's shell, each of Princess Artunis's limbs had been wrapped separately, as had each individual finger, exactly as the Egyptians would have done. Gul set Rana to the task of removing enough wrapping from the body to make some general observations about colour, length, width and the knots of the cloth.

The mummy did not have any nose plugs, and after unwrapping her further, Dr. Chinoy's face became grim. "You can see here, the vertebrae of the neck, twisted at a right angle. Her spinal column has been snapped in two."

Harry's eyes widened. "Could it have been an accident?"

"Possibly. But I still don't think so," said Dr. Chinoy. He pointed. "See her lower back? I was right about that. There's significant disruption. I think she was hit in two places—her neck and her lower back. It would have had to be a very odd accident indeed."

What confronted them now was not the beauty of a gold mask or chest plate. There was nothing serene about the skeleton laid bare on the table, its jaw bound, its body broken. Gul peered at the face of the woman. There was something in her mouth. With Harry's help, she unbound her jaw and removed what she could. White powder, the smell of chemicals. Drying chemicals. Bicarbonate of soda. Salt.

In near silence, they collected samples of bone and tissue, which they would send off for carbon dating. They cleaned up the body and placed her back in her now open shell of resin. After replacing the top of the resin shell on the body, they returned her to her resting place in the vacuum chamber. Then they packed up their things and left.

Everyone except Gul, who sat in darkness in the room, keeping vigil. She couldn't bring herself to leave, not yet. She placed her palms on the glass that separated her now from the body, and then rested her forehead against it too, the grief now too much, too unspeakable.

She was worried that Mrs. F had been right from the beginning, that this case was tipping her over into somewhere she had no control. But there was too much at stake to stop now.

Stop being so insane.

Over the next few days, Gul threw herself into work. She took taxis to the museum at the crack of dawn and returned home long after dinner. She finished all her paperwork, which delighted the Anwar brothers, who had been chasing her for expense sheets for three months. She was even charming to Ali Mahmood, even though she'd caught him haranguing a junior curator. When Harry had to go back to London to teach, she accompanied him to the airport and forced herself to cheerfully wave him goodbye. And then she waited.

When the first of the results came back, dating the straw mat and the wooden box, there was a certain inevitability to it all. The mat was only three years old. So were the fused pieces of metal on the casket.

And then the rest of the news followed.

The girl who'd been mummified was about fifteen years old when she'd died. Dr. Shuman, the forensic pathologist at

Oxford to whom Gul had sent all their findings, felt that the body may have been hit by a car at high speeds, the impact hitting her on her lower back. The force of it would have sent her flying. And when she fell, she might have landed and broken her neck as well. It would explain the dispersion, and the blunt force. Either that, or someone took a heavy club to her, and deliberately hit her with such unimaginable force that her body had fragmented. Gul felt queasy at the thought.

And then the final piece of the puzzle. Carbon dating and chemical analysis undertaken on bone shavings of the body, sent to the Quaid-i-Azam University in Islamabad, came back with indisputable findings. The body was only three years old as well. Princess Artunis had died three years ago.

Gul barely paid attention to what followed. The police opened a murder investigation. The body was found in Balochistan originally, so the cops there were in charge, though DSP Akthar was acting as a point person in Karachi. Gul sent him all her findings as well, then left them to it.

She knew she was being foolish, because hundreds of girls went missing in the country every day. And yet, here was a girl who was fifteen when she died. And she had died three years ago.

Mahnaz had disappeared three years ago, only months after learning about the legend of the Lost Princess. And she had been fifteen when she disappeared. Mahnaz, with her thick, crazy curly hair, and her impassioned views on feminism, her love of eighties rock ballads and her obsession with journaling her every thought.

It was true that the person inhabiting the body had, at some point, broken her pinky. But was that really so uncommon? People fell from trees or tripped on the stairs or got hit by mistake, and pinkies were broken.

After the car accident, Mahnaz had cried and cried and cried,

*her hair still wet from the swim, her finger like putty, until it
swelled, and then swelled some more.*

But what were the odds that Mahnaz could be murdered
and turned into this?

Zero. Absolutely zero.

And yet, Gul could not banish the thought.

*Because where was she, if she was alive? How could someone
just disappear for three years? Nobody vanished off the face of the
earth in the digital age, not unless some harm had come to them.
Why did she have an email address and social media account
nobody knew about? Was it just Mahnaz being a teenager, or was
there more to it?*

There was no way the body could be Mahnaz. It was ludicrous to even think it.

But what if she was. What if she was . . .

Images of Mahnaz flashed through Gul's head, a supercut
of memories. Mahnaz as a baby, drooling on her shirt and
making funny, giggly noises. Mahnaz as a toddler, holding
on to the side of the table as she learnt how to walk—on New
Year's Eve, no less.

In the day, Gul went about her duties, numb but
functional. At night, however, her thoughts twisted onto
themselves. She pored over Mahnaz's diaries, falling asleep
beside them. She thought about all the times Mahnaz had
disappeared from her life. The first, the nearly seven-year
ban imposed by Bilal and Sania after the car crash had been
awful; but at least then she'd known the girl was healthy and
well. The last three years had taken everything from Gul.
Now, as her thoughts spiralled, she began to think about
the fact that Mahnaz had disappeared even before she disappeared.

There it was, the thing that plagued Gul the most. A few
months before she vanished, Mahnaz cut her out of her life.

It wasn't simple, and it wasn't clean. It was a cold and calculated intersection, one instigated by Mahnaz herself.

Oh Jane, I've been waiting for you. You missed our Wednesday crumpets. Is everything well?

It was two days before she got a reply.

Sorry, Gul. Been busy with school.

Gul. Not Agatha. Gul had seen that text and swallowed. She knew, she just knew, that something was wrong.

Tomorrow, then?

Afraid I can't this week.

She'd tried again the following week.

Jane, do you want to come and see the new Indus Valley pottery we just got in?

There was no reply.

Mahnaz, I hope everything is okay.

In the end she had tried Sania and Bilal, who told her their daughter had a lot going on, including her exams. Gul knew that—she'd been helping Mahnaz study, not that she needed it. The girl would ace every subject with ease. But Mahnaz was fine, going to school, volunteering at the shelter, doing her homework in the evenings. It was just Gul she'd frozen out.

After a few weeks, Gul came to the house and had tea with her family. Bilal was his usual pompous self, while Sania acted like they had tea together every week, instead of it having been a year. Mahnaz was polite. But beyond that, she acted like Gul wasn't even there.

She knows, Gul thought.

And so she'd decided to leave Mahnaz alone, to give her space. And when she'd just about decided Mahnaz had had enough space, that she would force the issue, Mahnaz disappeared. And that was that.

It was evening now, and Gul knew she should go home,

but she remained at the museum. As she had almost every night, she brought a chair next to the body, sitting in the darkness, letting her thoughts turn on themselves. She told herself that she was missing Mahnaz. That was why she was having these moments of wild imaginings. She needed closure. The body, whoever she was, was going to have to provide that closure.

So she gathered the others. They all knew, of course, about her vanished niece Mahnaz. They'd been with her long enough. They knew the toll that her disappearance had taken on Gul.

"I want to do a DNA test," Gul told them simply. "I want to rule out the chance that this is Mahnaz."

She saw them all exchange glances. Hamza cleared his throat. "Apa, there's no chance . . ."

She watched Mrs. Fernandes elbow him in the side.

It was Rana who stepped forward. "Of course, Apa. We can contact Mr. and Mrs. Delani. The DNA sample would be better coming from Mrs. Sania Delani, as the mother of the potential sample match. Will you speak to them, to get their permission?"

"We don't need it," Gul replied, turning back to the body.

"Well, of course, we could take your DNA, but a direct parent would be a better match. That's not to say, of course, that there's even a chance that the body . . . that the body could be . . ." Rana stopped now.

Gul turned back. "You'll take a sample from me," she said, crossing her arms.

"Are you sure?"

Mrs. Fernandes came and put a hand on her shoulder. "Gul, you don't have to do this."

Gul shrugged it off. "Forget Bilal and Sania. You'll take a

sample from me, and it will be more accurate than any they could ever provide."

She watched Rana and Hamza look at each other, watched first the confusion, and then the growing realisation, as the words sank in.

It was time. It had been time for a long while now. Gul exhaled, deeply. "Bilal is not Mahnaz's biological father, and Sania Delani is not her mother. Mahnaz is mine. I'm her mother. Or at least, I was."

CHAPTER 20

IN THE YEARS AFTER Mahnaz's disappearance, a stray thought would often catch, and linger.

Hindsight.

Gul would find herself wondering about it as she brushed her teeth in the morning or got ready to give a lecture to her students in the afternoon, or when she was crouched deep in the earth with a trowel in her hand, wiping sweat off her brow.

What would she do if she could rewind the clock? Would she still have given birth to Mahnaz, knowing what she knew now? Would she have allowed herself to love so deeply, if she had been aware of how much she would lose? Could she have faced it all, once she understood the pain and the fear and the never-ending hollowed, gnawing ache that would come to take her over?

The answer was always the same. Of course she would. Because the idea of a world without Mahnaz in it was simply not something she could even begin to accept.

Gul squeezed her eyes tight. Today would be hard enough, without allowing more pain to find a way in.

She was in a rental car, parked in front of a set of imposing black gates, guarding the palatial home she knew well. The car was the exact same model and colour as her existing Suzuki. She had chosen it especially, to avoid anyone asking her any questions about what had happened, and she'd picked it up earlier that morning from Avari Towers.

And now she was here. The Big House. But she had yet to press on her horn, or to make her presence felt, the familiar feeling of dread giving her pause.

Get on with it. Get it over and done with.

Gul swallowed, and honked the horn several times in short staccato bursts. She had grown up in this house. There was no need for her to feel like an outsider.

A girl opened a slot in the metal gate, peeked through, and then briefly disappeared. She heard a familiar creak as she pulled the left gate open and made her way to the right side. She stared at the girl. It was Bisma. They had met at the shelter a year earlier, and the kid couldn't be more than fifteen. It was typical. Were Bilal and Sania really helping children from the shelter, or using them as cheap labour?

People always talked about what pillars of society her brother and sister-in-law were. Watching her now, Gul felt sorry for Bisma, who clearly had little or no choice in her employment. Still, she thought her knuckles would stay permanently white, and permanently fossilised to the steering wheel by the time both gates were pulled back, the right one eventually juddering to a halt against the wall. She wanted to get this over with.

She parked her car behind her brother's Mercedes, next to the Toyota that the driver used to chauffeur Sania around. She walked past the garden, which was looking particularly verdant, with its scatterings of laal saag and gul-e-mehndi, partially shaded by the thick almond tree she had often leaned against as a child, book in hand. And suddenly she was at the front door.

Gul made her way to the right, while Bisma went to inform her brother and sister-in-law of her arrival. They would take their time, she knew, a silent rebuke against her just turning up uninvited.

Well, they would just have to deal with it.

She found herself in the stifling drawing room, full of expensive doodahs, the little, fiddly trinkets that Sania had placed for maximum effect. There they were, her family, in shiny silver photo frames, exuding so much smugness that it permeated the whole room.

Her grandparents, in black-and-white, next to Jinnah, at the founding of Pakistan ceremony. When Gul's grandfather had set up Delani Investments, it was the first homegrown financial institution in the country, and he'd been a keen ally of Jinnah's. In the photo, all three of them were stiff, as though the weight of the moment required it. In another silver frame, a picture of her father at the Karachi Stock Exchange, shaking hands with a former prime minister. And here was Bilal at the office, looking managerial in his Savile Row suit. Gul had to admit, her brother's success at business galled her sometimes.

Not that he lorded it over her anymore. Bilal had long stopped talking to her about the business, or about the Delani Foundation, or anything family related. But she still had the shares she inherited from her father, and used the dividends to supplement her meagre salary. Every year, a physical glossy annual report from Delani Investments fell through her letter box, celebrating the firm's many achievements. No wonder Bilal thought the universe revolved around him. Anyone making his kind of money would.

She picked up one of the photos. Bilal and Sania with Mahnaz, somewhere on holiday in Europe—some palace behind them. They were all windswept, Mahnaz's wild curls blowing into her face. It must have been taken the summer before her disappearance, on their trip to Spain. Bilal was unsmiling, arms behind his back. Sania, of course, looked well manicured, her smile perfectly curated. The perfect family—until they weren't.

Gul sat down on the sofa, feeling queasy. She pressed her hand against the pale green, raw-silk upholstery. It had been beige once.

She got engaged to Adil on this sofa, both families surrounding them, everyone beaming with happiness. She'd put her hand in his, on this very spot. For a moment, she had actually thought they were going to make it.

"Well. This is unexpected."

Gul looked up. There was her brother, annoyed, but trying to hide his irritation. Somehow, no matter what she did, she managed to get under his skin. "Bilal. Hello. We need to talk."

As he walked into the room, Gul noticed the tight expression on his face. He came to sit across from her on an armchair. "Talk about what, exactly?"

The armchair was a new addition, tacky, ornately carved and gilded. Sania's doing, obviously. Bilal, for all his faults, would never have bought something so gaudy. "What happened to Ammi's rocking chair from Jamnagar?"

"It got old, and creaky. You can have it, if you want. We've put it in storage. Now, what did you want to talk about?"

"About Mahnaz."

Bilal brought a hand to massage his temple. "I don't see what else we could possibly have to say to each other. The police have shut the case, Gul. Get over it. You're welcome to continue to hate me, but it was the right call."

"It's not exactly about that," Gul said quietly. "I wish it were."

He lit a cigar but said nothing.

Gul waited for him to exhale a couple of puffs before she spoke again. "Princess Artunis is a fraud."

"Who?"

"The mummy. She's not from the Achaemenid Empire. Someone stumbled upon an old legend in history about a Lost Princess and some missing gold and used it to set up a remarkably sophisticated hoax. I suppose they were trying to sell the body to a treasure seeker for a lot of money."

"All the more reason to rebury her and put an end to this. I thought you were here about Mahnaz?"

"The girl, the mummy, was most likely fifteen when she died. And she's been dead for three years."

Bilal exhaled. "So?"

"Do I have to spell it out for you?"

After a moment, he blinked. "You can't be serious, Gul. Have you lost your mind?"

Gul stood. "Is it so wrong to want answers? We can't keep living like this, Bilal. You, me, Sania. We are prisoners, trapped in limbo."

Bilal shook his head. "The mummy is not Mahnaz. No right-minded person would think that she is. You are the only one, off in your own world, as usual."

"I've given them my DNA sample," Gul replied. "I wanted to come and tell you that. I'm not saying it's Mahnaz. But what's the harm in removing all doubt?"

"The harm? Can you really ask me that?"

"You don't want the truth to come out. Is that it? My team is discreet. Nobody needs to know."

Bisma suddenly appeared, armed with a tray of coffee, and got on with the business of pouring the milk and sugar. For a moment, neither of them spoke.

"We should never have taken her," Bilal said at last, when Bisma left. "We thought we were doing the right thing. But look at the heartbreak it has caused. For all of us, including you."

Gul felt the flush heat up her cheeks. "Don't start rewriting history, Bilal. You begged me for her. You even got Ammi to support your cause. You were desperate, when you realised you could never have children of your own. I'm the one who should never have listened to *you*. I should have kept her with me."

"What, so you could raise her as a single, unmarried mother, in Karachi?" He exhaled smoke in her direction. "Don't be ridiculous. Even you wouldn't have had the balls. She would have been stigmatised by our society if Sania and I hadn't stepped in. Can you imagine any families from our community accepting her? Anyone from any community for that matter. Do you know any unwed mothers, Gul? Because I certainly don't, not unless they're from the streets."

"You chutiya," Gul choked out. "We would have been happy. We could have gone away. I should have seen that at the time, but I was young, and you and Ammi were relentless."

"Not this again. For fuck's sake."

"Adil was bad enough, but then you made me feel so alone. All of you. You made me feel like I had no choice, not if I wanted to keep her safe."

"Same old shit. Everything is my fault, right?"

"No. You have no idea how much I hate myself."

Bilal stood suddenly and began pacing the room. "And what? She wasn't happy here, is that what you're saying? You think we did a bad job raising her?"

"That's not what I . . ."

He turned, looking furious. "Don't you think I want to know what happened to her? Don't you think, as her father, I have had sleepless nights and days of anguish? She was my little princess, Gul. I loved her more than anyone in the world. I'm the one who raised her. But she's gone.

Something happened to her three years ago. She vanished. Just like that." Bilal snapped his fingers. "And now it's over."

"It's not over. It will never be over, not until we know. Someone kidnapped her right in front of the school gates."

Bilal sat down, heavily. "This fantasy of yours. It has to stop. How many times are we going to have the same conversation? You're like a bloody broken record. Nobody saw anything, nobody heard her screaming. We've talked about this. Even the police have tried to explain it to you. Whatever happened, she was no innocent bystander. She left her bag at the school gate and had to have walked away or met someone. There were no signs of a struggle."

Gul's heart was pounding and she struggled to keep her voice calm. "Do you know any teenager who would leave her mobile phone voluntarily?"

"Well, if she was running away . . ."

"Running away? You can't still believe that. Not after all this time. She wouldn't be so cruel. She wouldn't put us through this."

"What else are we to think? There was no ransom, never any demands, nothing. The police went through every inch of that phone to see if she'd been groomed or coerced into meeting someone. So did we. But there was nothing. Why can't you accept that?"

"And you never thought it strange that a fifteen-year-old girl would one day just voluntarily vanish?" She took a deep breath. "Do you really think that's normal behaviour?"

"Exactly my point. She was running away. Probably with some low-class boy who we wouldn't have allowed her to marry. That's the only reason I can think of, anyway. But whatever happened, she instigated it. She was independent and emotional. Just like you. We never could control her."

"Who was she meeting?" Gul pressed. "Why is there no trace? Why have we never uncovered the answers? How could you have stopped the investigation?"

Bilal shook his head. "Here we go again. You've spent years harassing her friends, everyone at her school, all our neighbours and the whole Memon community at large. You've embarrassed us by not letting it go. How many times have I had to apologise to someone because you've called them, and called them again, and then even more times after that, to ask them questions? It doesn't help, it just makes our friends and family uncomfortable."

Gul glared at him. "You gave up too quickly. So did the police, thanks to you. But you didn't care, as long as the secret didn't come out. As long as people didn't find out she wasn't yours."

"Stop it."

Gul was so full of rage. She couldn't contain it any longer. "We should have kept looking. It took me a long time to understand why we didn't. But then I realised the truth: You didn't want anyone to ask any questions, did you?"

Now he was standing too, his face an inch from hers. "I said stop it."

"You can't have children, Bilal. But instead of just accepting that, you didn't want the investigation into Mahnaz's disappearance to go on, because you didn't want anyone to find out that she wasn't your biological daughter. Because your precious honour is at stake, and you would rather tell the community that your daughter ran away than let them know the great King Delani can't bear his own children."

"I said stop it!" He banged his coffee cup on the table with enough force that it shattered into several pieces, one of which went into his palm.

For a moment, neither of them spoke, watching the

coffee pool on the wood, then drip to the carpet. Bilal exhaled, slowly. "I'm sorry. I shouldn't have done that." He sat down again, pressing a handkerchief against his palm to staunch the bleeding. "I'm sorry I lost my temper."

"It's all right," Gul said, leaning forward to help pick up the porcelain. "I'm sorry for what I said."

"Leave it. The maid can do it."

"It's fine," Gul said.

"It's not. I never lose my temper."

No, he didn't. But it would have been easier if he did, Gul thought. Instead of hiding behind officiousness, it would be easier if they could just talk, like human beings. But Bilal never liked to appear weak or at a disadvantage. He always had to be in control.

"The DNA results will take a few weeks," Gul said quietly.

Bilal scowled. "You do what you have to do, Gul. Drag us all through the mud, if it will make you feel better. But do me a favour, and don't talk to me about my daughter again."

With that, Bilal got up and walked out the door.

AS GUL DROVE out of the Big House, a black jeep with tinted windows pulled in. The occupant must have noticed her, because the car stopped just outside the gates.

She groaned. Now bloody what?

Someone jumped out the driver's seat. It was Bob, Bilal's annoying cop friend, who waved an arm at her. "Gul."

Today he was out of uniform, wearing an aquamarine polo shirt and jeans, and Gul could see the outline of his biceps. Bob was in excellent physical shape. Perhaps it was his career as chief of police, or the fact that he was a shikari and spent most of his free time hunting every manner of creature in Sindh and Balochistan into extinction, but Bob seemed to never age. He had short, cropped hair, and an even more closely trimmed beard that almost veered towards designer stubble.

"Hello, Bob," Gul said as she rolled down her window.

Bob walked to her car. "It's been a long time."

"Indeed."

"I'm just here to see your brother."

"I figured as much."

Bob removed his sunglasses and stared at Gul intently. He was the same age as Bilal, and yet he looked at least a decade younger. It always amazed Gul that a man who radiated such an unassailable sense of authority would have befriended her brother, but the pair had been thick as thieves since their school days, when Bob was the most popular boy in his class, and Bilal, nerdy and needy, hung on to Bob's coattails. Bilal would have done anything to impress Bob, who, for his part, treated her brother with an amused indulgence. That dynamic hadn't changed. Perhaps it was their shared lust for power that brought them together, Gul thought bitterly. If it wasn't for Bob shutting down the police investigation, would Mahnaz be home right now?

Bob leaned into the car window and cracked his knuckles. He had done that the last time they met too, Gul remembered, when she had begged him to reopen the missing person's case about Mahnaz, and he had refused.

"You should go easier on your brother, Gul. He's under a lot of pressure at work."

"Why don't you mind your own business?"

"Bilal is like my brother. You know that. I'm just looking out for him."

"Go fuck yourself, Bob." Gul rolled up her window and put her car into reverse, fuming. She drove off muttering under her breath about Bob and Bilal, madarchods both.

The idea of going home filled Gul with dread, and not only because she was still constantly looking over her shoulder as she drove. Gul didn't want to face the emptiness, and the long, sleepless night that would inevitably follow. Another FoodPanda delivery for one was in the cards, the evening already stretching before her. She felt a heaviness, the weight of the whole situation left her physically exhausted.

As she pulled into the driveway, she left a message for DSP Akthar. She'd been chasing him since the morning to talk to him about the shrine, but today he was proving difficult to get a hold of. She thought about calling up some old friends, about going out to dinner and entering into some light, frivolous banter, but all they talked about was their children's sporting trophies and school results, their various causes or the state of the country—a conversation that never changed. Plus, she'd lost touch with most of them since Mahnaz's disappearance. In the first few months, everyone had been sympathetic. She was the aunt, after all. She was close to her niece; it was understandable that she would fall apart. But then, when she'd continued her relentless search for Mahnaz, despite her brother's decision to call it off, when she thought she had seen Mahnaz at the naanwallah or on the street and harassed everyone in society about their interactions with her, people started asking questions. What was wrong with Gul that she couldn't respect her brother's wishes and leave things alone? Why was she so obsessed? The girl had obviously been up to something—why didn't Gul seem to understand that whatever had happened, Mahnaz had been a part of it? Slowly, her friends stopped returning her calls. None of them wanted to spend their every moment listening to her half-baked theories, or to be asked to pull some strings, wherever they had them, to breathe life into the investigation. They dropped her, and Gul felt viciously betrayed.

It was dusty and humid outside. The air was stagnant; it felt like a storm might be coming. Gul opened her front door, tossed her bag near the whalebone doorstopper and walked down the corridor, kicking off her chappals on the way. In the morning she would head back to the museum. But for now, she would do some research to try to find out who could be involved in a hoax with this level of sophistication. To devise a mummy with cuneiform writing, bandaged correctly, carved with the rosettes of Persepolis, would require someone with an in-depth knowledge or understanding of history. There would have to have been someone with experience in mummification, and certainly, someone with experience in anatomy. The carving of the casket, the decoration of the sarcophagus—nothing about this was a one-person job. It would have taken a team to make the mummy.

Had Princess Artunis ever really existed, Gul also wondered. Could she still have existed, even if this mummy wasn't her? Despite everything that had happened, she so hoped the legends were real. For a brief moment, Princess Artunis had felt tantalisingly close, a woman of flesh and bone who had fought for everything she believed in. She wanted that woman to have lived, to have fought to protect those she cared about.

On her way to the kitchen, Gul stopped, confused by the aroma wafting towards her. She closed her eyes. Chicken achari. She would know that smell anywhere.

"You didn't have to, you know," Gul said as she continued towards the kitchen.

Mrs. Fernandes was hunched over the stove, stirring the pan, sprinkling in some fresh coriander. She'd already made some raita, and the rice, Gul could see. And there was a bag of her favourite milk toffees on the table, and even a pyramid of Coca-Cola cans.

"Wash your hands, then sit at the table. This is nearly ready."

Gul did as she was told.

Mrs. Fernandes had laid out two places. She'd even bought some tuberoses, and placed them on the table in an attempt to cheer things up.

"You are too good to me. You know that, don't you?"

Mrs. F ladled out food onto Gul's plate. "Shut up and eat, before it gets cold."

"Where's Francis tonight?"

"He's gone to Student Biryani with his girlfriend and some others."

"He finally told you, then?" Gul picked up her fork.

Mrs. Fernandes pursed her lips. "He also informed me about the Wi-Fi service you just paid for at the flat. I specifically told you we didn't need that."

"It was a two-for-one sale, Mrs. Fernandes. I called and upgraded Wi-Fi here and then the second line cost barely anything. He's too old to be traipsing to internet cafés or trudging back and forth to campus every day to try and complete his work."

"Eat."

They said nothing for several minutes. Gul let herself be absorbed by the food. When they finished, they cleared the table in near silence. Gul washed the dishes and made them both some jasmine tea. Then they sat on the sofa.

"Why did you never tell me?" said Mrs. Fernandes, eventually.

"I always assumed you had guessed."

"I did, after a while. She was too much like you. Physically, and in temperament."

Gul smiled. "You mean she was as bad-tempered and impatient as I am. You can say it."

"She was a firecracker. Unlike that slow-moving brother of yours. Or his insipid wife. That one doesn't know how to do anything besides shop and look good."

Gul would normally have laughed at this, but the gravity of the moment was too much to bear. She said nothing, and her living room was filled with brittle silence.

"You could have trusted me, Charlie," Mrs. F said.

Gul swallowed and looked down. She cradled the cup of tea in her palms. "It wasn't about trust, Mrs. Fernandes. It was about shame. What happened, how it happened, it has eaten me up with shame for so many years. It was my burden to bear. Not anyone else's."

Mrs. Fernandes put down her own cup, then reached out her hand. "You better start at the beginning," she said, firmly.

Little by little, as the evening eased into night, Gul found herself doing exactly that. She told Mrs. Fernandes about her childhood, about the sense of alienation that came from knowing how different she was from the rest of her family. About how she'd started reading voraciously when she was young, about her growing interest in ancient history, about a school trip to Mohenjodaro, and that moment when, standing alone in the Great Bath, she'd had an epiphany, and had known she wanted to become an archaeologist. She talked about spending all her pocket money on books on the Aztecs, Egyptians and the Minoans, instead of the Barbies or makeup that her friends seemed to covet. About digging up fossils in her grandparents' garden—the garden below them now—arriving home caked in dirt, much to the horror of her mother.

She told Mrs. Fernandes how it felt, as the years rolled

over on themselves, never to be taken seriously. Bilal was going to go to college in the United States, to get a business degree, and then come home and run Delani Investments. He would marry a girl from the right family—an industrialist's daughter from the same background. And he would patronise the Club and the many charity balls and live the life he was born into.

When it was her turn, however, it was a different story. When she told her parents that she wanted to go to university, they'd balked. It wasn't done, not in their community. Women didn't go abroad to study. This was blatantly false—several of her parents' friends had sent their daughters overseas. But her parents were more rigid, stuck to the old ways, worried that their wayward daughter would never return. Perhaps she could find something local—some class, somewhere, they said. The fact that there were no archaeology courses in Karachi did not sway them. They wouldn't even let her go elsewhere in Pakistan to study.

In a way, Gul's path was as mapped out as her brother's had been. When she left school, she would do some volunteer work. She was expected to marry well, to have healthy, overachieving children, at least one son. Her family wanted her to always be well put together and to find charities to devote her time to—when she wasn't looking after her children or her husband. It was such a ridiculous, painful, 1950s cliché. And yet, it was who her parents were, stuck in a time warp, a place where there was no room for the eccentricities of archaeology.

By then, she was dating Adil, another Memon from an industrialist family, one her parents knew and respected. On paper, he was perfect, and Gul had begun to realise that Adil was her way out. Adil doted on her. Her passion, her drive, her mad projects and explorations seemed to inspire rather than confuse him. Perhaps it was because he understood. He'd been studying for a PhD in philosophy when his parents had insisted he return to Pakistan and take over the family business. He was an outlier in his own way.

Gul was just seventeen years old when they met. He was a friend of Bilal's, and so their brief interactions were all very kosher. Nobody seemed to question the age difference, the fact that he was twenty-four. Both mothers were quietly delighted that their children had found each other, in what would be a "love match."

When Gul's parents refused to let her continue her studies, Adil had the perfect solution. He offered to marry Gul and take her to England. He would do his own PhD, he told her, while she studied archaeology. The parents would agree, if it meant the two of them would come back and start their lives together. He didn't want to see Gul's potential go to waste, her passion dwindle in a life constrained by society.

And she had gone along with it, knowing full well that she was using a man she liked, but did not love, to pursue her dreams.

If her engagement—when she was barely eighteen and still had a few months left of school—caused anyone's eyebrows to lift, she wasn't aware of it. Her own friends were supportive, and thought Adil was perfect in every way: rich, cultured, his own man. Plus, he was giving her the freedom she had dreamt of. And so, even they celebrated her news. How wrong they all were.

One day, in the last few weeks of term, she had a chance encounter with a team of Dutch archaeologists. They had come to do a talk, and Gul had practically harassed them, peppering them with questions, and then follow-ups, and then even more follow-ups. They'd been so impressed that they had invited her to their dig in Chanhudaro. Gul, in turn, couldn't contain her excitement. At first, Adil had been happy for her. It was a chance for her to learn so much. He agreed to talk to her parents, to help convince them to let her go. But then, Adil's friends—Bilal included—pointed out that Gul would be spending several nights there, in a tent, on a site where there was a group of foreigners—mostly men—without supervision. Worried about what people would think, Adil had changed his mind, and resisted her going.

With that resistance, Adil had confirmed Gul's worst fears. It was one thing to go to university. But after that, Adil would never let her work in the field, not in any meaningful way. He was yet another cog in the patriarchal system that held her back.

She broke up with him, to the horror of everyone. Adil didn't seem that upset or surprised, though. The whole Chanhudaro debacle had made him realise just how obstinate she really was, he told her. The things that had once enamoured him—her rebelliousness, her fierce independence—were now too much for him.

Six weeks later, Gul found out she was pregnant.

At this point in the story, Gul stopped, and sipped her tea. The rest was so painful.

"Go on," urged Mrs. Fernandes. "What did you do?"

"I told Bilal. I . . . I had to confide in someone. So I talked to my brother. He was upset, of course. But he told me that I had to marry Adil."

"And?"

"And it stuck at my throat, but I knew he was right. Not for me, I hated the idea. But I had to think of the child. If Bilal was right about one thing, it's that having an unwedded single woman as a mother in Karachi would have upended her life. But even after I put my own misgivings aside, Adil announced that he didn't want to marry *me*. His parents hadn't wanted the stigma of a broken engagement, and so they'd quickly found him someone else. A simple girl, with no career ambition."

"But what about his obligations to his child?"

"Oh, he told me he couldn't even be sure that the baby was his—not when I was the type of girl to go off on excavations and live so closely with other men. By then, he didn't want anything to get in the way of his new relationship. I told him that we could get a DNA test to prove his paternity, but he told me to get rid of it."

"Bastard."

"It didn't really matter." The tea was hot in her palm, but Gul cradled it, grateful for the warmth. "By then, Bilal had already broken my trust and told our parents the whole thing. They were horrified, as you can imagine. But he and Sania had already been married for three years, and nothing was happening in the baby department. He went to his doctor, who told him it was his low sperm count. And so he came up with this idea . . ."

And then they'd all ganged up on her. Have the child, they'd said. Do what the old families used to do, in less modern times. Gift the child to your brother. He would make such a wonderful father. Stay in the child's life. Be a doting aunt but go to university after all. Go and pursue a life outside of Pakistan, for a while. It was the best thing for everyone.

"It was such a difficult and confusing time," said Gul, rubbing the bridge of her nose. "My mother got sick right about then, too. My father decided it was because of all the stress and anguish I had put her through. She didn't want chemo, not when they told her how bad it was. She wanted to see the situation resolved, to live long enough to meet her grandchild."

"If that isn't pressure, I don't know what is."

Gul stood now and started to pace. "In the end, I thought I was doing the right thing. Bilal needed a child. And I had one coming that I couldn't even begin to look after. Sania was a great woman, for all her frivolities. We were friends back then. And they both assured me that I would be a huge part of the baby's life, as involved in raising it as they were. So I agreed."

Gul remembered that day, the day she, Bilal and Sania flew to Boston. She'd introduced herself to her obstetrician as Sania Delani, signing the baby's birth certificate with Sania's name, Bilal adding his own below hers. Bilal had gone through the trouble of getting a forged passport made in case anyone asked for ID, but the place was busy and nobody gave it a second glance. And nobody in Karachi batted an eyelid either—well-heeled people often flew off to various places to give birth, either for health reasons, or for much-coveted second passports. In this case, by being born there, Mahnaz would be a US citizen, something that many of Bilal and Sania's crowd aspired to for their own kids. As far as the world knew, Gul's parents had relented, and she was at university. And Bilal and Sania came back with their baby, to great celebration at their good fortune.

"They told me—you see, they told me I would always be a second mother." Gul looked at Mrs. Fernandes, imploring her to understand.

The other woman collected the teacups. "You have nothing to defend yourself against, Charlie. Not with me. You would have married that bloody rascal, if he had done the right thing."

"You don't understand, Mrs. Fernandes." And here it was, the hardest part. "I . . . I think Mahnaz found out. In those last few months, before she vanished, she wasn't talking to me. Why else would she have cut me out of her life? She must have known. I should have said something. I should have talked to her."

"You were giving her space."

"Maybe that's the last thing she needed."

"She would have come around, Charlie. She was big-hearted. Like you."

To her embarrassment, Gul's eyes filled with tears. "I really don't know how you put up with me, Mrs. Fernandes."

And then she found herself engulfed in a giant hug. "You silly, silly girl. You have let this experience, this horrible experience, colour your own sense of worth. Don't you see how much difference you make in the world?"

"I . . ."

"You think I've been blind, all these years? To everything you've done? To all the people whose lives you have touched? Look at Rana and Hamza. Where would they be without you? They worship you, but you are too stupid to realise it. And what about Francis and his bloody Wi-Fi? If you weren't so upset, I'd be furious with you right now."

Still bundled in the other woman's tight embrace, Gul let out a strangled laugh. "You are no picnic yourself, Mrs. Fernandes."

"I love you, Charlie," said the other woman.

And then Gul found herself really sobbing in Mrs. Fernandes's arms.

CHAPTER 21

THE NEXT DAY, GUL managed to get a hold of DSP Akthar and let him know about her concerns for Ejaz. She also asked for an update on the court orders. From his tone, it was clear he had enough on his plate without her adding more to it.

"The boy told you not to worry?"

"Yes," Gul said, "but he's been hanging out with that beggar gang near that shrine in Saddar. And now his phone is dead."

"He's a street child?"

"Yes."

"I wouldn't worry too much, Madam. He'll turn up when he's ready."

"Something is wrong, DSP Sahib, I can feel it."

"Even so, I'm afraid that your gut feelings are not actionable by the police force. I'm sorry, Madam. My resources are stretched thin as it is. I can tell you that the court orders have been issued. I had a lawyer friend in the Ministry of Law and Justice look at them straight away. As soon as there is some news I will let you know."

"But—"

"I'm sorry, Madam Gulfsa, but I have to go."

"Of course. Thank you."

Gul got ready to go to the shrine and check on Ejaz herself, for what good it had done so far. But then her phone pinged and she looked down. At last.

She had finally received a reply from her trusted antiquities contact, Iqbal Butt, a low-grade smuggler and middleman. He had agreed to meet her in town, at a doodh patti chai place that she loved. The owner had got used to seeing Gul by now, a lone eccentric woman, sitting in a sea of men drinking tea and eating parathas. Over the years she'd brought many dignitaries who were visiting the museum there.

Iqbal was waiting at a table when she arrived. He rose to meet her and motioned for her to sit down. "Please, Madam."

"Hello, Iqbal. How's the family?"

"By the grace of God, my son has finished his matriculation, Madam. Thank you for asking."

Iqbal had appeared at the museum one day many years ago, and offered her a bribe that was three times her annual salary, if she would help him "procure" a rare Gandhara Buddha that the museum had just been gifted. By the end of that encounter, after Gul had finished telling him what she thought of his proposal and where he could shove it, Iqbal had developed a headache. He apologised profusely for wasting her time and literally bowed his way out the door.

Now, they had an understanding. Gul paid him well for his information, even when things didn't go her way. Iqbal, in turn, kept her in the loop. There weren't many antiquities or art forgery deals happening in the city that Iqbal didn't have knowledge of.

As she sat with him now, Gul mused about Iqbal's fastidiousness. The man always smelt of rose oil. He was always immaculately dressed as well, always adorned in a white shalwar kameez that was crisp and sparkling despite the heat, his hands soft and well manicured. Iqbal had a monogrammed handkerchief he used to dab away the sweat at his brow. He was more junior clerk than smuggler.

They sat at a glass-top table, one that revealed the beautiful but battle-weary mosaic floor below, a relic from another era, when intellectuals visited all the Iranian cafés on this stretch of the street to discuss politics and literature. They placed their order, and over the clatter of teacups, she showed him a picture of the mummy.

Iqbal's expression barely altered. He handed back her phone.

"So?" Gul said.

"Madam should leave this one alone."

Gul ignored his advice and carried on. "She was found in some caves in Balochistan, in a drug baron's hideaway. Someone was trying to smuggle her out of the country, but we got her back and did an autopsy. She's a hoax, an attempt to make money off a historical legend, this mythical Lost Princess." Iqbal didn't look the least bit surprised, and Gul leaned forward. "Tell me what you know."

He shook his head. "This is not for you, Madam Gul. It is one thing to do business with thieves. But this is something different."

"I am well aware." The café was becoming busier now, the hustle and bustle picking up as patrons came in for after-work tea. She waited until their own chai came, and then she tried again. "You won't be in any trouble, I promise you."

The handkerchief was out now, and he was dabbing at his forehead. "You don't understand, Madam."

"Then help me to understand."

He put down the handkerchief and met her eyes. "Dekho, there have been all the time rumours in the city. For at least four, five years. There is a man. They call him Saayaa."

Gul nodded. "I am familiar with him."

Iqbal glanced around. "I have heard about this body of yours. It was found in his cave. Crossing him is a death sentence."

The volume of noise in the room increased. For a moment, they sat without speaking.

"Where is this man?"

"I do not know."

"Well, somebody has to know. If he's behind this mummy, then someone has to be helping him. He can't possibly pull this off by himself."

Iqbal said nothing.

Gul gave him a hard look. "The autopsy revealed that the girl was murdered, Iqbal. Someone knew about the legend of the Lost Princess and decided to murder an innocent girl and turn her into Princess Artunis for financial gain. Not just someone, many people. It would take an array of specialist skills to create a mummy with this level of sophistication. Someone with expertise in forensics, in anatomy, a master carver, a historian or Egyptologist, someone who understands or could have worked out the cuneiform . . . It's a huge conspiracy." She paused, expressing her fears out loud for the first time. "It could be someone at the museum, Iqbal. Someone I work with could have been involved in the murder of a woman."

Iqbal shook his head. "Maaf kijiye. I cannot help you. Anyway, you don't know that the woman was murdered. He could have picked up a dead body. There are always unclaimed bodies for sale in Karachi, if you know who to ask."

"Not in this case. This was cold-blooded murder. We have a duty here."

He did not look convinced. "It makes no sense. Why murder someone if you are going to wrap them up in bandages? Why not take a dead body from the morgue or cemetery? It costs less than you think to have one dug up. Same price as eating dinner in one of the fancy hotels. I think perhaps you are wrong, Madam Gulfsa. Let this one go. It's not worth the trouble."

Gul exhaled, thinking about how much to say. To hell with it. "Bodies can only be mummified within twenty-four hours of death, or the mummification has a high chance of failure. That's why he killed her."

Iqbal paled. "Are you sure?"

"Yes, I'm sure. They needed her body to be fresh."

"You know this for a fact?"

"Yes. I do."

"Well, if you say so . . ." Iqbal looked dubious.

"In ancient Egypt, young, beautiful women from wealthy families sometimes became failed mummies. Their bodies would fall apart. Do you know why?"

"I have no idea."

"Because the families waited a few days for the bodies of their loved ones to start to decompose a small amount before allowing the priests to remove them from their homes. The supposedly chaste priests were known for having sex with freshly expired corpses. That's why mummification has to happen with a fresh body. It doesn't work otherwise."

He began to sweat again.

"This is what we are dealing with here, Iqbal. A man who murdered an innocent girl—who broke her back and her neck so that he could have the perfect mummy. So, will you tell me what you know?"

Iqbal said nothing, but he was dabbing his forehead with ferocious concentration now.

"I'll make it easier. I'll tell you what I think happened."

Again Iqbal said nothing, but he looked straight at her.

"This Saayaa, he somehow came across the story of the Lost Princess. I don't know how. Whatever his reasons, he correctly identified that there are treasure seekers who would pay a lot of money for the princess. Am I correct?"

Iqbal hesitated, then nodded.

At last, they were getting somewhere. "So he recruits a team of specialists, kills a girl, mummifies her and buries the body for three years to establish legitimacy. And then what? He goes around spreading rumours about the Lost Princess. And he finds a buyer." Gul paused, then looked at him. "Several buyers?"

"From what I hear, there was a bidding war. But one collector in Doha won out." Iqbal pressed a fingernail into the table.

"How much was he selling her for?"

"Forty million dollars."

"Bloody hell."

"Rumours are the collector is actually part of a consortium that was planning to go and find the treasure, wealthy financiers who think paying up is worth the risk for the reward."

"How do you know this?"

"Please, Madam."

"If you can't help me find Saayaa, can you help me find his accomplices, the people who were involved in making the mummy?"

"No, Madam Gulfsa, I'm sorry, but I don't know how to find it out, this information. He is a dangerous man."

"So everyone keeps telling me." Gul wasn't going to give up, not now. Iqbal knew exactly what was going on, she was sure of it. "There is a man named Big Galloo. He may have helped him. He's connected somehow, Iqbal."

When Iqbal took a sip of his tea, the cup trembled in his hand. "Saayaa would kill us both for even having this conversation."

Gul leaned forward. "What about collectors? The treasure seekers? You said there was a bidding war. There must have been plenty of losers."

"Yes, of course."

"Can you find me one of those?"

"I doubt they would be based in Karachi, Madam."

"But you can try?"

Iqbal raised his cup to his mouth, refusing to meet her eyes. "I'm sorry, Madam. Truly I am."

She let it sit with him for a moment and gazed out at the tearoom. The tables were full now, the high ceiling fans doing little to shift the heat of the day. It was becoming stifling. Then she turned back to him.

"Iqbal . . ."

Iqbal put his cup down and looked at her. "They say that people who cross Saayaa . . . He performs laash ka muaina . . . How do you say . . . post-mortems . . . on them, but while they are still alive. He likes to use the old methods of torture. From what I've been told, he is supported by a league of evil djinns. His victims . . . they say they can never rest in peace, not until they find all their missing parts."

Gul found herself leaning forward again and speaking urgently. "Listen to me. I swear to you, Iqbal, that if you help me, nobody will know. I won't tell anyone. I'll keep you out of it, I swear on my life. This means more to me than you could ever know. Someone I care deeply about may have been hurt by this man."

Iqbal eventually sighed. "I will make some inquiries, Madam Gul. But I can't promise anything."

"That's all I could ask for, Iqbal. Thank you."

Gul left him, then made her way to the shrine, mingling amongst the pilgrims in the burial chamber itself, the smell of incense and roses lingering on her nostrils. Then she carefully walked through the streets and bazaars, making sure to stay in public areas this time. Ejaz was nowhere to be seen.

Eventually, she gave up and went home. Tomorrow, she would bring the whole team to the shrine. If DSP Akthar wouldn't help her, she would comb the place from top to bottom with every curator from the museum if she had to. What a sight that would be. She half smiled at the notion, and then rubbed the sides of her head. Her temples were throbbing.

She went straight to her room and downed some paracetamol with a can of Coke. As the day stretched to evening, Gul moved from the bedroom to her balcony. She took one of Mahnaz's diaries with her. She flipped through it, reading more slowly now. The diaries were all she had left; she had to savour them. This one was in a school notebook, blue and white, with a little school logo—a crescent moon and an open book—on the top right-hand corner. Again, there were no year dates. On the first page, Mahnaz was making fun of the end-of-school dance, which had been renamed a "prom."

> A Night in Venice. So original. And why are we perpetuating Italian clichés via American cultural appropriations in an English-speaking convent school, in a Pakistani city?

She was fifteen, Gul realised with a shock, touching the pages. Mahnaz was fifteen when she wrote this. She knew, because the *Night in Venice* prom had happened only a few weeks before her disappearance.

The police had interviewed a boy who had asked her to go with him. But Mahnaz had turned him down and told him she wouldn't be part of such stupid, patriarchal and appropriated traditions. The police had wanted to know if the boy had been angry enough to take revenge, but it turned out the boy had only asked her on a dare and was planning to take somebody else the whole time.

There were more pages. Poetry, some more quotes from Maya Angelou:

> I love to see a young girl go out and grab the world by the lapels. Life's a bitch. You've got to go out and kick ass.

Mahnaz had underlined the "life's a bitch" part several times. On other pages, there were musings on Arooj Aftab lyrics, a treatise on why *Emma* was Austen's best, a complaint against her mother for invading her privacy, something that looked like a sketch of a genome and then a blacked-out page.

Gul looked at the page and frowned. Again, Mahnaz had destroyed her own writing. Why?

Thoughtful, she retrieved the other journals and flicked through them. All Mahnaz, all writing from different ages and different levels of sophistication and length, interspersed with drawings and clippings from magazines, and photos. Some of the most recent diary entries had pages scratched over with pencil marks.

The marks made her think of the pencil mark on the sarcophagus.

Gul put the diaries down and closed her eyes. Mahnaz had disappeared one night. What if it wasn't a kidnapping? What if she *was* murdered, and Saayaa had targeted her for a particular reason? Maybe they had crossed paths at City Central University around the time of the PastMasters event. Could she have known about him? Could she somehow have stumbled upon him? What if he decided to use her for his fake princess, precisely because she was in the way?

The sun had moved, placing her little balcony in shadow. She shivered and brought the diaries inside. She shifted to her dining table, which was already heaving with books, the ones that wouldn't fit in the shelves that lined the walls. Her graphic black-and-white photos of the Chinchorro mummies of South America were framed and lay against the book piles. So were her pictures of digs in the Valley of the Kings, and of her in her favourite place, Saqqara, the necropolis of the ancient Egyptian capital of Memphis. Photos of her favourite Egyptian mummies, of her grinning inside one of the tombs, headband covered in sweat and dust, with other archaeologists—the life she once had.

She made herself a cup of tea. She'd given up that life, because the ache she had for Mahnaz had pulled her back to Pakistan. And that ache had kept her here after Mahnaz disappeared. For a moment, she allowed herself to feel the heaviness of it.

Then she shifted gears. She fetched the strongest lamp she had and plugged it in. Under the light, she tried to make sense of what things Mahnaz had wanted to keep hidden under her blacked-out pencil swirls.

She shook her head. Most of the blackouts were too effective, and she couldn't read a thing. Then she looked at the school notebook—the one with writing from only days before her daughter disappeared. This time, with the light behind the page, she could read some of what was there. She recognised the wide, looping, sometimes erratic scrawl. Mahnaz should have been a doctor, what with her illegible handwriting.

This is a filthy house of secrets and lies. It's time to do or die.

At that moment, there was a pounding on her front door, and Gul jumped, startled.

She walked to the doorway, expecting to see one of the cops patrolling the house, or Mrs. F, there to lecture her on why she should answer her phone and tell people what was going on.

But it was Ejaz, looking worse for wear. His shirt was torn; he had the beginnings of a shiner, and a cut above his lip. He was weaving slightly and clutching his side.

"Bloody hell," Gul said, ushering him in. "What's happened to you?"

"Could I have some water, Apa?"

Gul took him into the kitchen and poured him a glass. "We should take you to the hospital."

Ejaz took a sip, his hands trembling slightly. "No, no hospitals."

There was a first aid kit in the cupboard above the stove. Gul retrieved it now. "Sit down. Let me look at you."

Gul cleaned him up, wiping away the blood on his lip, icing his swollen cheek, watching him wince and touch his ribs. He could have fractured them. "You've been really hurt, Ejaz. It's time to let me know what you've been up to." She tried not to wrinkle her nose. The kid stank as well. He was covered in muck of some kind.

Ejaz said nothing.

Gul swallowed. "This is about the mummy, isn't it? You know, don't you?"

"Know what?"

"That she's a fake," Gul said, gently. "I think you've known all along."

Ejaz exhaled. He seemed to slump into himself. He was still a child, she thought. He was still a child, and he was caught up in something he couldn't handle.

Ejaz took another sip of water. "You're going to be angry with me."

"Why?" Gul brought some painkillers for him to swallow.

"For not telling you before."

Gul bit her lip. "Ejaz. I think you better let me know what the hell is going on. Right now."

Ejaz started to cry. "It's about Mahnaz."

"What do you mean?"

"A week before she vanished, I was in the bazaar near the shrine, selling my stash. I spotted her there. She was a total burger—that's what we call those rich Western kids with no sense of reality. She stood out like anything, but she was trying to scope out the place."

"Scope it out how?" Gul asked sharply.

"She was taking photos on her phone," said Ejaz miserably. "She was trying to enter from the side door. She said she had followed someone there, and she needed to find out about what was happening at the shrine."

"What do you mean? What did she think was happening?"

Ejaz gingerly touched the cut above his eye and then winced, sharply. "She wouldn't tell me, she just asked me to help her get into the shrine unnoticed. I refused. I told her the beggar mafia controls the shrine. She didn't even know that much. She has no idea what happens there. The shrine is famous for drugs, prostitution, sex trafficking and even kidnappings. Ask anyone around there—they'll tell you the stories. I told Mahnaz, those haramis watch all the worshippers who come in and out. She was so obviously rich and away from home, there was no way she could enter, not alone. They would have wondered what she was doing there. I told her to stop being stupid and to leave."

"Did she?"

He nodded. "Eventually, yes. After I insisted. But she asked me the strangest question."

"Ejaz . . ."

"She asked me if I had heard of any mummies being kept at the shrine."

Gul squeezed her eyes shut. "Oh my god."

Ejaz shifted in his seat. "I didn't know. I swear I didn't even know what a mummy really was back then. But she told me that if I ever heard any story of a mummy being found near the shrine I had to tell her immediately. I thought maybe someone was playing a joke on her, or she was being crazy. You know what she was like, always on one kind of mission or another."

Gul felt chilled to the bone. She rubbed her arms. "Yes," she said quietly. "Yes, I know what she was like."

"She told me not to tell you, not to tell anyone, but especially not you. Qasam ki baat. She made me *swear* it, Apa, that I would never tell you about our conversation, no matter what."

"Fucking hell."

Ejaz sniffed. "But then Mahnaz disappeared, and I didn't know what to do. I looked up exactly what a mummy was, and I thought, it can't have anything to do with what happened to her. And then, two weeks ago, I heard that one had been found and that somehow it had been sent to you for examination. And I knew I had to go to the shrine and learn what I could. I also had to see the body for myself. In case, in case . . . but the body was unrecognisable," he said bitterly.

It was sadness, more than anything, that Gul was feeling now. "You should have told me, Ejaz. Even if she told you not to, you should have said something. This week, if not before."

Ejaz clenched his jaw. "I know."

Gul wanted to yell. She wanted to tell him how much he had let her down. Instead, she wet a piece of cotton and gently dabbed at the cut above his eye. "You're going to have to have a shower before I put anything on this. What on earth are you covered in?"

"I tried to fix it," Ejaz said. "As soon as I heard about the mummy, I took a job running drugs for the beggar mafia. Some of the men there were talking about the mummy, about how they were waiting for a big payout. There's a basement at the bottom of the shrine. Nobody is allowed there; it is off-limits. Apa, it's where they torture and kill people. They told me that themselves. It's where they made the mummy."

Gul had to sit down.

Ejaz took another sip of water. "It took a while, but eventually I managed to slip inside. I wasn't even in there a minute before they caught me. They beat me up. They were planning to kill me, too, once all the worshippers left the shrine. Luckily I spotted a sewer grate in the floor behind some shelves. It took all my strength to lift it, but I managed. I crawled through the sewers to escape. It nearly killed me, Apa. There was so much to swim through."

"You were very brave," Gul said. Had they locked Mahnaz in that basement? Did they murder her there? What had she stumbled into?

He looked so young; his normally handsome face twisted with remorse. "Apa, the police could go to the basement, couldn't they? And check for DNA?"

"Perhaps, but whatever happened, it happened three years ago. And they may have cleaned it all up since then."

Ejaz started to weep again. "I should have told you. But after she disappeared, I thought I should keep my promise to her, and then some time went by and I didn't know what to say. She made me *promise*, Apa. She said she didn't know who she could trust anymore."

"It's all right, Ejaz."

He exhaled. "That's not all. At the shrine Mahnaz also told me there was something wrong with the shelter. She said that things weren't the way they seemed."

It was all too much, this effort to stay calm. Gul could barely breathe. "She never said anything."

"She told me she was handling it."

"What else did she say?"

"She just kept making me swear that I would never tell anyone that she'd been there or what we talked about, especially you." Ejaz flushed. "She said that a life may depend on it. Also . . . she was worried about keeping her diaries safe. She said they were important. But then she disappeared."

Gul thought about the pile of notebooks and journals that were resting on her dining room table even now, with their pieces of jutting-out scrap paper and funny illustrations. *It's time to do or die.* Could the answer to what happened to Mahnaz lie somewhere in her diaries?

CHAPTER 22

AS SOON AS EJAZ had showered and eaten, Gul updated the team and rang DSP Akthar, who seemed, at last, to understand the gravity of the situation, and sent a second police van to the house. But Gul was worried that they were drawing too much attention to themselves. If Big Galloo decided to look for Ejaz, wouldn't a house besieged by cops be the first place he would come?

At least DSP Akthar was now able to justify putting the shrine itself under surveillance. In the morning, the search warrant would come through, and the basement would be raided. Would it yield any real clues? It might be awash with forensic evidence, but whether any of that was linked to the mummy remained to be seen.

When they heard about what happened to Ejaz, the team insisted on coming over—eager to be of use and support. But Gul put them off. Ejaz needed calm and quiet. Gul had finally got him to fall asleep on the sofa but he tossed and turned, waking up alert and watchful every few minutes.

Hours later, when sleep had finally got the better of him and her own stomach had stopped its relentless churning, Gul was able to look down at the fan of books and papers, at the sticking-out brochures and photo collages, at the drawings and notations and science illustrations that formed Mahnaz's diaries. The diaries were another mystery to unravel. There was something here. Whatever happened to Mahnaz, the

answer was to be found in these diaries. Why else would she
have told Ejaz that they were important?

This is a filthy house of secrets and lies.

Gul rubbed her eyes. Gods, she was tired. She had nothing. Nothing concrete anyway, though Mahnaz's words
were reverberating in her brain. She picked up one of the
journals. There was no more time left to savour them. She
would have to treat them like evidence, as stories to be
excavated, like they were ancient artefacts. She would pore
over them for clues, for signs of who her daughter really
was. She swallowed down her emotions and started to read.
She didn't stop to dwell on the passages that made her gasp
with delight, that brought a chuckle or a tear, and ploughed
through. Mahnaz was prolific. She was someone truly
remarkable, a girl who could be funny, who made astute
observations, who was fierce in her feminism, and whose
intelligence took her breath away.

It was about twenty-five minutes later that Gul spotted
something odd. She almost read past it, but then, after a
pause, decided to double back. In one of her more recent
diaries, Mahnaz seemed to be going through an Egyptomania phase. Interesting. Gul didn't remember any Egyptian
phase, though Mahnaz loved all history with a passion.

But Mahnaz had translated Instagram memes into hieroglyphics, and had drawn characters of history, reimagined
and integrated into the jokes. Here was Cleopatra, saying,
"OMG, people think I'm a Kardashian but I have so much
more bling." But instead of writing out OMG, she had
drawn the hieroglyphics—a quail chick, an owl, and a jar
stand. On the page across, a sketch of the Rosetta stone,
with some of the hieroglyphics added, in tiny, tiny writing.

Gul had ignored it, because she'd read the fourteen lines
of hieroglyphics, the thirty-two lines of demotic script and

the fifty-three lines of ancient Greek on the stone so many times. But as she was turning the page, she paused and looked back. Mahnaz had coloured the whole Rosetta stone pink. She *hated* pink; she said the colour made her violently ill. Plus, she'd drawn glitter hearts around it, and Mahnaz's contempt for glitter practically made her allergic.

Gul stared. Mahnaz had only included the hieroglyphics, nothing more. But there were more than fourteen lines on this stone. Gul accepted that it was her own paranoia and neurosis that drove her forward. Nonetheless, she peered closely at the script.

The writing was so minuscule. She wondered if Mahnaz had used a magnifying glass when she was forming the pictographs, because she could not imagine being able to write in such a tiny, tidy hand. Gul went back to the dining room, opened a drawer in the serving table in the corner and pulled out her own magnifying glass. She held the diary close to the light. The text began accurately, the writing lauding the thirteen-year-old Pharaoh Ptolemy V. But after a few sentences, Mahnaz had added a series of nonsensical hieroglyphics, with what looked to resemble an @ rather than a hieroglyphic, then a dot and later a slash between them, before reverting back to the actual writings of the stone.

What the hell? Gul thought. Mahnaz was nothing if not exacting. She would not have included random pictographs and an @ sign and full stop for no reason, would she? Gul translated the extra letters into English.

kzprhgzmrqzmv@tnzro.xln/gsvnriilixizxpw

She stared. They made no sense. Was this a mistake? Had Mahnaz just included the wrong text by accident? Perhaps she was reading something else at the same time, as well as looking at the Rosetta stone. But why the @ sign and the full stop? And the random letters? And the colour she threw out of every colouring pencil case or marker set she had ever been given?

Hours later, after Gul had tried to translate the hieroglyphics into a variety of other languages, she gave up. This is what happened when she let herself grasp desperately at straws. She'd jumped into the rabbit hole where there were no answers, only conspiracies about colours and shapes and children's art materials. She wanted it so badly that she was assuming things, taking scribbles in diaries and coming up with fantastical theories.

Gul slumped on her bed next to the fan of diaries. Was she coming apart, finally? She had to stop, for her sanity. She curled up beside the diaries and eventually went to sleep under the whirl of her sleepy ceiling fan. She dreamt of Mahnaz. Mahnaz sitting by a crackling fire in the desert—the same stretch of the Thar Desert they had visited once in order to see the Milky Way, when they had camped out amidst the rolling dunes and thorny bushes, underneath a jand tree that offered little shade in the day and even less shelter in the evening. Mahnaz was writing hieroglyphics in the sand with a piece of wood, writing them backwards, the sand falling in and making each letter vanish within moments.

Gul's eyes snapped open. She sat up and turned on her light, her heart pounding. She was such an idiot. She grabbed the diary and a piece of paper. It was a simple cipher. Mahnaz had loved ciphers when she was younger, and when they visited the desert that one time, she had spent all her time writing out different codes in the sand. Another phase, another obsession. She was Miss Jane Marple, the famous sleuth, after all. Agatha and Jane, together, always.

In a few minutes, she had cracked it. Mahnaz had used the Atbash cipher, a substitution technique where the letters of the alphabet were reversed. It was simple, but effective, and one of Mahnaz's favourites. Gul stared at what she had translated.

pakistanijane@gmail.com/themirrorcrackd

There it was, right in front of her.

Whatever she was up to, Mahnaz had wanted to hide it from the world. What secrets did she have, what discoveries had she made that she didn't want her parents to stumble upon? Mahnaz had known about the Lost Princess. She had known there was an actual body out there, or that someone was intent on creating a mummy, at the very least. She had insisted that Ejaz not tell anyone, least of all her.

And yet . . . she had a second email address, and she had embedded details of that email address into an Atbash cipher. Who else but Gul would ever think to crack her code? Who else but Gul would look so closely at the Rosetta stone she drew, or would have known that pink was the colour Mahnaz would use to let people know that something was wrong?

Mahnaz had wanted her to find this. Why? Why not just come out and tell Gul what was going on? Why hide the facts from her, when she clearly didn't feel safe, when she thought Gul couldn't be trusted, and yet go through the trouble of leaving these breadcrumbs?

She logged into the Gmail account, and entered "themirrorcrackd" into the password field. Part of the title of one of Jane Marple's most famous mysteries, it was also Mahnaz's favourite novel. Gul tapped her fingers on the table as she waited for the page to load. And then suddenly there it was,

Mahnaz's other life. Gul's heart began to thud even louder. Other than what seemed to be some random spam or regular website notifications, there were no emails coming in or going out over the last three years. She closed her eyes briefly. What had she expected? That Mahnaz was out there somewhere, using this, her secret address? That finally there would be proof that she was alive?

She clicked through the emails half-heartedly anyway. Mahnaz had registered with many political and feminist groups from all parts of the world, and they were constantly barraging her with updates. There was nothing here. She loaded page after page, wondering just how much digital debris a person left behind when they disappeared, when she finally came across something of interest. She peered at the dates.

All the non-spam emails to PakistaniJane were *from* PakistaniJane. A few weeks before her disappearance, Mahnaz had used Gmail to send JPEGs to herself. Every email had one or two attachments.

Quickly, Gul began to print out everything she could. There were dozens of photos, and they seemed to be snapshots taken of a computer monitor, though Gul couldn't make much out, the images slightly distorted because they were pictures of a screen. She zoomed in. Each JPEG was full of columns of numbers. Bank statements, she realised. She was looking at pictures taken of bank account routings of some kind. Some of the photos were clear, others were skewed or cut off mid-number, as though the photographer was in a rush.

But there was plenty to make out. An account called the Darius Investment Fund had received a substantial number of inflows for exactly 999 dollars each, from a bank account in Zurich that had no name, only a routing number. She went through the printouts as carefully as she could. There were thousands of these transactions dating all the way back to 2015. The Darius Investment Fund was in turn transferring some of the assets to another account, which was based in Guernsey, called Orion Securities. Several million dollars had shifted hands over the years.

That wasn't all. One email had no photos but contained a hyperlink in the body of the email: *Welcome to Secret Seekers Alliance.*

Gul hesitated, and then clicked on the link. It brought her to a private Telegram chat room, and she was being asked for a username and password. She hesitated and then typed in Mahnaz's Gmail details.

And suddenly Gul was in a whole different world again.

Her eyes darted across the screen. PakistaniJane had communicated across multiple channels—Instagram, Gmail, and now Telegram. Mahnaz had an avatar—a curly haired cartoon version of herself, who, three years ago, seemed to be having a conversation with a group of people about the Lost Princess. Mahnaz had *started* the chat, talking about the City Central University event she had gone to and asking if anyone knew anything about the myth of the Lost Princess. There was a bunch of debate amongst users.

FortuneFinder007: If she's in Balochistan, she'll be somewhere near Hingol National Park. There is a labyrinth of caves over there.

LostRelicHunter: She could be anywhere between Balochistan and Oman. The answers will be in Persepolis somewhere. They will have tried to stop people worshipping at her resting place, there will be some scrolls somewhere.

FortuneFinder007: No way man. If they had found her, they would have destroyed her body straight away.

Cartographer: I would die to have her.

ArchaneArchaeologist: I would kill to have her.

Bloody hell. Mahnaz had been talking to a whole group of random people about the Lost Princess. That couldn't possibly be a coincidence. Not if, a couple of weeks later, she'd gone looking for a mummy, not if she had saved the link to the chat in her Gmail as some kind of evidence. Gul clicked through the previous chat history. Mahnaz had joined the Secret Seekers Alliance just after the City Central lecture. Had that event generated yet another passion that she decided to pursue?

Gul frowned when she clicked into a private chat between Mahnaz and someone named Goldilocks.

Goldilocks: So you think she would have a gold chest plate?

PakistaniJane: Y not? I've been reading up, there are plenty of examples elsewhere in history. Not just chest plates, but also masks. Do you know the ancient Persians had funerary masks? She could be a combination of Egyptian and Persian, that'd be amazing.

Goldilocks: What have you learnt about what she might have looked like?

PakistaniJane: Huh? Wdym?

Goldilocks: How do you think her sarcophagus would have been decorated?

PakistaniJane: Who knows. Anything is possible tbh.

Goldilocks: Egyptian or Persian iconography?

PakistaniJane: Could be either I guess, but it would be really something if they ever found a mummy with the iconography of Persepolis, right?

Goldilocks: Yes, really something. Do you know what sort of paints they used back then?

PakistaniJane: Wdym?

Goldilocks: I just wondered what types of pigments they used back then to paint on the sarcophaguses.

PakistaniJane: I think it was different for each colour. Like they used carbon for black paint and chalk for white paint and ochre for brown and orange but idk how they mixed them and stuff.

Goldilocks: Sounds like they were really dedicated. It would be interesting to see how they did that. Do you think there are still places where we mix paint that way today?

PakistaniJane: um, idk but ur questions r kinda sus.

Goldilocks: I just want to know, if I come across her, what would make her seem real?

PakistaniJane: Goodbye weirdo.

Gul sat back, stunned. Saayaa. It had to be. Through the channel, Mahnaz had come directly in contact with Saayaa or his forger—why else would Goldilocks have been asking such questions? But what had happened next? Mahnaz hadn't had any other contact with Goldilocks; she'd actually stopped writing much of anything. Was that because she'd disappeared soon after?

Gul picked up the photos. Where had these bank details come from? How could Mahnaz have possibly got her hands on them? None of this made any sense. And yet Mahnaz's disappearance was linked to Saayaa and whoever forged the mummy. Her thoughts were coming out so fast, they were tumbling over themselves. If she could find Saayaa, she would find the truth about what happened to Mahnaz. She squeezed her eyes now, as tightly as she could. There was no sense denying it any longer. Whatever happened, the news would not be good. Saayaa was extremely dangerous; everyone had told her that. If Mahnaz had crossed his path, what were the odds that she would have survived?

CHAPTER 23

IN THE MORNING, THE city was a haze of dust and smog. The sun was only just warming up the streets, and rush hour had not yet begun. For Karachi, it was a moment of calm before the chaos of the day. Gul drove her rental car down Mary Road and through Chartered Accountants Avenue, proceeding on to Khaliq-uz-Zaman and Lilly Bridge Road, ignoring the stray cats on the corner she normally stopped to feed, the barber setting up his chair under the kikar tree at the turning and the man at the nursery who was putting out a range of pretty plants and coloured plant pots for his customers. Very soon, she found herself at the only place she wanted to be—at Cantt—and parked on the street right outside Mrs. F's high-rise, her mind still churning.

Forty-five minutes later, after they had gone through every photograph and every bank account detail and she was fortified by cups of cardamom tea and Mrs. Fernandes's famous bun cake, they stopped to talk.

Mrs. Fernandes took off her glasses. "Definitely embezzlement or money laundering. See those figures of nine hundred and ninety-nine dollars? They are designed not to raise any compliance alarm bells, although it's amazing, in this age of scrutiny, that someone has managed to get away with so many transactions. There has to be some fraudulent behaviour here with one of the bank managers as well as the client."

"It's Saayaa, it has to be. Who else would be so connected? Can we trace the accounts? What do you think?"

Mrs. Fernandes pursed her lips. "We can try, but there are so many routings and reroutings in so many different jurisdictions. We can see what information is publicly available about Orion Securities and the Darius Investment Fund. The question is, is the money still in that account, or has it travelled further? You'd need to hire a forensic accountant or get the police on this; my bookkeeping skills don't lend themselves to this kind of work."

Gul stood and started to pace. "That will take forever, and I'm running out of time."

"You can always . . . I hate to say it, but you can always ask your brother? He knows this world far better than you or me, Charlie. He'll have some people who can look into this, I'm sure."

Gul shook her head. "He's angry that I'm following any of this up in the first place."

"He doesn't know what you know now."

"I don't trust him, Mrs. Fernandes. He had the investigation shut down once, he can do it again."

"So what, then?"

"I don't know."

Mrs. Fernandes went to the kitchen and came back with a fresh pot of tea. She was still wearing her long nightie. It had little embroidered red roses on it, and her hair was in the type of spongy curlers that Gul had only ever seen in eighties movies. She seemed smaller, perhaps. But not diminished. She was still a fiercely protective dragon, even without her helmet of hair.

She brought the teapot back and poured Gul another cup. "From everything you've told me, and everything I've seen here, Mahnaz was up to her neck in this. You must act, and you must act now. You know this. The police will take their time, but Bilal will move faster."

Gul sat down and accepted the cup back gratefully. "I just need a moment to think." She wrapped her palms around the mug and exhaled. And then she said what she had really come to say. "How could this be, Mrs. Fernandes? How could Mahnaz have gone through all of this and not even told me?"

Mrs. Fernandes grunted. "You must not think like this, Charlie."

". . . and Mahnaz. She got killed because of it."

"You don't know that."

"I accept it now. I have to accept it, after this." It was a shocking thing to finally say out loud. "She was the smartest person I knew. She was so unbelievably curious about the world and her place in it. That was probably her downfall."

"What on earth are you talking about?"

"My guess is her social media link to Yasmine Premjee led her to the City Central event, which kick-started a new obsession with the Lost Princess and with treasure seeking. It was so easy for her to get emotionally and intellectually invested in things, and I can just see how the story of Artunis would have ignited some sense of injustice in her."

"That doesn't mean anything, Charlie."

Gul stood. "It does. It means everything, don't you see? Somehow, someone introduced her to a private chat room on Telegram where she talked about the Lost Princess and tried to find out more about her. And that has to be where Saayaa found her."

"You don't know that."

"I know that she wound up at the shrine," Gul pressed. "That she knew that someone was making a mummy there, and that's where she went. And now thanks to Ejaz, I also know that the mummy was made in the basement of that shrine. A woman was likely murdered in that basement,

Mrs. F. And there's a high probability that that woman—that girl—was Mahnaz."

Mrs. Fernandes shook her head. "You mustn't think like that," she said quietly.

Gul sat down again, lifting her teacup with trembling hands. "It's all my fault. All of it. She's dead because of me. She knew that I was her mother, she felt betrayed by that news, and she couldn't tell me what was going on. And I couldn't keep her safe."

Mrs. F took the teacup very carefully from Gul and placed it on the table before leaning forward to take Gul's hands into her own. They were warm and calloused, and incredibly soothing. "You listen to me, and you listen carefully. Mahnaz was a child. She was a brilliant, staggeringly smart child, but she was a child nonetheless. You don't know what happened, but whatever it is, it's not your fault."

But it was. Oh Gods, but it was. Gul choked back a sob. "She understood well enough to leave me a message, and an incredibly sophisticated one at that. She was resourceful enough to find out the truth, but she felt she couldn't trust me with it."

"Gul . . ."

"A message so obscure that there was almost no chance of anyone finding it, only me, and only if I was really looking. Why? Why do that?" The tears came then, hot and fast.

Mrs. Fernandes squeezed her hands. "We may never know."

Gul wiped her eyes. "If she couldn't trust me, I don't understand why she didn't just go to the police."

Mrs. Fernandes crossed her arms. "Maybe she was aware it wouldn't get her very far. If she knew who Saayaa was, or knew that the people involved with the mummy had police contacts, she would have been wary of that."

"I don't want to go to Bilal. Really, I don't."

Mrs. Fernandes looked thoughtful. "Perhaps there is another way."

"Another way how?"

"Well, these printouts are from photographs she got her hands on, correct?"

Gul used her sleeve to dab at her eyes. "Yes."

"Well, from what I've always understood, everything digital has a fingerprint, doesn't it?"

Gul sniffed and nodded. "You're an absolutely brilliant woman, Mrs. F." Then she picked up her phone. "Hamza, I need you."

AN HOUR LATER, Hamza was sitting on the sofa in Mrs. F's flat. His normally gelled hair was a cluster of unruly tufts, and there was a trace of toothpaste on his chin. Hamza had rushed over only two hours after going to sleep, having stayed up all night to watch some online gaming championship, he told Gul. Even at the best of times, Hamza was not a morning person, and yet, he had picked up his phone when she called, and he had come, and Gul was grateful.

Hamza's head was now bent deep into his laptop. He had forwarded Mahnaz's photos of the banking transactions to himself, and was typing furiously.

Gul let him get on with it, preferring not to be a distraction. She stood and gazed out the window instead. They were five floors up, high enough that she could see the roof of Cantt Station, with the tracks behind. It was a view she had observed many times before. From this vantage point, the station's red-and-orange-uniformed porters looked like they were scurrying around the platform like fire ants.

This flat had always felt like a second home to her. It was a small place with only one bedroom and a little office with a rickety old pull-out sofa bed that Francis used, but it was cosy. And even though the kitchen could only fit a single person in it, Mrs. Fernandes still managed to cook for a small army from that little corner oven with only two work-ing hobs. She was there now, making some unda ki bujiya for Hamza, adding some extra mirch to the fried onions and scrambled eggs for an extra kick.

Gul turned and went back to the coffee table, pour-ing herself some more tea. For years, she had begged Mrs. Fernandes to let her find them some bigger, brighter accom-modation, to pay their rent, or at least part of it, so that Francis could have a proper bedroom. But the other woman had always refused and insisted they had everything they needed. Somehow, she was always able to put away a little something for the shelter, too, though she had allowed Gul to fundraise for that until Bilal had brought in the Delani Foundation money.

Now Gul watched Hamza, sitting on the same cane fur-niture that Mr. Fernandes had purchased forty plus years before from the cane market near Queens Road. How solid this place was. How soothing, and how different from the Big House, with its pompous silver-framed ancestors and fussy doodahs. After Mr. Fernandes died, Mrs. Fernandes had not changed a thing. A large photograph of him still adorned the peeling pale pink wall, next to a photo of Mrs. F's son and daughter-in-law in their Sunday best, a baby Francis in their arms. Francis himself was fast asleep on his sofa in the other room, secure in the knowledge that when he woke up, his grandmother would be waiting with bun cake.

She felt the ache in her heart. Mrs. F had lost so many people she loved, and yet, somehow, she endured. She had moved forward; she had built a life of meaning. Gul knew she would not be able to do the same, not without finding out what happened to Mahnaz, not until she buried her daughter and said goodbye. And even then, would her life ever feel whole again?

Hamza looked up. "I've got it."

Gul went to peer over his shoulder.

"See? Here's the metadata. Mahnaz never erased it. I can tell you that these photos were all taken at the same time, just over three years ago in April, on the fifteenth, around one thirty-three A.M."

"Only weeks before Mahnaz disappeared," Gul muttered. "Is there any way to tell who took the photos?"

"No, but I can tell you they were taken by an iPhone 12 Pro."

Gul nodded. "Mahnaz had that model. She must have taken the photos on her phone."

"Probably."

"What about finding out exactly where the photos were taken?"

"Just give me a minute." Hamza pointed to his screen. "I'm downloading an EXIF viewer."

"A what?"

"It's going to help us figure this out, Apa. If Mahnaz's location sharing was on, I can get some coordinates that I can convert into decimal degrees to use in Google Maps." He continued to tap furiously. Eventually he stopped, and looked at her. "I'm sorry, Apa, but Mahnaz disabled her location services. I can't find where these were taken."

Gul slumped. "Shit."

Mrs. F came back with the unda ki bujiya and a piping hot paratha, and for a moment, while Hamza ate and made appreciative noises, none of them spoke. Hamza was as scrawny as anything, but perpetually hungry. And though he wolfed down more food than anyone Gul had ever met, Hamza never seemed to put on any weight. Mrs. Fernandes made him a second paratha, which he practically inhaled. Eventually, he put down his plate and wiped his hands on a tissue. "I can't tell you where the photos were taken, but maybe I can clean them up a bit. It might help."

"Thank you, Hamza."

Gul sat on the cane sofa beside him now.

Hamza's hands moved across the keys so quickly, she marvelled, as image after image was pulled up, expanded, clicked on, and then removed, deemed not useful. But then he paused on one of the photos of the account details. "What's that?"

"What's what?"

"There's a light reflecting in the corner here. I am just going to expand here, hang on . . ."

He pushed the laptop towards her. "There's a mirror behind the monitor where Mahnaz took the photo—see? There's definitely light reflecting here, and I can make out some shapes. There's the shadow, it's clearly an arm, that must be Mahnaz taking the photo."

Gul's eyes widened. "How did I not notice this?"

"I had to clean up the image, Apa. It wouldn't have been very obvious. Even now, it's mostly just reflective light."

"Can you expand it further?"

"Hang on, let me try . . ." He pulled the laptop towards him and clicked furiously, before turning it around again. "There, you can make out something. There's a table behind her. Something's on there, I can't quite work it out. Is that an animal of some kind?"

Gul's heart raced as she stared at the screen. "Yes. Yes, it is. An animal. And I know exactly where Mahnaz took these photos."

CHAPTER 24

LATE THAT NIGHT, GUL pulled up across the road from the Big House, turned off the lights on her rental car and waited. The street was quiet, everybody likely asleep, even the chawkidars guarding the homes in this, the poshest of neighbourhoods.

The heat of the day had ebbed, and she stepped outside the car to cool off. She wrapped her arms around herself and looked out at the row of dwellings, each mismatched and different, from the large white mansions with their imposing façades and grand pillars, to the older cement-block structures, which were nowhere near as grand, but still managed to retain a quiet dignity. No matter what shape or size, these houses had one thing in common: high walls crowned with spirals of barbed wire. Even the heavy scent of jasmine and the lines of hedges and bushes couldn't take away from the fact that these were homes designed to keep unwelcome visitors out.

The slight creak of metal jolted her to attention. Bisma was there, moving stealthily in the shadows. She opened the gates and motioned Gul inside. Gul had been right in her earlier assumption that Bilal and Sania treated their maid poorly. Bisma had been easy enough to bribe when she'd stopped by earlier in the afternoon, in any case. "Thank you," she whispered as she crossed the threshold.

The girl nodded, unlocked the front door, and let her in.

Once inside, Gul nodded again and then sent the girl away. She did not want to cause her any further trouble.

In the landing, silence hung heavy. Gul turned to the right and carefully opened the study door, using her phone as a flashlight. There it was, sitting behind the desk. The large bronze panther she had caressed so much as a child that one side of it was shinier than the other. In the photo, it had looked like the shadow of an actual animal, but Gul had recognised the sculpture immediately. How many times had she wished she could have taken it from this house after Baba died and kept it for herself, a precious memento of the few happier times of her childhood?

Gul stepped inside the study, nearly knocking a vase of flowers from the heavily carved console by the door, exhaling with relief when she was able to right it, and noting the art deco mirror just above, the one that had arrived with her grandmother as part of her wedding trousseau. The mirror had reflected the image in Mahnaz's photo; it had to have. This had to be the place, especially given the time the photo was taken. 1:33 A.M. It would have been easier for Mahnaz to sneak downstairs and rifle around, but much harder for her to sneak out of the house without being noticed.

Gul made her way to Bilal's desk and sat down on the leather armchair. From her satchel she pulled out a device—not much larger than a credit card—and connected it to one of the USB ports. Then she turned on Bilal's computer.

She rubbed her arms. She and Hamza had gone over this, several times, and yet she was nervous that she was going to mess this up somehow. The device looked like a giant computer chip, but Hamza had explained to her that it was pre-loaded with a program to crack passwords through brute force. It would try the most common passwords first, and then move on to the more complicated configurations. Hamza had taken down dozens of pieces of personal information about Bilal, like birthdays and anniversaries and family member details, which the device was designed to initially tackle. Neither of them knew how long this would all take, and Hamza had pressed to come himself, but Gul had refused. If she was caught, then let Bilal's ire fall on her, not on those without the power to stand up to him.

Besides, there was not much Hamza would be able to do. If Bilal's computer had been set up by the IT guys at Delani Investments, it was likely they would have ensured it had a strong password, or two-factor authentication, and all this would be moot. But Gul was betting that Bilal relied on this device for his own personal use. And he was as technologically inept as she was.

Gul smiled grimly when she was proven right. It was only minutes before a password was accepted, and that password was . . . Mahnaz's birthday.

She exhaled, and lost herself in the world of Bilal's desktop. File after file after file. Bilal was meticulous in many ways; she wouldn't have expected anything less. Tax returns and car payments and medical reports, family pictures and scanned copies of passports and birth certificates and other critical documents. Everything orderly and as it should be.

It was nearly an hour later when she found, amidst a folder marked "Accounts," another folder marked "Orion Sec." Gul's heart quickened. Orion Securities. She clicked that folder open and saw the familiar pages of bank statements, the ones Mahnaz had photographed. Her stomach clenched. It was all true then. Until this moment, she hadn't wanted to believe it. Bilal was involved in some shady financial transactions, likely working for Saayaa. She peered at the dates. The last transaction was only two weeks ago.

Quickly, she plugged in the memory drive Hamza had also given her and copied across all the files. Then she went online and looked through Bilal's search history, but found it did not go back three years. Hamza had warned her that it was likely she wouldn't find anything here. But then she logged into Telegram. They'd discussed that too. If Mahnaz had taken photos of the site from this computer, then it was worth having a look, just in case . . .

Gul's worst fears were realised when she saw the username and password prompt, already filled out and ready for her to log in. It was Bilal's email address, not Mahnaz's. And the username affiliated with Bilal's email address was Goldilocks. In the darkness, Gul shook her head. Jesus. *Jesus.* Goldilocks wasn't Saayaa, it was Bilal.

She trawled through his messages. Goldilocks had joined the Secret Seekers Alliance only two days after Mahnaz. Goldilocks was asking everyone all kinds of questions about what the body of the Lost Princess might look like, what would make her credible and what would make her unique. And later . . . Gul swallowed . . . later, Goldilocks was talking excitedly about what such a mummy would be worth. And bloody hell, Goldilocks was still active. Only last week, after the discovery of the Lost Princess became public, Goldilocks was swearing that he had seen Princess Artunis's body for himself, and that she was legitimate.

She closed her eyes, the shock of it almost paralysing. Bilal was one of the people behind the mummy. Somehow, Bilal was linked to Saayaa, and Bilal was the reason that Mahnaz was targeted. Could Bilal *be* Saayaa? No, no that was too much to even contemplate. Bilal didn't have the brains. He didn't have the network. And most of all, he didn't have the balls. Plus, his love for his child was real; he would never have allowed Mahnaz to suffer.

Gul shook her head and forced herself to deal with the task at hand. It wasn't enough to have a hard drive; anything could happen to it. Anything could happen to *her*. She copied all the files and did what Mahnaz had done—emailed them to herself. Then she thought through her options as she waited.

When the first rays of light started inching their way through the bottom of the study curtains, Gul rose and went to find Bisma. "Go wake up my brother. Tell him I've just arrived. Let his wife sleep."

If Bisma had an opinion about what was going on, she was doing a good job of not showing it. She climbed the stairs, looked down at Gul briefly, and then disappeared. Five minutes later, there he was, Bilal in a pair of shorts, his eyes still heavy with sleep.

"What?" he barked, his hand gripping the banister. "What is it? What's happened? It's the middle of the night, Gul."

"Come down," she replied calmly. "Come down and I'll tell you." She walked into the drawing room and waited for him to follow. She could hear Bilal muttering under his breath about his crazy sister, and shouting at Bisma to bring him some tea.

As soon as Bilal stepped into the room, Gul pulled the photos she had brought with her out of her satchel, and tossed them onto the coffee table.

Bilal looked weary. "Gul, I have no idea what this is, but showing up here at five in the morning with all these theatrics is totally unacceptable. You do know I have to be at the office in three hours?" He turned on the lights.

"Your secret is out, Bilal. There's no point trying to hide it any longer. You're done."

"What secret?"

She nodded at the table. "Have a look for yourself."

Bilal frowned. "You need a sedative. Something to calm you down. I know it's been a trying time, but this is

ridiculous. Let me send for Dr. Pirzada." Nonetheless he
made his way to the coffee table, and she watched his expression pale as he picked up one of the photos. When he put
the printout down, his body was rigid. "I don't know what
this is, but you need to leave."

"That's just a screenshot of what Mahnaz saw." She took
the USB stick out of her satchel. "I've got the actual files
here."

Bilal blinked rapidly, saying nothing for a moment. Then
he narrowed his eyes. "Give me that."

Gul put the stick back in her satchel. "There's no point.
I've already backed them up and sent them into the ether.
It's out there now, Bilal. You're either so confident in your
own superiority or so bloody stupid you didn't even bother
to cover your tracks. If I could find all this in a few minutes,
imagine what the police will be able to do."

"I have nothing to say to you."

"Who took Mahnaz?"

Bilal scowled.

"It's your fault she's gone, you bastard. Whatever they did
to her, they did it because of you."

"Will you please just leave, Gul? You have no idea what
you're dealing with here."

"Tell me what happened."

Bilal raked a hand through his thick, salt-and-pepper hair.
"You're mad."

Gul glared at him for a moment. Then she exhaled and
sat down. She could shout, she could scream, she was close
to shooting his bloody head off. But none of that would
work. Bilal looked small, small and scared and shell-shocked.
Whatever his involvement, and however much she was prepared to despise him, Gul knew that he was torn up inside.

"She's dead, isn't she?"

He stared at the floor, rubbing at some imaginary spot with his toe.

"What did they do to her? Did they kidnap her? Is that why you helped them? Because of what they were threatening to do to her? You can't carry this burden alone anymore, Bilal. Tell me. Please. You can't go to prison with this on your conscience."

Bilal's rigid posture simply deflated. It was such an unfamiliar image, her brother looking defeated, his customary bravado simply disappearing.

He slumped into the armchair, put his hands over his face, and started to sob. "I'm sorry. I didn't know what would happen, I swear." His whole body started to shake.

"Tell me. Tell me everything."

He shook his head. "You'll hate me. You'll never forgive me."

"I hate you already. Nothing is going to change."

He looked up, his face anguished. "Don't say that."

"Start speaking, then."

The door creaked. It was Bisma with the tea. Once again, the girl asked no questions. She set down the tray, paused for a moment, assessing them both, and then backed out of the room. In that moment Bilal straightened and gathered himself.

Gul leaned forward and poured him a cup of tea, as though this were any other day, any other moment of brother and sister catching up in a room full of family photos and expensive art.

"Here, drink it."

It seemed to help Bilal, this performative attempt at normality. He took the cup, nodding his thanks, and blew over the top. "It was Delani Investments. We made some bad bets—I made some bad bets. I leveraged some of our capital to buy riskier assets. In normal times, those investments would have paid off. But then markets became so volatile, and there were all these capital calls. Nobody could have predicted it, Gul, nobody." Bilal looked at her, his face puffy, his hair dishevelled, imploring her to understand.

"King Midas lost his golden touch. I get it. Skip to the part about Mahnaz." The lingering scent of yesterday's cigar smoke hung heavily in the room—the air felt stale and oppressive. From across the coffee table, Gul could smell Bilal's body odour. His eyes were bloodshot.

"It all happened so quickly. I didn't know what to do. It was pension fund money. The company would never have survived a loss like that. We were thirty percent down. So I borrowed the capital from the Delani Foundation to tide us over. That's why . . . it's why I shut you out after you were in that car accident with Mahnaz. I knew the other trustees would be easy to keep onside, but you would have scrutinised every transaction. I had to remove you from the board and from my life."

Gul's stomach clenched. For years, she had thought that Bilal hadn't trusted her to keep Mahnaz safe. The shame of that had stayed with her, something she had to carry and learn to live with. In reality, he had banished Gul from their lives just to protect his secret? "How long has all this been going on for?"

He couldn't even look her in the eyes. "It didn't even work. It bought me a few months, but despite my best efforts, I couldn't make that money back so quickly. It took me years to get out from under it."

"Bilal . . ."

"It started thirteen years ago."

"When Mahnaz was just five."

"Yes."

Gul felt a sharp twist of pain. Bilal had been cooking the books for all this time, going about his gilded life, hanging out in boardrooms and at charity events and being a man about town. And all the while he was knee-deep in the muck, in the filth of corruption. She looked about the room—at the shiny silverware, the expensive carved rosewood side tables, the elegant Turkish lamps—the surfaces all dust free and glinting, the raw-silk sofa cushions nicely plumped, looking like they could be showcased on a magazine cover. What a meticulously crafted façade it all was. "So what? You went to Saayaa?"

He rubbed his palms against the stubble on his cheeks. "I didn't know who he was. I swear, Gul. A friend connected me to the moneylenders. I thought it would be a short-term thing."

He blew on his cup again, keeping his head bowed. "Over the years I reimbursed those moneylenders every rupee, and I did it time and time again, but they kept raising the interest on the loan, and threatening me if I refused to pay more. I didn't realise what I had signed up for, Gul. They were never going to let me go. I was too valuable to them."

Gul stared at him, saying nothing.

He put down his cup and looked at her with an expression of anguish. "When I struggled, they made me a deal. Help them whitewash their cash, launder their assets, and they'd delay calling in my loan. That's when I first heard the name Saayaa, and realised who I was dealing with. Every time I hesitated in doing what they asked, they would send me little warnings. Our dog was murdered. Our poor cook had his thumb cut off in the market one day. No explanation. Someone just came up to him, grabbed his hand, and sliced. But I knew, I knew who had done it even before they mailed me the thumb at my office."

Bilal stood abruptly and walked to the console by the door, where he pulled out a cigar from a drawer and cut it. Coming back in his shorts and banyaan, grey hairs curling above the U of his vest, cigar in hand, he looked old and ridiculous. "I laundered their money for them in every way I could. I did it through my own companies, through shell corporations, through legitimate businesses I could connect to and even . . . God help me, even through the shelter. I also sponsored the museum with their money and then reimbursed them through legitimate Foundation assets."

"You filtered drug money through the Foundation?"

He hung his head.

"That's part of what Mahnaz uncovered, isn't it? She told someone things weren't what they seemed at the shelter."

"Yes."

"Makes sense. It's not like you to support important causes without an angle." Gul was surprised when, in the midst of her anger, she felt a sense of sorrow. How different things might have been if Bilal had been an honourable man.

"That's not . . . that's not it. I was trying to support you in my own way, and to support Mahnaz and her interests. It wasn't just because of the laundering."

"Okay."

"It's true. I'm not a bad guy."

"So why are you still in bed with them?"

Bilal said nothing.

He was in so deep, Gul realised with a pang. There was no helping her brother now. "I don't understand what this has to do with the mummy, or Mahnaz."

"I needed advice. I spoke to the friend who had connected me to the moneylenders and he suggested one big payout to finally get them off my back. But I couldn't raise that much cash. The thing about being a famous financier is that people always think you have more money than you do."

"How did Mahnaz get involved?"

He lit his cigar and exhaled, and somehow, the act of that made him calmer. "She went to City Central University and came back with the incredible tale of the Lost Princess. She was so excited about Princess Artunis. I dismissed it, of course. I had other things on my mind, but I think she must have told other people about what a potential mummy could be worth if it was ever found."

"Why do you say that?"

"Do you remember that Delani Foundation fundraiser we hosted here, the spring before Mahnaz disappeared?"

"No."

"We invited lots of donors, it was a thank-you thing. Huge event, live music, awards presentation, the works. We even invited some of your museum colleagues. You were on the guest list, but you never replied one way or another."

"I don't recall ever receiving an invitation. It must have got lost in the mail."

Bilal ignored her and carried on. "There were over two hundred guests here that night. It was a big thing. I think Mahnaz must have talked to someone about the legend of the Lost Princess. Probably, she talked to more than one person. All I know is that three days after that event, I got a call."

"A call from who?"

"From Saayaa's people. Saayaa had heard the tale from someone who had been at the party, apparently, and he'd done some research. Turns out, there's a billion-dollar black-market mummy trade going on every year. It was a preposterous notion, and yet Saayaa told me, if I could help him pull it off, it would be the score of the century, and my debt would finally be clear."

Gul stood and began to pace. "He wanted you to make him a mummy?"

Bilal couldn't even look at her now. She could see how much shame he was feeling from the way he hunched his body, in the way he was taking rapid sips of his tea, as though that would help him get his bearings. "I think he thought the whole notion was so absurd that it might just work. It certainly meant that I would be in his pocket for at least another three years while we buried the mummy to make it more credible, in any case. Three more years of doing his bidding, and moving his money around. I probably saved him millions that way." Bilal crumbled his cigar into the ashtray.

"What did you do?"

"I agreed, what else could I do? Anything to get out from under him. I never thought it would actually work. My role was quite simple—to compile as much research as possible on the Lost Princess, and bring in professionals to help create the thing and make it credible."

Gul shook her head. Her brother deserved to go to jail for a very long time. She could barely even process what he had done. She felt numb. And then it struck her. "Mr. Davar's library in Parsi Colony was ransacked. That was you, wasn't it?"

He shook his head. "Not me, no. Saayaa's men. But I pointed them there. After Mahnaz told me about the Lost Princess, I went back to the university and asked the people at the history group some questions. They didn't know anything useful, but one girl told me about the historian in Parsi Colony. So I sent Saayaa's men there to see if there was more information available on the mummy. There wasn't though. I had no idea they were going to trash the place."

"They didn't know what they were looking for," said Gul, quietly, wondering how much more she could take.

But the revelations kept coming. "Saayaa wanted you, you know. He knew exactly who you were. All about your career, somehow. He thought that with your help, the hoax would be easy to pull off. I had to tell him that you'd never go for it. I knew you would refuse, no matter what the stakes. But I also wanted to protect you from him."

"Jesus, Bilal."

"But neither Saayaa nor I counted on Mahnaz."

"She found you out."

This time, when he looked at Gul, Bilal's face was full of pain. "She was using the study computer one day. I don't know what she was doing, but she came and confronted me about setting up an account in the name of Goldilocks."

"You really are shit at logging out of things. You know that, don't you?"

"She wanted to know why I had joined a group that she had only just told me about a few days before. The chat is private now, but three years ago, it was open to anyone, and so I decided to create an avatar so I could learn from her and from others and see if the plan could really work. Mahnaz wanted to know what the hell I was playing at."

He swallowed. "I lost my temper. I told her to stop poking her nose around things that weren't any of her business. I threatened to have her institutionalised if she didn't stop acting like a lunatic, and that was the end of it, at least, as far as I was concerned."

"You didn't know your child very well if you thought that," said Gul softly.

"No, no, I suppose I didn't, but I thought she would have more sense." He looked down for a moment, inhaled deeply. "I knew I would need help implementing the plan, and so I arranged to meet Saayaa's people one evening to talk through the logistics. How much money were they prepared to bribe people with, how far did they want the circle to go, that kind of thing. Mahnaz went and stuck one of those Air-Tags in my car. She tracked me to the meeting. It turned out she'd been searching through all my files too, in the middle of the night, and she was connecting the dots."

It was still early, but Gul could hear someone coughing outside—probably the cook as he awoke and headed to the kitchens, grumbling about something under his breath. The sweeper must have started work too, because she could hear the familiar sounds of a jharu going back and forth on marble steps. Just another day, Gul thought. Just another day, even though her heart was breaking. It was all starting to make sense now. "You met them at the shrine."

He looked at her sharply. "How did you . . . never mind."

"How could you, Bilal. How could you murder a woman?"

"No, no," he shouted suddenly, getting up. "I didn't, I swear. I would never! They told me they would procure a body from the morgue, that I didn't have to worry about the details. I just had to connect them with the forgers who could help pull the whole hoax off. But then they spotted Mahnaz lurking around the shrine, and I knew I was in real trouble. I convinced them that I could keep her under control, that she wasn't a threat to them. They seemed to agree, but then they cut me out of the process. The minute I brought in the professionals they needed, they told me my part was done until it was time to dig up the mummy, that I should keep my head down and not say a word to anyone if I valued my life."

"And then?"

Bilal sat down again and gripped the sides of the arm-chair. "Then Mahnaz disappeared. And in those first few months, I searched frantically for her."

It wasn't true. Gul knew it wasn't true. If there had been a proper effort to find Mahnaz, Gul would have been a part of it, and maybe, just maybe, she could have fended off the depression that took such fierce hold of her. Bilal must have seen the scepticism all over her expression because he quickly interjected: "You don't remember because you lost your mind, but I did, Gul. I made Bob turn over every part of the city."

"You shut the investigation down after four months."

Bilal relit his cigar. "Because I received a note telling me to stop, or they would hurt her. You don't believe me? Wait here." He went out and Gul heard the study door creak. He came back momentarily, and stuck a square piece of paper into her hands. "Here. See for yourself."

The paper was white, a neatly edged rectangle, with typed letters: *Forget about your daughter. It would be better for her if you did.* It looked almost modern, like a logo for a cool drinks company or PR business. It was unreal. Eventually, Gul looked up. "This is a vital clue. It should have been given to the police."

Bilal looked so sad. "Oh, Gul, you still don't understand. Saayaa has the police in his pocket. He controls them. He controls everything. I thought if I did what they told me, they would let her go. But when she didn't come home, I knew they had killed her. They aren't in the business of keeping people they kidnap alive; it's too much effort."

"And you did nothing."

"That's not true! I tried to reach out to them several times, but they ignored me. Saayaa is powerful, Gul."

She could barely breathe. How could he? How could he have let this happen? "They needed a body for their mummy, and so they took Mahnaz. They took her because you put her in harm's way."

He started to sob.

"Who is Saayaa?"

"I don't know, I swear it. I met with some of his cronies at the shrine, but I was never allowed to meet him directly. Messages were passed back and forth."

"Big Galloo? Is that who you met with?"

He continued to cry. His chest heaved but he didn't say a word, looking at the floor once again.

"Who was the friend who introduced you to the money-lenders?"

"You know I can't tell you that. For your own safety."

At that, she gave him a look of disdain. "My safety? You know the madarchod tried to have me run off the road the other day? My car is a write-off; it's a miracle I survived."

At that, he paled. "Gul, I didn't know, I swear . . ."

"Who at the party could be connected to Saayaa? We'll need a list of all your guests, anyone Mahnaz could have come into contact with."

After a long silence, he finally looked up. "It won't make a difference. He's too smart to be linked to anyone."

"He's not going to stop, Bilal. Saayaa will never stop. You have to turn yourself in. It's the only way we'll hunt the bastard down."

"What good would that do now, Gul? They've killed her, and they'll kill me."

"I really don't care."

"You really don't, do you?" Bilal wiped snot off his face with his banyaan. "What happened to us? We were once so close, do you remember? We used to race up and down those banyan trees at Nani and Nana's house. You used to love them so much, and I would always slow down so you could catch up, do you remember? I looked out for you, Gul. I've always looked out for you."

"Will you do it? For Mahnaz's sake, will you find your honour and turn yourself in?"

Now Bilal's chin wobbled. "Sania would be ruined. The company would go under."

"Not if you resign and take full responsibility for your actions." She stared pointedly at the photos scattered on the coffee table. It wasn't as though her brother had much choice.

He followed her gaze. Eventually he nodded.

"You'll tell them everything?"

"Yes."

"Including the name of the friend who connected you to the moneylenders, and also the forgers you found to help you?"

"Yes, everything. But just let me change, Gul. I can't go to the police station looking like this. I'll call Bob. We can meet him in his office. We can handle this in a civilised way. Okay?"

"All right."

He nodded again, his face sagging, his body heavy. "Just give me a few minutes. I'll ask the maid to bring you some fresh tea while you wait, this one has gone cold."

She pressed a hand against her stomach, feeling the queasiness there. She wasn't capable of drinking tea, or anything else. "I am fine, thanks."

"Gul?"

"What?"

"I hope one day you'll see that I'm not evil. I hope one day you'll be able to forgive me."

"I don't think that day will ever come, Bilal."

He shook his head and walked out. She followed him part of the way and stood at the door of the room, watching him take the stairs one at a time, his legs slow and sluggish. Then he disappeared.

She waited, feeling numb, wondering how Sania was going to handle the news.

When Bisma came in a few minutes later, she shouldn't have been surprised. "Bilal Sahib said to tell you sorry, but he had to go. He told me to give you this." She handed Gul a note.

In contrast to the earlier missive, this was hastily scrawled on a pink Post-it.

Don't trust anyone at the museum. Forgive me.

CHAPTER 25

GUL WANTED TO GO home and scream into a pillow. Instead, she drove to the beach. The day had barely begun; the sun was still licking the horizon through the morning smog, but the smell of fish from the returning boats made everything seem sharper. It was too early in the day for the camel and horse rides, too soon for the hawkers and restaurants. The Arabian Sea itself was rough and grey in the monsoon, leaving little coastline. And the beach was covered in debris—the previous day's rubbish yet to be picked up. Gul got out of her car and started to walk.

As she carefully stepped over the odd juice box, chip packet or glass bottle, Gul looked out at the sea longingly. How beautiful it was, in its wildness. She wanted to be in the water, to forget her troubles by ducking under the salty, turbulent waves and disconnecting entirely from the world. But Karachi's monsoon currents were deceptive and treacherous. Last summer a boy had stepped into the water just up to his ankles. Within a minute, the current swept him away, and his father soon after, who had jumped in to rescue him.

So she contented herself with the walk instead, grateful for the solitude and the boundless reach of the sea as it melted into the sky, which made her feel like she could breathe again. She stopped when she saw a large shell poking out of the sand, and crouched down to extricate it from the damp earth. The shell was beautifully crafted, resembling a delicate Greek urn, with a wide opening and ship-like keel running along the bottom. She smiled when she realised it wasn't a shell at all—it was, in fact, the thin white shell-like structure of a paper nautilus, created by a female octopus to keep her eggs safe. Judging from its condition, the mother octopus had done her job well, and kept her children from harm before they hatched and went out into the world. Gul had never seen such a well-preserved example. She picked it up and placed it in her satchel. She would take it home and add it to the shells her grandparents had collected on their own walks along the Bath Island shore.

After a few minutes, when she felt less like screaming, Gul stopped walking and wrapped her arms around herself, thinking about what had happened. Bilal had disappeared, raced off in his BMW while Gul had stupidly been waiting for him. Why hadn't she foreseen that? Bilal would never put his own neck on the line, not for anyone. He was such a fucking coward.

She'd woken up Sania, of course, but her sister-in-law seemed to be struggling herself, not understanding what had happened, not managing to process what Gul was trying to tell her. Sania just stared at her, unblinking, and then suggested that perhaps it was better if Gul left.

Now, Gul had to decide what she was going to do. Bilal or Saayaa had hired someone at the museum to help with the mummy, from Bilal's note, that much was now clear. But instead of just pointing a finger, he had warned her not to trust anyone. Still thinking about saving his own ass, no doubt. Who could it be? Thanks to his years of patronage, Bilal knew everyone there. Director Raja. Ali Mahmood. The rest of the curators and support teams. One of them had to have been involved. Should she turn over her evidence to DSP Akthar and hope for the best? But how far would that get her, really?

She tried to calm down the thoughts swirling in her head. This thing went so deep, it was hard to know what her next move should be. But one thing she knew for certain. She would not stop until Saayaa had been unmasked and he paid for his crimes. If only the police would do their fucking jobs . . .

She stopped then and stared unblinkingly at the horizon. What was it that Bilal had said?

Oh, Gul, you still don't understand. Saayaa has the police in his pocket. He controls them. He controls everything.

In that moment, she knew what she had to do.

THE KARACHI POLICE Office was located just off Shahrah-e-Faisal, southeast from the Gora Qabristan, the "White Man's Graveyard." The Christian cemetery was famous for one formidable landmark—towering majestically above the cemetery's wrought-iron gates, a stark white cross jutted a hundred and forty feet towards the sky. Countless British officers and their families were laid to rest behind the imposing cross, Gul knew. So much of Pakistan's colonial history could be revealed by looking at those tombstones, but like many places in Karachi, the cemetery was struggling with its upkeep.

She parked not far from the KPO building, which was no mean feat, since the place was blocked by high barricades and a long length of concrete roadblocks. A recent Taliban attack on their headquarters had left the police scrambling to increase security, and it looked like they had succeeded. The blue 1960s-style block building was an impenetrable fortress of metal bars and criss-crossing window grills, gate checks and scanned searches.

She gave her name and ID at the checkpoint and was taken through a vast courtyard into the building, where a receptionist escorted her to a lift, and travelled with her several floors, saying nothing as the lift hummed softly. The doors opened onto what seemed to be an executive suite, which smelt cloyingly of polish or air freshener. A kaleidoscope of police shields and insignias adorned the halls, and Gul was escorted to a meeting room nearby. Inside the room, framed photos of serving officers, smiling, unaware of how soon they would die in the line of duty, took up most of the space on one wall. Near the other wall the flag of Pakistan held a place of honour, adjacent to a large picture of the country's founder. The long table had a conference system, two bottles of Nestlé water, a display of wilting flowers, and a box of rose-petal tissues on it.

Gul waited for twenty minutes, trying to distract herself from her mounting anxiety by checking emails and reading on her phone, until a cough made her look up. Bob was standing in the doorway in his police uniform, a leather-bound file in one hand. From his expression, she gathered he had been waiting for her to notice him for some time. She was glad she hadn't given him the satisfaction. "Gul. How are you?"

He didn't come towards her and she declined to stand. "I'm here talking to you. How do you think I am?"

Bob walked slowly into the room, watching her the whole time. "I must admit I was a little surprised when Sania called me this morning and told me I had to see you urgently. What is this business about Bilal all about? She says he's left town and that you will explain."

Gul watched as Bob took a seat at the head of the table, putting down his file and cracking at his knuckles. The sound made her wince. Would he ever stop with that maddening habit? He'd been doing it since they were kids.

In his uniform and with his chest full of brass, Bob was an imposing presence, though the semi-rimless glasses he was wearing made him seem a little bit more approachable. Gul knew from Bilal that Bob had plans to run for political office one day, and she could see him getting far. In the cesspool of Karachi's murky power players, Bob fit right in. She took a deep breath. "I asked Sania to say that, because I didn't want you to have any reason not to see me. But I think you already know why he left town, Bob."

He arched a brow. "I do?"

"He doesn't do anything without talking to you about it first. It's always been this way. You've always called the shots in his life."

Bob surveyed her for a moment. "Would you like something to drink?"

"I'm fine, thank you."

"Oh, come on. Have a cup of chai with an old friend of your brother's at least."

"I had some tea this morning. Then Bilal asked me to wait for him to get ready so we could come and see you together. Instead he ran like a coward."

Bob brought his hands together and leaned forward. "This is about Mahnaz?"

"Yes. It's also about the mummy I currently have at the museum. I'm sure you're aware of her. She's a hoax and a murder victim."

His gaze was sharp. "I thought that hadn't been proven yet?"

"It's been proven. Without any doubt."

"DSP Akthar is in charge of that case, I recall?" Bob straightened in his chair. "A good officer. Straight as an arrow."

"I wish the same could be said for you."

"What?"

Gul stood now, her stomach in knots. "Bilal confessed to everything. He told me how Saayaa had taken a fancy to the notion of selling a fake mummy for millions. Bilal agreed to help in order to cancel his debt to him."

Bob didn't even blink. "I see."

"And he also told me that he couldn't report Saayaa to the police, because Saayaa had the police in his pocket. Why would he have said that, Bob, when you are his best friend of nearly three decades? Why would he have hesitated to bring the law into his situation—which I have no doubt you're well aware of—unless he knew that there was nothing you could do?"

Bob motioned for her to sit down, but Gul shook her head. He stood himself then, and came inches from her. "Are you accusing me of some sort of wrongdoing, Gul? Please be careful what you say. I am the IG of Sindh."

Gul held her ground, even though his breath was hot and heavy and far too close. "I am merely pointing out the logical and obvious case here. Three years ago, Bilal wanted the investigation into Mahnaz's disappearance to come to an end. Despite my best efforts, you did as he wanted. Why? To support a friend? Or was it because you knew what was at stake? I think you've known about Saayaa all along. Maybe you're working for him too, or maybe you're just turning a blind eye. Either way, you're complicit."

For a split second, Gul could have sworn Bob smirked. Then he sat down once again, opening his file of paperwork. "If you really think that, then ask yourself this. Why would I have allowed DSP Akthar to pursue the case?"

"Because even the Inspector General of Sindh needs to keep up appearances. How many investigations can you arbitrarily call off, before people will start calling you a corrupt cop?"

His face darkened. "I think you should leave now, Gul. I've seen you, out of respect for your brother and for your parents, who I was very fond of, God bless their souls. They would be saddened to see what has become of you."

Gul's laugh was bitter. "Do you really think bringing my parents into this is going to change anything? Who is Saayaa, Bob? Where does he operate from? If you refuse to bring him to justice, I'll do it myself."

He cracked his knuckles again. They popped loudly. "I think you need to be very careful here, Gul. Tread lightly. You've already been in a fair amount of hot water, from what I understand. I wouldn't want things to get worse for you." He walked to the door and held it open. "Will you see yourself out?"

"Go to hell, Bob. And take my damn brother with you."

She felt him watching her the entire way down the corridor.

WHEN GUL GOT home, Ejaz was no longer there. The kid had neatly folded up his blanket and slipped away. He'd left a note. *Gone to the shelter. Don't worry about me.* She cursed. Ejaz was meant to stay put until it was safe. She rang the shelter to make sure he was there, and then left strict instructions with Farzana not to let the boy out of her sight.

She made herself some toast, burning it just slightly so it was crispy enough, before lathering it with butter. Comfort food. She needed comfort food if she was going to think things through. She ate on the sofa, looking at the sunlight and the shadows coming through the slatted balcony doors. The light was transformed into dusty beams and danced about her bookshelves in a way that was strangely reassuring. The world may have gone to hell but here, in this flat, nothing ever changed. There was not much more she could do, Gul realised. Not in the short term, other than to make sure Ejaz was okay.

Her doorbell rang just as she was reaching for her car keys. It was Mrs. F. Gul stepped back to let the other woman in.

"I forgot your keys at home. Good thing you were here. Nobody seems to have known your whereabouts this morning." The statement was pointed.

Gul said nothing, but walked towards the balcony. She opened the doors and stepped into the sun.

Mrs. F followed. "You look like shit, Charlie. And Hamza told me what the two of you got up to last night. You foolish girl. You could have been in real hot water."

"Why do people like that phrase so much?"

"What?"

"Never mind."

"Well, you made it out of there, and you didn't call, which means you found something that upset you. So, tell me. What was it?"

Gul stared at the floor. "He's complicit, Mrs. F. Bilal has been working with Saayaa this whole time."

Mrs. Fernandes's eyes widened. Then she took Gul's hand. "I'm sorry."

Gul felt her eyes moisten. "I'm sorry, too."

"Come. Sit. Tell me everything."

Gul shook her head. "I can't. Ejaz has gone off to the shelter. I don't want him running away again, it's not safe for him on the streets."

"I left him there before I came here. Don't worry. Farzana is watching him and I told him myself, if he wasn't there when I returned I would beat him with a stick, the rascal. He has sworn he will stay put."

At that, Gul half smiled.

Mrs. F narrowed her eyes. "Sit down, Charlie. We'll figure this out together."

Gul did as she was instructed. On the balcony, she filled Mrs. Fernandes in on everything. For a while they sat in silence, neither of them really knowing what to say.

When her phone rang and she saw that it was DSP Akthar, she picked it up.

"What did you do?"

"What do you mean?"

"I am under strict instructions to remove the police escort from outside your house, Madam Gul. Apparently your safety is no longer a priority for the Sindh police."

Gul closed her eyes. "That's not a surprise, DSP Sahib."

"A review panel has been called for next week. I'm facing misconduct charges."

She swallowed. "I'm so . . ."

"Please, don't." DSP Akthar cleared his throat. "We both know what this is. But I'm afraid my hands are tied now. I'll need to step back from this investigation and let the Baloch police run point on the murder case."

"What about the shrine?"

"There's to be no more surveillance, no more investigation. It's been deemed a waste of police resources. I would stay away from there, Madam. I'm afraid you're on your own for the moment."

"I understand. Is there anything I can do?"

There was pained silence on the other end. "Just hope that justice prevails."

When she hung up, Gul almost threw her phone across the room.

CHAPTER 26

GUL CRASHED OUT ON the sofa. She slept until the late afternoon, waking up bleary-eyed and disjointed. After a quick shower and a cup of coffee, she jumped into her rental. Mrs. F had gone back to the shelter, and Gul planned to meet her there. Now that there were no police outside her house, she was even more worried about Ejaz.

On the way, she got a phone call from Rana. "Apa, where are you?"

"I'm heading to the shelter, why?"

"You should come in."

"What's going on?"

Rana was practically whispering. "The Minister of Antiquities is here. He found out the mummy is a fake, and he's just fired Director Raja for incompetence. Director Raja is being escorted out of the building."

Gul's grip tightened on the wheel. "We haven't made anything public yet. Ali Mahmood must have tipped his uncle off."

"I don't know, but there's a news story out already and some social media posts."

"Shit."

"Apa, Director Mahmood is in charge now. He's already asked to see you in his office."

"He can go fuck himself."

"I agree, but I'm sure he's saying the same about you."

"Can you do me a favour?"

"What?"

"Can you find out what type of car Ali Mahmood drives?"

"What type of car?"

"Yes. I've never seen him pull in. I think his driver usually drops him off and then picks him up at the end of the day."

"I've never paid any attention, but I can ask around. Do you need anything else?"

"No, thank you. But if you could find out soon, I would appreciate it."

THE ELECTRICITY HAD gone off at the shelter, and the place was sweltering. Still, the dormitories were full, the kids had nowhere else to go to get out of the sun. Gul spotted Mrs. Fernandes setting up some thermoses with water and oral rehydration salts for kids who were coming in dehydrated.

"Have you seen Ejaz?"

"Don't worry. I've been keeping an eye out. He was in the kitchen a while ago."

Gul exhaled in relief. "Good. I was worried that he was going to do something stupid again."

"Well, he was deep in conversation with Farzana, learning how to heal toothaches through witchcraft, if that counts."

Gul's phone pinged on her way to the kitchen. A WhatsApp message from Rana. That was fast. The girl never failed to disappoint.

Director Mahmood drives a silver Pajero, she wrote.

Then: *Asif Anwar told me that his wife usually drops him off and picks him up because she uses the car in the day. But apparently the car is in the shop, because the Anwar brothers have had to pick him up and drop him home the last few days. They're getting really annoyed about it actually, because he lives in KDA and they live in Nazimabad but he's insisting nobody else is available to drive him. Does this help?*

Gul stared at the messages for a while. Then she turned around, marching back to where Mrs. F was pouring sachets of ORS into cold water.

"It's . . . Ali Mahmood."

"What's Ali Mahmood?"

"Ali has been working with Saayaa."

Mrs. F put down her thermos. "Are you sure?"

"Rana spoke to one of the Anwar brothers. They've been driving him back and forth to work because his silver Pajero is being repaired apparently."

"So?"

Gul hesitated. Then she filled Mrs. F in on the events on Clifton Bridge, when she had almost been run into the concrete.

Mrs. F looked at her for a long time. "Why are you only just telling me this now?"

"I didn't want to worry you."

"You're lucky I don't kill you myself, Charlie." She walked to the stairs leading to the dormitories and sat down heavily.

Gul came and sat down beside her. "I know you're upset. But can we please deal with that later?" She put a hand on Mrs. Fernandes's knee. "We need to focus on this right now."

"Owning a silver Pajero is not enough proof to damn a man."

"It may not be proof, but it's plenty enough to damn a man like Ali Mahmood."

"What will you do? Call DSP Akthar Sahib?" Mrs. Fernandes placed her own hand on top of Gul's, and Gul knew in that moment that she had been forgiven.

Gul shook her head. "I wish I could, but he's in the firing line because of me. He won't be able to help."

"So what?"

Gul bit her lip. "I don't know, not yet. If I go back to the museum, I'll be fired. I have to come up with a plan before then."

Mrs. Fernandes looked pale. "I don't like this, Gul. I don't like this one bit. These people are dangerous. They almost bloody killed you. And now your brother has fled because he knows exactly how dangerous they are. The police are up to their necks in the whole thing. It's not safe for you to be here anymore. You should leave."

"They killed my daughter."

"I know."

"So there's nowhere else for me to be."

Mrs. Fernandes squeezed her hand. "What do you need me to do?"

"Nothing for now. But I'll let you know."

CHAPTER 27

GUL COULD SMELL THE aroma of frying onions even before she walked into the kitchen. There was a large handi on the stove, which could only mean that Farzana had made a mutter biryani for later. A rare treat, the biryani was a great favourite at the shelter because it was filling, but also unbelievably delicious. Farzana's spices were still out, adding to the smell of masala—large plastic jars of haldi, zeera powder and adrak. The large sink in the corner was piled full of chopping boards and fry pans, which Ejaz was washing now. He had the grace to flush when he saw her.

Gul put her hands on her hips. "You couldn't just stay put?"

"The idiot's been asking me about the shrine," Farzana grumbled, giving Ejaz a light thwack across the back of his head. "He wants to know how they could get a body out of there without anyone noticing. As if I would know."

"Aree, you're there all the time," Ejaz mumbled. "I'm sure you see things."

"I'm there to pray to the Shaykh, not to support the mafia," Farzana replied. "And if you had any sense, you would do the same."

Ejaz straightened. "I'm trying to find out the truth."

He had a hell of a black eye, Gul thought. And his lip was still swollen. She sat him down as gently as she could. "Ejaz, it's time for this to stop. This is my battle, not yours."

"If we can find some proof . . ."

"We will, I promise. You have to trust me. We'll find out what happened. But not with you going back there."

Ejaz said nothing for a moment. Then he nodded, and got up to pour himself a glass of water. "Are you going to teach today?"

With a shock, Gul realised it was Tuesday already. "Yes, I suppose so." She watched Ejaz closely. He wasn't going to let this go. It was obvious.

Farzana looked up from the potatoes she was peeling for tomorrow's aloo ki bujiya. "You should go get ready. Good luck—they're hot and hungry. I don't know how much they'll be paying attention today."

Gul smiled, picking up a stray piece of chopped carrot from the counter and putting it in her mouth. "I'll do my best to be entertaining." It was one way to keep the kid out of trouble, at least. "Ejaz, come help me."

AT THE END of the class, after the stragglers left, Gul got up, cracked her back and stretched. Hopefully the kids hadn't noticed how distracted she had been throughout class—how she had simply gone through the motions with Ejaz doing most of the actual teaching.

Gul walked over to where Ejaz was putting the workbooks away and put a hand on his shoulder. "Thank you. Having you here really helped today."

He flushed. "I can be more helpful if you'll let me. If I go back to the shrine, I'm sure I can find out . . ."

"Ejaz, no," she said softly. "Please don't put me or yourself in that position."

"I can't just sit here, Apa."

The determination in his expression was unmistakable. "If you really insist on helping, there's something you can do."

"What?"

"There's a man at the museum, a man named Ali Mah-mood. I need you to keep an eye on him. Call your friends. I'll pay them good money to watch him."

His eyes widened.

"I can give you his address," she continued. "And the model of his car, which may or may not be in the shop. But cover his home and the museum. If he leaves either, let me know. Don't let him out of your sight, but do not in any circumstances make yourself known to him, no matter what. And go in pairs, so nobody is alone. Can you do that?"

He didn't look happy, but eventually he nodded. "This is really going to help?"

"Yes. Yes, more than you know. This man is working with Saayaa, but he's dangerous, Ejaz. Don't go anywhere directly near him. Just watch from afar, and let me know if he leaves the museum or his house."

He nodded. "Me and the boys can handle that."

"I know you can."

SOMETIMES, WHEN THE sea breeze was blowing and the sun had set, Karachi could be a beautiful place, Gul thought. Tonight, so close to Independence Day, many buildings were garlanded in lights. Some were white, but even more were green. Some were a combination of the two. Some twinkled, like glitter.

As she drove up Bridge Street, Gul turned on some music to soothe her. Marvin Gaye wasn't working his usual magic though. She tried Smokey Robinson, and then the Supremes, and then the good old-fashioned Pindi band Vital Signs, but they all made her heart pound faster. Ejaz had messaged to say Ali Mahmood had left the museum and driven straight home. Was that it, then? The mummy was now publicly a hoax. Would Ali just slink off and lick his wounds, now that Princess Artunis had been exposed? She was at a loss. How was she going to get him to reveal who Saayaa was?

Resisting the urge to turn around to check if any of the cars she kept spotting were actually following her, Gul headed back to Bath Island.

At home, she sank into the sofa and picked up her phone. *Any news?*

Ejaz messaged back immediately: *He's still at home. The boys are at his gate, watching. They'll update if anything changes.*

Good, Gul responded. *Why don't you come back here and get some sleep?*

When her phone pinged a few minutes later, she assumed it would be from Ejaz, telling her not to worry about him. Instead, it was a message from Harry. He would have probably just come out of one of his seminars at UCL, and no doubt wanted an update on what was going on.

She would have ignored it, but Harry had sent a video. *Urgent. Watch this right now.*

Gul clicked on the video and felt the blood leave her body. It was Harry. Not in London after all. No . . . evidently, he'd never made it to London. Instead he was tied to a chair, a cut on his forehead, a gun pressed into his temple. He looked up, his expression bleak. There was a man holding the gun, but she could only see his arm.

Then the phone rang and she answered.

"Come to the shrine. Come now if you want to see Professor Gilbert again."

"Saayaa."

The man said nothing.

"How do I know you won't kill him anyway?"

"Tell anyone, and Professor Gilbert dies."

The phone went dead.

CHAPTER 28

AT 3 A.M., THE shrine was quiet. The food vendors had left for the night, the garland stalls were shut, the worshippers asleep, and the bustle of the day briefly put aside. The whole place had a sense of abandonment about it. Gul stepped out of the car and navigated her way to the entrance steps, careful to avoid a variety of debris—rose petals heavily trodden on, litter not picked up, and inexplicably, an unopened bag of candy floss.

Gul paused at the steps. What the hell was she doing? Heart in her throat, she weighed her options once again, as she had done every few seconds on the drive over. If she called the cops, Saayaa would know, and he would kill Harry. If she walked through the doors, they could both die.

She berated herself for the thousandth time. When she had gone to see Harry off at the airport, why had she turned away before he'd gone through the double doors and checked in? Instead, she'd left him at the entrance, waved, and was gone, so fixated on Mahnaz that she had paid no attention to anything else. And now Saayaa had probably been holding him hostage all these days. What state was Harry going to be in?

Standing in the breeze, Gul reached the same conclusion she had when Saayaa first contacted her. There was a certain inevitability to her being here. She was physically and emotionally spent. Saayaa had tried to kill her once already. If he decided to keep trying, it was simply a numbers game.

Eventually, he would succeed. She was so damned tired; it was time to bring the game to an end. Still, she wasn't entirely stupid. Before she left her flat, Gul had strapped her father's old service revolver to her chest. She normally kept it unloaded under her bed. In fact, she had had no intention of ever using the bloody thing, but in a city with rocketing crime rates and daily burglaries, it brought her some consolation. She was grateful for it now. If Saayaa decided to kill her, then she hoped she would have the opportunity to shoot him in the eyes before she died.

There was nothing for it: Gul would have to deal with whatever was waiting for her. She swallowed. It was her job to convince Saayaa to let Harry go. To find out about Mahnaz. At least she would finally be face to face with the truth, in whatever form it took. And there was peace in that.

As she walked up the steps, Gul scanned the area around the shrine. She tried the door, and it was unlocked. She pushed it open and peered into the room. Empty, save for the sarcophagi of the Shaykh on his latticed *Arabian Nights* bed and the ones of his family, which lay in the shadows. Then fluorescent tube lights flickered on and Gul straightened, blinking in the glare. She was no longer alone.

The man standing opposite her had long, curly, well-oiled hair and a thick beard. He was as wide as he was tall. "Big Galloo, I assume?"

He smirked. "Gulfsa Delani. The boy whore's adopted mother."

When he moved, she saw the other man now stepping in front of him and her eyes grew in disbelief. And then she heard the familiar sound of cracking knuckles.

Still in his uniform, Bob smiled.

The feeling that flooded over her was more akin to grief than fear. All this time. All these years. Saayaa had been part of her life, camouflaging himself as her brother's best friend. She knew that now with complete certainty. And she had never guessed.

"You always were an asshole," she whispered.

Bob walked towards her. Always a dominating presence, he seemed taller somehow, straighter, even more in control. "You really know how to complicate an already complicated situation, Gul. So . . . let's talk. But first, your gun, please. And don't bother pointing it at me." He waved around with his hand. "We have people stationed everywhere."

It was true. There were men standing in the corner of the room—blank, expressionless faces. She crossed her arms. "I don't have a gun."

He smiled. "What is ironic is how predictable you are. Your father told me about his service revolver many times. He was so proud of it, though as far as I could tell, it never saw any real action. And then Bilal was all bitter when you took it after your father's death. You two amused me, with your inability to get your shit together."

"Go to hell."

"Let's see . . . where could you have hidden it? Your kameez doesn't appear to have any pockets, and your jeans don't have big enough ones. I don't think you'd put it down your pants, but I could always be wrong. I'm guessing it's down your shirt, am I correct?"

Big Galloo's beefy hands were all over her then, and Gul winced as he pulled the old revolver from its wrapping around her chest. He grabbed her phone out of her jeans pocket for good measure, threw it to the ground and stomped it.

Bob shook his head. "You know you could have just taken out the SIM and reset the phone and that would be enough to stop people tracking her, right? What a waste of a good device." Then he looked at her. "You see? You're predictable. I knew you would never betray a friend and colleague, and I admire that. I also knew you wouldn't turn up without a weapon."

"Where's Harry?"

"He's safe."

"What about Bilal?"

"I honestly have no idea where that little shit has got himself off to. Clever of him to bail, though he should have taken you with him."

"Are you going to kill us?"

"That really depends on you."

"What do you want?"

"What does anyone want?" Bob raised a hand. "It's not personal, Gul. One day, I'm going to run for office, and after that, I'm going to run this country. But unlike the rest of you, I wasn't born with a silver spoon in my mouth. I was the scholarship kid who had to prove himself time and time again. Do you know how many people you have to pay off or woo to win an election? The army brass for a start, all the local runners, the various divisions and vote banks. It's millions of rupees before you even begin."

Gul couldn't help but stare. Police corruption was one thing. This was something else entirely. "So you became Saayaa? You started all these criminal enterprises?"

Bob shrugged. "Like I said, I needed the money. It was all low-key at the beginning. I was able to stay one step ahead of the police, for obvious reasons, which gave me an important advantage. But then I realised how easy it all was. I hooked up with Big Galloo over there and our business interests expanded. I thought, why not run the country and make sure I have enough for my retirement as well?"

Big Galloo grunted.

Bob crossed his arms. "Day to day, Galloo runs the show. I take on a more strategic role, given my time constraints. We share the profits, and I ensure the police leave him alone. Things got even easier when I started spreading rumours about Saayaa within the force itself. Imagine a gangster nobody has ever seen, but who every police officer shits their pants at the mere thought of. My PR has always been bigger than my reality."

"Those cops that stole the mummy were on your payroll."

"Yes. A few of them are. Cops need to feed their families too, Gul. Do you know how badly paid we are? If you want to be upset about something, be upset about how this country treats the people who risk their lives to protect it every day."

"If you cared about cops, you wouldn't put them in harm's way, chasing you."

He scowled. "Are you talking about the shootout at our cave? It should never have happened. The body was all set to be shipped. Sadly the intrepid DSP Akthar was able to stage a raid without me even knowing about it. He's been playing his cards close to his chest. I've neutered him for now, but he may become another problem to deal with."

Sweat was pouring down Gul's forehead and into her eye. She wiped it away with the sleeve of her kameez. "You tried to have me killed."

His eyes narrowed. "Actually, I thought perhaps Big Galloo had been too hasty when he tried to run you off the road. But after your idiot brother started squealing, and you came to see me, I realised he was right. It would only be a matter of time before you started making trouble for us."

"Does Bilal know who you are?"

Bob smiled and leaned against the Shaykh's resting place. "Of course not. He's a great guy, but not very bright. When he shat the bed with his investments—which I of course encouraged him to make, you know how much he looks up to me—I suggested introducing him to some moneylenders. So he met with Big Galloo, and from that day, I have had your brother in my pocket. Big Galloo handled the communications, Bilal could obviously never meet Saayaa. Then I went to that silly fundraiser of his, and Mahnaz, bless her, was so excited about the story of the Lost Princess. She was telling everyone about it. I've been watching your career, Gul. Lots of high-value items cross your path. So I asked her what a mummy like that would be worth, and she told me tens of millions of dollars. Imagine. So I thought, why not have a go? Why not get Bilal to set something up for me? I had nothing to lose, after all."

Gul could barely breathe. "You've known Mahnaz her whole life."

"Which is why I didn't hurt her."

"I don't believe you."

"That's up to you."

"Why don't you just kill me now? What's the point of all this talk?"

"Luckily for you, I have been persuaded that there is a plan that will make it possible for both of us to leave here happy. You should be thanking me."

"What do you want?"

"I want us to work together."

Gul looked into his eyes and saw a man entirely unrecognisable to her, a man brimming with confidence and something else, something much, much harder, the glint of cold steel reflecting back at her. "I don't understand. Work together how?"

He took her to the latticed bed of the Shaykh, brushing away rose petals left by worshippers during the day. "Please,

after you. It is, in fact, remarkably comfortable. Oh no, don't
worry, there's no actual grave here to desecrate. We got rid
of the bodies years ago. Tombs are a useful place to stash
other things."

Gul sat on the velvet cloth that draped the bed, amongst
yesterday's rose petals, which were letting out a waft of per-
fume that was both pungent and sickly sweet. What was
under the marble slab below them?

Bob came and sat on the opposite side of the bed. "You
have questions, I imagine?"

Gul felt sick. "You claim you didn't hurt Mahnaz. If that's
true, who is the girl you killed?"

"Who knows," Bob said. "Some random whore we picked
up. Random whores, I should say. It took us a few tries to
get the body right."

It was sick. It was so fucking sick. They were so evil. How
on earth had this happened without anyone except Mahnaz
noticing?

"Oh, don't feel too badly, Gul. They were addicts and
living utterly useless lives. Do you know what it's like on the
streets of Karachi? We probably did them a favour."

Gul inhaled deeply. She was here for answers, and she
meant to get them. "Bilal told me that all he did was connect
you to some experts, and that you ran things from there.
True?"

Bob cracked his knuckles again. "Yes. I couldn't leave
your brother in charge. I knew he doesn't have the stomach
for this kind of work."

"So Ali Mahmood helped you?"

"Who?"

"Ali, from the museum."

He shook his head. "Can't say I know him."

"Then who? Director Raja?"

His smirk was quick and devastating. "Rahim Raja can't even bear to get his hair tousled. Can you really imagine him getting his hands this dirty?"

"So who?"

"Well, at this point I suppose it can't hurt to tell you. I have several chawkidars on the payroll. And that nerdy accountant of yours."

Gul's eyes widened. "The Anwar brothers?"

"One of them, anyway. Quite a gambling habit he has. You'd never guess, would you?"

She exhaled. Asif Anwar was the one who had told Rana that Ali Mahmood drove a silver Pajero. Was that even true? More likely, it seemed, he had made it up to throw her off the scent. And then she had another thought. "The pencil mark . . ."

Bob's expression darkened. "All that work . . . Can you imagine if something so simple had given us away? I put Anwar in charge of following your every move and reporting back. He listened in to your phone call with Raja, and when you left, he erased the pencil mark."

"He's got no forensics experience. He couldn't have put the mummy together for you. There's someone else on your payroll."

Bob nodded. "You're right. We're quite a large team. And now you're going to be part of it. You're going to help me convince the world that the mummy you found really *is* Princess Artunis."

Gul stared at him. Bob had lost his mind. "She's already been exposed as a hoax. She's been autopsied. The media has reported it. There's nothing left to say."

Bob waved his hand in dismissal. "Nothing official has been announced, and we can fix her. We can let it be known that sinister forces tried to suppress her discovery and spread fake news about her. Imagine what my clients will think when the very woman who uncovered the supposed hoax tells them that the mummy is real. They'll be desperate for her. I may even get them to up their price."

"You're crazy. It would never work."

"It works every day, Gul. That's why the world is burning. People believe what they want to believe."

"Why would I help you?"

He leaned towards her and cracked his knuckles again. "Because I'll give you a cut. Four million dollars. Anyone who knows me knows how generous an offer I'm making. You can leave the country. Your museum has treated you so shabbily. Your family hates you. You can start again. I've known you most of your life, Gul. I know how much you've been dying to get back to Egypt. Why don't you just go? Draw a line under this."

"And if I don't help?"

He paused and shrugged. "You know the answer to that. And before you think about being noble, consider this. I know who you care about, who you love. Do you think it will just be you who suffers? I care about your brother, but every-one else in your life is fair game, especially that Christian secretary woman." His expression was devoid of any emo-tion, but she could see the hardness in his eyes. Whatever he professed, he would kill her before she even left this latticed bed, if it suited his purpose.

"And Harry? If I do this, will you let him go?"

He let out a bark of laughter. "Oh, Gul, you're not as clever as you think." He turned his head. "Professor Gilbert, you're up."

Harry emerged from the shadows. The truth was written all over his face. His expression was shrouded in guilt and remorse, and his eyes darted away.

No. Not him. Please Gods, not him. "Oh, Harry," she whispered. "How could you?"

He didn't look at her.

Bob jumped off the bed and dusted rose petals off his clothes. "Really, you should be thanking him, too. He's the one who convinced me that the mummy is still salvageable, that you can make the world believe she is real. If you can do that, then we can all part company with no ill feelings. After all the time and effort and expense I've gone through, surely you owe me that much."

Harry looked up for the first time. "Gul, please. We'll host a press conference. We'll tell the world that the rumours about her being a hoax are untrue. They'll believe it, coming from you."

It was pure fury that took over. "Go to hell," she hissed.

Bob clicked his tongue in annoyance. From nowhere, he pulled out a knife.

"We had a deal. You promised not to hurt her," Harry shouted.

From the other side of the bed, Big Galloo stretched, and then casually pistol-whipped Harry across the face. Harry fell to the floor and clutched his forehead above his eye, blood seeping through his palm.

Bob shook his head. "I was worried that you were going to be a problem in the end. Take them both downstairs, let them cool off. The press conference will need to be first thing in the morning, otherwise my buyers will get spooked. I'll give you an hour to decide what your future will look like. And Gul, remember, it's not just your life at stake here."

CHAPTER 29

IT WAS QUIET AND dark in the basement of the shrine, the dimmest of light coming from a single bulb hanging down a long cable. Their captors had tied them before they left the room, binding their arms behind them to two chairs a few feet apart. Metal shelves lined the walls, displaying mainly paints and hardware, though Gul also spotted a stack of prayer mats and beads. Near a dripping patch of ceiling, a battered suitcase sat ominously in a corner. Her heart thudded as she thought about what, if anything, the suitcase might contain. She focused on catching her breath. First Bilal, and now Harry. How could it be Harry?

She looked at him now, slumped in the chair a few feet from her, his head hanging. Just to see him there . . . The force of his betrayal left her incapacitated. She thought about what it would take to forge a mummy. Someone with understanding of forensics, of anatomy, of history and archaeology. Someone with enough precision and expertise to create elaborate duplicates . . . then she thought about all the years they had been colleagues, about his many trips to Pakistan, supposedly to investigate antiquity, when all along, he was here to help Saayaa.

Harry's muscles taut, his hair damp with sweat. What of the last few weeks? Why had Harry bothered to join the investigation? All the files she had entrusted him with, all the data he provided—the transcriptions. She pushed down the pain of it. Harry knew her well. And she, in turn,

had respected his expertise, enough that she let his excitement over the mummy override her own doubts. Had that
been his plan all along? To ensure that she wouldn't get too
suspicious? It was staggering.

Harry looked at her for the first time, and Gul saw the
shame etched across his features. "Gul, I'm sorry."

Gul blinked a few times and took some deep breaths.
She flexed her hands, trying to loosen the rope she was tied
with. "Spare me the contrition, Harry."

He nodded. "I deserve that. But would you believe me if
I told you that I never thought anyone would be hurt? Bilal
told me that Saayaa would bribe someone to remove fresh
bodies from the morgue. I thought he was an opportunist,
not a murderer."

"Surely you can't have been that stupid?"

Blood dripped from the wound over Harry's eye and ran
down his cheek. He said, "It's true. I trusted your brother.
He gave me his word."

"Then you're a bloody idiot. Why would you do this? You
make a decent income."

He swallowed.

"Though evidently not decent enough for you. That
inheritance from your aunt, the house in the country and
the flat upgrade in London . . . that was all this, wasn't it?"

He shook visibly. "I didn't think it through, Gul. Bilal
approached me a few years ago when I came to visit and
offered me a great deal of money to connect with his contacts. He put me in touch with Asif Anwar. I only discovered
Bob's identity when they kidnapped me at the airport, I
swear."

"And what did Asif tell you?"

"That he would procure a freshly expired body, and I
would show his people how to mummify her, and that's all.

A teaching job, in effect. I agreed to help with the cuneiform and act in an advisory capacity, *only* in an advisory capacity. Nobody was meant to get hurt. At least, that's what I thought until Dr. Chinoy told us the girl was a potential murder victim. I swear it, Gul, on my own life. I felt the same shock you did."

"And you didn't bother to ask any questions, did you? How many times did you try and fail at the mummification process?"

"Gul . . ."

"How many, Harry?"

He slumped. "Four."

"And those women, those *girls* were just lying about the morgue conveniently, every time you needed one? Do you know how few morgues there are in this city?"

He shook his head. "Please. I know I made a mistake. But your brother vouched for them . . ."

"All this time, I thought I knew what I was doing." Gul was annoyed at herself when she heard the crack in her voice. "And yet the whole time, you were pulling my strings, weren't you? When you arrived with the transcriptions, when we went to Parsi Colony and you hypothesised about the hidden treasure, and told me you felt the story was credible when I thought it was ludicrous. I should have known better than to get carried along on the adventure of it all, I should have been more logical right from the beginning. What was your plan? To keep the façade going until the body could be sold?"

He tried to push against his ropes as well, scraping his chair in the process, but gave up after a moment, frustrated. "I had no choice, Gul. I knew if you got too suspicious, you would start asking questions. And then they would have killed you."

"Well your plan failed, because they tried to kill me anyway."

At that, Harry flushed. "I didn't know that, I swear. Until you told me what had happened that day at the entrance of the hospital, when we were scanning the body, I had no idea. I was furious. I told Asif Anwar that I would expose them all unless they backed off. He said that one of Saayaa's men had acted on his own when he tried to run you off the road, and that it wouldn't happen again as long as you played nice. They were planning to steal the mummy back, to try and sell her again, but it was proving difficult with all the media exposure."

"And I was in the way?"

"Yes, but I was going to tell you that I thought I had found the location of the caves in Balochistan, and distract you by insisting we visit there. Just to delay things. Unfortunately, they never managed to get the mummy back. Now that the police have been called off, they plan to steal her again, during the press conference, in fact."

When Gul said nothing, he swallowed, loudly. "Tonight I convinced Bob that we could still salvage the mummy—for *your* life, Gul. I did it for you."

"And what, do you suppose, would Saayaa do to you if you lost him a forty-million-dollar contract? Don't do me any more favours." She jerked against her binds again and felt some movement. The ropes were loosening; someone had made a mistake when tying her. She pushed and pulled, and yes, they were definitely looser.

In the near darkness he laughed, bitterly. "This would all be over if you just give him what he wants." Blood had trickled down his forehead and to his lips, and he spat it out. "It won't cost you anything, Gul, but as usual, your stubborn pride comes first."

"If you really think that, then you're stupider than you look. As soon as we're finished doing what he wants, Bob is going to kill us both. Do you really think he'd reveal himself to us if he had any other plans?"

Harry's eyes held anguish. "Tell the world the mummy is real. It's the only way out. Bob will never harm you then, not when it would cause questions if you were to disappear."

"Did you kill Mahnaz?"

Harry seemed crestfallen. "Oh, Gul. Whatever you're feeling about me right now, surely you can't think me capable of hurting a child, least of all a child you love? Of all the things that galled during this whole experience, that was the worst, that you could possibly think Mahnaz was murdered and mummified. Do you know how hard it was to watch you these last few days?"

Gul wanted to kill him. She wanted to reach over and strangle the life out of him. "He didn't take her?"

"No."

"Are you sure?"

He nodded. "I worked on all the bodies myself. For all I know, she's still alive, Gul. Maybe she ran away."

"I don't believe you."

Harry slumped again. "No, I don't suppose you would."

"We have to get out of here."

"How?"

She jerked at her restraints, moving her head. "They kept Ejaz down here. He escaped through the sewers. I'm hoping they haven't had time to block them up yet. I'm going to try and make my way towards you. Whatever they bound us with, I think mine's loose enough to unravel if you help me."

"And if they've blocked the sewers up?"

"Then we're going to have to fight our way out."

"Jesus, Gul . . ."

"We don't have any choice, Harry." With effort, she lifted her chair and slid herself towards him, inches at a time, grunting with discomfort, and pausing between every scrape and squeak, in case she was heard.

"Are your fingers free?"

He flexed. "Yes, I have some movement."

"Good, I'm coming behind you. Work on untying me."

"Gul . . ."

"They'll never let us live, Harry, no matter what they say. We'll do our press conference, and then we'll die in some accident that nobody can question. A car crash. Or maybe a fire. They'll never let us live after all of this."

He was quiet for a moment. Then he exhaled deeply, almost as though the fight had gone out of him. "Try and come a bit closer."

She moved back again, achingly slow, until she felt his fingers fumbling around and touching her own, and she pushed her arms as far back as they could go to give him as much access as possible to her wrists. It was several minutes before they could work loose the rope that had secured her. Quickly she flexed her wrists, circulating blood. With her hands free, she was able to loosen her feet as well, and then she reached for Harry's ropes.

They'd just freed his hands and feet when she heard the basement door open. Light came from the stairs above. "Quickly," she hissed. "We have to find that sewage pipe. Ejaz said it was behind the shelves somewhere."

They rushed to the shelves at the back of the room but didn't immediately see it.

Footsteps came down the stairs.

She caught sight of a corner of the grate then. The shelves mostly obscured the opening. "Help me," she whispered, pushing at the shelves with all her strength. He started to push next to her and the shelves toppled over, paint cans and kerosene flying in every direction. Frantically they pulled at the sewage grate, even as they heard the exclamations, as the footsteps began to run towards them.

The grate came off in her hands with a jerk, and she was knocked backwards. "Go," she shouted at Harry.

Harry looked down. "I won't . . . I can't fit," he said. "I'll drown."

Gul stared down the sewage pipe. It was narrow. Their arms would probably have to stay at their sides as they went through it. It was also almost entirely full of liquid, which meant they would have to swim with whatever little movement their legs afforded. Would they be able to make it?

"We'll have to hold our breath and swim through. It can be done. Ejaz did it."

"This is only the manhole. We can't see anything below it, we don't know how it opens up to the sewage system. It could narrow even further. I could get trapped, but you're the same size as Ejaz, you can do it. You go. Hurry," he hissed.

There was no time to argue anymore. She jumped into the manhole, racing down its iron rungs, pausing long enough to hold out her hand. "You can do it, quick."

But Harry's body was jerked away, and she saw another man take his place. She recognised the man. She had maced him in the alleyway a few days earlier.

Gul dropped down the rungs as fast as she possibly could, took a deep breath, and plunged into the gelatinous gloop, swimming quickly through the narrow sewer pipe. The liquid was too murky, too dense to see through, and very soon her chest and eyes began to burn. Even shutting them didn't help, it only seemed to make the burning worse. She struggled not to gag through the overpowering smell of sewage, rancid and pungent, and forced herself to move faster. Ejaz had done this. She could do it too. As she kicked she felt her legs knock against the sides of the narrow pipe. The lack of space slowed her movement, and she started to panic. She had to hurry. She was running out of air. Then she heard the shot, echoing against the walls, even under all this fluid. She kicked wildly and wriggled through as fast as she could.

Just when she thought the pain in her lungs would get the better of her, that she would pass out, the pipe turned and widened, and she could use her hands to move faster. Then she was propelled forward out of the tunnel, into a reservoir of muck and trash and sewage water. She sat up and spluttered, barely able to breathe with the smell, desperately clawing the sludge off her face, half spitting and half vomiting into the grimy basin. She looked around. She was outside, in a canal of sewage, surrounded by floating piles of plastic, crows hovering above as the sun began to rise. She could see some makeshift buildings on the left, but there was no way to reach them from her lowered position. She was just going to have to keep going down the channel until she found a way out.

From the pipe behind her Gul heard grunting. The man was trying to find a way through but was probably too large to move quickly. It would buy her a few precious minutes, unless she got lucky and the bastard drowned before he could reach her. She pushed through the chest-deep sewage, trying furiously not to breathe in the waste that clung to her like a second skin. She could hear him now, the man. He'd made it through and was making his way in the water. He pawed at her leg, and she kicked out as hard as she could, satisfied when she heard the heavy grunt that followed.

For several minutes, Gul held the lead, the man close behind, twice reaching her, but then falling back when he slipped in the slimy waters, and at last she managed to pull away.

Spotting steps on the wall to her left, Gul raced for them, clambering up just as he reached her again. This time he had a proper hold on her leg, and she was in danger of falling back into the canal. She managed to half turn as he pulled at her, and swung the heel of her free leg into his face as hard as she could. She heard the crack of his nose and watched him falter, his hands automatically reaching for his face. She didn't waste any more time. She turned around fully, lifted herself out of the shit of the city and ran as fast as she could.

CHAPTER 30

GUL LOST THE MAN by ducking through some alleyways by the main road. Maybe he was winded, his broken nose giving him trouble, or maybe he took a wrong turn, but she found herself twisting and shifting her way through a small slum that had grown around the sewage canal. At one time the canal may have been a source of fresh water, because little mud-and-brick houses had sprouted up along the pathways, some with corrugated metal roofs, others simply covered in sheets of plastic. The road, such as it was, was covered in plastic bags and extra sewage pipes. Mosquitoes hovered around stagnant pools of water. But somehow, the place thrived.

By the time she stopped to catch her breath, the sun was inching its way forward. She tried to remain in the shadows, well aware that she was still close to the shrine.

A woman leaving her house carried a baby in one arm and an empty plastic water container in the other. Gul approached her, and the woman jumped back, startled.

"As salam alaikum. Please, I don't mean you any harm," Gul said, looking around quickly. "I need a phone. Do you have one? It's an emergency."

The woman did not have a phone, but there was a shopkeeper in the next alley, she said, who would be able to help. Then she rushed off, glancing back a few times, eager, no doubt, to be rid of the wild-eyed, sewer-soaked stranger, who, despite the stench, probably seemed like she came from wealthier parts of town. Gul could only imagine what a sight she must be. She was cloaked in wastewater from top to bottom, her hair matted to her head, scraping sludge out of her eyes with a kameez that only smeared the mess further. Only in this moment did Gul notice the absence of one of her chappals. She must have lost it somewhere during her adrenaline-fuelled escape. She kicked the remaining one off and headed to the next alley.

When Gul reached the shop it was closed. It was a khoka in the wall, nothing more than a little ledge under a window that was shuttered. She banged on the shutter as hard as she could. Thankfully, the shopkeeper opened up almost immediately, his sleepy eyes widening at the state of her.

"What do you want here?"

"I need to borrow your phone, Bhaijaan, please."

The man shook his head. He looked shocked to see her, and automatically wary. He was still in his banyaan and shalwar and she had caught him midshave, she realised, when she saw the lines of foam still on one cheek.

"It's an emergency, and I'm a woman on my own." While it galled her to say, she knew they were words that spurred most Pakistani men to action.

But not this particular shopkeeper. He peered over her and then glanced up and down the alley. "I don't want any trouble."

"And you won't have any, not if you let me use your phone."

His eyes narrowed. "You're not from around here."

"No."

"Go away."

"I can't, Bhaijaan, please. Someone's life hangs in the balance."

"You're going to scare my customers away. Be gone with you, or I'll call the police."

Gul exhaled and nodded. "Good. Call the police. Call them or I'll smear this shit on my hands all over your precious little shop."

BY THE TIME Gul had galvanised DSP Akthar, told him not to trust anyone but his key men, and met him back at the shrine, at least forty minutes had passed. DSP Akthar's people surrounded the place.

He already had his pistol cocked as he got out of his jeep. "You have to wait out here, Bibi."

"But . . ."

He raised an arm and signalled for his men to move forward, ignoring her entirely.

Gul waited. The muck of the sewer had dried now. She tried to brush it off her face. Only minutes later, DSP Akthar walked down the steps, raking a hand through his hair, a grim expression on his face.

"It's empty," he said. "There is no one inside. Even the shrine's custodians have disappeared."

Gul pushed past him.

"What are you doing?"

"I need to see."

He followed her up the stairs and into the main room, where the sarcophagi of the Shaykh and his loved ones rested. She examined them each in turn. When she reached the tomb of the Shaykh's mother, she paused. "Open it."

"What?"

She pointed at the rose petals scattered on the floor around the tomb. "Earlier these petals were covering the velvet cloth on top of the grave. Now they're on the floor. They were in a rush; they didn't properly cover their tracks."

Together, she and DSP Akthar lifted the velvet garment draped over the tomb and found themselves staring at the marble slab that covered the grave. The slab was heavy. It had clearly been put back in a hurry and left slightly askew.

Which was a lucky thing, Gul thought later, after DSP Akthar ordered his men to push the slab with all their strength. They winced as the marble hit the ground with a dull, heavy ring. When they peered inside, Harry stared back at them.

CHAPTER 31

MRS. FERNANDES HAD BAKED some almond biscuits and her famous bun cake. Hamza's mother had sent cauldrons of Gujrati food, which Ejaz and Francis were now industriously heating up, and Hamza himself was busy setting up some high-speed Wi-Fi system that meant everything in the flat could be controlled from Gul's phone. Rana, for her part, had presented Gul with a playlist of trance music that was meant to be healing, and some CBD oil she'd got her hands on from somewhere, to ease Gul's aches and pains.

Over the past few days, Gul had agonised about what she had lost. But these wonderful people constantly reminded her of just how much she still had. And that included her life. As she watched them now, making themselves busy while she lounged about on the sofa, she marvelled at the quirks of fate, of instinct. Instinct had ensured that she went back to the shrine and examined the tombs individually. Perhaps it had been the goddess Hemsut herself who had made sure that Bob and his goons didn't properly reseal the tomb, leaving a flow of air for its occupant.

They'd found Harry alive. In the end, he'd jumped on the man who had tried to follow her into the sewer and tackled him to the ground. He'd taken a bullet for her. Two bullets, in fact. One had lodged just above his lung, the other between two ribs. Neither had killed him, but they had allowed him to play dead.

From his hospital bed, Harry confessed. Four years ago,

on one of his trips to Pakistan, Bilal had approached him, and offered half a million dollars for his participation in a "little project," as he'd termed it. All he had to do was advise Bilal's acquaintances on how to make a mummy, provide the technical expertise that would allow the body to pass muster. Harry had agreed.

In light of all this information, the newspapers were having a field day. Was King Delani a murderer? Questions about his missing daughter, Mahnaz, began to surface, as did queries about his own whereabouts. A warrant was issued.

Harry also pointed the finger at IG Bhatti. Bob immediately went on the offensive and railed against criminals who made outrageous slurs to try to get off leniently. Still, he had been suspended pending an official investigation.

That investigation would be short and farcical, Gul knew. No government official with any clout in the country was ever prosecuted for long, not once strings were pulled and power plays undertaken. Politicians and their government cronies seemed to enter and exit jail with the ease of a revolving door. She herself had never given a statement to the police. Gul had been due to give one once she had sufficiently recovered, but she'd returned home from a hospital check-up two days after the attack at the shrine to find a perfectly wrapped box on her doorstep. Inside was a silver-framed photo of her with Mrs. Fernandes, Rana and Hamza, from Rana's university graduation. All of them beaming. Nothing else, nothing sinister, and yet the meaning was entirely clear. Gul did nothing further, needing time to think. Still, her stomach clenched at the thought of Bob living his life with no repercussions. Unless she prevented it, IG Ibrahim Bhatti would soon be back at his post.

Gul inhaled deeply. At least Saayaa's activities had been

curtailed. Just that morning, DSP Akthar had paid her a visit. They had a cup of coffee together and shared some gulab jamuns and nankhatais.

"I don't want him to get his job back, DSP Sahib. What was the point of all of this, if that level of corruption and evil doesn't stop a man from gaining power?"

DSP Akthar looked exhausted, but he gave her a reassuring smile. "At least Saayaa is gone for good, Bibi."

"Is he?"

"IG Bhatti would never risk reviving him, not now, not after all this scrutiny."

"What will happen to his drugs business? Will Big Galloo call the shots?"

"No, no I don't think so," DSP Akthar said. "Big Galloo is in the wind, he knows we're after him. Unfortunately, others will pick it up. There is a power vacuum in the criminal underworld, and they'll start killing each other off until one of the local gangsters prevails."

"Jesus."

DSP Akthar gazed into the distance for a moment. "It is no longer my problem."

Gul was quiet, not knowing what to say. DSP Akthar had come to say goodbye. He was being "promoted," he told Gul, and being sent to the backwaters of Balochistan. He also let her know that Asif Anwar had taken a leave of absence. The police had launched an investigation into him as well. His brother was devastated.

"I cannot thank you enough, DSP Sahib. You saved Harry's life. Many future lives, no doubt," Gul said eventually.

The cop smiled and took off his cap. "It is I who should be thanking you, Madam. We would never have closed this case without you."

"Yes, well, I don't think it's anywhere near closed, do you,

DSP Sahib? It must not be closed until IG Bhatti is held to account."

He arched a brow and smiled wryly. "Knowing you as I now do, Bibi, I would say it is only a matter of time."

"What will you do?"

He shrugged. "I will take my promotion and my pay raise and settle my wife in Bela before starting my new post. And hopefully, soon, I will return to Karachi."

"You're married?"

"Two years now. Inshallah, we have a baby on the way." He reached across a table and helped himself to a gulab jamun, wiping his chin with a tissue when bits of sugar syrup escaped.

She beamed. "I'm very pleased to hear it, DSP Akthar."

He put down the tissue, looking suddenly self-conscious. "Madam Gul, it was an honour to meet you. Should you ever have need of me, you know where to find me."

"And you me, DSP Sahib. I'm sure our paths will cross again."

His smile was wide now. "And I can honestly say, though it has come as a surprise to me, that I look forward to it."

After DSP Akthar had left, Gul received a phone call from a nurse at the hospital. Harry was asking to speak to her, and once again, she declined to take his call. His testimony was damning, but it seemed the authorities were eager to get rid of him. He was fined eighty lakhs, well below the half a million dollars he made from the mummy. They were planning on releasing him soon, and he would never be allowed back into Pakistan again. Either way, his career was over.

Harry had sent several messages begging her to come to the hospital before his extradition proceedings. So far, she had refused.

Now, Gul gazed at Mrs. F, who was admonishing Francis

for not heating up the food properly. On the other side of the room Rana was arguing an impassioned point about the Indus Valley script with Ejaz, who seemed not to really care and was lying back on the sofa with a soft smile on his lips, which only seemed to irk Rana further. Hamza was still under her desk; she could see his well-scuffed trainers and jeans poking out, and Gul felt at peace for the first time in a very long time. She stood, and brushed off biscuit crumbs from her jeans, despite a cacophony of protests about how she had to rest. "No, no, I'm fine, thank you. I'm sick of this whole invalid nonsense. There's absolutely nothing wrong with me that a ton of preventative antibiotics haven't already helped me with. And all of you, too. It's time to get back to work."

Hamza pulled his head out from under a mass of cables. "What do you mean, Apa?"

She smiled. "As it happens . . ." She'd been waiting all day to tell them this, and she couldn't hold it in much longer. "I'm stepping into a new role at the museum." Their shocked expressions delighted her.

And then she shared the news she'd held on to until they were all together, the news that was at once gratifying and bittersweet. Ali Mahmood had resigned from his role as director of the Heritage and History Museum. After all the negative press about the museum, several women had come forward and accused him of sexual harassment. Rather than face them, he had handed in his notice. His uncle had got him a cushy job working directly under him instead, in the Ministry of Antiquities. One day, Ali would probably run the place, the chutiya.

Director Raja, meanwhile, burnt by his own experience, was moving on. He had taken on a role at the Louvre in Abu Dhabi at six times his existing pay. He was fed up, he told her, of the backstabbing, ingratitude, and the nepotism, not to mention the newfound discovery of smugglers and murderers, and he had recommended her to the board to take Ali's place. "You're the only one stupid enough to really want this job," he'd told her. For some reason, the powers that be had agreed.

"Director Delani," whistled Rana.

"I'll always be Apa to you," she said.

Hours later, after they'd gleefully made all sorts of plans for museum projects, and the team were practically bouncing off the walls in excitement, she kicked them out, lovingly. It was getting late, and she was tired. While she was happy about their enthusiasm, she still had to let the whole thing settle. Was becoming director what she even wanted anymore? Maybe Bob had been right about one thing. In an ideal universe, it was time to cut her losses and move away. But until she found out the truth about Mahnaz, and until she saw Bob on his knees and Bilal face justice, this was where she had to be.

The team left, but Mrs. Fernandes lingered. Gul began cleaning up, carrying dishes into the kitchen.

Mrs. Fernandes brought in the glasses. "You shouldn't get them so worked up, Charlie. They'll get their heads full of notions. You and I both know you've been hired back so that the government can put an end to this mummy business. They'll slash your budget, and they'll wait for you to fail. Watch your step. There will always be someone wanting you to fail."

Gul put the plates down, reached out, and hugged the other woman tightly. "Today is a good day, Mrs. Fernandes. Why don't we just let ourselves enjoy it?"

Later, when she was truly alone and couldn't sleep, she padded into the kitchen to eat some of the leftovers. She dipped some dhokla into green chutney and ate while leaning against the kitchen counter. And then she thought of Mahnaz.

She squeezed her eyes shut, so tightly that it was almost painful. Mahnaz. Thinking about her made her feel physically ill and so she stopped. It would do no good now to spend time lost in the shadows. Not today. Let her have peace on just this one day.

She drank a glass of water and went to bed.

CHAPTER 32

THE NEXT MORNING A courier arrived with her new contract and a mountain of other paperwork from the museum. Gul's official start date was the following week, but already there was a lot to be done. Requisition forms to sign, the payroll to deal with, some urgent budgeting to go through and a couple of fundraising proposals that had to be sent out soon. On top of that, the museum had forwarded her all the mail that had accrued since Rahim Raja and Ali Mahmood left.

She stood on her balcony and sorted through the pile. It was the usual stuff. Invitations to exhibitions, research proposals, the odd invoice that should have gone to accounts. Amongst it all, she spotted a manila envelope addressed in her name.

Gul lifted it out of the pile and frowned. When had this come? She opened the envelope.

DNA Maternity Test Report. Gulfsa Nilofer Delani and Unknown Female.

Gul's heart skipped a beat. The DNA test on the mummy. The results had finally come. Her eyes skimmed past the columns of DNA markers and numbers, directly to the result itself.

The alleged biological mother is excluded with a probability of 98.99998%.

Who knew that relief could be so exhausting, she thought, as she physically slumped onto the ground, the paper still clutched in her hand. Harry and Bob had not lied. The mummy was not Mahnaz. For the first time in weeks, she felt like she could breathe. And in the quiet stillness, she began to contemplate things.

Gul wasn't sure how much time had passed, hours probably, because the sun was beating a steady drum into her head when the doorbell rang.

She got up and opened it. Sania looked like she had just come from the beauty salon. "Gul. You haven't been picking up your phone."

"Sorry. I'm still waiting for a replacement."

Sania cleared her throat. "Yes, well . . . I've come to tell you, your brother has been in touch."

"Where is he?"

"He went to Peshawar to stay with that army friend of his, the one with all the government connections. He's hoping that his friend will pull some strings and help him get the case against him dismissed. But that doesn't look likely, not now. He's looking at jail time, at least, until they can sort out this mess."

If it wasn't for the way she was smoothing her hair back into its already perfect shape, Gul would never have guessed anything was wrong with this impossibly implacable woman. "Is he coming back?"

Sania flushed. "If his name is cleared, I suppose. In the meantime, your brother and I have decided to settle things amicably. We're getting a divorce."

"I see. Do you want some tea?"

Sania hesitated. "All right."

Gul left Sania on the balcony and set the kettle to boil. She placed the remaining almond biscuits on a small plate and put two Lipton bags in the pot. Her stomach growled. She hadn't eaten all day.

When the water was ready, she carried everything outside on a tray, and set it down.

They sat quietly, sipping the tea for a while.

Eventually, Gul put her mug down. She gazed out at the banyan trees. "You were right, by the way."

"Right?" Sania turned to look at her.

"That mummy was not Mahnaz."

"Oh?"

"The DNA test report came back."

"I see. I'm sorry you didn't get the answers you were hoping for."

Sania picked up an almond biscuit and nibbled on it delicately. The way she was going, that one biscuit was going to last her a whole hour. But that was Sania. Nothing to excess, nothing to be enjoyed or not enjoyed. Just . . . nothing.

"Actually, I did find some answers."

"Oh?"

"I thought to myself, what were the chances that Mahnaz found out about a potentially horrific injustice, angrily confronted her own father and Sania had no clue about it? Would you like some more tea?"

"Gul . . ."

"And then I asked myself, what were the chances, the *real* chances, that Sania would have stopped looking for Mahnaz, given that she loved the child as much as I did, unless she knew her disappearance was voluntary? Because that's what happened, isn't it? Either they killed her to keep her quiet, or she vanished, to keep herself safe."

Sania bit her lip. Once again she smoothed down her hair. "We didn't set out to hurt you."

"She's alive?"

"Yes."

The weight of that and the weight it lifted hit her in

equal measure. Neither of them spoke for a minute or two, until Gul eventually took another sip of her tea, trying with difficulty to keep her composure. "Where is she? Is she in Pakistan?"

Sania shook her head. "She's finishing her education abroad. Under a different name."

"You let me think she was dead. You lied to me for over three years as I continued to search for her. You let me go crazy with grief."

"I know. But it had to be done, Gul. For all our sakes."

And now Sania was holding her hand. Gul stared at it, dainty and perfect, her wedding ring glistening, resting in her own rough and calloused palm. "You have to understand, there was no other choice."

"Who else knows?"

"Nobody."

"I think you better tell me everything. And Sania?"

"Yes?"

"If you lie to me about even a part of it, I will kill you myself, I swear to all the Gods."

And so they sat, long enough for the sun to make its way across the sky, and for the evening breeze to bring a welcome respite from the heat. Gul listened, and Sania talked. At times, Sania wept. As she did, Gul realised she had never seen her sister-in-law cry. Not when Mahnaz disappeared. Or before. Or even after. Though she had little sympathy for her now, listening to the words pour out.

All those years ago, Sania had watched Bilal try to impress Bob and the rest of the world with his financial prowess, investing in things he had no business messing around with, too arrogant to understand the true moral of the story of King Midas. She had known about the missing funds, and about Bob's suggestion that Bilal turn to the moneylenders

to hide his clients' losses, because Bilal had told her everything. She'd even helped him cover up the embezzlement at
the Delani Foundation. It had actually been her idea to cut
Gul out of their lives after the accident, so they would have
time to replace the money before anyone got suspicious, and
later, so that Bilal could continue to launder money through
the shelter and museum.

"Don't look at me like that. You're always so quick to
judge. You who have never had a sense of obligation to anyone, not even your own child."

Gul got up, and Sania raised a hand. "That was out of
order. I'm sorry."

They were quiet for a moment, Gul trying to calm her
pounding heart.

Sania started to speak, stopped, and then tried again.
"It's just that you don't understand. You have no concept of
what it's like. You are content to live on the fringes of society. Those of us who want a *real* life here, who want to raise
children who can make their own way, know that without
money and status, there is no future."

"That's not true."

"Isn't it? This is a country that is run on relationships
and networks. On lineage. It's a place of corruption and
darkness, where you need power just to survive. You have
to buy your way to safety in this country, Gul, especially if
you are a woman. There is no room for goodness here. You
know that much."

"Sania . . ."

"Who would talk to Mahnaz again if Bilal went to jail for
fraud? Who would have paid our bills? Fucking Bob? You
know he made a pass at me? Lots of passes, in fact. He's even
asked Bilal what I'm like to fuck. Sometimes he comes over
and just stares at me, and all these years, your brother has

done nothing about it, because his only mission in life is to impress that man."

Sania fumbled around in her handbag and pulled out a packet of cigarettes. Gul didn't even know her sister-in-law smoked.

She lit a cigarette and inhaled deeply. "Unlike you, I'm a realist, Gul. When Bilal lost all that money, I helped him because I knew it was a temporary setback. But I didn't know about Saayaa and all that tamasha until later, when Mahnaz confronted him. She did that in front of me, and after he yelled at her, he took me aside and told me everything, about making the mummy and the fact that we were being threatened by an elusive drug lord named Saayaa. Can you imagine how I felt? I did what I had to do. I helped him cover up the money laundering, so that we would all survive."

"Why didn't you go to the police?"

She snorted. "Really? After everything I just told you? Bilal would have gone straight to Bob, of course. He's always been enthralled by him, but Bob doesn't do anything for free. Plus, you've single-handedly proven how terrible an idea that would have been. I still can't wrap my head around the fact that Bob is actually Saayaa."

Gul swallowed. "What about Mahnaz? Why didn't she just come to me? I would have helped her. I would have helped you both."

Gul could see how agitated her sister-in-law was from the quick but deep drags she was taking on her cigarette. "This is not a game, Gul. There was too much at stake. I knew what would happen if she told you the truth. You're reckless. You wouldn't let this go. In your attempt to be noble, we would have lost everything, maybe even our lives. So I might have twisted the facts of her birth a little. I told her you didn't want her, that you begged us to take her from you so you could pursue your life of adventure. I told her it was one thing for you to have her around when everything was going well, but when the chips fell, you would always look after yourself."

Gul squeezed her eyes shut. "And she believed you."

"She was a teenager who had just found out that the aunt she worshipped was actually her biological mother. She reacted emotionally."

"Which is what you were banking on."

"Yes. I'm sorry to say I was." But she didn't look sorry as she crushed her cigarette out. "But what I didn't expect was that she would start an investigation of her own and put herself in so much jeopardy. When Bilal told me she had followed him to the shrine and had been spotted there, and that he had had to smooth things over with Saayaa, I knew I had to do something. So I arranged for her to go abroad under an assumed name until the danger was over. A diplomat friend helped with the logistics of getting her safely out."

"You couldn't have just sent her away without all the drama of a disappearance? Just sent her to live abroad. We could have gone to visit her."

Sania shook her head. "No, she needed to vanish, and she needed a new identity. Bilal told me that Saayaa has connections everywhere. What if they had decided to go after her, to control Bilal? And letting her stay here was out of the question. I couldn't trust Mahnaz to keep her mouth shut if she was here. No matter what I said or did, she would have kept investigating if she thought a woman's life was at stake—she's so impetuous and foolhardy. It was only after I convinced her that all our lives were in peril if she didn't go quietly that she agreed to leave. She wouldn't go for herself, but she was prepared to go to keep me and Bilal safe."

"How? How did you do it?"

"We sent her on a US government flight with the outgoing American ambassador. There was a delegation going and the ambassador pulled some strings."

"Are you telling me the Americans were in on it?"

"Only Barbara. She's a close friend. I told her it was a death threat and that we had to get Mahnaz out as quickly as possible, without too many questions. Mahnaz is an American citizen, as you know."

"And Bilal never knew?"

Sania exhaled. "No. Barbara assumed he did of course, but since leaving here, she's been posted to Guatemala and hasn't been directly in touch with him. Mahnaz has had no desire to speak to him either, so it made things easier."

"What about the police investigation? If Bob had nothing to do with her disappearance, why did he warn Bilal off searching for her?"

Sania shifted in her seat. "That was me."

"What?"

"I typed the note Bilal showed you. I sent it to him because I wanted to scare him into dropping his search. I didn't want Mahnaz to be found, least of all by your brother. He's a coward. I couldn't trust him with the fate of our child." She said this with scorn in her voice, and Gul wondered whether Sania had ever loved or even liked the man her parents had arranged for her to marry.

"So what did he think happened to her?"

"He thought they killed her, in the end."

"And you were happy to let him live with that? How could you be so heartless?"

Sania looked at her coolly. "My plan was to bring Mahnaz

back eventually, when things calmed down. Until then, he deserved nothing more. Mahnaz agreed with me, by the way."

"What about the diaries? Mahnaz left clues for me there. Why?"

Sania poured herself another cup of tea. "Those bloody things. If it wasn't for them, you'd have left well enough alone, the mummy would be sold and Mahnaz could have come back in due time. When Princess Artunis's story made it into the press, Mahnaz called me. She asked me to leave the diaries somewhere for you to find. She didn't feel guilty about leaving her father in the dark, but I thought perhaps she was feeling some guilt about you, because she said they would bring you some consolation. I have read them. I thought they were innocuous, and so I did as she asked. I wanted to bring you closure, I thought that I was doing a kind thing for you at a difficult time. She told me that if there was any hope of redemption, any chance of a relationship between us in the future, I had to do what she asked. Little did I know that she had saved all her evidence and made a backup plan. More fool me."

"She was just a child," Gul said brokenly. "All this, and she was just a child."

Sania's hand shook as she lifted her teacup. "Yes. And even so, she went away for our sakes. But she left clues for you. She was testing you, I think, to see if you would come through, if you understood her enough, loved her enough and were capable of ending this whole bloody business."

"Why didn't she share the diaries with me sooner?"

"Why do you think?"

"Because she couldn't get past the fact that I was her mother?"

"I told her you abandoned her, Gul, and the news

devastated her. For that, more than anything, I'm sorry. She was always so close to you, closer than she has ever been to me. Do you know how hard it's been for me? You may have given birth to her, but I'm her mother."

Gul stared out at the horizon. "And now it's too late."

Sania shook her head. "Actually, I think perhaps she is finally ready to forgive you."

EPILOGUE

GUL WALKED IN THE dust.

She passed lines and lines of terra-cotta mounds. They were indistinguishable from one another, save for the pieces of rough wood jutting out of the earth, which gave each one a number.

There were no mourners here, in this baking earth. There were no tears. For this was the place of abandoned souls, the nameless and the faceless, the cemetery of the unknown.

Gul walked until she neared the very end of the mounds. It took a long time, picking her way through. There were so many of them. Then, finally, just when the sun's heat threatened to become unbearable, she was where she was meant to be. She stood in front of the one that was different. This grave had a marble headstone and a stone frame. This grave had been tended to. Loved, even.

Gul crouched and put down her bouquet of roses. Then she stood and stepped back. There was no number on this grave. There was only one name.

Artunis.

She closed her eyes and invoked a prayer to all the deities she knew. May Artunis, whoever she was, know peace, at last.

As she turned and walked away, Gul thought about what was in the back pocket of her jeans, even now. A postcard, one she had received just that morning. It was picturesque. It had a snow-capped mountain on it, with a little lake below.

Dear Agatha, wish you were here. Jane

It was enough.

꧁

AUTHOR'S NOTE

THIS NOVEL IS A work of fiction, but it was inspired by real events. In October 2000, police in Karachi arrested two men on suspicion of "selling a human-sized gold sculpture" for eleven million dollars. The sculpture turned out to be a mummy, adorned with a gold face mask and crown, which lay in a wooden coffin covered in royal symbols from the Achaemenid Empire. It had a gold chest place that stated, in cuneiform: "I am the daughter of the Great King Xerxes . . . I am Rhodugune."

The body eventually made its way to the National Museum of Karachi, and at a preliminary press conference it was announced that archaeologists had uncovered the remains of a mummified Persian princess dating from approximately 600 BC. Authorities in Iran immediately demanded the mummy back, and the Taliban asserted its own rights to ownership as well, all under the glare of the international media.

But Dr. Asma Ibrahim, real-life archaeologist and museologist, a.k.a. "Madam Museum" in Karachi, was suspicious from the start. Over several months, after carrying out an autopsy and scientific analysis, she systematically proved that the mummy was a clever forgery and also unearthed disturbing evidence that the woman inside the sarcophagus could have been murdered. The world lost interest in the mummy once she was proven to be a hoax, but Asma never did. With the help of the Edhi Foundation, Asma arranged for her to be buried in an unmarked grave. The body's true identity remains unknown.

Asma is a remarkable woman who has battled misogyny throughout her career, and has made a huge impact in safeguarding Pakistan's heritage. I hope one day she writes a book about her own adventures and experiences—until then, she will always remain an inspiration.

Another inspiration came in the form of Dr. Salima Ikram, a Pakistani Egyptologist who really did find herself face to face with a cobra when excavating a tomb once. I owe Salima a debt of gratitude for talking to me about mummification and introducing me to other amazing Egyptologists. Any errors and inaccuracies are my own.

Finally, the Princess Artunis never really existed, though I really wish she had. King Xerxes was actually murdered by Artabanus, commander of the royal bodyguards. I have also made up the timelines and circumstances around his sons' murders, and Amytis's role in them, but the Achaemenid Empire really doesn't need any embellishment from me—it was a fascinating time in history.

ACKNOWLEDGEMENTS

THANK YOU TO DR. Asma Ibrahim, Dr. Salima Ikram, and Dr. John J. Johnston for guiding me through the world of mummies, and to Gillian Slovo and Kamila Shamsie for telling me there was an incredible story I just had to hear.

A huge amount of gratitude to Nick Whitney, editor extraordinaire, Rachel Kowal, and the entire team at Soho Crime. Thank you also to my wonderful agents Margaret Halton at PEW Literary in London and Stephany Evans at Ayesha Pande Literary in New York, and everyone else who provided editorial support, particularly Tahmima Anam, Erum Sultan, Aisha Rahman, Mahnaz Hadi, Simon Edge, Doug Young and Bill Massey.

Many other people also helped with research, logistical or other support in and out of Pakistan, including Adnan Noon, Saman Shamsie, Susie Orbach, Joelle Harari, Fabiana Werdum, Sarah Trueman, Priscille Falconer, Farid Azfar, Osman Hadi, Taniya Zaffer Khan, Lulu Nana, Bee Rowlatt, Dermot O'Flynn, Diya Kar, Mahvesh Murad, Rosey Strub, Anoushka Beazley, Kamiar Rokni, Abi Hardwick, Omar Shahid Hamid, Harriett Gilbert, Paula Garrido, Jamie Gibbs, Zain Mustafa, Jumana Dalal and Ann Herreboudt.

Finally, my biggest thanks to my family, and all the Warducks and Jals, particularly Damien Phillips, Tia Noon, Fahad Khan, Nina Khan, Aliya Yusuf, Jaffar Khan, the Khan-Mowjee clan, Ayesha Tammy Haq, Christine Lacote, and Marie-France Phillips. Ro Khan-Phillips, I love you, you are always my inspiration for everything.